D1355929

The
DARK DAUGHTERS

BY

Rhys Davies

LONDON

READERS UNION

WILLIAM HEINEMANN

This Volume

was produced in 1948 *in Great Britain in complete conformity with the authorised economy standards. First published in* 1947 *by William Heinemann, Ltd., it was set in Garamond* 11 *point and reprinted at The Windmill Press, Kingswood, Surrey. It is one of the books produced for sale to its members only by Readers Union Ltd., of* 38 *William IV Street, Charing Cross, London, and of Letchworth Garden City, Hertfordshire. Membership of RU may be made at all bookshops and particulars are obtainable from either address*

CONTENTS

Part I

THE FATHER

Chapter One

IN 1895, wearing a smart frock-coat and an even smarter puce cravat, Mansell Roberts opened his chemist's shop at the base of an arboreal North London hill intersected with rows of solid new villas. The wholesome breezes of Hampstead Heath blew down over the hill before losing themselves with a different odour in the clotted lower-class districts far below. Among tasteful scrolls heading the new chemist's bills—and much more imposing than the actual premises—was an engraving depicting the shop's exterior with two smart carriages drawn up at the kerb. Mansell had ordered many packages of these bills.

He was by nature averse to giving credit but he trusted those villas with their horse-shoe drives, stucco porticoes, flowering urns, and their roomy basements for several domestics. And to make more certain of laying a solid local foundation, he had become a worshipper at decorous St. Mark's, though again his nature was averse to the Established Church; he preferred those small dissenting sects catering for the less orderly souls of England.

He was materially ambitious, had a peasant's respect for facts and figures, and looked out on the world with enquiringly nimble eyes. Yet, as if his being had a network of secret veins feeding him with a mysterious life, he could isolate himself in an austere brooding during which, judging from subsequent pronouncements, he was occupied chiefly in combats with a sinister power specially roused to obtain possession of his soul. This was no mere sensual man. In addition he owned a darkly handsome presence, was dignified in address and gesture yet gracefully quick in movement. He wished to spread himself, not in the sense of showering his fruits on the earth but of attaining solid position for himself. Particularly he wanted to own houses.

"Property," he told his wife, "it seldom lets you down, Arabella, except by Acts of God. No stocks or shares for me."

The only child of a Welsh farmer who had lost all his money in a pioneering mining venture during the seventies, he had cause to know how treacherously gold coins could behave, how hostile they were to steady ownership, how they could be the carriers of disease and death. The excited but ignorant coal-mining company in which his father was induced to invest—he even mortgaged the farm—operated in the new El Dorado of Glamorgan, two counties distant from the farm. The experimental, costly shaft was not sunk deep enough and, finding no coal, the Company sold the land for a few pounds. But a few months later the new owners, digging deeper, discovered the richest seam in the county and began to make one of the famous huge fortunes of the district. When he heard of the discovery, Mansell's father became struck with a sort of paralytic grudge against the world and completely lost interest in his farm, a bladder complaint also descending upon him.

An aunt married to a publican in Somerset had then paid for 'putting Mansell into the world', this including the bare cost of keeping him in lodgings during his three years apprenticeship to a Bristol chemist which—the world then not being so particular—was his sole training in pharmacy. But at nights he diligently studied books, on Sundays listened to English preachers to perfect his language and accent, never associated with other young men or with women, but enjoyed the anonymity of a Debating Society formed to scrutinise theology. Even in those days he walked with a shut-in, single-minded air, like a young wolf. No child ever asked him the time, no grown-up the direction to the Town Hall or railway station. He looked a young man who holds a goal in brisk view and is determined not to be side-tracked or delayed.

He had worshipped his father and fully understood his inability to bear the disgrace of losing money, allowing his life to whittle away into melancholy distrust of the world and early death—worshipped him even though the father rarely allowed conversation, was totally lacking in affection demonstration and, after the financial catastrophe, remained isolated in Biblical studies. Yet the two lived in a world of silent identity with each other, a male exclusiveness. His mother toiled about the mortgaged farm heroically; the amount of energy she possessed was amazing, and this was her sole legacy to her son. She was a small bird-like creature whirring in and out of the house in a sphere of her own.

The death of his father was like a little death within himself. It was some months before he regained some of his former buoyancy. Four years later, and by then a fully-fledged chemist's assistant earning twenty-five shillings a week, he went home from Bristol to bury his mother. But on this occasion he wrote first to an acquaintance, Miss Arabella Williams, daughter of a moderately prosperous local cattle-dealer, saying he would like to see her on important business immediately after the funeral; he had to return to his work next day.

Smartly black-garbed in the English style—his only, and wise, extravagance—he laid his proposition before her. He needed a wife, a business of his own in London, and capital to launch these ventures. Brisk, already speaking in a polished English way, and with a black imitation opal in his cravat, it was not often that such a local young man reappeared in that sluggishly beautiful countryside. Arabella consulted her father the same evening. Calling next morning before dawn in the trap taking him to the station, the orphaned son of a respected old friend was welcomed by the cattle-dealer, who was still in a nightshirt. A dowry of two hundred pounds it would be.

A*

"Be ready in three months," Mansell told Arabella. She was of the old obedient race of women. There was still something wiltingly soft and pretty in her manner. Nothing much had been allowed into her head. But it had been her girlhood dream to marry a missionary and to live in quiet service with her man in Africa, a countrified land across a stretch of water like Ireland, while she sewed endless white pinafores and drawers for the loving blacks. However, Mansell and a chemist shop were not to be despised.

He left his job in Bristol, went to London, and took a bedroom in Camden Town. London excited him. The new Babylon, richly swollen through the long Victorian triumph —this was his kingdom, wicked though his upbringing declared it. Instinctively he straightened his figure, so that he looked even taller; his face bloomed into health, and he waxed the ends of his moustache. With his well-cut figure and his curved nose quiveringly awake, women looked at him with a beady interest. He strictly went to church on Sundays, in a good district, and admired the full portly congregation, his eyes fastening on the many half-sovereigns in the collection plate.

One evening he went into a Camden Town theatre and was most pleasantly impressed by a raffish comedienne then in the full roar of her deeply-embosomed voice. She seemed to throw out a rousing challenge to the males in the audience. Florence Delorme she called herself. Befeathered, strutting from easy haunches, her golden hair frizzed out like a sun in full beam, this daughter of London had a victorious quality that invigorated him. Though her roots were planted in a sooty befouled soil she flared in gigantic sunflower vitality. He sat in startled admiration.

This was the kind of woman an ambitious man ought to have behind him! She generated confidence. She'd also be a beauty in the bed. Nevertheless, not yet free of the plain bread and butter of his upbringing, he felt a wariness. The soft candlelight of Arabella was safer in the long run than this brilliant gas-mantle of a woman. And less expensive too. Swinging his new malacca cane, he walked to his lodging in an affable mood. Florence Delorme supplied him with a vicarious sense of possession, pride in his own powers, and further satisfaction with the abundant wealth of this city.

It took him over a month to find the unoccupied shop under Maitland Hill. It was one of a semi-circle of five, with two floors of living quarters, in addition to a spacious room and kitchen behind the shop. The other premises were occupied by a butcher, a dairy-grocer, a fruiterer, and a barber who also repaired umbrellas and sunshades. Behind were the dung-smelling mews where some of the Hill people kept their carriages and horses; coachmen lived in the lofts. The solemn chime of nearby St. Mark's could be heard. A public-house in a garden of acacias stood at an opposite corner; and in the centre of the broad road-junction skirting the shops was a horse-trough and a cab drivers' shelter where tea was brewed. It was a route, though not a popular one, to the salubrious Heath.

After carefully examining steep Maitland Hill and the genteel intersecting roads containing less imposing houses, Mansell made enquiries of the dairy-grocer. A bootmaker, he was told, had occupied the empty shop but went bankrupt, the gentry preferring to order their boots down in the West End. No, there'd never been a chemist, and speaking for himself he'd welcome a chemist; he had to go down to Camden Town for even a bit of corn-cure. The empty shop was owned by a widow in Finchley; she'd let it reasonable, he reckoned; the place had been empty for two years. The district was all right for shops catering for everyday wants, which boots were not. He thought a chemist would have to be a high-class one. Credit was apt to be long-standing.

Mansell fingered his moiré gloves. He could make it high-class all right. He imagined fine ladies buying his perfumes and his green bottles of smelling-salts. And he knew a formula for a headache powder—it would be a district for languid afternoon headaches—concerning whose virtues he could speak a sermon. These leisured ladies, their husbands remote in the City—he knew how they enjoyed lapses into vague indispositions. How deft and tender he could be in oblique allusions to the liver, the overweighted stomach, the sluggish bowels. He would become a family friend. It was a nuisance he did not look older; few women were impressed by a young chemist; and he decided to grow, with the aid of macassar oil, a less juvenile moustache.

Within a fortnight he had moved from his lodgings into one of the rooms over the shop, buying a second-hand double bed. The death of his parents had been valuable even if there was not a penny left after them. He stood alone, and a young man standing alone in his emotions either sags hopelessly or soars energetically. True, the image of his father was embedded fast—and alone—in his heart, and if he had paused to dwell in visions (but he was not then aware of the visionary quest dictating his activities) perhaps he would have seen that he wanted to be successful to ease his dead. The family money that had gone down the barren coal-shaft would be resurrected in medicinal gums, curative herbs and flowery perfumes: the sale of sick-chamber utensils and surgical belts, being infrequent, was less advantageous. Ailing humanity, he ruminated while at two a.m. he scrubbed the fixtures left by the bootmaker, could be very profitable; next came the vanity of women—both gifts of the devil.

Despite sharply economical buying, an unwearied attendance at auction rooms, and a trip to Brighton to acquire very cheaply the stock of an imprisoned chemist, he had to write to Arabella to tell her another hundred pounds was necessary. She came up with the money. Her father had told her she must see the shop before parting with it, but she handed it over on arrival at Paddington station, clinging to Mansell's arm, intoxicated by the long train journey.

He was filled with a sort of second-hand tenderness for her.

"Now you've gone to the expense of coming up," he said in the hansom cab he treated himself to, "we'd better get married here soon as we can: a lot of work to do on the premises yet."

"Hard faces the people have got here," she whispered, looking frightened out of the window. "And there's dressed up they are!" These people were not the simple blacks of her missionary books, waiting to welcome her and her rolls of calico.

They bought a few more articles of furniture and lived in amicable but celibate tally for three weeks before the wedding, she working hard on the premises while he, wearing his frock coat, pranced off to the wholesalers. They married the day before the shop opened. In the evening he took her to a music hall in Islington; he had found that Florence Delorme was appearing there that week.

Arabella, wearing a grey pelisse, nestled closer to him on their bench in the pit. She had never been in a theatre before. A man came round selling hot polonies and meat pies. She had glimpses of gold ropes looping up sumptuous claret curtains, naked cupids, draped women with trumpets, extravagant lights, and great barrels of beer on a counter behind the benches. This was a still further cry from her old dream of setting into life with a quiet but brave missionary. But she felt in her bones that Mansell was destined for success. And already she had satisfactory cause to know the strong vein of austerity in him. During their three unmarried weeks, though they had occupied the same bed because they couldn't afford to buy another, he had respected her.

She laughed obediently when he gave a loud unexpected guffaw at one of Florence Delorme's quips, though she did not follow the joke. She had liked better the sad ancient monkeys of the previous act.

"I forgot," said Mansell, as soon as the curtains closed on Florence Delorme, "to turn the gas out in the back room upstairs. Let's go now." Though she insisted she had turned out the jet herself, they left the music hall. It was as if he couldn't bear to stay there any longer, and must get home. With her.

In the morning, a married man and the owner of a chemist shop, he opened his door to the public at eight o'clock. A stray gent might want something on his way to the City, or a coachman a bottle of linseed oil. The magohany drawers and glass cupboards gleamed spick and span from Arabella's polishing, the coloured round bottles shone like bubbles, the canisters of herbs, though battered, were clean. On the counter were flasks of lavender-water, a basket of pink soap-ovals, a box of Dr. Mackenzie's Complexion Wafers, and a glass shelf arranged with those curled fringes of false hair, in various colours and costing 10s. 6d., with which fashionable women were now draping their foreheads; there was also a little pile of scented booklets called Papier Poudré. Just visible over the partition enclosing the dispensary a bundle of trusses hung discreetly from the ceiling. There were bottles of rosy curative sweetmeats and chocolate of an evil tint for children's worms. Porcelain utensils gleamed pallidly in glass cupboards.

Behind was the parlour with a sagging horse-hair sofa, chairs, engravings of the Queen and the Baptist preacher Dr. Spurgeon, huge twin vases painted with biblical scenes, and a bobbined mantel-drape. Here, in addition to living peacefully with Arabella, he hoped to give consultations. He knew that the establishment did not look very high-class or well-stocked but was sure he would make up for these deficiencies by earning the repute of a sterling chemist. Besides, the people of this district would distrust flashiness.

"Wear black. You must look very respectable," he told Arabella unnecessarily. "And older too. No good chemist's wife looks under forty. We better have three children. A chemist who is a family man gets family custom. A whooping-cough mixture that cured my own child——"

Though he had sent to all the villas very courteous

letters soliciting patronage, not one customer entered during the morning. In the afternoon a spectacled black-clothed young man with a sheaf of handbills came in. Mansell leaped forward. The youth gave him a leaflet. "Sunday next at eleven, three, and seven, sir," he said heavily. "A special visit from the Gipsy Evangelist."

"Here," called Mansell, "wait a minute . . . That boil!" he cried in anguish, pointing at the ripe protuberance hanging over a soiled celluloid collar. "If your collar cuts into it you will be poisoned. Let me lance and dress it."

"They trouble me a great deal," faltered the young man damply.

"We'll soon cure that. . . . Step into my dispensary. You are from the Gospel Hall in Laburnum Road? I want to pay you a visit. Ever heard Roderick Hughes? Now there's a preacher for you——" Talking without stop of a sermon the celebrated Hughes had given, he lanced, dressed and plastered skilfully, only pausing to sell the youth a blood-mixture, all for half a crown.

"Arabella," he barked wolfishly upstairs, where she was hanging curtains, "a customer! A theological gentleman from the Gospel Hall." The previous night they had both knelt by the bed and asked for success on the joint venture of shop and marriage.

She came downstairs smiling and, in her mild snowdrop way, looking quite pretty. "Start coming in they will now, you see," she said, with that quiet feminine assurance that gives refreshment to such men as require it.

And it was true. He had scarcely lit the gas when a cantankerous old man came in for soda-mint tablets, and a villa maidservant for oil of cloves for toothache which was driving the cook mad. But though he kept the gas burning till ten o'clock the whole day's takings did not exceed fourteen shillings. There was not one applicant for opening an account.

"I'll buy a parrot," he said. "Bird-seed I can get cost price."

And the next Sunday morning he sacrificed going to St. Mark's, went to a bird market in the East End which the butcher told him about, and got a bird the colour of green-gages. Day after day Arabella hovered a hundred times near the shop door, like a hesitant customer, while Mansell, bending over the parrot's cage just inside, exclaimed: "Pills? . . . Perfumes? . . . Soaps?" For a long time the bird, looking sceptical, remained unaffected but one day broke out into the words with an easy readiness as if it had maliciously kept them in its throat all the time.

Thus passers-by became reminded of their wants by a screech which carried, however, a note of derision. Children gathered and adults paused, and casual trade certainly improved. But still no one opened an account. Mansell sent letters to four local midwives offering a generous discount on purchases. One came in and bought packages of cotton-wool, but only after Mansell had passed her on to Arabella and tea. She said the men of the district were prosperous but not real gentry; their ladies were frequently confined but high and mighty in their tastes, favouring shopping in town, where they could drive in their carriages like titled folks. But there was room for a chemist for servants.

Mansell was filled with a nervous rage. There was neither big money nor spiritual satisfaction in servants' trade. He wanted in his shop beautiful women drenched in perfume, and men who were pillars of the land.

His moustache waxed, and wearing the highest collar he could find, he approached the vicar of St. Mark's and begged to be appointed a sidesman. The vicar, whose sidesmen all kept carriages, said there were no vacancies but ordered a dozen tablets of oatmeal soap. On Sunday mornings his church was packed with the finest feather boas and freshly-blocked top-hats. His sermons were solid as a baron of beef or the British Empire. Mansell, though he sniffed the expensively pomaded and perfumed air of worship with a hungry anguish, was full of contempt for those sermons. He began to look fretful. Not only was London as a wealthy evil Babylon to be rifled still holding aloof, but his inner soul was famished.

Prancing with thwarted energy, he took to attending the Gospel Hall in Laburnum Road. There an ornate evangelism prevailed. He had been interested to find that a well-off, stout and elderly widow, referred to as Sister Crawford, was ruler of this church and sometimes conducted the service. He saw at once that she was subject to angina pectoris, that her silver hair was a wig and that she wore a Dr. Wardrop cuirass—of which he wanted to become local agent—to help flatten her stomach. In her apparel she did not disdain a fashionable flamboyance. And she kept a carriage. Bertram, the young man whose boil he had lanced, was a sort of secretary and curate.

Instinctively alert, he made further enquiries. Mrs. Crawford lived in one of the grander villas on the Hill; her late husband, who had been a ships' chandler in London docks, was strangled by swallowing a denture, and because the doctors had not acted quickly she bore a bitter grudge against them—the case was famous locally. Her church, the lease of which the couple had bought, belonged far away down the century to that famous evangelist who had styled herself the Queen of Sheba and drove about London and Brighton in a kind of chariot attended by a stalwart bodyguard on horseback: she also kept a seraglio of many husbands. But Sister Crawford had discarded most of the extravagant beliefs of her predecessor and was not really out of tune with the advance in taste and education made by the buxom century under the pilotage of Victoria.

"Sister Crawford," he accosted her politely after the service one Sunday, "I am the new chemist at Prospect Terrace, and I would like my name to be put on your books."

"We keep no books, brother," she said regally. "There is only one Book and that is kept by the Lord. Every name is already down in it." But she looked with interest at this tall young man bending reverentially towards her. "I have passed your shop. I was sorry to see those ridiculous women's hair fringes in your window. Only a few weeks ago I condemned them as foolish vanities."

"They are worse than that," he said at once; "they are a wicked waste of money. And they are made from the sweepings off barbers' floors. But as a Christian chemist I have my living to make. . . . Now——" and after telling her how much her sermon had nourished him he mentioned challengingly a point in it that had perplexed him.

Theological dispute was meat and drink to her. She ceased acknowledging the deferential bows of her departing congregation and for half an hour concentrated on this flattering keen-eyed young man. She then invited him home to cold supper. Bertram, her protégé, accompanied them; it turned out that she had taken him from an orphanage and was training him as a possible pastor.

At supper, in a house solemn with material prosperity, Mansell's agility in theological argument favourably impressed Mrs. Crawford. More important, there was established between them that mutual harmony of cells, nerves and brain, like a spiritual marriage, that happens occasionally in one's lonely journey through life. Before the session was over she signified her intention of closing her account with her present chemist. He was not surprised to find she was a great believer in medicines, pills and even herbal sachets, though with perfumes and toilet luxuries she would have no truck.

And at last a carriage drew up at his door. Mrs. Crawford was arriving to open her account, the first on his books. Her descent and majestic progress across the pavement, her mauve and silver head held high, was watched interestedly by the parrot, his head cocked aside. "Pills?" he screeched. "Perfumes? Soap?" She was followed by Bertram, who vaguely carried a closed watered-silk sunshade and a little pug-dog. Mansell sprang forward, bowing in front of the cage. "Blessings on you, Brother Roberts," pronounced the lady. "Praise the Lord."

"Praise the Lord," echoed Bertram damply.

"Praise the Lord," Mansell sang, still carefully covering the cage. The dog barked crossly at the parrot.

Mrs. Crawford creaked on to the one narrow cane-seated chair at the counter, while Mansell nipped behind. She wanted, first, to consult him about Bertram, who seemed to be wasting away and was of low spirits. Could something be done to revive him in every way?

"Revive him! Why, I can make him a tonic that will make him want to gallop all round Hampstead Heath."

He undertook a regular course of treatment for the secretive-looking protégé. Bertram was then sent back to the open landau to enjoy the sunshine, and Mrs. Crawford launched into herself. She had various ailments, most of them natural in a despotic rich woman who took no exercise except in evangelical wrestlings. Before the consultation was over Mansell had established, in addition to the previous spiritual harmony, a respectful though commanding intimacy with her physical envelope, of which she stood in a fear strange in a woman so occupied with the eternal. The bond was tightening.

"You will deliver all the medicines yourself, Brother Roberts?" she requested. "And take supper with me?" She rose in her billowing skirts of grey and purple; her gold neck chains and immense locket hung with stiff costliness. "I am now taking Bertram for a ride on the Heath." But she pointed at the little pile of Papier Poudré booklets. "A woman who uses those fast things," she pronounced, "would never be allowed in my church."

"Alas," said Mansell, dominantly, and subtly, standing firm, "at present I am at the mercy of this Gomorrah of a city. . . . But a man fights in his own way, Sister Crawford." At her passage to the door the parrot screeched something unintelligible. "My parrot bids you good day," he swung the tails of his frock-coat before the cage.

"They are not birds I favour," she declared on the pavement; "there is something heathen about parrots." But with her stately bow she gave him a sudden sweet smile of trustful liking.

He visited her regularly after this, particularly when itinerant evangelists were entertained at her house. Arabella was kept firmly in the background; indeed, she never met Mrs. Crawford. He saw that the childless widow of sixty was beginning to be disappointed with the ineffectual Bertram, who showed little sign of ever breaking into fiery battle with the morality of the times. Mansell, energetically swooping aside the tails of his coat as he sat in the huge arm-chair with its gold-tasselled antimacassar, his aquiline nose quivering to pounce on a debatable subject, supplied her with a sense of a successful son. He became adept in selecting occasions when *not* to be deferential or submit to her opinions.

He also noticed that Bertram became galvanised into a damply trembling attention only when the serving maid Agnes came into the room. She was a plump pasty-faced girl with a kitchen warmth around her. Mrs. Crawford would sit with her small fat feet up on a gilt-clawed stool and look less of a public woman expecting reverence. Mansell thought that on the whole she was unobservant.

"We must get the church members to support you, Brother Mansell—if I may call you that now?" she said. "Your medicines are really doing me good. I will mention your establishment in my address one Sunday when opportunity occurs. . . . It behoves us all," she continued with a rising inflection and easing, with a slight pant, her body in its cuirass after the generous supper, "to keep the vessel of the Lord in clean and healthy condition."

"Bertram," Mansell turned to the owlishly silent young man, "I have brought you a new medicine to-night. You must be sure to take it regularly. I shall bring you further supplies."

"Yes, Brother Roberts," Bertram said, starting out of his

reverie, but his thick flabby legs hanging loose. His gaze had been fixed on the door, where Agnes would come presently with coffee.

"*I* will see that he takes the tonic," Mrs. Crawford said.

One evening an American evangelist was entertained at the villa. He had brought to England a creed which included disdain of earthly medicines. All curative elements for the body, as well as for the soul, came from Above; and, no, he would not recognise even herbs of the field as God-given means for ointments, purgatives and tonics. His loud didactic briskness seemed to speak well for his creed. Mansell bristled in his chair but kept glancing satirically at the American's eyes which, despite his breezy loquacity, had a torpid interior dullness. He was not worried about the oblique attack on his trade, for he had seen that Mrs. Crawford was unfavourably impressed by the American's lack of pomp and circumstance in his loud jaw-masticated words—earlier at table he had said grace as if the Lord was seated there with them and would Himself enjoy the mentioned leg of mutton. And after the meal she had risen with an especially frigid majesty.

They were sitting in the conservatory; it was a warm June night. The light from the candles streamed over the garden rhododendrons whose furiously purple and creamy blooms expanded with a prosperity natural to that villa. The American continued with his bouncing attack on medicines. Mansell at last took his courage in both hands and said: "Yet, sir, if you will pardon my saying so, you yourself do not go to your stool as regularly as you should."

Mrs. Crawford quickly raised one webby eyelid—a habit of hers when her attention was specially arrested—while the other remained as if over a still deeply meditative orb. The eye swept over to Mansell in a momentarily startled beam.

"What's that, sur?" the American rolled, equally surprised.

"I am a chemist, and as such I am aware of your condition. You are constipated—a common complaint in your country, I hear . . . Now," he bustled, "if I gave you a pure medicine which eased this condition, would you still condemn the medicine as unnatural to divine law?"

"Waal," the American recovered somewhat, "I sartainly would not take the medicine. I would continue in faith, sur, till the condition had passed." Was this the famous British propriety?

"But meanwhile, sir?" Mansell insisted ferociously. "While you waited in your faith, day after day——?"

It was then that Mrs. Crawford interfered. And for the second time in his association with her Mansell saw her smile—this time, a sly comfortable smile of solid appreciation. "I think, Brother Mansell," she said smoothly, "you have made your point, and therefore the discussion can be terminated. I may add that for myself I do not see why a state of health caused by earthly conditions cannot be treated with earthly remedies. . . . We have an example here in the conservatory—Bertram. Two or three weeks ago he was very low-spirited indeed—he was reared in an orphanage——" she veered like a frosty wind on the American, "but a tonic of Brother Mansell has worked wonders; he is twice the young man he was and therefore doubly useful in my church . . . Bertram," she concluded, turning to him, "you will tell Agnes we are ready for the coffee now?"

Bertram jumped up quite smartly, swished aside the tinkling curtain of sea-shells, and disappeared. It was true that a kind of jerky vigour had begun to be manifest in him, though as yet it had not reached his tongue, and still no one knew what he was thinking (if anything at all; for the orphanage seemed to have ironed all character out of him, perhaps in the belief that an illegitimate child is best without one). Mansell watched his exit with justifiable satisfaction, and was not surprised that he was gone on his errand a long time. Conversation in the conservatory, led by Mrs. Crawford, took a less personal note.

But afterwards she told Mansell that from the first she

had distrusted the American and felt him to be a false prophet travelling more to advertise himself than the works of the Lord. Mansell also found that, half lost in her, there was a sly need of humour; and when they were alone together she would often remind him, with a pant of her highly-guarded bosom, of the way he had scored off that crank of an American.

And before long she invited him to give a Sunday address in her church. He took for apparent subject the evils of drink, working into the address many pieces of practical advice about the body—which, since all are troubled with one, even though it is only the vessel of something greater, takes precedence among interesting topics. The congregation was most attentive to the chemist's informative talk: up there in the pulpit the tall good-looking young man seemed entirely healthy.

True, the flock—the church was always full—came mostly from the district's fringes. It consisted of studious-looking minor clerks, heavily breathing women with turned-inwards neurasthenic eyes, girls of extreme pallor, earnest young men frustrated in some way from taking the Cloth, and—the greater quantity—obstinate rebels from the discipline of the Established Church. They all sang the rolling hymns with extreme fervour. Most attractive of all, a wide latitude was allowed in the sermons or addresses, and no one winced when Brother Mansell referred to diseases of the liver and kidneys.

2

"Arabella," he said one night, "we can sit back a little now. We are established." He was unusually meditative, almost rapt. He had just spent a couple of hours on his account books.

They were in the living-room behind the shop. It was very late but Arabella couldn't stop working; she was polishing the little chiffonier they had bought. Though she did not possess his healthy strength, the rhythm set by her energetic husband a year ago had caught her fast. Even that first year had made her look worn and over-dutiful; her hair had gone slack and she did not spread from her those rays, like a flower, that a youngish married woman should.

But she was pleased at Mansell's use of the unusual "we"; it included her so kindlily. She took advantage of it. "Perhaps soon we'll be able to send back that second hundred pounds to my father," she said, a little worried frown on her narrow brow.

"Good gracious!" he bridled in astonishment, laying down an illustrated brochure of graveyard memorials. "Arabella, you've been working too hard and staying at home too much. . . . On Sunday afternoon we'll go for a walk on the Heath." But he knew he would probably not succeed in getting her out.

Already she had become one of those women whose soul passes into the furniture and hangings of their home. As another woman will look forward to going to the theatre three evenings hence, so she planned to polish the brass candlesticks. She had no awareness of starvation. She accepted Mansell's absorption in Mrs. Crawford and her congregation as necessary if he was to become a man of substance; she had no word of complaint when he closed the shop, at nine p.m. now, and hurried off most nights to the villa on the Hill. . . . But he never told her that once a fortnight, when he closed extra early, he hurried down to Camden Town and went to the music-hall. Florence Delorme appeared there only occasionally. But there were other comediennes of her kind, and he rarely failed to be entranced by their radiant acceptance of the things of this earth.

A month or so later—it was not long after she found she was with child—he told her with a solemn look of fulfilment: "I have ordered a memorial fit for my father's grave. That little slab on it has always vexed me." His mother was not buried in the same grave.

"We can afford it, can we?" she asked vaguely, still full of her own important discovery.

"Arabella," he spoke with some affection, "you must stop worrying now and look after yourself. . . . A good wife you've been and a lot of sense I showed in marrying you." He shook his finger at her. "You show sense too and keep quiet and bring me a son in June. We will name him after my father." This terminated the discussion.

Mrs. Crawford, approving of his filial piety, had helped choose the memorial. But when he said he was arranging with the firm to pay in monthly instalments she was horrified; she advanced him the complete sum of ninety-five pounds; there was of course a world of difference in owing to a friend for a family tombstone instead of to a cold firm. Afterwards, in a reverie, he wondered whether he should have investigated the possibility of disinterring his father's coffin in Wales and bringing it up to St. Pancras' cemetery. But five years had elapsed since the burial, and even he shook his head.

By this time Mrs. Crawford was herself in a mournful mood, the aftermath of nervous shock.

One morning her excited cook had arrived at the shop and bade Mansell go at once to the villa together with restoratives. Leaving Arabella in charge of the shop and the respectable cook, who seemed to need something too but kept silent as to causes of this haste, he hurried up the Hill carrying his small leather bag. The daily rough help, a member of Mrs. Crawford's congregation, admitted him.

He found the mistress gasping on the drawing-room sofa as if her cuirass stifled her. The mauvish tint of her face had deepened slightly. But the shock, whatever it was, seemed more mental than physical. Quite a lively anger shot out of her pale eyes. Yet she whined a little when, cool and calm, he took her outstretched hand.

"Brother Mansell . . . ! Oh, the wickedness . . . ! And under my own roof!"

"There, there, dear Sister . . . quiet now." He opened

his bag and very attentively passed a new bottle of violet-scented salts under her nose. "Never mind what it is . . . *you* are first."

But, though appreciative of this soothing, she was bursting to speak. The awful tale came out in a torrent.

Late the previous night, cook had sought interview with her; already suspicious, she had just forced out of Agnes in the kitchen a confession that she was with child. But as to the father the sulky girl remained, as cook reported, "silent as a flat-fish." Mrs. Crawford was on her way upstairs to her meditations and bed; she had told cook she would go into the matter thoroughly in the morning. . . . But in the morning Agnes's attic-room was empty. And so was Bertram's room, just below the attic stairs. And his straw hamper, which she bought for him when he travelled with her to the Evangelist Convention in Birmingham, had gone too; his chest of drawers showed signs of hasty packing. And he had not left a word of farewell. Cook thought the two would go to Agnes's mother in Portsmouth, a mother of whom she had never liked the sound . . . But worse was to come. It had occurred to her that Bertram would need money for this flight with his paramour. He had looked after the church accounts and had a cash-box in which both the monthly contributions and the Sunday-service collections were kept. They had found the cash-box empty. It was then that she had sent for Brother Mansell.

On hearing of the cash-box Mansell for the first time in the recital looked shocked. But he allowed Mrs. Crawford to pant and breathe out her fill, only remarking soothingly when at last she had eased herself: "What can you expect, dear Sister Crawford? He was a love-child—as they are so pleasantly called—and brought up in a foundlings' Home. I always thought there was something missing in his soul."

"But he seemed to be getting on so well with me," she wailed. "Always so polite and obedient. Certainly his health used to worry me, but when he began to take your tonics three or four months ago he became so very active and lively I had every hope for him."

Mansell twirled the smart ends of his moustache, which, despite her criticisms of toilet vanities, he had cleverly continued to wax. "It's plain," he said caustically, "that my tonics couldn't reach his character. It seems to me, Sister Crawford," he added with a note of healthy decision, "you are well rid of him. Later on he might not have stopped at bigger crimes . . . Can I inform the police about the cash-box?" he asked, the man in charge of affairs.

At this she gave a little dramatic scream but completely recovered from her collapse. No, she could not have the affair becoming public in any way. She had already sworn cook and the daily help to secrecy. And as for her dear Brother Mansell, she knew his tongue was discreet. . . . Did he realise, she began to whimper a little again, that in her family circle he was her only male support, now that Bertram was gone? Her brother, who lived in Totnes, hadn't spoken to her for seventeen years; there had been a bitter dispute over their father's will.

The bond became complete. It was a few weeks after this that she aided him with the memorial stone.

Months afterwards he returned compliments by giving his child Mrs. Crawford's first christian name—Marion. She was highly gratified but still never expressed a wish to meet Arabella, though she sent black grapes and red roses after the confinement, together with a copy of her *Meditations*, a little book printed locally.

Of course the sex of the child had been a great disappointment to him. In some strange way it seemed to be a setback to a progress showing every sign of success. But now he was too busy to allow a brooding gloom into his days; after deciding on the name he relegated the child entirely to Arabella. Not only was trade in the shop increasing and there were several accounts with villa owners, but he had taken over the secretarial and business affairs of the Gospel Hall, and, unable to forget the snub he had received at

St. Mark's, he began a crusade, by way of printed posters, advertising, and getting vigorous evangelists to come on visits, to attract worshippers away from the Established Church with its high and haughty spire.

Yet for all the happy industry, Mrs. Crawford sometimes began to vex him. He found himself thinking that she was too much. And one or two of her activities in the church seemed to him to lack dignity. When she took the service herself he did not like the tone of her sermons; she was too autocratic (for a woman), there was a mundane flavour, she had no true mystical flight, no rapt vision. She would take it into her head, like an obstinate old woman, to lay down the law to her congregations on such matters as insurance policies, everyday apparel, and the choice of seaside towns for holidays. Directly she entered the pulpit a wayward oddness was apt to possess her, though she often managed to link up the subjects of her addresses with Holy Writ.

Once he nearly achieved a serious rift with her. It was over the subject of Canterbury lamb.

Her butcher—he had served her well for many years—had told her of the continued objection of the working-classes to the frozen meat coming in from such respectable British colonies as Australia and New Zealand. They viewed the joints—so much cheaper than the fresh meat of England—with an hostility rooted, apparently, in an indignant suspicion that profit-making Tory powers were bamboozling them into eating inferior food. Perhaps, too, dating from early in the century, there was still a horror of those wild countries to which England's criminals were transported. Such persons as took the frozen meat bought it furtively; they hated neighbours to know; it was a proclamation of hideous poverty.

Indignant at this obstinacy of the poor, she gave a Sunday evening sermon which she opened by saying: "To-day, dear brothers and sisters, I had Canterbury lamb in my house for dinner. It was delicious." At once she obtained the congregation's astonished interest; women in particular looked startled, as if she had heaved up into the light a shame private to them. Her sermon became a lecture with a banner, the ostensible text being the sin of ignorant obstinacy. The fashionable preacher then packing the Portman Rooms with his scourgings of high society could not have had more attentive listeners. And that week the sermon was reported in the local paper.

Mansell, however, was angry. He expressed his disapproval at supper in the villa that night, with cold Canterbury lamb on the plate before him. "It savoured of advertising the butchery trade," he said bluntly.

They were alone. An ominous silence followed his remark. She was still flushed from the courage of her sermon. It was not a good moment to choose. But in any case she never would brook real criticism, only welcoming reverential treatment of selected portions of her sermons.

Then, suavely, she said: "You forget, Brother Mansell, that my church stands for education of the poor in addition to bringing everyday spiritual nourishment. . . . You had no objection," she went on, her voice becoming silvery, "to my referring to the healing products in your shop a year or so ago. Has not your custom improved?" It was a reminder that she was no fool. Somewhere in that whaleboned, brocaded and frilled lump of English obstinacy lay embedded, like a diamond in clay, a lively shrewdness.

But she had deeply irritated and shocked him to-night. Her mind seemed to him of a low order, her vision petty. Women were ill-fitted to understand mystic things. And, since Bertram's flight, he was too often in her oppressively weighty presence (oh, what a relief it was to get away to the music-hall and sit in the dazzle of Florence Delorme and her like!) Also, since her 'loan' to him for his father's memorial, a subtle element of possession had come into her manner. It was as if she had taken a pair of silver scissors and clipped his wings.

Sulky and silent, he gazed at the slices of lamb on his plate, wanting to say something grossly rude to her. He sat in chagrin, squirming interiorly. . . . But she was wealthy. She could render him great aid yet. She was prepared to do so, as he was to let her.

Though it had been roused by something trivial, he experienced what he knew was an important battle with himself. She waited, in the ominous silence. He swallowed a piece of the lamb and said: "The meat is certainly delicious." But under his moustache his smile was wolfish.

"Ah!" she tinkled, very pleased. "You must tell your wife to buy it, dear boy; she will save money . . . And that reminds me. I would like to get a cradle for little Marion; you said she slept with you and your wife—surely a dangerous thing?" The rest of the session passed amicably. She told him a great deal about her late husband's affairs and how he had built up his ships' chandler business with financial aid from her.

When he left the villa he did not go home at once. He climbed to the top of the Heath. He wanted air and heights. And a sense of power. All the time in the villa he had felt tied by the leg. And he knew that virtue had left him. He also felt very alone.

It was a soft August night. Midnight was not far off: the Heath's pastoral knolls and dim green vales were deserted. There was a smoky light in the sky, a tawny moon-gleam banked about with sullen clouds. He stood under a tree. From those heights the great sprawling city was like a mirage. A phosphorescence glimmered along its labyrinthine ways, more twisted than the paths in a man's mind. . . . But it was no mirage. Solid property stood down there. The big money-changing palaces. Houses with majestic porticoes and solemn windows. The long rows of dwellings where lived the poor who were more industrious than bees. Down there, too, beckoned the soft daughters of the night, their breasts soft as poppies. Pairs of gleaming horses neighed in stables. And of these he had nothing yet.

A man stood alone. And if he is to live he must undertake

some quest of the spirit. He saw the long bare scrubbed table in his father's house and his father seated at its head, silent and never looking at anyone, clean and grey, the descendant of a long puritan line. He had died without giving a message or revealing a secret. But though shorn of his riches, as Samson his hair, power had not really gone from him. . . .

And the son, in his reverie, watched a shadowy figure going down the grassy slope below him. It had seemed to appear from nowhere and it went down with a soft effortless glide. It raised an arm. It could be . . . who? Someone laughing in his sleeve.

Chapter Two

I

T O a roll of drums the lights went down and the curtains parted. But Mansell did not return to his seat; Florence Delorme would not appear so soon after the interval, and the man he had met in the bar was both informative and friendly.

His dismal face was eased by a pair of bright, inquisitive eyes that even his dyspepsia hadn't blighted; short and thick-set, his bowler, pushed to the back of his head, reached to just above Mansell's shoulder. He was one of the confidential, sleeve-plucking kind, standing close to one and very open in revealing their affairs.

"But there ain't lashings of cash in the tattooing business. Not much for a go-ahead man." Through the glass partition enclosing the bar he had pointed out an oval advertisement on the fire-curtain lowered during the interval—"That's him, the chap I'm managing. Been trying to advertise him in all the 'alls this side of the water. But I ask you, how many people want to be tattooed? And me a married man."

"What were you in before?" Mansell enquired, drinking his ginger beer. Glancing through the partition he saw doves fluttering round a magician in a blue kimono who stood before a painted rough seascape where a young woman, possibly Grace Darling, frantically rowed a boat.

"Me? I been in everythink. Started as an office boy in Mincing Lane but couldn't stand a stick-in-the-mud job. Been on the 'alls too, as a feed, but wasn't any good—I got to be working for myself and now I never sink lower than managing a biz. . . . Now this tattooing, we get a worthwhile job with it sometimes. Bloke came in the other week wanting a fox's tail done on him—a rich bloke of fifty in a topper; wanted it whisking right up his back. Took fourteen bouts to do it and I made Fred charge double the usual; a tail fit for a king it was, a lovely red ginger tint . . . You a married man?"

"I am. I have two daughters, and another child due at the end of the year."

"I'm married too," said the tattooist's manager dismally, "and if it wasn't for my ulcers I'd be a happy man. I'm married to May Potter."

"Oh!" said Mansell, alert but not quite believing. May Potter married to this rather low-class chap with his melancholy face and squelchy voice!

"Steaks have been my ruin," groaned Miss Potter's husband. "Can't leave them alone and they're black death to me. One thing, though—I keep off spirits; I see enough of the harm *they* do." He nodded and closed one eye meaningly.

Mansell then said, with some pomp: "*I* am a chemist. My establishment is on Prospect Terrace up by Maitland Hill. If——"

"Know Prospect Terrace all right." He looked the kind of Londoner who was familiar with every cranny of the capital, a true son of muddy King Lud. "Coach & Horses pub on the opposite corner; got a nice garden. May and me had a drink there a month ago."

"I think I could treat your dyspepsia successfully. Of course you may have a duodenal ulcer. Do you vomit?"

To a clash of cymbals the curtains swept down, and rose to disclose a tank of water and two sea-lions situated in the Hall of Mirrors at Versailles.

"Ay. Black stuff like coffee grounds. I'll give you a look up; Wednesday p'raps. You not interested in tattooing yourself? Or anyone up your way? . . . Well, if you know anyone that'd like anything from a genuwine Chinese dragon done in all colours to a cabbage rose with a scroll of 'Mother' round it, 'ere's Fred's card, and my name in the corner, see—Walt Monks, Manager. Poor Fred, he's a queer bloke, a soaker. Would tattoo clusters of fruit on anybody's fanny for nothing, if I wasn't behind him. Cousin of the wife he is." He finished his stout, bawled "So long, Elsie," to the barmaid, nodded to Mansell and went into the auditorium.

It was the beginning of an association of importance to both. Mansell recognised qualities of metropolitan astuteness in Walt Monks, to say nothing of his having a foot in the nocturnal world of the music-hall. And to Walt, forty, seemingly honest after a fashion and an inquisitive collector of 'pals', a master chemist was a useful stand-by for his gastric trouble and perhaps other disasters (for he had a morbid interest in physical decay), besides appearing to be a man of substance interested in further commitments. A born 'partner', he was constitutionally unable to stand either on his own legs or accept the position of an underling. Perhaps this was because of his ulcers.

"A man like me," he said, as he sat on the counter chair, "is best sitting down watching and thinking . . . I see 'em," he brooded on another tack, "inside me like crabs getting bigger and bigger. If I ain't careful they'll up and choke me one day."

"You must take it after every meal," Mansell labelled the bottle. "But you've got to leave off those steaks and all fried foods."

"I'll eat a steak on my death-bed," said Walt malignly. "Nice bit of property you've got here."

"I don't own it," said Mansell cautiously.

"Trade's slow in these parts, is it? Natty district, but stand-offish. . . . I know a chap," he said, "a saddler, that's doing well taking over those big houses people are getting shy of now; he furnishes 'em and lets them out by the room. Puts a manager or manageress into 'em; met him at the Derby with a flash tart on his arm. . . . London's getting busier," he said, staring at the parrot complacently searching for lice under its green wing; "people pouring in. Since the Coronation I never seen London looking more prosperous. And here I'm sitting," he grunted, "wasting for lack of capital."

A slim fluffy-haired girl of seven or eight ran in with a hoop, causing the parrot to swing on its perch with a wrathful shriek. The girl put out her tongue at the hostile bird, flapped her nankeen frock at it, danced over to the counter and, putting her head sideways, asked for a barley-sugar.

"No, child: go in to your tea."

She tossed her head, gave Mr. Monks a vivacious glance, and ran through the dispensary. "My elder daughter, Marion," Mansell said.

"She'd make a good juvenile on the 'alls, should think," Mr. Monks gazed calculatingly after her. "A pretty voice and style. Friend of mine is making his ten quid a week out of his twin girls doing a few cartwheels and bit of tap-dancing. Audiences like children; takes some of the bad taste out of their mouths after the low comics."

"My daughter," said Mansell, with a pronounced frigidity, "will never go on the Halls, Mr. Monks."

"Call me Walt, for God's sake," he implored. "I'm known from the Elephant to the Heath as Walt. . . . You ain't religious, are you?" he suddenly asked, his glance cocked up in a bright agony.

"I am secretary of the Laburnum Road Gospel Hall," Mansell replied, not without pride.

Walt looked at him with a moment's wonder, but, with

the acceptance of true sophistication, nodded and said: "A bit of religion comes in useful sometimes. Flourishing concern, is it?"

There grew between them the attraction of opposites. Opposites at least in outward characteristics. Mansell, as a more or less established family chemist, was achieving a polished, rather handsome dignity. And his clothes were correctly dark, his linen, over which Arabella drudged thrice weekly, always spick and span. Walt, stumpy, wearing celluloid collars and false dicky fronts, and with a suggestion of furtively ducking his head from commitments which were too binding, part of his mind buried in his wretched stomach but most of it occupied in a sparrow-like watching for worldly opportunities, seemed remote from the dignity of his friend.

For friends they became; quite intimate friends. From the first, Walt's treatment of the chemist as a man of solid substance was exactly what Mansell, ever running from one part of his being to the other, required. On his side, he acknowledged in Walt a deep knowledge of this massive city with its peculiar opportunities down byways and back-washes.

One June afternoon he took Walt into the living-room for tea and to meet Arabella. After the visitor had gone even she humbly ventured a remark: "He doesn't look a man *you* can be seen about with, Mansell. Something to do with betting, is he?"

"Betting? Certainly not. He's interested in buying up old property."

"Is he married?"

"No doubt, no doubt. . . . Come, Arabella, look at the time. Did Marion fetch my best boots from the cobbler's? I'm closing earlier this evening. If Mrs. Perry comes to the door give her the package I've left on the ledge."

"Can't Marion take it up to her house?" She didn't like answering the door when he was out.

"No, certainly not. I cannot allow my daughter to go

to that house." More he would not say. And within an hour, dressed like a gentleman of means, he left the premises and vanished into the rosy evening.

"Where has my father gone?" Marion asked in a speculative way as her mother plaited her hair that night.

"To the Gospel Hall, or to Mrs. Crawford's house, I expect."

"I think he's gone to Richmond," Marion said with an air of authority. "I heard him tell Mr. Monks he would get to Richmond about eight o'clock. . . . Did you feed the baby?" she enquired, and, doubtless by an association of ideas, she went into the scullery and poured a saucer of milk for the cat.

Already her manner declared an instinctive awareness of her position as first child and of her power as a frizzy-haired child with whom strangers in the street and shop were delighted to pass the time of the day—and, more mysteriously instinctive, of her mother's isolation and wilting condition. One day her father had caught her tearing a leaf out of a Papier Poudré booklet and applying it vigorously to her cheeks. He had been very stern. Not a whit disturbed, she had listened, apparently with appreciation, to his point of view.

"There's someone knocking at the shop door," she announced, coming from the scullery in her nightdress; "I'll go." Surprisingly, her mother was sitting down idle and in deep thought.

"No, Marion. Run upstairs and see if Gwen is sleeping. Rock the cradle if she's awake."

"Where is her dummy-teat?" Marion asked busily. "Don't forget to cover Polly's cage. He was in such a temper just now he scattered all his seed." She placidly accepted the bird's strange dislike of her.

In the shop doorway stood Mrs. Perry. Arabella looked at her, then beckoned her in, closed the door and drew its blind. She did not quite know why she assumed a secretive manner with this youngish woman in her flamboyant silver-buckled green cloak, and whose head of rust-coloured hair was bohemianly hatless. Arabella understood that her medicine was for something quite normal and that her wild look was due to brandy-drinking.

Mrs. Perry had come for her laudanum. At her entreaty Mansell had lately increased the morphine in it; she paid him generously. She was one of those women who exhibit their sorrows at the least provocation; she found the world a callous, unforgivable place. After a brief career on the stage she had become an artist's model and finally married a stockbroker with whom she lived in a villa on the Hill. Mansell was partial to her in almost an avuncular way.

"Here it is," Arabella held out the package.

"As true as God's above," moaned Mrs. Perry, having sunk on to the counter chair, "one of these days I'll cut his throat."

"Now, now," breathed Arabella agitatedly, "that's no way to talk."

"You've got a husband worthy of the name. Not a bull of a man who turns out not to be such a bull after all and runs every five minutes to his mama for sympathy. I'll put a bullet in him some day. *And* her!"

Arabella looked about her in fear. So this is what went on in the high-and-mighty villas! She felt justified in her dread of this terrible city.

"I've just smashed some of his Crown Derby dinner-set," Mrs. Perry began to heave. "And he's gone off to his mother across the Heath again. . . . Why did I leave Sasha, poor though he was!" she broke into hoarse wailing. "Why did I think I could become respectable? . . . It's killing me!" she shrieked.

"Hush, dear, hush!" Arabella begged. "My baby is asleep just above you. And someone might pass the door."

"A good husband *and* babies!" wailed Mrs. Perry. "I wouldn't have a baby from that stockbroking stoat if——"

"Be quiet!" ordered Arabella, stern. "My daughter will be listening."

"Little Marion," crooned Mrs. Perry, suddenly calm, perhaps in exhaustion; "a sweet child . . . Oh, and your husband, you don't know how lucky you are, dearie . . . Pretty Poll!" she sang. "Pretty Poll!"

Arabella hovered pointedly near the door, but she asked: "Where is Richmond, Mrs. Perry?"

"A holiday place on the river . . . Ah," she said dreamily, "many's the evening I've spent there in a punt with Sasha. A lovely place for a good evening out. One day he sketched me sitting under a willow with my little dog looking up at me so sweetly."

When, sighing and whimpering, she had gone at last, Arabella went up to the top floor to see that Marion was safely tucked in for the night. Of course Mansell had gone to Richmond to look at some property with that Mr. Monks. He never did confide his business affairs in her, never. But of one thing she felt almost certain—he did not drink. Never the slightest sign of it. He wouldn't be so foolish, with him so closely connected with the Gospel Hall and Mrs. Crawford.

She stood at the top window stealthily looking out.

There was a view over the monster city, and in the sunset a glimpse of the Thames like the slime of a snail's path. Among the confusion of sombre buildings lay petals of smokily pink light and a huge dome floating like a blue bubble. She shivered. It might have been some barbaric and hostile city, an illustration in the missionary books at home in Wales. She went downstairs, slower than usual, her mind clinging to the thought of cleaning the cutlery. But first she went into their bedroom.

In the cradle Gwen, a fine plump two-year-old, lay fast asleep. She was little trouble, unlike Marion had been. A month after Marion's birth Mansell had insisted she should be fed on a new patent food he stocked in the shop. But years later, when she got stronger, he often pointed out to customers his lively pretty daughter as proof of the food's invigorating qualities, though otherwise his interest in

Marion had been slow in developing, and in her precocious way it was the child herself who insisted on his notice. Gwen he totally ignored, so far. He had even been indifferent that she should be fed with the patent food—after all, it cost half a crown a tin whereas Nature was bountiful to her mother, despite her worn and sallow look.

Arabella tidied the room. He had dressed himself with special care to-night, making a complete change of linen. She picked up a black necktie; her smoothing of its creases had the delicacy of a half-frightened caress. Downstairs she cleaned the cutlery and washed and starched yet another of his shirts. She ate a bowl of mutton broth; she kept looking at the clock. By midnight she had accomplished other tasks; she could not sit down. He had never been as late as this. *Was* he taking to drink with that Mr. Monks?

2

Her fears on that account were groundless. All Mansell drank that night was one glass of champagne—and that only out of courtesy. He was intoxicated by a more potent force than drink. For the first time he met May Potter.

It was her birthday. She was resting between provincial engagements. Mansell was highly gratified when Walt invited him to the picnic supper on the river, particularly as no one else was to be honoured. They met below the bridge. Walt had already hired a punt and conveyed the picnic basket to it. He sat in his braces reading *The Pink 'Un* while the chained punt gently swayed its splendid other burden. May Potter sat musing as though unaware of the strollers. Mansell, descending to the towpath, saw her before he noticed Walt.

A large spray of roses was pinned to her bosom. With a white-gloved hand she held a Japanese parasol against the strong sunset. Yellow curls played charmingly about her pink-and-white face. Her gown made one think of fucshsia and from a hat of milky straw two long velvet ribbons streamed down her back. Of course the passers-by were staring at her. Not only did she look striking but many must have recognised May Potter, even though her name on the posters, when she appeared in the West End, lay down among the 'wine and spirits'.

"There you are, 'ole boy." Walt looked sweaty. "Step in. Where'll you sit? Next to May? Or me? . . . Meet the wife," he said as Mansell cautiously stepped over. "We had our photos taken an hour ago—chap came along with his contraption and a black cloth big enough to cover the Albert Memorial. Quite a crowd collected."

"I've been at him about sitting there in his braces," were May's first words to her husband's friend. But she spoke without that vexation common in the voices of upbraiding wives.

Mansell was surprised to find her speaking voice almost made one think of a squeak. He had heard her sing at a hall in Islington; he had heard her ring out in Tosti's *Good-bye*, the lake of Killarney behind her. Her blue eyes— they were of an extraordinary purity like the blue of a wayside flower—were playing over him with the expertly aloof glance of the actress assessing an audience. At her next remark he felt approved: "Your friend could teach you how to dress, Walt. What's his name?"

"Mr. Roberts. Mansell Roberts. . . . When we first met," he chuckled, "up in the bar at the Bedford, I thought his first name would be Pharoah. But he ain't so starched as he looks—are you, 'ole boy? That's right, sit next to me. I'll have to get to the back and paddle her."

He sat facing May Potter. He sat facing her in a private boat! Save for "Good evening" to Walt (with a low silent bow to his wife), he had said nothing yet. His mouth was dry. Now the scent of roses reminded him. Formally he handed across to her the package he carried.

"I heard it was your birthday. With many happy returns from an old admirer of Miss May Potter."

Walt, getting up, cocked his eye. "Crikey, we ain't in Windsor Castle, 'ole boy. You'll be on your knee kissing her 'and next. She's bin wondering all day if you'd bring her anythink." It seemed to Mansell that he was being deliberately common of speech this evening.

"Oh, you liar!" Her cry was certainly a shrill squeak. But she was so pleased, opening the package with the hands of a greedy child, there was no wrath in the squeak.

"Them roses on her milkshop," Walt continued, taking up a paddle at the back, "cost Fred five bob. I was going to bring 'im but 'e's got a big job on tattooing a boa-constrictor all round the middle of a client I found for 'im—a seedy-looking bloke that hasn't got a chin. Besides, Fred's always in the glooms."

"Oh!" With a theatrical cry May held up the bottle. Even Walt forbore further comment, though the thought 'had it at cost price' was no doubt evident in his eye. "My favourite scent," May cried delightedly. "Thank you, Mr. Roberts." Then, winningly, even flirtatiously, she said: "I think I will call you Pharaoh. Can I?"

"Of course, of course." He would not have minded if it had been Solomon or Beelzebub. He felt extraordinarily roused, as though he had suddenly walked into a new careless world quivering with gay lights.

Squeezing up his face, Walt got the punt into mid-stream. He said they had steak for tea at an hotel. And in the picnic basket was a fowl, tomatoes, a trifle, maids-of-honour tartlets, a bag of cherries and—yes, he smacked his lips, a bottle of 'bubbly'. He then ruminated at some length on the prospects in the photography business. A chap he knew in Notting Hill was in it and doing well.

"I'd like the cherries now," May said.

She sat eating cherries while the punt gently sucked at the water. She sat daintily spitting out the stones into one pink ungloved fist, her luscious mouth never ceasing to work. "Spoil your supper," Walt said. "But you always had an appetite. Offer some to Pharaoh, greedy." She offered him a stalk of two. May Potter held up two cherries to him! Swans glided up to the punt. The sunset flared in deepening crimsons behind her. She closed the parasol. The evening was breathless. A petal fell from the roses at her breast.

Presently Walt steered the boat into thick clumps of bulrushes in a backwater; it was time for supper. And at his remark as he peered over the side—"Nobody left a young Moses here?"—his wife cracked into peals of laughter of the most abandoned kind. She seemed unable to stop; all her body was given over to it. Mansell could see right into the interior, moist as a peach, of her mouth. Her throat had the pulpiness of the singer.

"You 'ave got a cosy laugh, May," observed Walt, unpacking the basket. Yet Mansell, his senses trebly alert, wondered it that laughter was really the clashing of nerves roused like his own. After the presentation of the perfume only once had she looked at him, with a quick dart of those pure blue eyes.

"On the quiet side to-night, Pharaoh," Walt remarked.

"You chatter enough for everybody," his wife riposted, easing herself after the paroxysm. "Pharaoh's enjoying the quiet of the river." Yet still she did not look at him.

And still he sat in a muse. Ah, it was a far cry from the farm in Wales, austere as an Old Testament chapter, to this scene on the famous river where he sat drinking champagne in friendly intercourse with a music-hall star (well, almost a star; and surely she was still under thirty). The image of his father, dim and cloudy, haunted the edge of his reverie. Was not the son slowly but surely attaining the richness of which the father, lonely and disappointed, had been thwarted? By what intimacy of cell, nerve and sinew had he known that his father was a man enamoured of the world's abundance but, locked in an ancestral puritanism, dreaded his own passion?

"What's up, Pharaoh?" reiterated Walt. "The hoss didn't come in?"

"You do keep on," May protested, nibbling at a chicken wing. "He's quite happy."

"I *am*," Mansell averred swiftly, "I am." And in an effort to add to the conversation he told them about his queer customer Mrs. Perry and her begging for laudanum.

"A soubrette on the bill with me in Birkenhead was the same," May shook her head. "She had an awful set-to with the Blue Man from Borneo that she was living with. Drink I can understand, but not drugs, ugh!"

"You can understand drink all right," Walt winked at Mansell as he refilled her outstretched glass.

"Oh, you liar!"

Even in the going light Mansell noticed a fold in her cheeks, a thickness under her eyes. She hadn't what you'd call a perfect face. But that was how it should be. How awful if she was perfection, an angel! A man required defects for the sake of his confidence. He hoped she drank. And he spoke more boldly: "A little drink is sometimes of benefit along life's thorny path."

"That don't sound like you," Walt rebuked. "And you the secretary of the Gospel Hall!" This made Mansell flush.

"Don't tease him," said May in a high voice. "I won't have our Pharaoh teased."

"He didn't bring *me* a bottle of scent."

"Black draught is what I should have brought you," Mansell broke in at last. But not without a dim recognition of the vulgarity to which he was sinking.

And again May's laughter mounted up and up, to crescendo. They all laughed, Walt with a hollow *hoo*, *hoo*ing born in the roof of his mouth, not in his gastric stomach. But Mansell's light crash mingled harmoniously in the deep golden wash of May's cries: it was a delicious union in laughter, a rolling over of liberated beings. Finally she dabbed her eyes, peeping at him with wet little peeps. Several rose petals had fallen into her lap during the convulsion.

"Walt," gasped May, "you must take the punt to that place we passed. You know." She took from under a cushion a little silver-mesh bag.

"Ho!" observed Walt. When they got there May, assisted by her husband, heaved herself up while Mansell discreetly collected the débris of the meal. She walked into the dusky garden of what looked like an inn. With a fine strutting walk, a confident stage roll in it.

"It's been a wonderful evening——" Mansell began, in a falsely chatty way.

"Thought any more of that idea I put to you?" Walt enquired with the cerebral intensity he used in business topics.

"Well . . . *when* I've seen the premises, and *if* I can raise the five hundred, I don't see anything at present against a partnership." Actually he was very excited by the idea. But the exact opportunity to sound Mrs. Crawford, who was ill, had not yet occurred.

Walt gave his honest opinion of the prospects and his further gleanings concerning the district. Quite a while passed before he observed: "May's gone a long time." Mansell, preoccupied, decided that he had been left alone with Walt purposely. He also decided that a business association with Walt was desirable. When May returned at last she seemed distant and even sad.

3

He hastened to the villa on the Hill the next evening. After a restless night—Arabella had highly irritated him with her dumb look of reproach when he got home very late from Richmond—he had become more and more determined, churning up a dramatic air around him. Why had he delayed? Mrs. Crawford surely waited to be used. Sunk in her decline she was bored and her grasp of earthly matters was less shrewd.

Enthroned in the carved shawl-draped and cushion-padded chair, she was eating strawberries off a silver plate. Since her slight stroke she had given up her big suppers with their large helpings of meat and sturdy puddings. And the Gospel Hall did not see its Queen so often now. She was content to leave its affairs to her honorary secretary.

"Well, dear boy? You look very eager. Is it such a pleasure to see your old friend?" She whined a little. In place of the regal despotism was its penalty, loneliness.

Drawing a footstool close to the throne and sinking down so that his head was convenient for a touch, he plunged at once: "Yes, I am excited. Through a friend, Mr. Monks, I've had a wonderful chance to acquire a valuable property very cheaply. But I want your advice, my dear. In the first place, ought I to take advantage of the business innocence of a stupid woman?"

"Explain, dear boy." She was certainly roused.

"Mr. Monks—he's an expert on property—took me to see this lady at her house. Oh, a terrible painted woman—it seems she was kept by a married man." He shuddered. "She made eyes at me! But she's very silly. She did talk about putting the house in an agent's hands, but Mr. Monks has since told me that if I played up to her a little and offered her quick cash down she'd let me have it at about three hundred under to-day's value—of which she knows nothing."

"How much would she take?" clanged Mrs. Crawford, her face going solid. "A woman like that certainly deserves to be beaten."

"Eight hundred," he said, carefully lifting a strawberry stalk out of her satin lap.

"You've got eight hundred?"

"Of course not. I could only spare two hundred at the most and that would clean me out. What with Marion going to the private day school and this third child coming——"

"Where is this house?"

"Near Paddington station. Three floors and a basement; eleven rooms. The neighbourhood is getting very busy. Mr. Monks says if I let the house out in rooms I could turn over a clear ten or twelve pounds a week."

"You mean *we* could, dear boy?" Far within the creases of her face she smiled—that face so dominant in aspect and, like all dominant faces, wanting to be melted by the right appeal for help or protection.

"You'll come in with me?" he murmured.

"*Not* as a landlady," she wagged her finger; "I cannot accept the thought of my keeping lodgers. But I may be able to lend you eight hundred at some small percentage. You've given me and the church faithful service . . . I have not forgotten it already," she added with that impressive depth of meaning used by persons who have wills worth the making.

He said nothing. But his hand stole out tentatively, only to be withdrawn with a beautiful shyness.

"Of course," she said, activity beating up into her voice, "if you let the rooms furnished you'd get bigger rents."

"I had thought of that," he said. "But the expense of furniture! This lady——"

"Don't call her that, dear boy; she can't be one. . . . I will give you some furniture; this house is overpacked with it—what need have I of so much now?" she began to boom. "All these chairs in the house and so few people to sit in them! Stacks of linen. Can I take them to the eternal mansions? . . . And if there is not enough, you can buy the rest second-hand; it will be good enough for lodgers. I will advance you a thousand in all."

He took the last strawberry on her plate and slowly ate it. Then he carefully wiped Mrs. Crawford's fingers with his snowy linen handkerchief.

The interview was a lesson to him. Persons of standing liked to talk in thousands. He must extend both his courage and his vision if he was to become one of the commercial

princes of London. That very evening he vowed that he
would own a chain of houses, leading to the glory of hotels.

While the house transaction was proceeding Mrs.
Crawford—on Mansell's advice she was taking bromide—
asked a few questions but, on the whole, was amicable to
everything. She gave him to understand, vaguely, that her
three per cent on the loan would be inserted in the agreement merely for the sake of form and her solicitor. The
solicitor however was never consulted; neither was any
agreement drawn up. But she did ask how the lodging-
house was to be managed.

"A private residence for people of accepted position.
I shall require references."

"Yes, yes . . . but who will be on the premises in
charge?"

"Mr. Monks will rent a room there. He also knows of
a highly respectable Scottish lady who could be housekeeper; she's elderly and was the assistant matron of an
orphanage."

"Surely we could find someone among our flock for the
position? There is Mrs. Nudd, for instance, a widow and
penurious——"

"I feel," he coughed rather hurriedly, "the position calls
for a woman of very firm character. Apparently this
Scottish lady is so forbidding of manner that no lodger
would dare to trade on her Christian feelings."

"You seem to rely a great deal on your Mr. Monks,"
ruminated Mrs. Crawford, just a shade of hostility in her
voice. "Am I to meet him?"

"Why, of course. But he travels in the country a great
deal, inspecting property."

She never did meet Walt Monks. Walt himself did not
know of her existence. But his respect for Mansell increased
boundlessly when all the purchase money for the house in
Dover Terrace was produced. The painted lady, bodily,
was no imaginary creation; only her character was this; she
was quite aware of the value of her house.

Mansell spent one more bad night during this particularly busy time. These dark nights of the soul came down on him at intervals—ever since that midnight years ago when he had stood on Hampstead Heath and seen the Devil walk away from him laughing in his sleeve. Sleepless, but during the dragging hours falling into what seemed like trances more real in their activities than a wakeful state, he would toss among a confused mass of thoughts and emotions. His skull seemed licked by flames. Yet, though his limbs twitched, his body lay totally in abeyance, as if dead or anæsthetised. It was as if his spirit was unleashed from its physical bondage and thrashed within his head in chaotic mastery.

On this night, lying in one of these turmoils of apparent slumber, he felt his eyes slowly open. At the same time there was a far-away thought of being asleep. He found the room flooded with a dim reddish light. He saw fantastic objects in its dull glow. Above the bed his father's head, cut off at the neck like John the Baptist's. It vanished abruptly. A huge tank of water stood before the curtained window and a sea-lion lunged up, opening its snouted mouth to give a barbaric laugh that, though silent, split his skull. He saw a broken graveyard column and a marble dove. He smelt perfumes of carnations and lilies that by some strange alchemy of the moment became stinks in his mind.

He cried out—was there a cry?—as his body struggled up in anguish from its cords of death. Did he hear those cords snap like catgut? He found himself sitting up in bed. But he knew his agony was not yet over. Vestiges of the terrible sleep still about him, he had a sense of being hounded through mysterious lanes of the spirit. Towards a further mystery, a core, a palpitating heart of knowledge lying wrapped within a blood-coloured grove tangled with roots and hung with writhing branches like veins.

At last he became aware of the black stillness of the room. He felt himself a helpless child shivering among nameless terrors of the world. Dimly he sensed Arabella fast in sleep somewhere within that bed which now appeared vast, solemn and lonely. Presently he lay back and remained unmoving. Arabella had not stirred; she always seemed to sleep well, perhaps because of her physical industriousness. He lay still and exhausted.

There came down on him the consciousness, profound and certain, of the soul's unalterable loneliness.

As always after these strange nights he felt grey and older the next day. A dry ashy taste lay in the day. He attended to the shop in a mood of fretful dislike. Yet he couldn't bring himself to take a tonic or a sedative. Not because of an experienced chemist's contempt of his stock, but because of a half-superstitious dread. The agony of the night belonged to something that forbade the physical act of taking a drug.

What he did feel in need of was the company of Mr. Monks. That amiable matter-of-factness of May Potter's husband was, in its way, cleansing, despite his melancholic concern with his inside. To-night there was also the possibility that if her turn was on early in that music-hall across the water May would arrive home at a reasonable hour.

They lived off Holborn in a street of sagging-roofed houses smelling of cats and fungus-clusters. They occupied two basement rooms at twelve-and-six a week. Mansell had been surprised, and pleased, to find that May's earnings were on the paltry side. Walt drew a very small commission from the tattooing business and from advertisements solicited for music-hall programmes—Mansell had already given him one wherein his new creation, a hair-pomade made of genuine bear's fat, was tastefully announced at half a crown the bottle, post free.

He had not yet fathomed the mystery why May had married a man who seemed so totally devoid of any advantages, either physical or spiritual. But he did feel in need of his company to-night, ah, he did indeed! Luckily,

Walt was at home, soaking his feet in steaming water. Two pairs of kippers lay on an open newspaper on the table— "Got 'em in Aldgate; May likes 'em," Walt said. "I been on the go all day after ads. A glass of stout, Pharaoh? Over in the chiffinier there . . . I got to see an Eyetalian bloke ten o'clock in a coffee-shop by Drury Lane," he added—"about Fred doing the Bay of Naples on his chest; seems he comes from those parts."

"No stout," Mansell flicked back his coat-tails as he sat in the battered windsor chair. "Too hot." There was a fire in the grate, which was of the kitchen variety with hobs.

"That corn-salve of yours ain't done much good," Walt looked in dismal horror at a foot. "May's got a corn coming too."

"May can't have corns in her profession!" Mansell exclaimed; he jerked a little.

"Lord," chuckled Walt, "some of 'em on the 'alls are so corny you'd think they'd crawled out of the tombs in the Abbey." He dried his feet. "Must say, though, your white stuff is doing my old bread-pan good. Toast yourself a pair of kippers, Pharaoh. I got a steak for myself."

"I'm not hungry." Mansell gazed restlessly at the array of performers' photographs, all signed with a flourish and tacked to the fly-blown wallpaper. There was one of May.

"What's up, Pharaoh? Jumpy to-night, ain't you? Don't want to back out of the biz, do you? I saw that tart yesterday and she'll be leaving the house certain on the 30th."

"No, no; everything is going smoothly my end." He got up and wandered about the room gazing at the photographs while Walt laced his boots. "It's the heat," he said, stopping at May's portrait—surely not a recent one? She was looking downward, in pensive mood, a glacial beauty in the oval face. "May looks quite sad here."

"That? Taken in Blackpool. She'd just buried her sister and I took her up there to forget it."

"How long have you been married to May?" He turned round with an air of casualness.

"Me?" Walt cocked an eye up at him. "I ain't married to her."

Mansell sat down, his mouth open but silent.

"I got a wife in Canterbury, down Kent way," Walt fetched a bottle of stout. "A mistake, *she* was. Chambermaid in a class hotel at the time." He poured the stout. "So I can't marry May. Sure you won't have a drop? . . . Well, seeing that you and me's going to be close partners, you ought to know the worse—or best is it?" He cocked his eye again, drinking. "Me and May, we've got used to each other. I knew her when she had her 'air down her back— my dad lived next door to her cousin Fred's family, near the Elephant. But after dad chucked the bucket I went roving for a bit. I didn't see her again till I was a feed on the 'alls myself and the wife back in Canterbury—which she didn't ought to have left, with a temper like hers." His bird-eye squeezed up, he ruminated malignly for a space.

Mansell still sat in silence.

"No, May and me ain't married. She's never been married to any man. . . . But we ain't got kids to point the finger of scorn at us," he added unexpectedly; "that's one blessing. Ha, reminds me of that old chap who was dying and called all his fourteen to his bedside—'I got,' he croaked, 'an awful confession to tell you 'fore I go to my Maker . . . I wasn't married to your mother!' Terrible silence, the fourteen all turned white—all except one that stretched himself and said as the old man breathed his last: 'Well, I dunno about you bastards but *I'm* off to the Pig & Whistle.'"

Mansell still appeared to be gravely preoccupied. Walt gave him a shrewd glance and said sympathetically: "Born and bred in country parts, wasn't you?" He heaved a hiccupped sigh. "Where it's my ambition to end in peace 'fore my ulcers get me . . . a garden and poultry and all."

But the visitor was still plunged in reverie even when May arrived a quarter-hour after Walt had gone to his appointment—"No, you stay," Walt had said; "you've got the glooms, I can see. May will cheer you up, ole boy. . . . Expect you've been having a turn with your missus," he had added mildly; "we all get a dose of that."

She came into the gaslit underground room with a sweep of her fashionable skirts and her bust held up with the assurance of the actress. "Why, Pharaoh!" she smiled behind her white-spotted veil and, taking the pins out of her hat: "A treat! I'd have come earlier." Hat and veil removed, those pure blue eyes flickered at him. "Nothing gone wrong about the house business?"

"No, no . . . just a friendly visit."

She peeled off her gloves. And saw his quick pounce on her wedding ring. "Walt's told you then?" she said in a high voice. "I wear it to stop questions. He asked me if he was to tell you . . . Oh," her tone changed rapidly, "I'm happy to-night."

"Why?" He was still standing, gravely. She was powdered and rouged. Perfume came from her. There was a faint line of green fascinatingly under her eyes, where the thick flesh began.

"Why?" Her smile became mysterious; in it seemed that elusive sadness he thought he detected in her. "Oh, I don't know. Perhaps because we had a good house to-night. I had to give two encores." She began to laugh. "And there was such a row backstage. The Looe Sisters were on the bill, Eunice and Barbara—you know, they call themselves The Cornish Nightingales. Well, Snoddy Hayes made fun of them to their faces; said there had never been any nightingales so far west as Cornwall—best they could do down there was crows. '*Scarecrows*' somebody else bawled from behind a piece of scenery. My word, Eunice's language!" Beaming in malice, she took two cigars out of her silver-mesh bag. "The manager gave me these for Walt. You have one, dear . . . oh, you don't smoke." She took the toasting fork and sat by the fire with a kipper. Walt had already laid the table; two pint bottles of stout and one glass were included.

The mantelpiece clock ticked the golden moments away. For the first time he was alone with her. He sought desperately for words. She turned the kipper. "Hand me that plate, Pharaoh," she squealed, because of the grease. "This chimney wants sweeping. Don't you smell soot?"

"Walt was telling me you're troubled with a corn," he mumbled.

She gave a surprised little shriek. The note of intimacy in it was exquisite. "Why, I was only this second thinking of my corn. The heat of the fire brings it out. Oh, Pharaoh, we think together!"

"I was trained at Bristol in ailments of the feet," he said in a rushing voice as if some menacing force hounded him. "If Walt has a razor——" But he stopped, curbed.

"We'll see after supper," she said with a judiciously prudish turn. "Now a kipper for you."

"I cannot eat. I'm off colour."

"What! And you a chemist!"

"I am also a man," he smiled at last.

And then she dived into that torrential laughter of hers which was so shattering. Her flanks heaved like a boat's. The kipper fell into the grate ashes—"No matter," she skrieked, "it's worth it." She rolled in joy. Perfumes were released from her with the heavings. The room was very warm. Her yellow curls shook in the yellow unshaded gaslight. He saw her breasts tautly pointed up in the power of her laughter. He did not join in it but sat with a fixed smile. All fears had suddenly left him. Another force, ancient and conquering, had gained mastery.

Later he cut her corn. Her foot, though small, was not beautiful. But it had a soft childish roundness that pleased him; he smiled at it. Dipping the long shining blade in whisky he extracted the corn very deftly. He knelt on the floor; the foot rested on a soiled pink cushion. She gave half-playful squeals. When it was done he slowly rose, the razor extended in his hand. His aquiline nose seemed more curved, quivering and tight-stretched. He stood as though in a dream. A curious luminance, unearthly yet strong, shone in his eyes.

She pulled on her stocking and wriggled into her shoe. Then, after glancing from the clock to the open razor still in his hand, she said with a little quaver of mingled excitement and fear: "Walt will be back any minute now, I suppose." She rose. "I'll put his razor away; give it me."

He laid the razor on the table. And at the same time he suddenly looked depleted. A grey exhaustion slackened his face. She began to hum a tune as she collected the dishes on the table; it seemed she had no intention of otherwise breaking the silence. And he was glad of it. He sat down and, chin on hand, stared into the fire. But he knew that some day this woman would be his possession.

May brought out a bottle of brandy and he accepted a small amount. After this they sat subdued, talking of the house in Dover Terrace.

4

Arabella did not become aware of her husband's new business plunge until the transactions were completed. But that he was a new-born man was evident. He was kindly to her but preoccupied, flitting out every evening. At table he looked across at her with the polite abstraction of a man in an omnibus. Yet there was this strange blossoming in his face, as if whipped up blood left there a roseate tint and a happy confidence.

When, at tea, he told her about the purchase she seemed to crumple in relief. So it was merely that! "Mansell," she breathed, "there's glad I am you've found something else at last."

"It's only a beginning. I'm going to make big money. I can educate Marion and Gwen, and my son—I must get rich for him."

She sat in a dream. How right was her confidence in him when they married! And her own care and economies in the house were justified. He did not waste money out in the mysterious city nights. No doubt she had been unjust about that Mr. Monks too. She would not lessen her thrift; Mansell had a long way to go yet.

"I was thinking," he said, eating cake, "that to save buying furniture for this apartment house we could spare some from here; and perhaps some linen and so on."

Arabella slowly looked up. Her precious furniture polished with such jealous love through the years: the linen washed and ironed so carefully . . . friendly possessions, comfortable securities in this alien place far from her race. There was a blankness in her face, as of someone uncertain. Then the light of martyrdom flickered through, a gentle ecstasy of yielding.

"Yes," she murmured; "we can spare some."

"Some day," he looked up at the clock, "we shall live in a villa on the Hill . . . Well, Marion?" he said, vaguely parental as the child ran in from afternoon school.

"I want a kite." She put her head enticingly on one side.

"Kites are for boys. Or tomboys. *Not* little ladies." He patted her head with a remote grandeur as he passed, the consulting chemist and the man of property, on the way into the shop.

"I'll ask Mrs. Perry for one," she called, an affable threat in her voice.

"Arabella," he turned scoldingly, "you must be more firm with this child; she's getting spoilt. On no account is she to pester Mrs. Perry." He disappeared, Marion looking after him curiously. From the hearth-rug Gwen, solid in her dumpiness, watched with fat wide eyes; Marion always interested her.

"That's no way to talk to your father, Marion." But there was not much rebuke in Arabella's voice.

"Well," Marion said, a gleam of candour in her face, "he should tell me himself. He is always walking away. He doesn't bother with me very much, does he?"

"Now, now," Arabella seemed really vexed; "your

father is a very busy man." She got up and attended to her elder child's tea. Her pregnancy was very evident.

A son, he had said yet again. She prayed nightly she would have a son for him. His need had so entered the texture of her being that it had become a wearing and tiring obsession. Some afternoons—but with what a feeling of guilt!—she had to rest on the sofa. It wasn't that her body was tired. A strange blotting out of her mind plunged her mind into darkness, and her whole being felt empty, like someone weak from starvation or who lacks some vital necessity. She had not experienced these oppressive bouts when carrying either Marion or Gwen. But dimly she felt that the birth of this child would bring her life to its final stage, that thereafter she would settle down into a new happiness. She would be a completed human being with no more of importance to expect from the world.

Several pieces of furniture were taken from the house the following week; also both the rugs in their bedroom, a pair of vases and three engravings of biblical scenes. "It's nothing to what Mrs. Crawford is lending," Mansell told her; "but even so, Monks will have to search for a lot of second-hand stuff for me. I've got a sterling partner there, Arabella. When it's all ready you must come down and see the house before the tenants are in."

"How far is it?"

"Near Paddington station, where you arrived when you first came to London."

"An awful long way it was from here," she said. The vague distances of deserts seemed in her voice. "It's best for me not to go out now."

"As you like, as you like. Now, those towels——"

Walt was indeed invaluable. His knowledge of where and how to pick up bargains was astonishing. For days, accompanied by a downtrodden weed of a man with a barrow, he visited junk-shops and street markets, his purchases ranging from bedsteads and Indian bamboo furniture to a trout preserved in a glass cabinet and a hair-

tidy made of shells. One evening Mansell arrived at the
house and found in the hall an enormous oil-painting
ferociously depicting The Charge of Balaklava—"Had it
for ten bob," Walt preened himself. "Came from a duke's
house. Gone down in price since then; but it'll go up again,
you see! Give class to the first floor front . . . Look what I
got for five bob——" He held up a toy wooden cupboard
which sprang open to reveal a nude woman posed modestly
with an arm across her eyes.

Mansell made an annoyed gesture of dismissal and asked:
"Come, come; did you see the gas people to-day?" He had
wondered before if his partner concealed lecherous inclina-
tions beyond his stomachic gloom.

And the handy men and half-professionals Walt picked
up! He had a rooted objection to engaging for repairs and
decorations any recognised firm. Payment of these men
was done in a hand-slipping, lowered-voice manner, but
Mansell agreed their charges were very low and many
pounds were saved. Cans of paint and bundles of wallpaper
were usually delivered at the house late at night. "I don't
believe in middle-men," Walt declared stoutly; "they're
the curse of our country. I like 'aving the good old-
fashioned craftsman who works on his own and can drink
his pint of beer with the best."

Walt also suggested the appropriate rents for the rooms.
Mansell was astonished by their expensiveness. But Walt,
with May at the conference and nodding agreement, said:
"Better to have some rooms empty for a while than get
riff-raff in. We got to take the long view, Pharaoh, same as
in all solid undertakings."

Yet when the house was opened on August 1st every
room was let. "I've had intros. to 'em all," Walt said,
"through friends of mine and May's." Since Mansell was
tied to the shop it was Walt who had interviewed the
prospective tenants, sitting in the larger of the hall-floor
rooms which he and May, when she was in town, occupied
rent free. (The manager was also to draw fifteen per cent

of the rent roll.) A daily charwoman was the sole domestic help, a Mrs. Moon. She had lost an eye which, judging by her aspect, had gone in some fierce cat-and-dog kind of combat; but she adored May and had been a theatre dresser in her time.

Six women and one man took up abode in the freshly garnished house with its stucco smeared buff from the parapet to the area, where Walt placed a little monkey-tree in a tub. A basket of mossy ferns swung between the usually open front door and an inner white door of curtained glass panels. The attic sheltered a ripe barmaid, the basement a 'smoking-concert soprano' (as Walt called her). The grand 'first-floor front', which contained the Balaklava oil-painting and most of Mrs. Crawford's best pieces, was fittingly occupied by a lady of means and leisure who never appeared before four p.m. One of the other three ladies, Mansell understood, had a Dutch husband frequently abroad; another was in the artificial flower trade; and the third was a resting ballet dancer. All seemed colour-fully well-dressed. The middle-aged man tenant was connected, it seemed, with a theatrical agency; he was breezily corpulent and smelt of brilliantine and whisky.

"They all look showy to me," Mansell remarked one Monday evening: it was rent day. A certain frigidity held his eyelids; he seemed to find it difficult to look straight at Walt. "Come-and-go sort of people," he fidgeted. By dint of much evening attendance spread over a month he had at last caught a glimpse of his complete tenantry. He had also found that the barmaid, after a fortnight in the house, had left her job.

"Pharaoh," Walt squeezed up his face into a friendly distress, "'scuse me, ole boy, but you've never got shot of *all* the country bumpkin idears in your loaf. Top of that, too, you get jumpy through all those Gospel Hall fleas biting you. It won't do, Pharaoh, it won't do—not if you want to be a man-of-the-world . . . Because Lily Andrews," he reproached, "done her face up to-night like Fido's dinner

you get to thinking like a missionary. . . . Well," he said
with sudden, and firm, directness, "she isn't a tart! All she's
got is a chap high up in the brewery line that can't marry
her because he's got a barmy wife."

His feet up, he sat in Mrs. Crawford's green plush chair,
a lace-fringed round table holding a glass of ale beside him.
May, who that week was appearing in Reading, had arranged
the room cosily. To change the difficult subject Walt began
to relate how at last he was getting May on to the picture
postcards, plain and coloured. Mansell however did not
start into attention.

And neither did he go home at once when he left the
house at eleven o'clock. He walked to the end of the quiet
street where, not fifty yards from the house, an oval of
trees spread over palings a generous foliage. In this sombre
shelter couples often halted. He selected a concealed but
advantageous position and prepared himself for a long wait.
But there was much to occupy his mind; grave decisions to
be made.

The gas lamp opposite his house threw an angle of tawny
light across the dung-smelling road; a cat stalked through
it. An engine shrieked from the great sprawling railway
station. Through the vague acrid fog came the distant
jingle of hansoms. Whispers reached him through the
sprouting laurels and the swaying branches. They were
like whispers reaching down from antiquity, the eternal
murmur of the unquiet flesh. He had a vision of the dim
squat lineaments of this vast city lying in the womb of time.

He stood there for over two hours. Spectres occasionally
skirted the arboreal oval. A more factual person passed
close to him, came back, sidled into his shadow under the
overhanging branches, and in a very genteel way said:
"Lost the last train, my dear?" He could see the feline
glisten of her eyes, smell the wet sweetish odour of her
mouth. He said roughly: "Go away." She tossed her head
but muttered something about dirty spying: her skirts
swept the pavement. She wore long black gloves.

Later he got a hansom outside the station—he often travelled in them now—and arrived home at two o'clock. Arabella was still downstairs, knitting stockings. He said feverishly: "Why do you wait up in this senseless way?" On the table lay a tray covered with a snowy cloth. "I don't want anything to eat. Go to bed." She went away at once and in silence.

He flung himself into a chair, biting a finger-nail. That night he did not go to bed at all, dreading the upstairs room with its associations of nightmare and fantastic visions. But early the next evening, very much the righteous owner, he was back in the Paddington house. "Five of them," he stormed, "drove up and entered the house with a male escort—and I expect the sixth came later. Why haven't I been told of this? Are you straight with me, Monks?"

Walt, in his turn, adopted a deeply aggrieved manner. "If you was suspicious, Pharaoh, why didn't you ask me plain questions, 'stead of going behind your partner's back and stand watching out there like a blinking owl?" In his dark gastric eye, rich as mud, lay a sceptical gleam as he surveyed the indignant proprietor.

"You wouldn't have told me the truth," Mansell accused.

"Sure you didn't know it already, Pharaoh?"

"Don't call me Pharaoh," snapped Mansell.

"Your nerves ain't too good, seems to me." Walt scratched his head. "What's the matter? You ain't been looking too well for weeks. There's something else eating you, p'raps . . . Now what about a tot of brandy?"

"Never mind about my nerves." He paced the room. Then he whipped round—"Does May know about these women?"

"You'd better ask her yourself, ole boy. She'll be in London on Sunday. . . . She asked me to get those," Walt went on erratically, pointing to three bottles of brandy on the sideboard. "Got 'em cost price through Lily Andrews . . . Yes, you'd better ask her yourself,

partner. You'd best come here at six o'clock, if the Gospel
Hall can spare you. But don't ask me to be here too; I don't
like May in a temper, and she'll have one like a cat-o'-nine-
tails when she knows you've been spying on the house.
Any case, I got to see Fred Sunday evening. That smoking-
concert gal in the basement's found me a couple of customers
for tattooing . . . Now, Pharaoh," he dared, "take it easy!
The house is running smooth. A nice homely smell to it—
Mrs. Moon said it herself, and *she's* not one to have her
character upset."

"But the authorities!" Mansell still prowled about,
fuming.

"Well," Walt said cryptically, and with some meekness,
"I ain't a harping angel or a green choir-boy, and I 'aven't
trudged these streets of London for forty years without
learning how the law can be put in its place, like the monkey
with his nuts."

Mansell made a gesture of repugnance. Then, with an air
of postponing the important final decision, he announced:
"I shall hear what May has to say. It seems I can get no
further with you." And he left the house at once. He was
home by ten o'clock.

He looked worn out. Arabella dared not say a word.
Without breaking the silence, he preceded her to bed
immediately after his supper: he had eaten ravenously. The
deepening silence between them had assumed a quality of
acceptance. Arabella would not allow her mind to dwell on
it. It belonged to the mysterious male world where profound
activities took place.

5

On the following Sunday night, after being away for
five hours, he spoke to her with a great gentleness. It had
been an unusual Sabbath evening altogether. Arabella
herself felt that something exceptional was happening.

He had not gone to the Sunday evening service at the

Gospel Hall, telling her that important business required him at the Paddington house. Marion was sent up to Mrs. Crawford with a message that he would not be with her for supper: never before had he not missed Sunday supper with his patroness. And he had gone out at five o'clock dressed in his best suit and linen and with pomade on his hair.

By half-past nine he was back surprisingly in his home. "Oh," she exclaimed, "I haven't got your supper ready!" But at once she sensed that the recent tension in him had gone.

While she got the supper he spoke of the possibility of acquiring another house in a year. "So everything is going well after all?" she ventured in her obedient way. He nodded and asked for the coat which he wore about the house. She fetched it and said as he changed: "Your necktie is not so tidy as when you went out. And where's you tiepin—you haven't lost it?" A quick flush came to his cheeks as he exclaimed: "So that is why I was jostled by those men in the omnibus! . . . Never mind, it wasn't a good one."

Again he ate a very good supper. Afterwards, when she was making final preparations to retire, he said, gently and with a note of resignation: "Arabella, in future I want to sleep alone on the top floor. I can't sleep in our bedroom; I'm restless there."

She stopped in her progress across the room. After a moment she turned. The spaniel-brown eyes in the puffed face had a dumb shine; there was no expression, no surprise, hurt or bewilderment in them. "Very well, Mansell," she said.

He gave her a quick keen glance. The pin-point moment passed. She resumed her task of laying fire-sticks in the hearth to dry for the morning. He fetched his drugs-register from the dispensary and sat conning it.

"I think that's all for to-night," she murmured, looking round vaguely.

"Oh, Arabella?" He sounded casual. "I've been thinking . . . of course I know how you've never felt happy or at home in London—look how you won't ever go out either alone or with me—and I was thinking . . . perhaps you'd like to go back to Wales, to your father."

"That hundred pounds we are still owing him," she said unexpectedly.

"Come, your father is well-off enough. Even that third hundred pounds was a dowry, surely? . . . I thought you would like the child to be born down there," he resumed.

She shook out a cushion and arranged it in square solidity in its chair. "And for me to live there for ever, do you mean?"

"I didn't say so," he hedged. "But of course if you found you were happier down there, you could have the children with you and I would send you money."

"If a son it is——?" she said, straightening the runner on the chiffonier.

He thought for a minute and replied: "He could come and live with me later. You would have Marion and Gwen."

"I haven't wound the clock!" She gave it several quick turns, then said: "I don't think I am wanting to go to Wales, Mansell. Not without you—no indeed. Perhaps when you've made enough money you'll retire and go there with me."

"That is looking very far ahead, Arabella. Very far!" In his tone was a perceptible note of disappointment. He had even begun to jerk a little again, as if that tension in him was returning. "One can't tell; my business affairs may all crash."

She gazed round the room. But there were no more tasks before bed. As he turned a page of the drugs-register, she repeated: "No, I don't want to go away, Mansell. Best it is for me to stay here with you." She went to the door, hovered there a moment, and went out. He seemed intent on something in the book.

But a few seconds later he went to the door and called: "Can you take Marion to your bed to-night and I will sleep in hers?" Since the house had been denuded of all spare furniture Marion's bed was the only one beside their own. "We'll buy a new bed for the little back room to-morrow," he called.

For a second or two there was no reply from the dark staircase. Then her voice came down hollowly: "Very well, Mansell."

He fetched from the dispensary a few billheads and, after tearing off the heading—it still bore its picture of two elegant carriages drawn up outside the shop—sat writing for an hour. He couldn't stop himself writing. She was going to Chatham in the morning but would get the letter the next day. It would surely ease her mind a little.

He wrote ". . . I told her as soon as I got home that I couldn't sleep with her any more. This is right, is it not? It would be immoral for me to continue with her. But she will not go to Wales. Not yet, at least. I think she suspects I am seeing a customer of mine, the Mrs. Perry I told you about, the one who takes laudanum. This might be awkward as my wife sometimes serves in the shop when I am out. My wife, did I say? . . ."

Yes, it would ease her mind. She had made quite a little scene of horror, aimed at herself. Gusty sobs of self-reproach had shaken her. She also told him a good deal about Walt: they had "not meant that to each other for two or three years now." In any case Walt had never been what she called "a manly man"; perhaps this was because of his ill-health. His low and sly talk was only talk.

But she had been magnificent. And the locked door, the heavily draped window, the glasses of brandy, the golden woman unashamedly naked, the enticing whisper of adultery—was not all this a part of the mysterious destiny he had apprehended in his visions? He had been overwhelmed by a sense of something inescapable. The whisper of damnation became exhilarating: guilt freed and refreshed him. He was destroying the foreboding consciousness of sin that haunted him. He felt himself a reborn man. Yet, in the depths of abandonment, in the final moment of release, a fugitive realisation flashed through the recesses of his being. This was no last fulfilment! He remained alone. But this too vanished and he sank into a deeper release, dark and untroubled as death.

She had wakened him with another glass of brandy. And for a short while she indulged in another bout of self-recrimination. She said she didn't understand herself; but one thing she was certain of—she never wanted to do deliberate harm to anyone. For a few moments the sadness always running about somewhere in her being was recognised, faced, and allowed a voice: sitting plunged in heavy grief, she said the world was ruled by tykes. Then she had got up, sprayed herself with perfume, yawned, and, sitting beside him on the bed, concentrated her self-rebuke on a large hairy mole on her thigh. This blemish—it was certainly very unsightly—always made her feel disagreeable —"It's just my luck," she said, "if only it had been behind, where I couldn't see it! It's done a lot to take the push and ambition out of me, that big mole has."

"I like it," he had said. He sat watching her pull on a stocking. One man sat there on the edge of the bed looking in calm satisfaction at his possession. But, in the long wardrobe mirror opposite, another man sat as if isolated in forbidding repudiation. He had looked up and seen that other being.

The sense of dark release lasted. And his life at home became simpler than he dared hope. But it belonged to a man whom at times he seemed able to watch as another person. He apprehended that it was May who had achieved the cleavage that at last gave him quietude. With the advantage of this duality he had been able to steer the difficult first meeting with Arabella most successfully.

And there were no embarrassing moments during the ensuing business of his removal to the top floor back room. Arabella went about her tasks without apparent change. She prepared the small room carefully; she offered to occupy it herself but he firmly declined this and said he wanted the

c

room to be as bare and simple as possible. It occurred to him at times that she was glad of the new arrangement. He treated her with a kindliness he was careful not to make too pronounced. Conversation at table became almost entirely devoted to shop customers; he began to make fun of their ludicrous foibles about their health. He even cracked a joke at Mrs. Crawford's expense. And Marion's prattle became, for the first time, interesting to her father. He warned her that perhaps soon she would have a little brother; she declared decisively that she didn't like boys. Gwen also came in for more attention. One day he brought home an expensive toy for each.

On a December afternoon Arabella gave birth to a girl. It was a very difficult birth. Old befuddled Doctor Ross— he and Mansell got on quite well, the doctor having an atheist's argumentative taste for theology—had from the first been lugubrious about this confinement. Marion and Gwen were sent for a few days to Mrs. Crawford, whose cook loved children.

Arabella's cries startled her husband; he closed the shop. Doctor Ross came downstairs once and said: "I don't know what's the matter with her—I expected trouble but the child will be much below weight, I think. It's your missus is behaving badly; never seen a woman in such a state of fright. You'd better go up to her." But he had been unable to go up: he sat biting a finger-nail. When the child was born the doctor said it was undernourished; he did not expect it to live.

They named this third daughter Katherine. It was entirely Arabella's choice. Mansell was very attentive to her during the long rest which Doctor Ross—he shook his head commiseratively during a talk with Mansell—insisted on. Even Arabella gave way to this: her furniture and cutlery seemed to exist no more.

Katherine's convulsions were dangerous but she lived. The doctor told Mansell: "Afraid she's going to cost her mother something, though."

Chapter Three

I

GWEN, her straw sailor hat perched on the back of her head, came running. "Kate's let the kite fly away . . . look!" Far up, the taut blue paper triangle breasted the wind, dipped a farewell, and soared away for ever. "You ought not to have let her hold the cord," Marion scolded. She turned with her exaggerated outdoor primness to the young man sitting beside her on the bench: "My little sister is very clumsy; her hands cannot hold anything properly."

"It cost sixpence," Gwen said to him expectantly; "it was mine."

"Bring Kate here," Marion commanded in her cool grown-up way. "We must go home now." Gwen gave a disappointed look at the young man but walked up the ferny hillock obediently.

"You will appear out this evening, please?" Konrad pleaded. His deep heavy voice contrasted surprisingly with his appearance. "You will come to the door in the mews, yes?"

Shaking her head, she tightened the sash of her polka-dotted muslin frock. "I think my father is staying at home this evening." She peeped up at him under her lashes. "Did you mean it when you said we might become engaged, Konrad? I am only seventeen."

"But I am twenty. Next year, year after, the earnings will be of sufficiency to support us." He was foreign correspondence clerk in a warehouse near the Mint.

"Oh, you've been putting stuff on your moustache again," she tinkled, with a pretty gesture of annoyance. The valiant line of fair hair was seeded with brown drops melting in the heat. When he replied that he needed to look as old as possible to go and see her father she smiled pensively. He sat beside her, lanky and tenuous; his good looks were uneasy, not yet defined. She seemed older than him; her movements, though fluttering, were crisp. Already, in manner at least, she had the makings of a lady: not for nothing had her father sent her to Miss Shepherd's refined school on the Hill, and allowed her to take extra music-lessons with the expensive Madame Mizler whose nephew sat beside her now.

"I must go." She laid her hand in light regret on his arm. "You must not be seen with me on the road."

The miniature green vales of thorn, hornbeam and birch glistened in the sunshine. On the road above strollers were enjoying the Saturday afternoon tranquillity of the Heath; there were fashionable clothes, parasols and waiting carriages. "Kate! Gwen!" their sister called, distinct. A striped ice-cream cart under a yellow awning had drawn up for the more plebeian walkers. Gwen, running, asked for an ice-cream. Sulky and awaiting reprimand for the lost kite, Kate loitered behind.

"Certainly not," Marion commanded as Konrad carefully took out his purse; "they are not allowed ice-cream." But she blew a whisper to him with a gesture of farewell, genuine and tender: "I will put a note among the leaves——" Straw boater in hand, he stood smiling uncertainly, stiff in a salute but a running glow in his cheeks.

"I'll tell father you've been courting," Gwen promised as they reached the high road.

"You foolish child!" Marion spoke with such superb disdain that Gwen recanted and said she'd only tell him a man had followed her about. "And as for you, Kate, why do you always walk looking on the ground, child? You'll have to give Gwen sixpence out of your money-box."

Tall, slim, with graceful deportment, she swept along and crossed the carriage road to the path which led towards Maitland Hill. Gwen trotted sturdily by her side. But Kate constantly lagged behind. Already she looked permanently hostile. She was destructive too. Only the day before she had screwed off the head of a celluloid doll and poured into its inside a bottle of camphorated oil stolen, despite her terror of her father, from the upstairs stock-room.

"Why don't we ever go on the roundabouts?" Gwen asked as they skirted the little fairground.

"They're for public-house people . . . I do hope mother is better by now," she mused. "She seemed so unwell to-day." Yet she had insisted that Marion should take her sisters to the Heath; insisted with a strange, far-away obstinacy.

"Oh, mother is always unwell," Gwen protested. "Mavis Jackson goes to the Crystal Palace nearly every Saturday."

Two customers were waiting in the shop when they arrived. Gwen bounded through. Their father was making up a prescription behind in the dispensary; as Marion crossed it to the living-room door he glanced aside at her. There was something aloof, almost anonymous, in the glance. "I will be closing early to-night, Marion; I'm going out," he informed her. "I will have my tea at six o'clock." Gwen had already run into the living-room with a shriek—"Kate let my kite fly away." But her mother wasn't in her chair.

It was Marion who found her lying on the first floor landing outside her bedroom.

She lay there as if she had been crawling to the door. The daughter saw her livid blue lips, the saliva curling down her chin; she heard faint choking throat-sounds. Backing away she uttered a thin cry. "Gwen!" she called then, sharply. Gwen ran up and, after staring in astonishment, shouted over the banister: "Kate, Kate!"

Marion advanced again, tentatively, calling with a humble softness: "Mother?" Gwen kept by her side and suddenly wailed: "Mother, get up, get up." Kate reached the top stair and, her arm round the banister post, stood looking with round eyes of fear. "Mother?" Marion whispered, touching her shoulder. She dropped on her knees. "Oh," she sobbed, "she has fainted. Get a glass of water, Gwen."

She knelt helpless and whimpering while Gwen scrambled downstairs past the watching child at the banister.

"Did you tell father?" she faltered when Gwen had returned with the glass.

"No . . . Shall I call him?" Her whisper, as she crouched beside her sister, was secret. "See if she will open her eyes first . . . she will be angry if we disturb him in the shop."

But the glass shook in Marion's hand. She shrank back from the long hollowed face with its blue lips. She wailed at last: "We must call him . . . tell him to come." She laid the glass on the floor and took her mother's hand. "It's cold," she whimpered. "Call him."

Kate gave a peculiar strangled cry and ran from the banister to the furthest corner of the landing. And she made another flight when her father strode across the landing, his face pale and his nostrils quivering as though in anger; she flew to Marion and Gwen, who had withdrawn together into another dim corner. The three watched silently while he knelt beside her and felt her wrist and lifted her eyelid. He wiped her lips gently with his handkerchief; he called her name quietly—"Arabella?" Then he lifted her in his arms—for she was no great weight—and called to Marion to open the door of the bedroom he had not entered for years.

Afterwards he sent Gwen for the doctor and told Marion to look after the shop. They scampered. His manner was important and authoritative.

The collapse lasted four days. On the third day she seemed to be getting better. Mansell remained calm and attentive, never leaving the premises even in the evenings when usually he went to visit his properties down town. During the day he frequently called Marion to look after the shop while he sat with his wife. His friend, old Dr. Ross, was in constant attendance.

"The wonder is," the eldest daughter, tip-toeing into the dispensary one morning, heard the doctor say in the shop, "that she's kept going so long in her condition. There's that complication of her last baby too. You'll have to prepare yourself for the worst, me boy; she'll never get over this."

"She always was frail. But what a worker—I could never stop her, and she'd never go out or take a holiday. Years ago I tried to pack her off to Wales but she wouldn't budge. Obstinate, my word! One of these women that can't tear themselves from their homes."

"Will-power kept her going," the doctor grunted. "Her body's got no more strength in it than that bottle of patent tonic there—why d'you stock 'em, you rascal? You chemists ought to be put in gaol, every man jack of you."

"The trouble with atheists is," her father observed, "that they've got no understanding of human nature. There's as much comfort in that bottle of tonic as there is in believing in the miracle of loaves and fishes——"

"Ha——" began the doctor with a snort. But Marion, with a shiver, crept back into the living-room. Once more she became aware of the closed privacy of the male world.

Women suffered unspeakable torments and terrors. And men, talking among themselves in security, watched from afar. Kate's birth . . . she remembered her mother's gaunt face and stricken eyes when she and Gwen had returned home from Mrs. Crawford's. But chiefly she remembered the curious slack odour of her body, unknown and sickening. She shivered again and ran up to the top floor to make her father's bed. When Konrad had kissed her once at the mews door she had drawn away. There had been something in the grip of those warm lips. . . .

She was late this morning. Mrs. Hancock had sent to say she couldn't come because her daughter was confined. Gwen and Kate would be back from Miss Shepherd's at twelve. As she made the bed a feeling of maturity came to her. She knew now why her father slept up here, in this comfortless room, with only a cheap mat on the floorboards and that photograph of a grave in Wales over the narrow bed. It had been whispered to her yesterday . . . But had it been the imaginings of a wandering mind?

Before going downstairs to fetch the cup of milk and brandy she slipped into her own room, tore a leaf out of a Papier Poudré booklet and rubbed it over her nose. Then she put on her finger a red-stone ring. They were consolations. She was not going to her music-lesson to-night and as her father would be home she doubted if she could slip out to the mews door either. After an intent scrutiny in the mirror she flew downstairs for the milk. Taking it into her mother's room she walked with a hushed demeanour. She saw herself as the perfect nurse.

Arabella's head turned from side to side. But her eyes were closed. Her cheek-bones protruded sharply; her iron-grey hair, surprisingly strong-looking and coarse, lay in a bound skein on the pillow. The doctor had said something about getting a professional nurse, but after a conference with her father apparently it had been decided to wait a few days.

"Mother," called Marion, tenderly, "here is your milk."

The lids slowly lifted: the eyes were startlingly bright. But the lips' blue was less livid. Marion, her movements exquisitely gentle, held the cup to them. "A little," she coaxed; "just a little." Half the milk was laboriously sipped. And Arabella asked the time. She was constantly asking the time. The daughter sat on the bed and stroked her hand. "You feel better to-day, mother?"

"He will bring her here," her mother suddenly said, in quite a strong voice. "I can't keep her away any more."

"Keep whom, mother?"

The over-bright eyes became fixed into a sort of animal obstinacy. "I told you . . . that woman. He spends money on her. He's rich. Perhaps she has a son. He wanted a son . . . Take care of Gwen and Kate, Marion."

"Who *is* she?"

"I don't know. It's that Mr. Monks has led him astray.

. . . He's rich, Marion; I know! But it's all wickedness. They are houses for bad people. He told me, the day when the man came from the police; he told me. He went upstairs to pray. He had to go to the Court and Mr. Monks was put in prison. The piece from the local newspaper is in my drawer over there. . . . The gold locket is for you, Marion; my father gave it me for my wedding." Her voice began to sink. "The sun is shining to-day," she turned her head restlessly.

Marion, looking alert, took up the cup of brandy-laced milk and coaxed more into the sunken mouth. "Rest a minute now, darling mother," she murmured; "you mustn't talk too much."

"You won't forget? And take care of Gwen and Kate . . . Kate——"

"I won't forget," she soothed. "I think father is a very foolish man," she added in a high tone. "And he's a hypocrite as well." She looked at her mother, like one woman at another, in bridling indignation.

"Yes," Arabella whispered. "But he's afraid of God."

"He can't be; he wouldn't behave as he does."

"Always religious, he was," the voice began to revive again. "He can't forget God. Brought up very religious, in Wales. . . . He wanted to get rid of me," she went on, "he wanted me to go back to Wales with you and Gwen, before Kate was born; to my father. But I wouldn't go, no indeed, not even when my father died; ashamed I was to go for the funeral and——" her voice became inflexible—"he might have brought *her* here; he might have stopped me coming back . . . I never left the house," she said on a rising note of triumph, "I never said anything to him, but never would I leave the house, I was here all the time." A petal of red burned on her cheek-bones.

"You ought to have been quarrelsome with him, mother." Smiling, Marion stroked her mother's hand.

"Not a man for that he was. Always shut up in himself, so full of himself. A man with a high stomach we used to

call such. But very proud of him I was when I got married."
She suddenly gave a frail smile and turned her face into the
pillow whispering: "Take the locket now; don't you let
him find it."

It was her last bout of confidences with the daughter who,
even as a precocious child possessed of a cool individuality
of her own, in some curiously intangible way had always
been her associate and witness. That night Mansell sat up
with her; Doctor Ross called during the evening and
advised it.

Not long after dawn he roused his daughters, even the
nine-year-old Kate. He was calm but grey-faced.

They came in their nightdresses into the room. Two
candles were lit on the dressing-table; the window blind
was still down. Marion, approaching the bed, gave a
sobbing cry. Gwen put her hands on the bed-rail and
watched, Kate secretly hovering behind her. Their father
loomed tall and authoritative. But his face was drawn and
old-looking. "Kiss your mother," he commanded. "She
called for you."

She was still. Her eyes were open. Marion, sobbing,
kissed her. Gwen silently followed and, after lightly kissing
the cheek, paused and gave her mother a long attentive
look. But Kate hung back; she began to retreat from the
bed. "Come, Kate," her father said and lifted her against
his chest. She wriggled her arms free and, her face darkly
malign, pushed his face away with her two hands. "Put me
down, put me down," she screamed. He put her down at
once. And stood looking at her as from a great distance.

She shrank to a corner by the window, the furthest point
from the bed.

"Mother has gone?" Marion faltered, twisting her hands.
Gwen stood close at her side. There was no sense of a
presence in that bed. In the room itself an atmosphere of
vacancy seemed to hover. The candle-lit room looked
unreal. There was not a sound from the street.

"Your mother was a good woman," he whispered. He

stood looking down at his dead wife. His daughters had drawn away.

A spent repose already glazed her face. The haggard features were old. Yet she was only forty-four. She had fulfilled her destiny as a submissive woman with a character pliant as the stalk of a flower. And though ten years ago she had made her stand as the legal wife in this house of scrupulous furniture and chaste curtains, she had paid for her obstinacy. Perhaps she had known it was the final sentence.

He stood whispering by the bed. Was he praying? Or whispering to his wife? Or to himself?

The eldest daughter tried to hear his words. But she too, with Gwen, had retreated towards the window, where Kate huddled against the curtain. Suddenly he uttered a groan and fell on the bed. His arms embraced the dead body. Marion beckoned to Kate. The three crept to the door. They heard his groans. Marion shut the door silently. On the landing she said to her sisters: "Go back to bed. I must dress."

When she got downstairs her father was already there putting on the kettle in the kitchen. He did not look at her. There seemed no evidence of the torment that had made him throw himself with those awful groans on his wife's body. He told his daughter she must look after the shop that morning; no prescriptions could be made up; Gwen and Kate must not go to school. At half-past eight he went up to the doctor's house. He wore a black tie and fresh cuffs and went out with the incisive air of a man on important business.

Marion had carefully made him breakfast, boiling an egg exactly as he liked it.

2

Always, from childhood, she had possessed a detached identification with him. But her mother had forced a starved adult affection on her and she had responded with a quick inquisitiveness: in an artificial way they· became united against this aloof and mysterious master of their lives.

An air of artificiality had indeed haunted the house. It had forced the eldest daughter into a false maturity; it gave her manner its hints of shallowness and even crookedness. But it also gave her her detachment. She could watch her father untrammelled by emotion. On occasions his airs of despotic grandeur even amused her. She could afford to be attentive to him. At the same time watching like an interested little adder.

Six days after the funeral he said to her, rising from the tea-table: "You will look after the house in the future. Of course Mrs. Hancock will still come in to do the rough work."

Prepared for this, she said at once: "Father, I want to take up singing. Madame Mizler says I have a good voice. I would like to go to the Academy she told me about. You can get a housekeeper surely?" She looked down her straight nose like a young lady.

"No, I don't intend getting a housekeeper." He spoke with marked decision. "Later I may have other arrangements." He stood in the doorway leading to the shop. "And I don't intend letting you take up singing, Marion— at least not in that professional way. But you may continue with your piano lessons here, if you wish. I have thought of turning your mother's bedroom into a drawing-room and buying a grand piano for you."

"A grand piano?" she said attentively, turning the jet bangle on her wrist. And, aware of the cold still power emanating from him: "Very well, father."

He took a step into the shop but turned. "Oh, Marion, who was it you were talking with at the mews door last night? Did I hear a man's voice—a deep voice?"

"It was Madame Mizler's nephew." She placed the cover on the butter dish. "He wants to become engaged to me."

"He does, does he? And you go to the mews door like a servant. Is he a groom?"

"Don't be foolish, father," she tossed her head. "He is the clerk for foreign business in an important City warehouse. He is of German birth," she added romantically; "his name is Konrad."

"A warehouse clerk; a German! . . . I will talk to Madame Mizler when next she comes into the shop. Meanwhile you *must not* see him . . . Marion," he said, with a different, well-disposed note, "you may be a rich young lady some day. I do not want you to cheapen yourself."

"I am very fond of him," she said in a warning voice. But he disappeared, pulling the door to with a slam.

If she had seen her father's angry scowl as he went into the shop she would have been very interested. It was his aloofness that made her toss her head in vexation.

Mansell was deeply shocked. His daughters thought they could mix with whom they chose, did they! His daughters, so admired locally, with customers always enquiring after their welfare. They were his possessions, and of value as well-behaved girls who looked neither to left nor right. They were of more value even than this shop, now so well-established as a respectable family business. Fine-looking, quiet girls who were the admiration of all the neighbours. He didn't begrudge a penny of their expensive education.

Frowning, he looked round the shop. He must make new plans now. But would it be prudent to abandon the shop? He was often exasperated by the way it tied him down and he could well afford to give it up and devote his energies to acquiring more property. He remembered his dreams of owning a chain of hotels. But something had happened to him. A halt of his ambitions. A deadlock held his soul, a sloth his mind.

The huge coloured bottles in the window were coated with dust. He rarely changed the window-display now. Sometimes he forgot to keep up the stock of emulsions and cough-mixtures in time for the first November fogs. But he was careful—since nowadays nearly all women powdered —to keep pace with the developing trade in cosmetics though he automatically disapproved of this sign of an increasing self-assertion in the sex, which was almost matched by the nefarious growth of Socialism among men.

The self-imposed week of stay-at-home penance and mourning had passed with leaden slowness. In a black alpaca coat he stood moodily looking into a glass showcase while the parrot nibbled at his finger-nail. Those porcelain utensils needed washing. He would ask Marion and give her some trinket; besides, she liked showing herself off in the shop. . . . Of course he could engage an assistant. But, no, a stranger wouldn't do. The ladies of the villas expected his personal attentions, and they preferred the shop to be untidily old-fashioned, erratic as to its closing time and himself stern and pessimistic about both their physical and spiritual condition. Of course they never really followed his advice; but they enjoyed his solemn concern with their state and readily bought his mixtures.

A stout coachman came in carrying a whip. "Well, Pearce," the chemist said patronisingly, "come in for your new truss? Go behind." He followed into the screened dispensary and turned the key in the living-room door.

Since his daughters were growing, the old horse-hair sofa had been moved into the dispensary. Pearce, a talkative man of fifty, took off his trousers and long woollen underpants, removed the old blackened truss—it was renewed every two years and paid for by his employers—and lay on the sofa. Mansell took a pole and unhooked the cluster of stiff leather trusses hanging under the ceiling. They were dusty too; one, almost as large as a child's hoop, had been in stock since the shop was opened in 1895.

"Seen the posters for the old Gospel Hall, Brother Roberts?" Because the coachman had been a worshipper at the democratic-seeming Hall in Mansell's time there, he adopted an annoying familiar manner. "Who'd 'ave thought our old church would be turned into one of these 'ere living-picture palaces? What would the old lady 'ave said!"

"Times are changing," Mansell said shortly, unravelling the trusses. "People are less Christian nowadays."

"That's true enough. I feels less Christian myself, 'specially when I got to wear a new truss like that, they pinch like 'ell till they get softened and set into the body. I want a bigger size this time, don't I? My belly's hanging down and going so soft, my missus she's been calling me old jelly-belly; it's all the bread I eats. . . . Aye, a cinema! Sister Crawford, I bet she's turning in 'er grave. I miss the place myself, I do; it was a cosy 'all and on Sunday nights made you feel full as a bag of oats."

"Mrs. Crawford should have left the means to continue the Hall as a church." He fitted the truss roughly.

After two years he still felt sensitive about Mrs. Crawford's posthumous behaviour. But even during the last few months of her life she had turned odd and choleric. It was as though her approaching dissolution gave her a perverted vision. She seemed to despise and distrust everyone around her, all her loyal associates, both secular and religious— had she become aware of the ultimate sterility of all earthly associations? A dreadful arrogance, far more pronounced than hitherto, possessed her. Mansell himself was treated with short shrift; and her faithful cook, who had been with her for thirty years, wept continuously.

But on the day of her burial he had shut his shop, drawn the blinds, and gone to her funeral in the deepest mourning. The Gospel Hall members attended in force, and in a grave-side oration he praised their Generous Benefactress in very high terms indeed; she might have been as famous as her early predecessor at the church, the evangelist who called herself the Queen of Sheba and piously reigned over an empire of small churches and a harem of husbands. . . . Then there had been the bombshell of the will. Abolishing her old hints and promises, both Mansell and her cook were left out of this new will drawn up three months before her death. All her twenty-five thousand pounds went to the Devonshire brother with whom she had waged family warfare over decades. Even the Gospel Hall was left totally unprovided for. Perhaps Sister Crawford, who so often showed a carnal shrewdness mingled with her flighty evangelism, foresaw that the day of her church was done. In the last sermon she gave before her forced retirement she had bitterly attacked suffragettes.

However, she had been the backbone of his prosperity. She had made him three separate advances to purchase houses and not once had there been anything but a verbal agreement concerning repayment. The solicitor and the brother made no enquiry regarding these large sums, doubtless imagining they were payments for the upkeep of the deceased client's religious commitments. But he had expected at least a couple of thousand or more from the will and intended buying a sable fur for May's birthday. The disappointment still pierced him unpleasantly when he was reminded of it.

After getting rid of the coachman he fidgeted with a prescription or two and then, having broken a beaker, went in to tell Marion that he would have to go into town early that evening. The week of mourning that he imposed on himself was not concluded until to-morrow evening. He spoke half turned from his daughter; in the darkening doorway he looked saturnine.

"Yes, father. There's some cold ham for your late tea," Marion said with cool disinterest.

At six o'clock he left for the Paddington house, extravagantly taking a hansom all the way. Six awful days of sackcloth and ashes. Of fear and dreams. In the evenings he had sat studying Darwin's *Origin of Species*, lent him by Doctor Ross. And there had been letters to write to Arabella's relatives in Wales. None of them had come up for the funeral. She had drawn herself away from them so drastically, ashamed and guilty that he had not repaid that loan from her father when she got married. Poor woman!

No doubt about it, the Terrace was deteriorating and getting low-class. But after the police raid he had ordered the stucco and woodwork of the house to be repainted and now it was occupied by eight steady persons. True, the basement tenant looked a shifty woman, but May assured him she was only a retired palmist living quietly on a small fortune made on some seaside pier and thinking of nothing but her cactuses in pots. May was strict. After the raid she had been furious with Walt for his slackness. "Trouble with him is, he's too soft-hearted," she had boiled; "no one's a dirty beast for Walt." She was entirely in charge of the house now, using the two adjoining first-floor rooms.

He found her in the front room, lolling under the Charge of Balaklava oil-painting. Dressed in shot silk edged with not quite clean swansdown, she was eating with her fingers a plate of tinned pineapple while she scanned *The Era*. She seldom ate anything but snacks, particularly of fruit, though she often bought half a chicken at the ham-and-beef shop opposite the station, eating it in her fingers just the same.

Of course there was the drink too. He was always telling her to feed herself more with proper sit-down meals. But he never protested about the drink.

As always now, her first glance at him was sombre. She returned desultorily to *The Era*, swallowed a chunk of pineapple, and said: "I *thought* you'd come to-night. Got a housekeeper or something in? No?" She bridled. "You've left those girls of yours alone in the house?"

"Marion is quite a capable girl. She's seventeen." Drumming his fingers on the mantelpiece, he entreated: "May, don't drink that juice like that!"

"I like it, Pharaoh." She waddled her lips expertly in the plate of syrupy juice. Afterwards her small plump hands, on which half a dozen rings sparkled, brushed her corsage with a quick prettiness, like some animal. "I eat oysters like that," she said, more amicably. "Now you're a widower we'll go down together to Brighton one Sunday and have a good feed of oysters in that bar where everybody goes. When you're out of mourning, of course . . . My God," she surveyed his clothes with a grimace of which he was uncertain, "you are a black eyeful!"

She had never really forgiven him. When she found herself pregnant she had stormed for weeks. Her stage career would be ruined. She would be set back for years. These days a star couldn't afford to lie low even for three months; there was so-and-so and so-and-so only waiting for her to drop out for a while with pneumonia or a twisted ankle.

But when the child was born she had her revenge— "There you are," she said. "The Almighty won't let you have a boy, see!"

Really her pregnancy had been of great value to her. She had found something genuine on which to blame her lack of engagements, especially in conference with other pros., for none of whom the word 'failure' ever existed though it haunted their vicinity. She would never have become a West-End top-liner. Her voice was going, and her style. And also there was that peculiar inner stagnancy of hers, a dusty sadness that could make her look at times like a monument of grief. Perhaps it was that which had attracted her to her Pharoah, whose material prosperity might also bury awareness of professional collapse.

"I've had a busy week, May——" he began grievously, still drumming his fingers restlessly.

"I don't want to hear about the funeral." She shuddered. "Have a whisky. You're looking pinched round the beak again . . . But there," she sighed, rising from her chair, "you never was one to sit down solid. Always with the

fidgets——" She yawned, looking at herself in the long
gilt-framed mirror hanging between the two windows.
"Sure you don't want a whisky? . . . Get away with you,
pulling that face! Run along then; I'll be there in a minute."
As he opened the door into the next room she went to the
Chinese cabinet Walt had found in those auctions he was
always going to. It contained a full store of drink.

Walt himself dropped in about ten o'clock. As adviser
and general overseer he constantly travelled between the
houses, though Mansell did not think it prudent for him to
live in any of them; he now lodged with May's cousin, the
tattooist Fred. Since being gaoled his manner towards the
owner of the houses owned a guilty humility. To have
been nabbed like that, him, Walter Monks! Yet the three
months in gaol seemed to have done wonders to his gastric
stomach.

"Getting back to normal, Pharoah?" he cocked a clearer
eye at his employer. By that time Mansell had accepted a
small brandy from May. "Pity you and May can't take a
holiday together now."

"I was just telling May there's nothing to prevent us
getting married now," Mansell said, in quite a pleasant
manner.

"You'll have to stay in mourning for a while," she
murmured, occupied in some reverie. "Of course, there's
my little Laura to think about. Do they become proper if the
parents marry soon?"

"Well," said Walt, "there's an old custom I heard about
when I was up North, though it was in the days when women
wore big skirts. The mother used to hide her love-birds
under her skirt when she walked to the altar, just like
chicks in the old hen's wings; and there they stayed till the
parson said the last word and made them lawful."

May jerked up with sudden savagery. "I've had about
enough of your jokes, Walt," she fumed. An awkward
silence followed this, broken by May herself with a loud
hysterical laugh. Mansell looked distantly at his deplorable

manager, whose services however were still very valuable.

"Fred and me," Walt changed the subject, "got an idear. Down Waterloo Road the other day we met a bloke, name of Ted, that's just left the Hussars. A fine picture of a man he is, used to be in the fairs before joining up. Well, 'tween us we're thinking of putting him on the halls tattooed all over; he's got two bits on him already, a wild rose on his arm and 'I love Jenny' somewhere else——"

"That will do, Walt," May reminded him again majestically. "I s'pose," she resumed the subject of her reverie, "Laura will have to stay a love-child."

"You *are* going to marry me?" Mansell began to jerk.

"What, and live behind the chemist's shop? With your three daughters and all?"

"They are well-bred girls," he said with some haughtiness. "When she's a little older you can bring Laura to live with us."

"I'm not sure she won't be better off at Barnet," May brooded. "It's good country air and I must say that woman keeps her clean and fat." But a crooning note came into her voice, a yearning into her face. "All the same, a mother needs the love of her child."

"And you ain't getting any younger, May," said Walt, who had not been offered a drink. She only shot him a sultry look. Their long association permitted him many impudences.

"I wish to know," Mansell pronounced, "how I stand. I have plans to make. May, you must make up your mind. For myself, I'm tired of makeshift, and I am not happy living in an immoral way; it isn't necessary now, either."

"Pharaoh speaks right," said Walt with marked admiration.

"It wouldn't look decent for us to marry so soon," May brooded.

"I didn't suggest we married at once," Mansell's voice began to rise again. "I only want to know for certain, to make my plans and prepare my daughters."

"A widower," said May, dreamily, "couldn't leave off mourning for six months. Even nowadays. It used to be a year." Was she listening to the roar of applause as the plush curtains swished down?

Walt said: "May always was a one to put things off until next year's Old Moore's Almanack came out." He appeared to be innocent of malice as he added: "Expect she's been having a confab. with that baggy-eyed palmist down in the basement."

"Oh, I never have!" shrieked May. "I never see her except when she brings me her rent."

Mansell rose from his chair. He stood authoritative and stern. The master of the house. The man of means. "If," he said, "I discover any signs of wrongdoing in this house I will turn everybody out at once. Everybody! You hear?"

At this May bowed her head. Her handsome bosom heaved. "No need to talk like that, Pharaoh," she grizzled in a woebegone way. "I got nothing to be ashamed of. But you're not yourself, I can see, dear."

Walt, also getting up, broke heartily into this awkwardness. "You'll be down to-morrow night, Pharaoh? Right'o, I'll bring the books. There's those dilapidations at Number Nine to see about too, and I've been making enquiries about gas-stoves for Number Nineteen, though Alice Corby says don't 'ave 'em, they encourages suicides . . . and we don't want another of those, do we?—not after Doris Lawrence and her cup of poison."

"But we can charge more rent," Mansell said, brisk now. "There's a percentage on the slot-meters too . . . May, my dear," he turned, "Walt needs a glass of beer."

"It's more than the old crab deserves," May said crossly. But she obeyed.

3

Despite May's continued shilly-shallying during the next two or three months—that crochety, lumpish sadness seemed to possess her more and more—he prepared his eldest daughter for the arrival of someone very pleasant.

He was a little surprised that Marion made little comment or show of feeling. But then she always had been a self-contained girl, her attention engaged on herself. Perhaps she was stupid as well as vain. He could not understand the light feathery glances of her empty-seeming eyes. He had bought her a brooch. Then a day or two after his final declaration that with three daughters on his hands he would have to marry again, she asked if she might have a string of pearls which she had seen in a shop window. He gave her the three guineas, but with a rebuke. Too much jewellery wasn't suitable for a young girl. He was obliged to tell her also not to sing at her work; customers in the shop would hear and it didn't sound well while they were still in deep mourning.

More difficult was the affair with the youth Konrad. The aunt, a thick-set, arrogant German whose charges for music lessons were very high, instantly agreed with her chemist that the courtship was scandalous; indeed, something in her smouldering concurrence while she was buying a bottle of eau-de-Cologne, made Mansell frown; and he took advantage of the occasion to give notice that Marion must terminate the music-lessons.

"Ach," Madame Mizler seemed to spit and snap her fingers as she waddled towards the door. "Zome impudence it is. My seester, the mother of Konrad, she is the Baroness and will be in anger . . . Ha!" she exploded at the parrot, her voluminous flannel skirts flouncing, while Mansell stood behind his counter in icy hauteur, "ha, the girl is not of advantage, and I go, I go. Bah, Englishers, zey require the whip." He stood amazed, his fingers spread on the counter.

Marion also showed high temper when he told her of the interview. "Father," she bristled, "you are interfering. I am quite capable of deciding whether Konrad is a suitable friend. He is teaching me German. He respects me and reads poetry. His family is quite distinguished, in Berlin. I think it is ridiculous to be so superior about foreigners." The fees of Miss Shepherd's high-class establishment were bearing fruit.

"These people," he said, calm, "come to England only to make money. They are adventurers. You are to take your music lessons with someone else, and in this house. I told you I would buy a grand piano; you may choose it in time for your eighteenth birthday." In his frigid demeanour was the contained force of a man who occupies a powerful, unbreakable world.

She seemed to wilt. Putting a handkerchief to her face she scampered upstairs dissolving into little whimpers. When later she came down, wearing the pearls with her black frock, and served the light meal which he took before going out, he warned her that if she continued to see the German he would discover it without fail. This time she listened without comment, fingering her pearls.

Two or three weeks later the problem solved itself. Both Madame Mizler and her nephew disappeared; a shop customer told Mansell. They vanished as abruptly as birds, Madame not even informing pupils who had paid for a term's lessons. "There!" he told his daughter, "I warned you they were adventurers. London contains many such people."

"I knew they were going," Marion replied composedly. "Konrad said there is going to be a war. He has gone to serve his country."

"War?" Her father stood still. Certainly there had been one or two small items in the papers. "War?" He had just acquired the lease of a new house. "Were they spies, then?" he pondered.

"After the war Konrad will come back for me." She put

her head on one side. "I have still been seeing him occasionally, father."

Then, for the first time, he struck his daughter. He smacked her face. Slowly advancing, he did it with a frightening deliberation. Both Gwen and Kate had just come in from Miss Shepherd's school. Gwen stolidly went on eating currant cake. It was Kate, sitting with two cushions under her, who broke into a howl. Without another word their father walked back into the shop. There were beads of sweat on his forehead.

Gwen said: "He hit you, Marion! I'll steal a bottle of scent when he goes out and sell it to Mary Ferguson to-morrow . . . Hush, Kate," she ordered, "*you* haven't been hurt, have you!"

Marion had reeled into the arm-chair. But she lifted her head. Her left cheek was crimson, her eyes frosty. "I didn't deserve it," she said, calmly. And as she looked at the doorway through which he had stalked, her whole roused face looked efficient.

After August Bank Holiday and the declaration of war he became very active. Decorators came to the house. All the furniture in Arabella's bedroom was taken away, and many other pieces she had loved and polished. Miss Eliott, the respectable music-teacher living in Albert Road, was sent with Marion to choose a piano.

He had the look of a man who is feverishly gambling. Perhaps the hectic brass-band days of war were affecting him. Marion herself was excited by them; when he left her in charge of the shop while he pranced out on purchasing expeditions she often took a few shillings from the till for her private use.

Costly new furniture began to arrive, and thick Turkey carpets with wonderful strident designs, curtains of mansion brocade. He rearranged the bedrooms. The three girls would occupy the entire second floor. He would sleep in the room across the landing from the new drawing-room. It had been used as a stock-room for the shop; for it arrived a large luxurious bed and a set of solid mahogany furniture. It all took nearly two months. People said the war would be over by Christmas.

One Sunday afternoon late in September he told Marion to take her sisters for a walk on the Heath and not to come back till five o'clock. When they returned Marion found that a large slice of sponge-cake had been eaten, though her father had not made his tea. She also noticed a faint scent of violets lingering around her grand piano in the new drawing-room. Her lips curled in and she hissed to herself. Prowling further, she picked up a hairpin in the new bedroom. She placed it markedly on the white pillow and left the door wide open. Downstairs her father spoke to her kindlily. He told her she could order some new clothes for herself and her sisters from a dressmaker who was a customer of his. He did not go out that evening. He looked as if victory had come in him.

It had. That afternoon May at last fixed a date for their marriage. The house met with her approval.

But really it was the war that had jolted her out of that vexatious torpidity which had engulfed her since the child's birth and her retirement from the halls. She had become very patriotic, boiled against the enemy, and in the overflow of roused virtue decided in favour of domestic tradition. "Mind you, though," she warned, "I won't make a good wife to you, Pharaoh."

Perhaps she had caught her patriotic fervour from Walt, who in all her new material prosperity had remained a sort of anchor as she lay like a ship becalmed. The war made him particularly truculent. He wished to go and fight, but of course his gastric trouble and age made it impossible unless men became scarce later on. And he bore with pride the recall to the colours of the ex-Hussar who was to have been Fred's masterpiece of tattooing and who went back to his regiment with half a Chinese dragon on his chest, though the garland of dahlias round his middle was complete.

"You needn't worry about the houses, Pharaoh," Walt

declared one evening in the Paddington headquarters. "War's sure to bring 'em luck, see if I'm not right. It's a time when the Old Nick takes over the reins." But Mansell had winced and looked sourly at this associate clinging to him as loyally as a limpet. And he had been angry at May's sentimental suggestion that Walt should come and live with them at Hampstead—— "But children always take to him," she defended; "they can tell he's a good full-sized man that doesn't care a hang for police, parsons or parliament."

One evening in October, while Gwen was putting Kate to bed, he told Marion: "I am not opening the shop to-morrow."

"I saw the notice in the window," she remarked.

"I am getting married," he said, lacing up his boots. "It's going to be quietly in a registry office."

"But we're not out of mourning yet," she objected. She took up the table-cloth.

"Marion, I am best judge of this. It's not right you three girls should be here alone."

She shook the cloth into the hearth. "Mother told me you had a fancy woman. Is it the same one?"

He stood up. For a moment it seemed as though he was going to strike her again. He was glaring. But the grey mask-like frigidity settled into his face. She had turned from the hearth and was looking at him with a bright considering gaze. Was there an elusive light of malice in those innocent eyes? "I shall leave the house at nine o'clock to-morrow morning," he said curtly, "and I shall be back with your stepmother in the late afternoon. You will see that everything is tidy. Explain to Gwen and Kate who is coming."

When he had gone she sat down and cried a little. Then, with a little grimace, she stood up and in her careful, refined way went on clearing the table.

She looked very slight and willowy in her black. But she walked with a poise that was one of the specialities of

Miss Shepherd's school. Her skin gleamed with a pastel-tinted, bird's-egg purity; her ears were fine and delicate as her hands. To-night she would have very much liked to droop and sigh in Konrad's arms under the wistaria of the mews door. Instead she went to the sideboard which had replaced the old marble-topped chiffonier and fastened yet another new brooch in her blouse.

4

It was past five o'clock when they arrived the next day. She waited with her sisters in the drawing-room over-looking the fork of the roads with its cabmen's shelter and horse-trough. Gwen was in her second-best frock but the only concession allowed Kate was a new ribbon in her plait. The two had made little comment on the information that a stepmother was going to come that day; backing into silence, they awaited their decision until they saw her.

Tired of watching at the window, she went to the piano, sat arranging herself there and trying out various glances at the door—frigid, indifferent, haughty—and finally began singing:

> " *'Gaze not on swans in whose soft breast*
> *A full-hatched beauty seems to nest,*
> *Nor snow which, falling from the sky,*
> *Hovers in its virginity.*
>
> *'Gaze not on roses——'* "

"There's a cab!" Kate warned in her queer voice, surprisingly low and throaty in such a young girl. Her nose, with Gwen's, was pressed against the window-pane. But Marion, in a voice of light serenity, went on singing absorbedly. Miss Shepherd had said she sang that song very well; she had learned it in her last year at school. "No, it's not for us," called Gwen, giving Kate a push.

" '*For if my emperess appears,*
Swans moulting die, snow melts to tears,
Roses do blush and hang their heads,
Pale lilies shrink into their beds——' "

She wore deep black. And her pearls. Her fair hair was coiled up into a firm, decisive-looking heap; it displayed her reedy white neck. But she dare not wear the ear-rings bought with her filchings from the shop till; not yet.

"There's one!" Gwen shouted, jumping. Kate said, low: "It's coming to our door." Marion stopped playing but did not rise. They ran to her at the piano. "They've come," Gwen urged. "We saw her . . . What's the matter, Marion?" she plucked her sister's sleeve.

"He's got his key," Marion said, stiffly. "Let them come up here." Her sisters stood on either side of the piano stool; she placed an arm about their shoulders. They could hear the cabman assisting with luggage. The cab crunched away. . . . There was a long silence. They listened. The daylight was beginning to fade.

"Marion?" called her father's voice up the staircase. And again, nearer: "Marion, where are you?" Then, fainter: "Yes, come up; they'll be in the drawing-room, I expect."

When the door opened she slowly rose. She did not take a step towards the woman advancing towards her; she stood with her reedy neck soaring nakedly. Her hand still lay on Kate's shoulder. Gwen stood a little apart now, stolidly observant.

"Why, my darlings," exclaimed May, who had not forgotten how to make an entrance, "how pretty you are! . . . Quite a picture, aren't they, Pharaoh! . . . Oh!" she placed a softly plump hand over her mouth; he had asked her not to call him that now. She gurgled: "I've been reading the Bible, my dears. Come, let me kiss you." She smiled with a dazzling fixity. "You are Marion."

The large woman, still wearing her furs, a neck chain of mixed stones glittering among them, planted a full kiss on

Marion's lips. There was a smell of violet cachous mingled with something else. A high colour burned in her cheeks. Gwen, unwavering on her strong legs, was then bent over. But Kate fled: she fled with a single agonised cry to the brocades flowing richly in the window-space.

"Kate is a highly-strung child." Her father wore a dark grey frock-coat; there was an opal in his silver-grey cravat. "Kate," he called, quite kindly, "your new mother is not going to eat you. Don't be foolish, child." But Kate was not to be drawn.

"What a beautiful piano," May exclaimed and, perhaps with excellent tact, sat before it in her furs and brilliant hat with its spreading jay and multi-coloured delphiniums.

"You've not seen it before?" Marion enquired. "Father gave it me for my birthday. It is mine."

Nodding and smiling, May strummed a bar and broke into song. She sang 'The Bell Goes a-Ringing for Sarah.' Large smoky audiences had been subdued by that song. She lost a note or two now. Her breathing was constricted. Looking up winsomely she said: "It's all that champagne, Mansell, and the excitement."

"Come," he said, "come to your room and take off your hat." The grey October dusk hovered in the corners.

She began to sweep with careful deliberation towards the door. But her arms seemed to flap like the agitated wings of a great bird. He took one of them. She giggled. "Oh, it's so queer to see myself here. But we're all going to be happy . . . We ought to have brought Walt with us, Phar——" She giggled again. "Pretty children," she crooned. "Any man would be proud of 'em."

Marion's watching of this exit was remotely chilly. To Gwen she murmured as the door closed behind the two: "She's nervous." Lightly flicking a handkerchief over the piano keys, she called crisply: "You are silly, Kate, making a fuss."

"Kate's highly-strung," Gwen repeated with satisfaction. "Kate, you do behave stupidly sometimes. Hush, Kate."

"I don't like her," Kate snarled in extreme hostility. "She's too big." She broke into more weeping; broken raucous sobs very trying to hear. Gwen went to her and clumsily pressed her into the solidity of her chest. The sobs dwindled.

Marion went across to the window-space. "Let's sit here," she whispered intimately. They settled together on the long brocaded stool.

They sat there a long time. Marion's whispers went on in the thickening dusk. There was no other sound. The house was silent. Once Gwen asked, hushed and turning to stare at the dim door: "Has she gone to bed already?" Presently, entwined grey forms in the thicker grey air, they seemed like a piece of statuary sealed into the quiet of that room. But at intervals the whispering was renewed. Outside, the lamplighter made his pausing ascent of the hill; they heard the *snap* when he set his pole to the three-branched standard above the horse-trough, and a darkly yellow light streamed in over them.

Chapter Four

I

WITH legs opening and closing like shears, Mansell pranced round the young man and the new motor-car he stood beside. His voice too hopped in fury: "How dare you come up that drive with your car, opening my gate without permission! Do you take this place for a public-house? Is nobody's privacy to be respected? . . . Go away." Distorted in bitter agility, he disappeared behind the ever-greens. The three spectators in an upstairs window leaned less secretly out of the curtains.

The hatless young man—he looked pleasant enough, with oiled hair correctly parted and a linen handkerchief neatly in his dark jacket—had not attempted to reply to this wrath evoked by his introductory sentence. He might well have done so, for he was not there entirely without invitation. Gwen looked down in guilty apprehension.

"Shall I call to him?" she quavered.

"I wouldn't, dear," advised Marion. "Father will never welcome him now . . . I must say you were rather foolish to suggest he came to the house in this way."

Gwen saw the young man get into the car without a further glance at the house. He slammed the door hard. She watched the shining car's progress down the drive. In a slackened, emptied voice, she said: "But when Mr. Llewellyn was here, father said he might get us a car some day."

"You are so simple-minded," Kate said contemptuously. ". . . Anyhow, I don't think he's much of a catch. Looked quite ordinary to me." And Marion, crossing to the dressing-table, asked: "How many times have you seen him, Gwen?"

"What has that got to do with it?" Shoulders hunched up, she still paused at the window.

Marion, while Kate locked the door and took out a packet of cigarettes from her knickers, inattentively replied: "I don't see that a woman can properly fall in love with a man just by talking to him about bicycle tyres in a garage." She scraped a large powder-puff over the bottom of a bowl. Three tea-roses leaned in a silver vase under the mirror. "I'm out of powder again. I wonder——" She had already stolen spoonfuls from her stepmother's room.

"I *had* come to an understanding with him."

"Of course," Kate remarked in her concrete way, indifferent to the emotion involved and puffing at her cigarette, "we have the reputation of being well-off. I suppose we *appear* to be prizes. . . . Does his father own that garage?"

"Yes. They're not poor. They can't be; they actually sell motor-cars. They live in one of those villas overlooking Tremartin park. Ivor has sold five cars this year."

"Well, he's put paid to coming to this house." Kate

sounded deliberately final. She had seen her sister quickly rub her hand across her cheek before she turned from the window. "But imagine *any* young man coming to court here! Think, Gwen, do."

"You could run away with him," Marion suggested idly—"if he asked you . . . But judging by the look on his face when he got in that car, dear, he's been frightened away for ever."

Gwen, pacing down the room, took these comfortings wrongly. "Are you jealous?" she demanded. "No one in this district has paid any attention to either of you."

"We're not allowed to live that kind of life," Kate replied briskly. Without resentment, she added: "And I don't think we've got it in us to attract young men so that they'd sweep all obstacles out of the way. We're like those flowers that bees won't go to."

Marion, intent on fumbling among the crowded contents of a drawer, pouted: "But we are women."

"Oh, hush, both of you," Gwen snapped.

She sat on the bed. Striped skirt ending at the knees, her legs were long and supple. She was a handsome young woman: the aquiline nose, firmly-moulded lips and high-sweeping cheek-bones gave her an air of authority. But there was a curious blankness in her gold-speckled eyes, a stoniness. Her good colouring lent her a look of warmth: it was only a skin-warmth.

"Why, Gwen," Marion tinkled, peering into the mirror, "are you upset? . . . Look, you've always wanted this, haven't you?" She took from the drawer a waist-belt of dull silvery metal, a fine piece of imitation Renaissance work. Its medallions, linked by a chain, were engraved with a history of a human life, the cradle of the first medallion held by a snake-clasp to the coffin of the last. With an eldest sister's generosity, a flowing gesture of maturity, she handed the belt to the surprised Gwen. "Now you'd better go down and lay tea, dear. Try and get that woman to come down; I want some more powder."

That afternoon May did go down from her gabled room at the other end of the house. She heaved up from her afternoon nap in sufficient time. Her husband's furious voice below her spacious window had wakened her, and the interesting sight of the car and its driver made her feel active. In the country one is glad of any trivial event, especially in the afternoon.

The hall-gong struck with massive and extra violence. She knew her stepdaughters' different summonses to meals: Marion's fussy patting; Gwen's ponderous arm-swinging knell; Kate's impatient kick. The few occasions when Laura used the gong it drummed in subdued moderation. To-day it was Gwen's, only more so. She was not incommoded by the noise. The trouble with the country was that there was rarely any clatter, except that made by temper. Often the silence got badly on her nerves: sometimes she made to herself loud observations about it.

For instance, it was exasperating how quiet were cattle. Only yesterday she had made a scene about those thirty sheep. By arrangement with some farmer, they were spending a week on the grass of the so-called orchard—it was not her idea of an orchard—almost directly under the corner window of her room, where it was her custom to sit for hours. Their grey miserable faces, their silent following of each other, incensed her. Stupid, stupid creatures, with their daft lack of character, their sightless staring as they plodded along at each other's rumps. She really preferred cows, on the whole she did; they made her heart wobble but they did pay attention to one. The only thing these blessed sheep did not do in unison was when one stopped to let out black droppings or a squirt of water. It was concerning this she bitterly complained when Mansell came to bed. Almost right under her window! The orchard was already a mess of black heaps.

"It's good for the ground," he had said. "You can't expect sheep to go into a shed to oblige you, and you're not bound to sit in that window or keep it open." For the

◗

hundredth time she grizzled: "What a blasted fool I was to come to the country." It had led to more.

She shouted over the landing banister: "All right, you. No need to bang that thing again. *I'm coming down.*"

For all her uncorseted waddling, legs jostling against each other and breasts flaccidly loose, she descended the staircase—it seemed constructed for an opulent descent such as this—with the deliberation of a style learned in a hard school. Her flounced but strained poplin dress ended below her calves: she considered the modern craze to display the full leg to be immodest: besides, she had varicose veins. She held her great chin well, with the line of one accustomed to facing gigantic audiences both in London and the more difficult areas of Northern England where one turned one's back at one's peril. Within yellowish pads of flesh glinted, small but certain, a pair of wonderfully blue eyes: a crystalline baby-blue, but apt to blaze.

To-day, as she reached the hall, those eyes sidled about in readiness for anything. It was only rarely now that her face displayed a completely mollified look.

"Where's Laura?" she demanded of Gwen. Carrying a plate of scones across the hall, the stepdaughter shook her head for reply. The question was really an oblique reminder that despite her frequent isolation upstairs she was not forgetting a maternal superintendence. "Where's Laura?" she repeated in the dining-room. Tea was spread with some respect for its importance, since the other meals were on the spare side. Placid sunshine gleamed at the window. A bowl of snapdragons burned on the table.

Kate, already eating bread and butter, replied: "She can't have run away. . . . Perhaps she's gone for a walk."

"Don't you bark at me like that, girl!" Seating herself by the six cups and saucers, she demanded: "What was all that row going on outside the house this afternoon? One would think we were in a slum."

"You'd better ask father," Gwen sniffed. He was coming in. "Pour mine strong, please."

"Some whippersnapper of a commercial traveller," Mansell said crossly. "Llewellyn was telling me the other day they've taken to calling at private houses. . . . He wanted to sell me a car!"

"Well, why didn't you buy it? A man in your position. Here we are in August again and everybody going for holidays except us. I'm sure we all need a change."

"May, *I don't like cars*," he exclaimed.

Already the curved nose, thrusting out sharp, was quivering. That lean hungry wolfishness of his had become more pronounced. Yet he was not a slight man. His hair, still thick and vigorous, was whitening. The gaze of his restive eyes emerged erratically; their real absorption was inwards. The knuckles of his long thin hands cracking, he ate with a famished austerity, as if the food, which nervous exhaustion demanded, gave him no satisfaction. Since his retirement to the country he had grown a fierce little beard.

"You don't like them," May said; "but others do. If you bury people in the country you ought to study their comfort." Gwen politely offered her the plate of scones, but she waved it away: she never ate much.

"They have their legs," he said tartly. "And there are three bicycles here."

"Everybody hasn't got your crazy energy," she riposted. "Digging away out there like mad," she went on, unnecessarily brushing her corsage with quick and still pretty hands. "I've always wondered why people break their backs growing potatoes when they're so cheap in the shops. Apples I can understand, a tree doesn't need all this digging and looks nice . . . Where have you been, Laura?" she demanded in prompt but not displeasing scolding. Then the blue eyes flashed. "What!" she cried shrilly. "Hoo, look at her—my word!" She burst into fond laughter. "Oh, my beauty! Let me see you behind."

Laura, with an embarrassed simper, turned on the hearth rug. She had put her hair up. Jabbed with prongs and a comb, it piled up blackly, lustrously firm. Its ebony sheen set off the pulpy, pink-tinted creaminess of her face. She was suddenly a young lady.

"Where did you get those prongs?" Gwen asked.

"And that comb?" added Marion, who had just swept in. Laura rudely turned her back on her. "You've been skulking into my room again."

Laura blurted, raw: "Well, I saw you coming out of mother's room a minute ago; you steal her powder."

"What!" screamed May. "I *thought* my powder had got low." Spectacularly she half choked on her tea. Her eldest stepdaughter incensed her much more than the other two. Marion's false but calm air of being real mistress of this large house, if only by virtue of being a lady, had riled her from the beginning.

"I have helped myself to a little face-powder." Marion sat down coolly. "Father pays for it, does he not?"

"Good God, the woman's off her chump. And what in heaven's name does she want to powder herself for in a God-forsaken place like this where there's never a smell of a real man? . . . Oh, you pour her her tea," she blew at Gwen, forgetting her own daughter, who sat in the chair at her other side. Gwen was obliged to pour for both.

Marion did not deign to reply further. She sat in a stiff vacancy. The plait of fair hair coiled round her head gave her a look of efficient primness. Perhaps it was her delicate skin and slim bearing which made her look younger than she was. Also something in her was still paused in youth, though this arrested girlishness seemed brittle, superficial, as if one single day it would swiftly plunge into decay, like a rose.

At the other end of the table Mansell sat removed from this scene of squabbling women. It might have been a lot of duck-noises. But, another little dispute brewing, his hand trembled as he laid down his cup. "You're all too idle—that is the matter here," he interfered. "All of you."

His wife gathered herself up from her chair and went to the door with a rolling magnificence. Her irony was tremendous: "What do you expect *me* to do? Keep pigs or something?" She turned for her exit. "Let me find you stealing things again, my lady, and *I'll* take the starch out of you." After this—and she left the door open like royalty—she could be heard making a tour of inspection of the ground floor. She had not been downstairs for four days.

"Little tell-tale," Gwen cooed privately to Laura. "You do look a sight with your hair like that . . . Let me do it properly for you after tea," she suggested with a peculiar coyness, one eye on her father. Listening to his wife's progress, he seemed unaware. "You've got lovely hair but you don't know what do to with it."

"I'm satisfied with it like this," Laura scowled. Her face had become squat and heavy.

"If she wishes to make herself look even plainer than she is——" Marion leaned across, whisperingly. And Kate, who had maintained a contemptuous silence—she was usually like that at family meals—couldn't resist: "It's coarse hair, like Italians have; it never looks quite clean to me."

Beard raised, their father rapped his knuckles on the table. "Be quiet," he ordered impatiently. "This everlasting bickering!" But the fuming was entirely interior, self-preservatory. As if the little feminine cluster down there was without importance.

Marion shifted her string of beads. "Father, cannot you buy us a car . . . please?" The after-word sounded teasing.

"I would drive it," Kate said. Her broad face, hard flat hands and clipped decisive voice bristled with a need to exercise dammed-up energy. "I'm sure I could learn in a day."

"A car would make things easier for us," Gwen said blandly. "Laura," she asked, offering her the last scone, "wouldn't you like a car to take you to Tremartin for your singing lesson?"

"I have my bike." Laura looked quickly at her father. Agitated at being forced into the open like this, he was getting up. "It's strange how you imagine I'm made of money. . . . I keep you in idleness," he jerked querulously to the door, "when most unmarried women nowadays work at careers. But you're never satisfied."

"Careers?" Marion lifted her head. "You never encouraged us to take up careers. In fact you were positively against it. You remember, don't you, that I wanted to become a professional singer?"

"Besides," said Gwen, "we look after the house. You won't spend money on servants——"

But he had vanished. Marion turned crisply to Laura, who was beginning to look restless. "Who would have thought this family could produce two vocalists. . . . Assuming you're going to be one, dear."

"I can't quite see Laura on a platform," Gwen's eyes surveyed her, kindly, while Kate promptly observed: "Judging by that girl who sang at that concert in the Parish Hall, she needn't get too depressed."

Laura stalked to the door.

"You can't bear it, can you, that father bought me that music-case last week." Now her piled-up hair gave her an unready, immature look.

"It's your mother that got it for you," Gwen flung a last taunt; "don't deceive yourself." She went to the door and, opening it again, left it ajar.

They heard their stepmother soundly rating the Tremartin licensed victualler on the telephone. Not only was his delivery a day late but if he thought that last lot of port fit for a human being . . . As they listened there was no bitterness in their faces. Marion even tittered. But Kate darkened in contempt: when May shouted, "If you were in trade in London you wouldn't last a month," she jumped up impatiently, spitting: "The woman's a disgrace."

In the drawing-room the parrot let out a long extinguishing screech.

"No wonder we're talked about in the district," Gwen said. "No wonder we're nicknamed Petticoat House."

"*That*," Kate said, flat, "is because there's four obstreperous women here to one man."

"Not counting Laura," Gwen said.

"But it's wrong," pouted Marion. "A pair of trousers rules us."

"Hark at her," Kate growled as May continued to hold contact with the outside world.

"Why doesn't she go?" Marion seemed to sing a little song, putting her head on one side like Desdemona. "If only she would go! I think we could manage father if only she was gone."

"With her silly daughter." Kate planted herself, her legs sturdily apart, at the window. Gwen noiselessly assembled the tea-things—"I think I'd miss Laura," she said.

2

In January of that year May had been on the point of a dramatic departure. Especially dramatic because the house was marooned in the snow and no man, beast or machine could approach for five days, not even that unsung gallant of isolated rural parts, the postman. But for the upset woman those rolling billows of snow and the buried road did not register as a difficulty; she had gone on packing a trunk.

Whether or not the sense of being cut-off, flowering at last into a great dread of the alien district, had been the subconscious cause of her decision was unknown to her stepdaughters. They favoured the opinion that the non-delivery of the weekly crate of drink brought about the exciting event.

True, this had not been mentioned (as far as they could gather) in the man-and-wife battle which took place in the corner bedroom with its gable bay, though, hovering in the passage, they listened very carefully. The amassed complaints of the years since he had retired were hurled at the husband. Chief of these was that he had deliberately imprisoned her in country which must drive any sociable woman mad. Another was that if he had let Walter Monks come there with them he would be alive to-day, besides being company for herself.

But she was sick to death of it now, she was, and she was going; she would get her trunk down from the tower-room and go in the morning. "May," he had shouted, "if you go, you won't get a penny from me. Not a penny."

"Keep your dirty money. I'll sing in smoking concerts. . . . Ha," her voice rose to a new malevolent note, "you think you're the only man I can rope in, I s'pose?"

"If you leave here you go for ever. And alone. Laura shall not go with you." At this the three sisters looked at each other in dismay.

"What?" Her voice became even fuller. "How could you keep her? She'd come with me, *me*."

"You're very sure of yourself," he derided. "But I tell you this—if you got her away I would go to law, I would show you were unfit to look after a young girl."

At this there was a pause—before the cataract, beginning slowly, and mounting to full release: "You'd go to law . . . he'd go to law! Him! . . . Ha, ha, that's funny, that is. To law! He'd step into the box looking shiny as all the twelve apostle spoons. *Him*. He'd speak like a slice of the Bible. Him, that made a fortune out of cat houses . . . And me— oh, I'd be sitting there with my hands in my lap and mum as a worm!" The voice ripped like a sheet. "Get out of my sight, you God-damned hypocrite. Out . . . out——"

She then broke into a howl that after a few seconds became a long convulsive wail on a lower note.

At the creak of the opening door the three had hastened away across the landing. But, while Gwen and Kate flew into the opposite passage, Marion stopped.

She stopped and turned; she stood drawn up in the centre of the landing which even on bright summer days remained shadowy. His head ducked, he approached; it jerked up as he realised her presence. Did she see guilt in the drawn grey face? Or only sense it in the rat-coloured winter light? Did it give her the added courage to smile—tranquilly, remotely? He went past her at once, without a word.

Later that afternoon May, with the aid of her daughter, had noisily got a trunk down from the tower-room; thus the great decision was announced to the house. All the rest of the evening the sisters hovered in turn about the landing, getting excited, doubtful, thwarted. May did not leave her room. But Laura, bewildered and tearful, fetched and carried. She refused to be waylaid by her stepsisters.

"Silly thing," Gwen remarked to Kate, "she doesn't want to go. Her mother frightens her; she feels safer with him."

"The worst of it is," Kate said gloomily, "no one will be able to go to-morrow unless there's a big melting of that snow to-night. . . . It's just like her to decide to go when it's impossible. She's dotty."

"Drunk! She always keeps a couple of bottles of whisky for emergencies."

Yet, though that night the weather had changed to a southern mildness and by the morning the snow was melted sufficiently to allow an exit to the railway-station two miles away, the Ruthin Arms car was not ordered. All the morning silence wrapped the bedroom. Mansell went downstairs at his usual time, eight o'clock. He looked nimble and decisive. In the kitchen he enquired considerately of Gwen, who had preceded him by a few minutes: "You have enough coal in for the stove? It's milder, but keep a good fire going." He never begrudged coal; he seemed to need much heat himself.

Later, Laura had trotted about with a look of release, though she still skirted away in wary secretiveness from her stepsisters. At breakfast her father (he had not so far displayed interest in the lessons she had begun to take in Tremartin) asked her questions about her progress and the

D*

teacher. After advising her to practice diligently on the drawing-room piano—she could have a fire there as often as she liked—he announced that he was going to Tremartin himself to see Mr. Llewellyn. This implied that he stood in deep need of a session away from this house of women. It also implied that the air of peace hovering in the house was secure.

The trunk, however, never went back to the tower-room. It remained in May's bedroom till her death.

And from that January day she left the room less often. Mansell himself carried up coal for her fires. Laura ran errands and took up the tray of paltry snacks. Her mother ate little and irregularly, though she liked a lot of fruit, both fresh and preserved. She became even more addicted to writing for London drapers' catalogues and ordering an abundance of clothes, this causing more conflicts with Mansell ("If you needed them, May!" he would yelp. "If you went out!") But, as with her drink—which he still did not begrudge—she got all she wanted. She ordered two expensive evening gowns: she got extra clothes for Laura too: on one surprising occasion she even bought for her stepdaughters a dozen pairs of stockings and sent Laura downstairs with the package and a note flourishingly signed, as in her music-hall days: 'With May Potter's compliments.'

On another occasion she posted to the Tremartin wine-merchant a coloured postcard of herself in her sumptuous heyday, accompanied by the message: 'Yours truly of the other side orders six bottles of rum to be delivered before Sunday.' The victualler, dull as an ox, propped it against a display of beer-bottles and attention was often drawn to the celebrity. Eventually Mansell got to hear of this, and there was another bitter quarrel upstairs.

One afternoon, as the mild wet spring of that western land drifted sweetly into summer, she had remarkably descended to the garden. But not without careful defences against the sunshine. Flowing draperies of chiffon hung from her ample shoulders, a long tatter of lace protected her throat, a wide poppy-wreathed straw hat was securely pinned. In the porch she paused and looked at the lustrous patina of the landscape, with its far blue-cut line of enclosing hills, its green and buff rise of lonely fields, its quiet-locked woods and remote white clusters of farmsteads, and she shuddered. But, Laura at her side with anxiety and pleasure congested about her nose, she successfully reached the lawn. There, a pathetically noble ruin, a once-jocund Venus gone recklessly over-ripe and lustreless, the sunlight picked out the fatty yellow pouches in her face. It also struck from her eyes a bluer, more crystalline purity.

"Pinks," she pointed in her slow brooding tour of the borders flanking three sides of the lawn. "What are those?"

"Gilliflowers. Gwen and Kate know how to make flowers grow, don't they! Look, here are the first roses." With an approving nod or two May passed on. A swollen yellow finger caressed the curling lips of a rose. She lowered herself, breathing heavily, and picked herself a double marigold. "Will we take a bunch?" her daughter asked; but with an instinctive glance back to the house.

"No, child; wild flowers depress me now. I used to have the best out of florists' shops."

"Look at that little birch tree at the edge of the lawn! Marion wanted to cut it down because it spoiled the view from their window, but father wouldn't let her."

"Don't speak so *fast*, Laura," her mother pounced; "you don't give yourself time to open your mouth properly, girl. Now listen——" Declaiming a music-hall rhyme as example and sweeping over to the white bench, she launched into an elocution lesson, unacademic.

Once sunk on the bench she did not move for half an hour. She lost the drift of her lesson and a silent passivity wrapped her. But from this brooding in the sunshine she roused herself now and again to look at her daughter with a troubled yearning; she even fumbled sentimentally for her hand and pressed it with a sigh. As if she much needed to breathe out a private revelation, perhaps a confession, but

was baulked by delicacy . . . or the instinct to let well
alone.

Yet within that yearning lay a steady pin-point of satisfaction. This daughter was no disgrace. She was a fulfilment. And now her arrival, which had robbed the stage of
one of its most promising delights, could be forgiven. By
now retirement—at least from Number One dates—would
have been unavoidable: her voice had let her down. What
did it matter now? The years robbed one of everything.

So this belated fondness burst into life. The illusion had
served its purpose. . . . But facts had to be faced. Except
some that on the whole were better left in silence. What
purpose would be served by telling Laura she was born out
of wedlock? She wished this deep hankering to tell her did
not come so often, with its under-feeling of pleasure. But she
could not make up her mind. Would it be better to tell her
before those stepdaughters, who would twist the story this
way and that, got it in? They wouldn't dare reveal the
secret while their father was alive. But who knew what
would happen to either herself or Mansell, some sudden
drama—you never knew with a man of his kind—that would
leave the young Laura at her stepsisters' mercy?

The huge poppy-wreathed hat nodded. She lapsed into
a doze.

Behind the little birch tree, from within the tall narrow
window of the downstairs corner room they had more or
less appropriated as a parlour for themselves, the sisters had
watched the leisurely tour in fascination. Gwen had hastened
in with the news that the woman was coming downstairs
dressed to go out. There was an excited scamper to the
window, even Marion becoming alert.

"Good gracious, doesn't she look sad!" Gwen admired.
"Except for those clothes, anyone would think she was
going to a funeral."

"She's acting sadness," Kate remarked.

"She's so capricious," Marion sighed, with a criticism
that sounded like jealousy. "I wonder will she ever go?

I wish she'd go. It would be best for herself. . . . She does look stupid twirling that aster."

"*Marigold*," Gwen corrected, putting a chocolate in her mouth. "It's strange father didn't want her to go that time when she packed the trunk," she mused.

Kate gave a cynical laugh and said it wasn't strange at all—"He couldn't bear the disgrace of his wife leaving him; not down here in his native place. . . . Besides," she added in a flash, "she belongs to him too much, to all he's done. Such people don't walk out on each other; they can't. That's why there's murders."

"Of course he's killing her with the drink," Marion asserted, not for the first time.

"And by bringing her down here," Kate added. "As he killed our mother with cruelty."

"If not by other things," Gwen put in.

"Her face," Marion peered, "is yellow as that aster. Poor woman, it would be a mercy for her to die."

They hadn't seen a hat on her head since her one and only trip, in a hired car, to Tremartin the summer after they came to live in the house. Then she caused quite a sensation in the old grey town—it had been market-day—both men and women pausing in astonishment. But it had been a secret lesson for her husband: he became certain of what he suspected—that she did not, after all, add to his local prestige. He had progressed into worldly success and knowledge; these people remained unchanged in their antique traditions. It was all very well to see such women on the stage; in the daylit streets they were unnatural mistakes.

3

The afternoon trip into the garden became, in a way, decisive. From it May dated her physical decline, complaining she had caught cold in the small of her back. "A nasty wind sprang up and nipped me there," she would complain. 'The country' could never be trusted. It was double-faced, treacherous, malign. It was naturally anti-pathetic to civilised human beings, and weather, both hot and cold, was always worse there than in those self-protec-tive products of man, the great cities.

"The fact is, May," her husband accused in one of their milder moments, when defeat seemed to govern both of them like a pain, "you look for excuses for laziness."

"I didn't marry a well-off man to make beds and cakes and wash his shirts. . . . And you didn't marry me," she reminded him sombrely, "for those things either."

"I married you because you were a fine-looking woman." A dead anguish lay down in his voice.

"I was that, Pharaoh," she admitted, passively accepting the past tense. Except in the strictest privacy she never called him Pharaoh now, agreeing it was unsuitable in the presence of his children. "I often turn over my old photo-graphs and my album of press-cuttings," she went on, "and I think—'my God, I could have had dukes and lords if I'd had the push some of the pros. of my time had.'"

"You flatter yourself too much. You had several faults. They were what attracted me to you, I was sick of my first wife's virtues. . . . And you've done well for yourself," he assured; "if it wasn't for me you would have sunk to a low-class Pimlico room with Monks."

"And then perhaps he'd be living to-day."

"Or have died sooner."

"Poor Walt," she mourned, "I let him down. Funny, he was never my proper husband, but he lasted; something held us together . . . If you had let him come here with us," she grieved in dreamy rebuke, "the country wouldn't have seemed so bad . . . with these oil lamps," she added concretely.

"Now, May," he said, testily then. "It would not have been proper. Besides, he'd have wanted to bring Fred down as well."

"And why not? Heaven above, we got to stick close to each other on this earth, haven't we? We're not here so long that we can afford to neglect old friends. Fred's decent even if he does like his drop, and he could have set up in that Tremartin place with his tattooing; if sailors and soldiers can be tattooed, what's wrong with farm labourers getting done? Besides," she rambled, "Fred knew how to stuff birds. Way back in olden times his family came from the country."

"I daresay . . . Be quiet now; I want to sleep."

"*I* don't sleep well here," she grizzled. "You didn't ought to have retired so soon from the chemist shop. I got to like going in the shop and listening to the customers . . . And," she said, dreamily again, "I could make trips to the houses and keep a strict eye on 'em. . . . What a fool you were," she began to bristle, "to sell that house in Maida Vale for three thousand, I can't forget it. The way that old tart talked you down, I could have knocked her head off. Anybody would think you'd lost hold of yourself. It riles me now to think I didn't get my stays off with her. . . . But no," she fumed, "you got that silly bee in your bonnet about coming here and turning respectable, all so sudden when you were making packets of money. Bee in your bonnet—no, the wind-up in your guts——"

He drew the bed-covers over his ears.

In late September, a few weeks after the occasion of the car-salesman's visit, she developed jaundice. She blamed the approach of autumn with its damp and its yellow leaves. With the drawing-in of the evenings a deeper melancholy settled in her and she confessed to her daughter her dread of another winter in that house. The jaundice was no light attack but, after at first consenting and when the arrangements had been made, she refused to go to the county hospital: the doctor wished her to go for a thorough overhaul. That inbred passivity took complete hold, though not in the sense of submission to other wills.

It aided her in enduring the illness. She sank into a

stagnancy where she lay as though impervious not only to all external activity but to her own state. The doctor—he was a real little old countryman of local roots—visited her daily; she treated him with the vague remoteness of a goddess scanning the unimpressive lineaments of a pigmy. She did not drink for two months, and lost flesh. By December she had recovered from the jaundice but looked a wreck. One afternoon she sat bolt upright in bed and asked for her hand-mirror.

"My God," she muttered into the oval, "true enough all good things come to an end." She laid the mirror down. "That's the last time I'll look into a glass like that." Then, more briskly, she demanded: "Now, Laura, my bunch of keys—over there . . . My rings began to fall off in bed," she went on, gazing at her fingers; "my lady Marion remarked on it, she's always got her eye on jewellery. . . . Found those keys? Go to that cupboard . . . I hope you haven't been missing your singing lessons, dear? . . . There, on the bottom shelf, bring all that's there."

"But mother——" Laura quavered uncertainly.

"Am I to get out of bed to fetch them?"

Laura brought over the four bottles of spirit. Her mother directed her to place three under the bed and to fetch a glass. This done, she said: "Yes, dear, I know. But it's no good you sulking. I can't help it now . . . And I wouldn't let you see this if I thought you'd take to drink. But you won't, you're not the kind—as far as a human being can tell now. But if you do, God help you—and you remember those words, my girl. . . . How have they been behaving to you while I've been lying here?" she asked, pouring.

"Oh," Laura tossed her head, "just the same. But I get even with them."

"Do you? . . . One of these days," the mother's eyes seemed to meet in concentration, "*I'll* put the fear of the Lord into them."

During the illness the sisters had made dutiful, almost

official, visits to the room they never otherwise entered. They always filed in together. Once May crackled into a laugh, her orange face squeezed up so peculiarly that Kate, who for all her hard demeanour was still high-strung, retreated into the gable window. "You make me think of the Eskimo Triplets," the stepmother gurgled. "They used to be on the halls. Never one without the others. A dresser told me they shared the same soup plate, like little pups."

"I'm glad to see you are back a little to your old self," Marion said carefully. And Gwen proceeded, calm: "Tell Laura when you feel like a custard or a jelly." Kate came out of the bay window and nervously examined the unframed photographs pinned on the walls—all were signed, and every face, except that of Dan Leno, kept a successful smile.

Whether it was by the aid of drink or not, she got up the next day.

But it was for the last lap. During the following months she did not leave her room to go downstairs more than half a dozen times. She went down for Christmas dinner and ate a small slice of the turkey Mansell got from Garth Farm in barter for an oil painting of the Charge of Balaklava. Yet, in some elusive way, the illness seemed to have rejuvenated her. She was certainly better-looking, less puffy; her movements were more graceful. She began to drink more than ever. But still Mansell made no attempt to curb this.

It was during this period that, descending to the drawing-room one afternoon in a new lacy tea-gown and wearing all her rings, she struck out for Laura's future and obtained by threats four hundred pounds. In addition, though the transfer was not done for days and meanwhile she drank heavily, she saw that the money was placed properly to Laura's credit and the deposit book actually put into her hands.

"But do you think I'm going to leave my daughter in the lurch?" Mansell protested fiercely. They were alone in the drawing-room.

"I don't like the way you are going," she replied obstinately. "You've got some queerness at the bottom of your soul. . . . It's all got to do," she admitted, "with something I don't understand. But I do know it's leading to nasty habits with your money."

To Laura she said: "Now, dear, here's four hundred pounds for you to spend when the need comes. Maybe some day you'll want to get out of here and try your hand at a job. . . . Do you feel you want to go on the stage like your mother?" She scrutinised her doubtfully. Laura did not seem to possess the style she was familiar with. But styles had changed, and not for the better.

"I would like to sing," Laura replied, fascinated by the wallet-like object her mother had taken from under the mattress: she thought it contained the actual money, and she was already alarmed by thoughts of burglars—and of her stepsisters, who the last day or two had been watching her like particularly aware cats. "Miss Edwards says I'm getting along nicely."

"Well, *I* don't know about your voice," the experienced professional observed. "You might make a soubrette, in straight stuff . . . Were you thinking of grand opera then?"

"No . . . o," Laura murmured.

"I can see you in operetta," May pronounced; "doing a bit of acting and singing, perhaps a bit of dancing. You'll be short and well-covered but not fat," she continued, "you've got a good swing of the hips and your eyes are dark and can roll about like a Spaniard's. They'll cast you for gipsy or Spanish parts. Always see you get bright clothes. But you'll have to get rid of that scowl of yours, girl. Practice every day before the mirror—start to-day. You depress me sometimes. . . . A cheerful face," she said mechanically, "is necessity number one on the road to the West End."

Laura felt depressed herself: by this wallet, this sudden fixed attention on her future and this vague suggestion of parting in the air. She had never been able to penetrate into the mystery of her mother's character. The occasional maternal gestures she made embarrassed her. Capricious, heavily yearning (in comparison with the care of other girls' mothers—as far as she could judge) these gestures possessed no system and gave no feeling of satisfaction.

Her mother went on to explain the deposit book. And if the money was not used for a professional training it was to be a nest-egg for marriage. "I decided to get it for you that day when you walked into tea with your hair up," she said with some emotion. "You gave me quite a turn, and when I got upstairs I cried. You've grown up before I've had a chance to look at you properly. . . . Children, you think they're children for ever, and then one day you get a kick from them that knocks you down and makes you feel old as the sorrows of Satan."

Then she gave the London address of a retired professional friend who would help Laura in every way— "She's a bit of an old hen but her heart's good as gold: she won a pile in a sweepstake." The friend, with whom she still exchanged Christmas cards, was married to a famous singer.

"Thank you, mother," whispered Laura, appalled by the responsibility of so much money.

"Your father can well afford it." She looked out disagreeably at the torrential April rain sweeping across the landscape. "That chemist shop made a mint of money—though you wouldn't think it, so tatty and old-fashioned it got. . . . Lock that book in your dressing-table, my girl, and hide the key. I bet those stepsisters of yours have sniffed there's something going on and they're sure to go prying around."

"They've been saying some spiteful things to me the last day or two," Laura admitted.

"They have, have they! Ha, one of these days——" She ruminated darkly.

Laura, glad to stir from the oppressive discussion, tidied

the room. Her mother, in a fluffy sateen bed-jacket from Oxford Street, remarked that the trouble in the small of her back had got worse because of the rain. Getting up from the fireplace Laura noticed tears rolling down the tinted face: not many, and the face remained monumentally still. About her, the flowering of an old sadness, was the sense of a fixed, private grief, not to be approached or touched. Instinctively the daughter knew it.

When she had been brought from Barnet to live at the chemist shop below Hampstead Heath she had turned to her father as a more recognisable and a safer person. Lately she decided it was only the drink that made her mother into a special being so often shut away in a complex world of her own. Still she preferred the mystery of her father, more acceptable because it was a male mystery. She liked to think of him digging in the garden, growing vegetables like any ordinary man, taking trips to the town—but she always wished he would take her with him and not leave her alone in the house with the others. His quarrels with her mother she had begun to accept as normal, though when they happened they still made her feel sick and at the mercy of threatening terrors.

Her stepsisters she accepted without criticism as natural enemies; she saw now that it had been like that from the first and was bound to be, like something in the Bible. They were the only occupants of her world about whom she was quite clear: she was able to assess her forces against theirs, and was perfectly aware they would be victorious. They had such advantages—age, experience, close knowledge of their father and of the long mysterious life in London before she was taken to the house there. But also she knew now that where he was concerned she too had an advantage. She was not included in that secret but continuous ebb and flow between him and his three daughters. That wave of feeling which in the fibres of her being she had come to recognise, without enquiring into its origins, as hatred.

4

Blaming the weather—no one, she accused, could go out into it—May began drinking early that day. By the evening she looked ill and was extremely irritable. She even turned on Laura for bringing her up some mutton broth: specks of fat glistened on its surface. When her husband came into the room while this one-sided row was proceeding his first glance at her was a chemist's glance. He suggested she saw the doctor next day. She flew at him.

The next day she went downstairs to tea. She seemed mollified but sat almost entirely silent, only looking now and again at her stepdaughters with a speculative but seemingly well-disposed examination.

A few days later Mansell went off to Tremartin after the mid-day meal, to see his only local crony—the Mr. Llewellyn who wrote sermons for his own pleasure though he was no preacher; he was an astute and well-off business man, dealing in property and also very successful with stocks and shares, to which rumour added that he 'carried on' with a woman in another town. Laura, going to her music lesson, accompanied her father on the outward journey.

She went off perplexed but pleased by her mother's signs of activity. May had instructed her daughter to collect, unobserved, the keys of every door in the house. There were nineteen altogether, including the two of the downstairs exits from the house.

At three o'clock, after listening from the landing, May crept downstairs. Clocks placidly ticked in the afternoon repose. The parrot knew this quietude and, unless encouraged, never disturbed it. Washing-up done, the three sisters had retired as usual to their parlour.

In one hand she carried two keys; the other held an oval hand-mirror. She noiselessly locked the front door. It was more difficult to creep past the parlour near the kitchen and lock the back door, but she achieved it undisturbed. Her breathing was heavy, and she walked with a solid, uneasy little roll. A purple undertint smouldered in her face. She put the two keys into the pocket of her cashmere jacket.

She crept to the parlour door and threw it back. "*Now,*" she boomed, entering, "what are you three plotting, hey?"

Kate's feet dropped from the mantel-side and she eased herself up quickly, throwing her cigarette into the fire—her father was hostile to women smoking. Gwen, rearranging Marion's coiffure in a new style, gaped; her eyes travelled to the hand-mirror. Marion had uttered a little shriek; for a moment she looked at the intruder sideways, recoiled into herself.

Menace thunderous along her cheeks, May advanced a step or two. "Sitting here like three spiders every afternoon," she breathed.

Marion was the first to become vocal. "The woman's mad!" Her thin cry was curiously chilling, an undernourished noise. But she looked calculatingly at the door. To reach it she would have to push past the large figure of this purple-faced mænad—and in its wrath it seemed very large indeed. At the same time she clutched her hair with an annoyed gesture; it was only half arranged, and a comb, prongs and several hair-pins fell from her lap as she jumped up.

"You call me mad——" May's voice growled, boweldeep. "You bundle of old tricks, you, I'll smash this mirror on your head." But she advanced no further from the strategic position covering the exit. The air of menace exuding from her seemed to crackle in its strength; an odour, the petrifying odour of wrath, ran in it. Blue eyes biting, she stared in scheming enmity, awaiting her opponents' move.

In those lightning moments, compounded of astonishment and fear, it was to be expected that the ambushed

sisters would make a tactical error.   Both Gwen and Kate
had become pale. But, perhaps because she was more or
less in a state of *déshabille*, it was Marion who was most
unnerved. May, facing her like some great realistic fact,
completely undid her. Again she uttered her chilling
hollow shriek, and, swooping bird-like, made a dash for the
door. Gwen and Kate, discomposed further by the shriek,
at once ran after her.

Their stepmother made no effort to detain them. Neither
did she lift the hand-mirror. But she went in pursuit.

Oddly, Marion had run to the front door: the back door
was nearer. She was still pulling hysterically at the handle,
her sisters by her side, when May heaved into the hall.

"I'll give you *mad*, my fine ladies . . . And I'll teach
you to respect my daughter."

They ran again, scrambling confusedly up the staircase.
But Kate was whispering something. Amazingly quick,
despite her weight and condition, May heaved not far from
their heels: as she reached the top stair only the landing's
width lay between them. Then, neck sunk into her chest,
she drew up in the middle of the landing.

A door handle was rattled. A moment later there was a
rush of skirts across the landing towards the opposite
passage. Another rattle. And a wild beating on a door
panel, as if in call to someone within. And Gwen's cry:
"She's locked all our doors!"

May appeared at the passage entrance. The sisters rushed
to the far end where the window looked over the house side.
They crouched there together. May drew up a yard away
but did not cease to heave in her terrible not-to-be-appeased
fury. "I'll teach you to leave my daughter in peace." The
pronouncement was not screamed but uttered in that low
hideous growl.

They hurled past her again. Still she made no attempt to
intercept them. A tumultous trio skipping across the
landing, they rushed into the narrow arched entrance where
the curved stairway led to the tower room. But May did not

pursue up there. She only went to the archway and stood filling it, peering up.

"Ah, my fine ladies!" She gurgled now. "Ah, my fine ladies!"

A long, thwarted wail from Marion went up and up. And Kate's hoarse, cursing voice broke: ". . . every door. . . ."

"—Every door!" The clap of laughter below crashed up, strong in the narrow confined space, and echoing.

"Oh, what shall we do?" wailed Marion's voice.

"—teach you a lesson!" It sounded final, a last appeased taunt.

She left the archway, trod heavily across the landing, went into the short passage on the left, unlocked her door and slammed it.

They came down. Their thrust-out faces peered cautiously from inside the narrow darkish aperture. They stepped out to the landing. And, neck swirling up and face undiminished, May came out from against the passage wall. "I'll teach you who is mistress here," she growled. With a single united cry, they scampered.

Down the staircase. But Kate, who was last, shouted in barking wildness: "The 'phone! 'Phone for help. She's out of her mind."

Descending with awful certainty, the hand-mirror pressed against her thigh, May invited: "'Phone then. Get the police. A van-load of them. And the fire-engine to get you out of the house." Majestically bedraggled, she descended without the aid of the banister. Her face seemed eyeless, the sockets closed.

Though they scampered this way and that across the hall, completely without direction, they yet seemed hypnotised by the descent. But Marion shrieked: "Don't get the police. Not the police."

"The windows," Gwen screamed.

"Ah!" May stood blindly on the third stair: the sigh contained a huge pleasure. "Ah!" And she moved no further. The closed fleshly face was lifted in a listening rigidity.

Marion had run to the nearest door; it led to the dining-room, and it opened. She gave a cry of triumph. Gwen shouted: "That window is jammed." It was. Then the parrot, caged in the drawing-room, swiftly screeched. "Tea-time," it announced, "tea-time." Another screech followed, madly indignant. Kate, who had skipped near the telephone in an agony of indecision, suddenly stood arrested.

From the stair May threw two keys to the floor. Then she turned and, a hand on the banister, heavily began to climb. Below, the three watched.

They stood huddled together, their faces crumpled into pallid relief. Marion recovered first; she put a hand to her disarranged hair and patted it. Gwen whispered quaveringly: "Blind drunk, of course. We ought to have stood up to her . . . three of us." Their stepmother disappeared.

"We couldn't." Kate still gazed up, with eyes wide and fixed in wonder, as though for the first time she had looked upon some unholy mystery. "We couldn't touch her."

Marion gave a constricted yelp: "Touch her, indeed, touch her! I'd have died."

Gwen picked up the two keys and unlocked the front door.

"She's coming back," Kate whispered, staring up.

A shower of keys fell down the staircase. A moment or two afterwards a door slammed.

"We'll leave those keys," Gwen said. "Father must pick them up . . . or Laura."

"Get tea, Gwen," entreated Marion. "You can finish my hair afterwards."

Except that it was May's last flourish, the outrageous scene seemed to cause no particular repercussions. When Laura, swinging her pigskin music-case, returned a couple of hours later, the sisters totally ignored her. There was no tea laid for her. She saw the scattered keys and collected them. She had quite forgotten about them. A young man had followed her about in Tremartin, right to the bus.

Her mother was asleep on the bed. Incoherent mutters came from her throat and her face twitched. Vaguely disturbed, she returned downstairs and prepared tea in the empty kitchen, eating it there, hungrily. It had been exciting in Tremartin. He had looked like a nice student—perhaps he studied the violin—but she dared not go into the park though she had half an hour to wait. Not with her heart palpitating like that. In the market-square she made friends with a dog, patting its head and keeping close to it. Safe on the bus, an enormous satisfaction eased her. And she had decided to ask Marion to practice with her to-night. One could forgive. After all, Marion was quite old.

When Mansell arrived, his eldest daughter called him into the parlour. He rarely entered this room. Very much mistress of herself now, Marion related the afternoon's event. Kate and Gwen, sitting calm as judgment, supplied one or two extra details. "Of course, father," Marion said remotely, like someone speaking on the telephone, "we realise she was intoxicated, but we do think she should be spoken to and our position here made clear. We do not ask for respect, but it's hard to be actually threatened and even attacked."

Gwen said: "I'm sure she needs a change. Couldn't she be persuaded to go to London?"

"Laura is impertinent to us often enough," Kate said. "But we don't complain."

He had listened with a growing querulousness, tugging his beard and moving about the room. Silent, until he burst out: "I cannot interfere in these women's quarrels. I don't understand them. Men seldom do." He opened the door. Not once had he looked at them directly. "Don't trouble me with them again." Going out with an untidy hopping, he pulled the door sharply.

"Coward," Kate softly rapped.

"Liar," Gwen whispered.

"Really, such a perfect hypocrite one can almost admire him," Marion said. "Of course he's entirely at her mercy," she granted. Her expression might have been one of satisfaction.

But May's real decline set in from that day. She never went downstairs again. After a fortnight of steady drinking bouts, alternating with fits of extreme irritableness (one day she boxed Laura's ears), it became plain that she was very ill. She ate next to nothing, and at last, when she had vomited blood, she consented to see the doctor. He decided it was cirrhosis of the liver and on this occasion ordered her instant removal to hospital.

She looked at him from the shreds of her profound contempt for 'the country' and all to do with it. "I'm going to die in my own bed," she croaked. At his clear professional warning, something of her old jaunty spirit bounced up, and with no respect for his age she cut at him: "Look here, my fellow-me-lad, I got no use for hospitals because they have women nurses."

And she would not budge. She lay in a huge apathy; it was disturbed only by her obstinate call for drink. Laura became an entire nurse, though her mother insisted she went to her singing lessons. The three sisters kept aloof but gave such aids as impersonal servants would render. Laura herself they treated not exactly with silent indifference but with the calm of those who can afford to bide their time. That last outburst of May's might yet prove her most stupid action.

She lingered on for months, and—it was like a relief— her illness dominated the living conditions of the house. She lost weight, she incessantly complained of feeling cold. Mansell bought a narrow iron bed and slept in the tower-room. The doctor had given him a liquid to reduce the alcoholic content of the bottles still arriving from Tremartin: he did not interfere with them, though he put some away in the cellar. As the weeks wore on May actually drank less. She was so often sunk into a daze, almost a coma. Wearing all her rings, she slept well at nights and seemed not to need an attendant.

Her last known words, muttered while Laura was in the room at evening, were: "I ought to have gone to America." She died, alone and apparently in her sleep, that night. It was September.

Mansell put on a black tie and, after the doctor had been, prepared to go to Tremartin on the melancholy errands. Laura, after much weeping and hysteria, begged to go with him: she had kept him in view all the morning, following him about. After a cross refusal he consented at the last moment. The sisters were intent on their own arrangements. But Gwen cornered him and thrashed out the matter of cash for mourning clothes. He reduced her estimate of fifty pounds to thirty: this was for them and Laura. Clearly his need to impress the district had lost its first strength when, besides installing the telephone, modern fireplaces and plumbing in the villa, he had erected an expensive bronze weathercock on the tower parapet. He had even contemplated erecting a flag-pole too.

Laura never forgot the two-mile walk to the village to catch the afternoon bus to Tremartin. He did not say anything at all, and walked fast. Yet presently he took her hand in his. A few tears had been running down her cheeks; at the touch of his fingers they coursed out in a flood she thought would never stop. But she too did not utter a word. Tall, walking like someone who has never lost sight of the important goal of his life, he remained closed in his man's being. By the time they reached the village an exhausted peace calmed her.

In Tremartin, where he left her alone for an hour to amuse herself among the shops, she suddenly felt a clear need to see again the young man who had once followed her. If he appeared now she would consent to a walk in the park. Instead she met Miss Edwards, her music teacher, who took her into a café and lent her a powder-puff. But the town's activity was soothing. The world was here in miniature. And when she returned home with her father she felt resolute and capable. It was like a little leaf broken out from its seed. She need not stay in this house with them for ever: trains ran every day to London.

During the five days before May's burial peace held the house. True, Marion asked if she could have one of the eight rings the layer-out had brought downstairs, and was refused with a sharp display of anger she accepted grace- fully. And Laura caught a glimpse of the sisters examining her mother's packed wardrobe and reported it to Mansell. He locked the room. Marion, however, arranged two vases of flowers to be taken up. May's only close relative, a sister living in Ireland, wrote to say she couldn't come to the funeral. He did not communicate with her cousin Fred.

5

On the day before the funeral he became very restless. His energy—the previous day he had cleared out the rubbish accumulated in the cellar—seemed a burden to him. He had got up very early. His daughters saw him go into the garden: for minutes he stood at the lawn's edge. His head, its thick whitening hair wind-blown, was lifted as though he searched the heavens. About his figure was a final unapproachable loneliness. And even a look of nobility. He was like a man who prays to be freed of earthly terrors.

Stalking about the house, he drew away at the approach of others. Late in the morning he left without a word.

He climbed towards the blue range of foot-hills. Beyond were the mountains. Within an hour he entered the cemetery and stood unmoving by his father's grave. From another part of the slope he heard a shovel's clatter. And voices. They were finishing her grave. With a pen-knife he scraped thin moss out of the lettering under the broken column. Then he left the cemetery, striking out above, on the crisp rough mountain grass. From behind sullenly moving clouds a greenish-purple light spilled down.

To stand on natural heights is often a necessity in man.

Or an urge. In purifying calm, or in sorrowful weeping, the domains of the world below become his. Mansell stood on the edge of a crag overhanging an immense drop. Beyond a granite sweep in the far distance the sea moved her great primeval body like an elephant. The sea, closed eternally on its mystery, only trafficking with the lonely moon. Inland a silver shower of rain slanted like a benediction on the veined face of a hill. Below him, in a deep stone-brown hollow, gleamed a clear sheet of water. The world tilted towards him as he stood at the dangerous edge of the crag.

He wanted to die. To die in a lonely marriage with this natural mystery, to go down into a silence knit with unknown whispers of eternity. Ah, to cast off this burden of old guilt that vexed and hindered the soul!

Was there a laugh in the wind? Did someone touch his elbow? There was no one. Looking down again, he saw that a shoelace was undone. He stepped back and tied it. And his mind opened like a purse. What had he been thinking? What was this strange being that could possess him? Why should he die? He had money and health. . . . But as he walked away, across the chill green upland, he felt a great fear. Would that other self one day enter into complete possession?

His steps became quicker: sweat broke on his forehead: a vein beat in his temple. He tried to think of to-morrow, the factual arrangements of the funeral, and of the problem of Laura left alone with her stepsisters. But his mind couldn't fasten on these matters. Something was opposing the return to his real self. He walked still faster, untidily descending now.

An hour later, exhausted, he asked for bread and milk at a small farm standing off the Tremartin road. A flat-faced woman big with child, like a peasant in a medieval painting, stood skinning a rabbit outside a lean-to. She attended to him while a white terrier yapped at his heels. He sat on a bench outside the house. A fern in a pot had been brought out to enjoy the moist day. The woman recognised him as the owner of Petticoat House, knew of his bereavement, and after offering him blackcurrant wine chattered with a roundabout inquisitiveness. In the yard a dozen black pigs, white-ringed round the belly, snuffled with little agonised squeals into mud, pushing each other away, heads eternally down, jealous, rapacious, angry.

The woman's unsatiated voice became meaningless. His being was squeezed into the snout of one of those beasts: he knew that inescapable search of the mud.

He got up, muttered a word or two, and walked off. The woman stood gazing after him until he was out of sight. Then she gave a little pleased tug at her extended skirt and went back to the rabbit. It seemed to have done her good to see him in the depths of melancholy. When a man lost a wife it was right his world should fall to pieces.

The afternoon light began to fade. The windy clouds thickened. He walked on and on, always away from the direction of his house. Skirting the town, he struck out from its far side, crossed fields and rights-of-way, and, from a ring of trees slanting in the wind, saw at last the farm of his childhood. Since his return he had never visited the place: something forbade it. Hidden under the trees, he stood gazing with bright secret eyes. The plain square house looked unchanged. How often with his father he had worked in that field of wheat stooks. The wild light cast shadows on it now. An elderly man in shirt sleeves crossed from a barn. At sight of him he turned abruptly and walked away. A spatter of rain hit the leaves. Strung to a branch a shot crow danced on the wind.

He knew now that he no longer hungered after the luxuries of the world. Should he give away all his money? Begin again at an everyday task, in some place of strangers, alone with his soul?

But deeper than this was a recognition. And a lamentation. It was too late. A man possessed but one soul. Llewellyn, after one of the theological discussions to which he escaped when the house became like a prison, had told him that his soul was sick—"And that can be a healthy sign," he said, "bad illnesses, of soul or body, can give a man rebirth . . . Trouble with you is you've got too much of the old Adam in you. You ought to be more humble before the works of God. You're tied by the leg to your own proud nature."

And there were his three daughters. Always at his heels. Never to be escaped. Damnable with their silent knowledge. There was no place of strangers where he could hide from them. They would always follow now.

Dusk was falling through the rising wind. In the town, puddled with rain, he went in the direction of Llewellyn's house, but swerved away. He felt a repugnance for the company of anyone but strangers. People looked at the bare-headed man hurrying along, his unkempt hair wet. Some instinctively drew away from him. He set out on foot towards home. An awareness of to-morrow's duties began to gnaw him. . . . But he did not want to go to her funeral. He wished she had relations who would claim her body. He remembered her rose-hued flesh, the golden fruits of her breasts, the lustre of her skin. These did not belong to this place. He did not want her buried here. And he wished he had arranged for a cremation. But the crematorium was such an expensive distance away: use of it was against his principles too.

The wind was howling. A brackish odour, like that of a tarn thick with rotting leaves, recurred on the winged air. It returned in swirls and swoops across his lifted face. The broken sky staggered like the sea. And through the primitive wind, howling with old catastrophes, desolate with memories, he seemed to hear the movements of the massing clouds. The last light was extinguished.

It was nine-thirty when he arrived home. Laura came out of the drawing-room, skipped towards him with a little cry, but drew up and half turned away: she wore black. For a few moments he stood in the lamplit hall looking at nothing, a stranger unconnected with the house. Then from upstairs appeared his three daughters. They came down the staircase together. Marion stepped first; in an old dark dress Gwen had altered, she reached the bottom stair and stood with her hand on the newel looking at him interestedly. Kate drew up a couple of steps above her; she too was silent but watchful. But Gwen, a tape measure hanging from her neck, half invited explanation—"Why, father, you've been gone a very long time . . . we were worried," she added in a cool, steady voice.

He began to walk towards the drawing-room. "Are you wanting supper?" Gwen called. It sounded oddly like a taunt.

"No," he replied. Laura subduedly followed him into the drawing-room. The door closed.

At sight of him the parrot rocked its green body and broke into chuckling cries. And, cocking its head with the concise eye shooting recognition, it repeated again and again: "Fine day to-morrow . . . Pills, perfumes, soap?" Laura said shyly: "It's such a bad night, I lit a fire here for myself." She put on another log. His slippers lay conspicuously in the hearth. "Be quiet, Polly," he ordered, raising a finger. There was no anger in his voice: the bird had always been his pet. But: "Fine day to-morrow," the derisively optimistic voice shrieked. And again. And again. In the mad burlesque of the human voice seemed all the indestructible repetition of life, in the bright ridicule of the eye a bitter tenacity.

Chapter Five

I

WITH sidelong glances he watched his first daughter approach across the orchard. She had come in by the side gate and made a brisk détour towards him. It was like a swoop. She had something to say.

His instinct was to go up the ladder into the thick-

entwined tree where the fruit hung in bustling clusters of
green and scarlet, fresh as paint. But, turning his back on
her, he stooped and continued to pick up the fallen apples,
throwing them into the baskets. She carried a bunch of
chrysanthemums and a little pannier of eggs. The afternoon
was clear as glass, the enclosing hills lay relaxed in the
thin purple of early autumn. The rustle of her feet in
the grass stopped.

"Father," she asked at once, in the manner of one raising
some small domestic matter, "is it true that you intend
marrying again?"

He lifted himself and faced her. Yet he seemed to be
shrinking away from the light gaze of her eyes, empty as
ice. He could never fathom her calm but he was afraid of it.
Her artificial manner, shallow yet somehow steely, set up an
inward dread. He snapped irritably, apparently dismissing
her as a vexatious child: "You have been listening to gossip
at the farm, have you!"

"Gossip seems an ill-chosen word," she began primly.
"Looking at it from a daughter's point of view, I would call
it important information. It was hard to be told it by
outsiders. . . . You know," she continued, laying the
chrysanthemums lightly on the eggs, "how they talk in
country parts. They heard you are courting a Mrs. Parry,
who has inherited property from her husband. . . . Are
you hungry, father?" she broke off. "You look quite
famished. Why don't you eat an apple?" He had jerked
back to the baskets, sorting the bruised fruit from the good.
"I hope you make a good profit on the apples this year," she
said; "then perhaps you will give us a little extra money for
the housekeeping. It doesn't do for a family in our position to
be suspected of parsimony. We might forfeit local respect."

"I have to support three idle women."

"*Four*, if one counts Laura. But in a servantless house the
size of ours 'idle' is an untruthful word. Would this
lady you contemplate adding to the ménage ease our
burdens or increase them?"

He walked away, over to the next tree under which stood empty baskets. He went with a jerk of his shoulders, repudiating her. But in his thinning face, that was becoming wrinkled as a walnut-shell, there was the curious look of hunger. She followed him, composed and straight, her formal demeanour unquenched, stepping carefully among the apples shining in the grass.

"Father, you give me so few opportunities to talk to you. I do wish you wouldn't shut yourself away so——"

"Leave me alone," he said, a little squirm of anguish down his voice. But he suddenly whipped round, an angry parent troubled with a foolish daughter. "What do you wish to say?" he demanded testily, as though she hadn't spoken at all yet.

With the lightest of emphasis, she replied: "I think you would be foolish to marry again. Gwen and Kate will be quite shocked. I cannot speak for Laura, but I'm sure you'll marry without the approval or support of any of your daughters. Don't we deserve some consideration, father? Surely Gwen, Kate and I run your house most competently, you have every material comfort according to the means placed at our disposal. And a third wife somehow seems *undignified*, father. . . . Surely," she went on with growing rapidity, in her artificially stilted way magnificently controlled, "you are not marrying this woman because she has means? And after four years you must be accustomed to a state of celibacy? In fact, I would say you were naturally a celibate. No one would call either of your previous marriages a success, father——" A note of rebuke entered her voice.

"You are insolent," he blazed, raising an arm.

She did not shrink back. "I am sorry if I seem so, but as your eldest daughter I do feel justified in venturing an opinion on a matter which is going to concern your children so intimately."

"You gabble, gabble," he fumed, stooping and with nervous gestures flinging apples into the baskets. "Say what you've got to say and go."

"Very well." She took up the bunched chrysanthemums again and gave them a calculated sniff, like someone on the stage. "It is this," she resumed: "I cannot lend you support in this marriage—and I'm sure I'm speaking for Gwen and Kate too. I shall do all in my power to prevent it."

"Your power!" he sneered, flinging an apple so that it went wide of a basket.

"Yes," she said, "my power."

He rose and stalked over to her, staring intently into her cool, well-behaved face, so totally devoid of emotion, the blue of her eyes the steely blue of ice. His own eyes burned, but unsteadily, a broken conflagration. They faced each other at the distance of a yard. Still she did not shrink.

"Who are you?" he breathed. "What are you?"

"Your daughter Marion. And I have your interests at heart, besides my own and my sisters'."

"Do you know that I could turn you and your sisters out of my house? I could lock my door against you. You have no talent. You would be obliged to find a situation as a domestic servant."

"Come, father, you forget that you allowed me to take first-class pianoforte lessons in London. I could earn a meagre living teaching in Tremartin . . . or in any other district you chose to live in——"

"You mean you would follow me," he said, low like a whisper.

"I could disgrace you wherever you were," she said tranquilly. "The past is not so easily disposed of, father. . . . But of course such behaviour is not going to be necessary," an earnest note came into her voice. "You are making me miserable, father. I am not naturally a bitter or spiteful woman, and I want us to go on as we are now, unnecessarily economical though our living is these days."

"I will marry again," he said, "I will set my wife above you and your sisters."

"You mustn't be so foolish," she implored, though without flamboyance. "My personal feelings to this marriage apart, you have no right to marry again because you could never make a woman happy; as a woman I can tell that. You're too self-willed and too closed in on yourself. And in your heart of hearts you despise women. You should have been a monk, father, and used your life searching for God. . . . Do you know why you want to marry this woman?"

"Go on," he invited mockingly.

"Because of cowardice," she said. "You think you want a protection against us, though heavens knows we're under your will enough, especially where cash is concerned. . . . Of course you're looking for forgetfulness as well. Well, you'll never find it that way."

He thrust his head nearer, the eyes searching her face, but vainly. "What are you?" he whispered. "A she-demon risen from hell?"

She pouted deprecatingly. One hand fingered a chrysanthemum as she turned down her face. "I can't follow you when you talk like that. Perhaps I'm not religious enough. But I'm not going to allow myself to be upset by being called a she-demon. My feelings are only those of a daughter upset by this danger of your marrying again and, besides your making another mistake, also making yourself look ridiculous and a subject of malicious gossip. You know we're called Petticoat House already."

"If you and the others do not approve of my marrying, the door is open for you to go." He turned from her abruptly.

"*I*," she said, also turning, "haven't the slightest intention of going through it so melodramatically, and I feel Gwen and Kate haven't either. You would have to forbid us your roof in some disgraceful manner that would become the talk of the district. You would earn the reputation of being a heartless eccentric, father, a cruel man casting off the daughters who have sacrificed their lives for your comfort." With this she left him.

She walked away with assurance. His daughters were of

good repute in the district, admired as educated women who kept within a formal pattern of behaviour.

He stood half hidden under a tree. The world had become empty. He was hungry for love, he needed the gesture of affection, the gentle touch of a hand's warm flesh. And he wanted about him now a woman who was quiet, a stranger knowing nothing of himself but who accepted him as a companion without question of the past years. He had come to the archway which looks on the last fields and he did not want to go down to them alone. He felt he had not the strength.

When Marion turned at the house gate to close it he stood looking at her. She moved gracefully, with an ease that was almost stately. Who would think she concealed such venom! How pretty she had been as a child! But he had not touched her, he had never seen her being, and she, like her sisters, had grown to womanhood without his knowledge. He had been a father only in name. He had looked upon them only as his possessions and as examples of the good odour of his life in London. But now, out of the privacy of their secret life, their power had become manifest and they united to destroy his peace of mind. Why did they not go their own ways as women? What had he to do with them?

His lips moved soundlessly. He was praying: "Father, my daughters gather themselves against me. Give me your strength to withstand them. Tell me the secret." But there was no reply. He stood among the loaded trees in the sunlight, white-haired, the proud nose lifted, his eyes unseeing. And his loins, his knees, the rivers of his blood became his father's. But there was no reply. The dead took their secret away for ever. He was alone.

Later he heard the click of the gate-latch again. With an alert side-glance he saw, not the three advancing in united purpose, as might have been expected, but Laura. She came towards him with the slow, half-hesitant walk he had noticed in her lately—she, who used to half skip or run towards him as if in need of protection. Had Marion conveyed information to her already?

But she had come to help him carry the filled baskets to the barn. Yesterday she had remained with him in the orchard all day; to-day she had been to Tremartin for her singing lesson. She stood for a moment not looking at him, as if uncertain of her reception or the necessity to speak. A look of palpitating unease had developed in her lately.

"You have picked a lot to-day," she said awkwardly. "Will we carry them in now or pick more? Gwen is preparing tea."

He knew that for weeks she wanted to tell him something of import to herself. He had felt her hovering in calculation of the right opportunity. And he did not want her to speak: he sensed a disclosure which he did not want to know. This daughter caused him a different pain; she was a sin in which lay a secret seed of pleasure. The glimpses of her mother in a turn of the head, a flash of the eye, even a bridling of the unripened breasts, brought to him a ghost of the old tumult. This he wanted to repudiate too.

"We'll carry these baskets in," he said in an exhausted voice; "I've finished for the day then."

At tea, laid formally on the dining-table, Marion kept up her usual brittle chatter. He rarely listened to it. She sat at the head of the table and talked of the cushion-covers she and Gwen had embroidered for the church bazaar. But he saw at once that information had been conveyed to Gwen and Kate. Gwen sat solid but flushed high in the cheeks: Kate's voice barked more staccato in contempt. They ignored him. And Laura was not included in the church bazaar conversation. She sat next to him at the other end of the table; since her mother's death, that had been her place, by her own choice, a wide section of the table lying between them and the three sisters. Usually there was silence at their end. But occasionally, and especially lately, Laura had given vent to a raw outburst, usually over her share of the food served out by Marion.

There was one to-day. A dish of sponge-cake slices was not passed down to her when she asked for a piece. Marion's fingers groped among the heap and selected a piece as she said with apparent vagueness: "Pass me Laura's plate, Gwen."

"I don't want that burnt piece," Laura cried shrilly.

"Burnt, Laura?" Gwen held the plate, smiling inside her lips. "All the pieces are caught a little. Good gracious, you're not a child of six."

"Why can't you pass me the dish?" Laura flared at Marion. "Your fingers don't look clean to me. You chose that piece deliberately," she cried madly, jumping up so that her chair stumbled back noisily.

Marion coolly held up the dish. "Let her make her selection Gwen; her singing lesson must have made her bad-tempered."

With a sort of prowl, electrically crouched in herself, stretched-out neck thickened, Laura crossed the room and paused near Marion. "You . . . you *snake*," she whispered, choked. And, in a huddle, she rushed from the room.

"She *is* getting difficult," Marion sighed, swinging her ear-rings.

"She suggests arrested development to me," Kate barked, her square flat face aggressive. Ignoring her father, she boldly took out a cigarette.

"Four years ago I would have taken her and thoroughly smacked her bottom," Gwen murmured. "I don't know what to do with her nowadays except make her wash her own undies; I've slaved enough for her."

Their father had sat as though unaware. There had been so many occasions such as this: women bickering and squabbling in their world of petty spites and meannesses. They were trivial; he refused them acknowledgement.

"Some more tea," he snapped, pushing his cup down the table. Marion would not reign over the tray down there much longer.

"I do think it too bad, father——" Gwen began, but was

quickly interrupted by Marion, who tinkled: "Gwen, perhaps you'd better go and try to pacify that girl; she didn't have much to eat, and I suppose she's still growing."

Gwen shook her head and resumed, while Marion helplessly fluttered her hands: "I do think it too bad, father, that . . . that you're keeping only the bruised apples for the house. I would like to store a basketful of good ones for the winter."

"They're all sold," he dismissed her. "You eat too many apples."

"Heaven knows we need them," Kate put in, sharp.

"I forbid you to give apples to your horse, Kate," he said.

"I only give him my share of the bruised ones," Kate answered, in her rude, swearing voice. "He's getting thin."

A year or two ago marvellously she had succeeded in making him buy a horse. His friend Mr. Llewellyn had got it cheap for him. But he could not be induced to add a vehicle for private transport from the isolated house. And to motor-cars he still had a strong aversion. Gradually the horse had become her possession. She would go for long rambles on him, wearing farm-labourer's cotton breeches, and when she returned behave in an obstreperous domineering fashion. The horse seemed to supply her with a kind of masculine courage.

Both Gwen and Kate looked as if they were restraining themselves with difficulty before their father. He was rising from the table. Kate looked at him in smouldering derision. Gwen's folded-in smile, as she held up her handsome head and fine bosom, was ominous. But they kept silent. Only Marion complained: "Oh dear, all this is trying for my nerves, I really feel I will go into a decline early in life."

"You're in it already," Kate said. "The three of us are."

He was at the door. "You may leave my house whenever you wish," he said.

"Father, don't be foolish," Marion sang out in quite a confident voice. "Where could we go, unless you gave us the means to live?"

E*

But he had shut the door.

"Bah," Kate said, "he at least is going into his dotage early."

"I thought you were going to tell him, Gwen," scolded Marion, petulant. "You would have if I hadn't kicked you. I told you I'd decided it's best for us to act on our own first. . . . Why are you so stupid always?" she asked irritably.

"You call me stupid—stupid yourself! Anyone would think no one's got nerves except you. . . . Hold your tongue!" she hissed as Marion attempted to speak. "Nothing but a bag of old tricks!" She was fluffing herself out like a turkey; Marion tossed her head. "Do you know that your neck is dirty," Gwen went on, baleful. "Going over to the farm like that! Or don't you mind?" A shadowy ring certainly encircled Marion's throat, behind the two rows of yellowed pearls.

"You're so coarse, Gwen. If father turns us out, you at least will find sanctuary in the kitchen of some moderate-size mansion."

"Oh, shut up, you two," growled Kate, flicking cigarette ash into her cup.

Gwen rose superbly from the table, addressing Marion: "For that, my lady, you'll cook your own dinner to-night. I'm going upstairs and I'm going to stay there." She swept to the door and left it open.

"There you are!" warned Kate. "You're too bossy, Marion."

"She's so touchy these days," wailed Marion. "And just now when we've got to stick together and plan something . . ."

"You'd better get her a box of chocolates to-morrow," advised Kate, indifferent.

"I haven't any money this week. Can you lend me a shilling?"

"No. . . . Ask Laura." Kate gave a hoarse bark of laughter. "Or steal it from her room. The silly little bitch is saving up money like her miser of a father."

From the drawing-room came the parrot's screech:
"Fine day to-morrow. . . . Pills, perfumes, soap?" Marion
pressed her hand to her head. "You can wash up at least,
Kate. I haven't made my bed yet."

"I wonder how much longer you'll be able to lie on it?"
Kate flung her cigarette end into the fireplace and gave her
hard bark of laughter.

Marion sat quite still for a minute. She sat dwindled and
spent-looking. Her thin rouged face, released, looked
pathetic. "It's disgusting," she whimpered, "I feel nothing
but shame." A couple of tears ran down her cheeks. "Sometimes I feel quite tired, Kate." Astonishingly more tears
fell. Kate pretended not to notice and strode over to the
window, standing there with her legs apart like a man. "We
seem to be in some sort of prison," Marion wept; "perhaps it would be best if he threw us out."

"What would *you* do?" Kate said, deliberately incisive.
"Gwen is capable, I could take a job in the riding stables at
Tremartin, but God knows what you're fitted for."

"I . . . I could teach the piano. Or go as companion to
some old lady . . . or be a governess."

"Oh, for God's sake stop wailing!" Kate barked, striding
back. "Take a couple of aspirins and go and rest. I'll see to
the tea-things."

"Yes, Kate, I think I will." She sounded femininely submissive. "I'm only just feeling the shock of this afternoon."

"I expect you'll be fit as a fiddle by to-night," Kate
remarked.

"Kate . . . Kate, dear," Marion lifted an earnest face,
"I believe the three of us should somehow *break out*. . . .
The years go on and we don't realise what they're doing to
us. I don't mean making us older, but each day moves us
one step nearer to something dreadful, without us realising
it . . . because it's slow, slow and quiet . . ." She
paused: a haunted look passed like a shadow across her face.
"Sometimes," she said, "I feel quite separate from myself, as
if I'm two persons; I can watch myself, and grieve—yes,

grieve. I seem to go into a trance . . . I often wonder," she went on, erratically, "if there's something in spiritualism and a presence is dictating to me from another world."

"Dictating what?" Kate clattered the tea-things together.

"Not to forget." Already she was far away, her eyes unconnecting. "I often wonder if it is our mother trying to grope her way through to me. . . . One night," she said, "lying in bed, I felt someone kiss me—oh, so lightly! I woke up to the touch and had a distinct sense of a presence beside my bed——"

But Kate was carrying the trayful of things away, a fresh cigarette stuck in the corner of her mouth. Such unearthly flights were beyond the scope of her mind.

When evening closed in, a brownish still evening thick with autumnal air, the house lapsed into tranquillity. It was recognised even by the parrot, who brooded quiescent as an owl. No one lit the lamp in the hall. At the bend in the staircase the arched stained-glass window filtered violet, green and rose lights into the dusk. Kate came from the stable after bedding the horse; since the day's shock had finally given Marion a bad headache and Gwen still sulked in her room, she had agreed to prepare some sort of supper. Their father had left the house an hour ago and gone for one of his mysterious evening walks, though it could not be to visit this woman, who lived in Tremartin.

Upstairs Gwen silently passed across the landing, crept down the passage and stood for minutes listening at a door. Slowly she turned the crystal knob, without noise, not hearing her own hard breathing. The door yielded soundlessly. She crept in. From the window the last russet light picked out a bed on which a figure reclined on its stomach, its head in an arm: the light breathing was reposeful. The pages of a letter and an envelope lay on the bed. Gwen picked up the pages and crept close to the bed and stood beside it for a minute or two. Then with a swift dart her arm shot out and two fingers grasped the lobe of the sleeping figure's ear and twisted it.

Laura gave a little dazed shout, squirmed round on her back, and shrieked. "Little lazybones," hissed Gwen, still bending over her, "you expect me to cook a meal for you as usual, don't you! . . . I . . ." she half laughed, "I'd like to tie you to this bed and starve you! . . . What's this . . ." she brandished the letter. "A letter from that butcher's son that's gone on his holiday? Think I don't know about it?"

With another cry Laura attempted to snatch the letter away. One leaf tore in half. She grasped Gwen's arm; it pushed her victoriously back on the bed. She bit into the arm. Gwen, with a bellow of pain, recoiled for a moment, then swooped on to the bed and beat her fists with light but deliberate emphasis into the open face, into the neck as Laura, screaming, twisted for protection into the pillow. The blows ceased; lying full and heavy on the girl's body, Gwen pushed the head deeper into the pillow. Her breath came in hard gasps: she whispered abuse. But Laura gave a violent heave, twisted up, got free of the whirl of limbs and ran screaming from the room.

She had reached the bend of the staircase as her father, who had not long returned and was feeding the parrot, hastened out of the drawing-room. He had lit the hall-lamp. Seeing him, Laura, for some reason, sat on the first stair below the bend, sobbing more quietly. A moment or two later Gwen began to descend the upper flight. At the same time Kate, oddly wearing an apron, came hastening into the hall from the kitchen, and Marion, in a tattered purple dressing-gown and a hair-net tight over her head, inquisitively descended a step or two behind Gwen.

"What does this mean?" Mansell demanded, irritable.

"She bit me," Gwen announced, passing Laura. She pulled back the sleeve of her frock and showed a smear of blood. "The iodine is in the kitchen, isn't it, Kate?" She had snatched a crumpled page of the letter and held it.

"Bit you!" Marion exclaimed. "Good gracious, what a little beast! Bathe it at once, Gwen," she advised, glad of the opportunity to pacify her sister. "I'll bandage it for you."

"Why did she bite you?" their father snapped, trying to assert himself irritably into the feminine clangour.

Laura was still rocking herself on the stairs. "She crept into my room when I was asleep," she wailed, "and attacked me. She wanted to frighten me, she stole my letter, she twisted my ear. . . . She's wicked," her voice rose hysterically, "she's mad and wicked."

"That Tremartin butcher's son has been writing her," Gwen addressed her father. "And a fine reputation *he's* got! Even though the girl who sued for a paternity order against him lost her case, poor thing. The Don Juan of Tremartin!" she said grandly. "With his racing car! That's what your daughter does when she goes off to her singing lesson, carrying her pigskin music-case so important."

"Is this true, Laura?" her father demanded up the staircase.

"Here is some of his letter," Gwen held out the crumpled sheet. But he thrust her off impatiently.

Laura had got up. Her face closed heavily sullen, thickened with dark obstinacy. "Yes," her voice rang dramatically. "But all I want is to get out of this house . . ." She looked at each of the sisters in turn. "I'd like to kill the three of you."

"Don't be foolish, child," Marion attempted to take charge. "Someone has to think of your welfare. You can't run about as though you're a chorus girl already."

Mansell turned and, with a single violent gesture of his arm, banished the three sisters from the hall. They huddled into the kitchen passage together, even Marion retreating from the blaze of that gesture. But her voice could be heard, censorious: "Of course she's got her mother's vile temper and nature."

He stood on the bottom stair, not approaching further, while she remained at the bend, looking down at him sullenly.

"You are friendly with this young man, Laura?"

"Yes," she said. "We . . . we might marry," her voice suddenly faltered.

"What!" Slowly he mounted several steps towards her. She seemed to be spellbound, fascinated by his approach, unable to move. "This butcher's son of bad repute . . ."

"Living in this house . . . with them . . . it's enough to drive me to anything," she said in a stronger voice.

Still he advanced, scrutinising her. "You are in love with this young man?" he asked.

"No," she said. And her face shut again; she lowered her lids; the moist red-curled lips shut sulky. The plaited black hair swung shining like whips.

He was standing a step below her. "Yet you are allowing him to write you——" Somehow the words seemed of no importance, though his voice was penetrating.

"I want to get away from this house," she faltered again.

"What?" he exclaimed, quick. "At your age, eighteen!"

"A Tremartin girl I know has gone to London by herself and she's only seventeen. It's different now than in your day."

"You must not go," he said in a low, vibrant voice; "not you. You must stay with me."

Still she did not look up. The anger-thickened face was very pale. Slowly he stretched his arm, as though in wonder, the long thin ascetic's hand touched her shoulder, the palm opening on her flesh. "Stay with me," he whispered. She lifted her head. And into her face, for a moment, came a beseeching hunger. Then, with a moan, she sank to the floor. She would have fallen down the first flight had his hands not stayed her.

She lay with her eyes closed, whiter, sweat breaking out at the curves of her nostrils. The fibres of her throat throbbed. He knelt over her, rubbing her hands, whispering her name. When she opened her eyes she gave him a long slow look as if from a profound distance where she was still locked. For a moment there seemed no recognition in those eyes, only the mystery of a being eternally isolated, removed from all exterior power. He drew back sharply.

"You fainted," he said, in the testily impatient way that had become usual to him.

"You touched me," she whispered. The black fathomless eyes seemed to palpitate now, as full awareness coursed back.

"Go and rest," he said irritably. "You're not well."

Without his help she rose, turned, and slowly mounted the upper flight, not looking at him again.

"I will tell them to bring you something," he called.

"No," she cried, "no." And he heard her weeping, her desolate weeping as she disappeared into the darkness above. He took a step or two upwards, then stopped, his hand trembling on the banister.

2

Marion, with her most gracious air, eased herself into the chair offered her and smiled very sweetly at Mrs. Parry. Gwen sat more rigidly on the sofa, a look of reserving her opinion firm in her face. Both were soberly dressed, even to hints of shabbiness, though Marion's demeanour conveyed familiarity with regal ball dresses and tiaras in her time. It had been decided that Kate's presence would give the visit too much the look of a deputation arriving: besides, she was so incalculable.

"What a very comfortable drawing-room," Marion remarked, after the briefest of glances. Gwen remained stolid during the preliminary courtesies. She had thought that a definite attitude of intimidation would be best, but she was willing to allow Marion to set the first note.

"A woman with a pride in her home I am," Mrs. Parry declared in a quick sing-song.

She behaved like a startled partridge. Short and plump, she whirred about the room uneasily, unable to settle. As Gwen said afterwards, she had expected her to disappear under the plush-draped table. She seemed about forty, and she certainly possessed warmth, a physical and energetic heat.

"Mrs. Parry," Marion said, "my sister and I have come on a delicate mission. We have been surprised to hear that you may marry our father."

"Oh well, now indeed!" Mrs. Parry gurgled, her chin sinking into the rosy folds of her neck. "People do talk! Some property of mine he was going to buy, through Mr. Llewellyn before he died, and he came here to see me about it." Still not sitting down, she peeped sideways at the nicely poised Marion.

Marion smiled encouragingly. This woman of peasant stock, who had gone up in the world but failed to cope with the progress however wealthily she was ensconced amidst her fat furniture, chenille curtains and galloping bronze horses on the marble mantelpiece, was almost exactly what she had expected. She possessed health, abundance of physical presence, and obviously all the domestic virtues. The villa, in the best part of Tremartin, was spick and span as a half-crown fresh from the mint, and its owner respectable as the Baptist chapel at which she worshipped with unbreakable regularity.

"Will you allow me to ask," said Marion gently, yet not without a note of firmness, "if you really intend marrying him?"

"Oh dear!" bustled Mrs. Parry, and she moved a spray of mother-of-pearl flowers from a bureau-top to the table centre. " 'Yes,' I have said to him once, twice I have said 'No,' and 'Yes' once again. . . . There's glad I am," she went on in the pleasant sing-song of her upbringing, "that you have come to see me." She seemed to have decided that they were meeting to discover if they would take to each other.

Marion still smiled graciously, while Gwen still looked forbiddingly reserved. "It is a pleasure to meet you. But father is so strange and secretive, we have had to come without his knowledge, I'm sorry to say."

"He does things on the sly," Gwen put in.

"A religious man he seems to be," remarked Mrs. Parry and, looking grave, pursed her lips.

"He is religious in a topsy-turvy kind of way," said Marion.

Arrested now, Mrs. Parry sat down; but at quite a distance, like a servant. "How are you meaning?" she asked.

Marion appeared to be tranquilly reflecting. "Well," she said, slowly, "he puts the cart before the horse. It's himself first, then God. Sometimes I think he believes he *is* God. There is no true repentance in him. He is a proud and haughty man. Everybody must minister to his comfort, including God." Suspecting that all this, however calmly and distinctly stated, possibly meant little to Mrs. Parry who was of the kind that relied on smelling the air around a person, she proceeded: "He won't go to church any more, though in his own way he certainly does want to repent of all he's done. He is unable to bow to the discipline of church or chapel, he cannot give way." She paused as if in tidy consideration of further words.

Mrs. Parry's mouth hung open. After a moment she said, more to herself than her visitors: "All he's done——?"

Marion did not appear to hear. "If only he could give way! He's unkind to himself as well as to his daughters. For instance, he's got quite enough money but he wants more. And what he's got he locks up. . . . Mrs. Parry," she sighed, "we live very simply, very sparingly. Do you think you could improve matters if you married him?"

"Because we," said Gwen, sounding a trifle ominous, "intend staying with him. We three daughters, I mean. Our stepsister we can't speak for, she's extremely wayward and difficult."

Mrs. Parry's body moved in bewildered unease in the chair: her mind, like her eyes, seemed to be rolling about, unable to settle. They waited for her to speak.

"A lot of hints there are in what you are saying," she half gasped at length. "Married twice I have been myself, and your father twice; I was thinking when we met about the property that lonely we were the two of us and the two born and bred about by here and the two settled and with means; a tidy thing it seemed for us to set up, for I do like looking after a man, and lowering to the spirit it is to live in a house without a man and lock the door at night on myself alone." She panted a little, seemed to shake herself, and turned a dismayed but not unchallenging eye on Marion and then on Gwen. "But you are not wanting me to marry him. Why now? Speak plain."

It was a decisive moment. Gwen peeled off a repaired cotton glove in heavy thought. But Marion, after only a moment's hesitation, replied earnestly: "Isn't it natural, Mrs. Parry? Is a stepmother ever really welcome? And we've already had one. And it's not as though we are children, we are women perfectly capable of running our house and looking after our father. Besides, we know his moods, we know how to deal with his bad tempers. . . . Now, Gwen," she turned, sharp with pride, "there's no need to give way like that."

Gwen, her shoulders hunched, had lifted a handkerchief to her eyes and begun to shake with sobs. "We have sacrificed our lives to him," she wept. "He always hated us to have friends, especially men ones. And now he wants to cast us off. But he won't give us any money, we couldn' live."

Mrs. Parry bustled up and violently struck a small brass gong. "I will tell my Jinny to get some tea. . . . For goodness' sake don't you be worrying about me. A bossy woman I am not. . . . Tea on the tray, Jinny. In the silver teapot."

"Mrs. Parry," resumed Marion while Gwen pulled herself together, "there is now a serious matter I would like to discuss. . . . Has my father been honest with you?"

Mrs. Parry sat on another chair closer to Marion. It was an instinctive woman-to-woman movement, willing but wary, the movement of natural allies who yet distrust each other. "How are you meaning, honest?" she asked in a hushed voice.

"About his second wife and our stepsister Laura?"

"Heard I have of the second wife." Mrs. Parry's nostrils were sensitively awake. "She drank."

"I wasn't thinking of that," Marion shook her head, adding reflectively, "though she only began drinking heavily after she married him. . . . But did he tell you that our stepsister is illegitimate?"

"He lived in sin with that woman in London," Gwen burst out, half choked, "while our mother was alive."

Marion corrected: "You use words wrongly, Gwen. He lived with our mother but at the same time carried on secretly with Laura's mother. That made it far worse."

Mrs. Parry's mouth opened soundlessly again. She had been struck. She looked alarmed, even slightly grey of skin; her vigorous bosom seemed diminished. Marion's repeated question was unnecessary: "Has he been honest with you about this?"

"No . . . indeed no," answered Mrs. Parry. But as she slowly looked at Marion, then at Gwen, her eyes became filled with alarm of them. There was a silence. The comfortable room, stuffed with the costly accoutrements of a safe and solid everyday existence, seemed heavy with menace.

"I thought he had not," Marion said easily, without even the ghost of passion.

"We decided it was only fair to come and tell you," Gwen added, fully recovered.

"But I am surprised," Marion said, severely, "that he should choose a respectable woman for a third wife. It would be bound to lead to strife. With his nature it would be wiser if he chose some slut whose past could match his."

Mrs. Parry made an effort. "Isn't it that he has repented full now?" she breathed. "A man unhappy in himself he is." But she seemed to be speaking more in self-defence of having admitted the mysterious suitor into her house without a stricter scrutiny of his credentials.

"Repented?" Marion said. "Well, we can only speak

from our own experience of him. He may have repented and therefore forgiven himself his sin, but he certainly hasn't forgiven me and my sisters for knowing all about his life in London . . . and I have not told you all of his scandalous life there," she inserted with firm crispness, "I do not wish to talk about all of it. But we *know*, and that is why he behaves harshly to us, stints us of money and wants to get rid of us." Then, with swift thin passion, she cried: "Is that the proper way for a father to behave to his daughters?" Upraised in her chair, she suddenly looked starkly attenuated; her skull seemed to be visible.

Mrs. Parry had made a little recoiling movement. But, in a sudden automatic way, she asked: "How are you behaving to him?"

"We are at his mercy," Marion replied. "We have no real advantage with which to retaliate. How can we punish him?"

"You have come to tell me about him," Mrs. Parry pointed out, her eyes beginning to dart, half shrewd, but still frightened of this alien intrusion among her furniture.

"Yes. But didn't you wish to know about him? Would you have preferred the risk of marrying such a man?"

Mrs. Parry looked in anxiety at the door. When would tea come?

"Of course," Gwen sailed in, "we don't know how he would treat you. He does get ashamed of himself sometimes. The night our mother died he threw himself across her bed and cried to her spirit to forgive him. But that didn't stop him marrying his fancy woman a few months later and not long afterwards bringing his bastard daughter to live with us . . . *Us!*" she raised her voice passionately like Marion, but with less effect.

Mrs. Parry remained in conclave with herself. Her energetic physical brightness seemed gone. She looked her real age now: it must be fifty. Life was not so simple after all, even with money. These two woman were thrusting her along dark passages hitherto unknown in her own life.

Their assurance held a dread from which she drew back like a well-fed cat roused in its comfortable basket by some rough hand.

"Perhaps," Gwen further addressed her, "he thinks you can help him to forget the past and that's the only reason why he wants to marry you."

"No," said Marion decidedly, "he wants both to punish us and to protect himself against us. Being a guilty man, he's afraid of us. . . . But, of course," she held Mrs. Parry's eye in calm calculation, "he won't be rid of us so easily."

"*I* think," Gwen said, "he'll end by going mad."

Mrs. Parry jumped a little in her chair, perhaps because the door opened. The maid brought in a massive embossed silver tray.

"What a beautiful tray," Marion remarked.

"Presentation it was to my second husband," Mrs. Parry's voice rose in relief. "Treasurer of the Chamber of Commerce he was for many years."

"He must have been highly esteemed," Gwen said in the sententious manner she assumed sometimes. "You've lost two did you say?" she asked, socially sympathetic as the maid vanished.

"The second went natural," Mrs. Parry poured tea, apparently eased in the fresh atmosphere; "much older than me he was. The first went down at sea; Captain Matthews he was, son of the minister of Salem. His picture is over by there."

"A fine-looking man," Marion craned her long graceful neck.

For a while they drank and ate in acceptance of the tea-tray's sacred conventions. Then Marion resumed, delicately tentative: "Mrs. Parry, I hope we haven't shocked you by revealing this about our father. And I know, of course, you will keep it all strictly private."

"If he is a bad man," Mrs. Parry said with warmth, perspiring a little from the tea she had drunk too hot, "not likely I am to show off that I was letting him court me. To those that know of it, just say I will I have changed my mind and give no reason."

There was a little hush. Then Gwen, smiling, said: "If we seemed to exaggerate you should consult him be-fore——"

"It has cost us a lot to come here," Marion interrupted, not smiling. And, a sad note in her voice, she added: "We do not go out much . . . and it is not really because we are kept without money, it is because we are ashamed."

"Oh, well indeed," Mrs. Parry remarked in a new assured manner, "seeing you in the street I would not say—there go two women who are ashamed of something!"

Marion sighed: "We have learned to conceal our feelings from the world, we want nobody's pity."

"That is true," Gwen lifted her head.

After the second cup of tea, Marion asked: "Are we to take it then that you have decided not to marry him?"

There was a long pause. Looking refreshed, Mrs. Parry darted several lively glances at them. Then she rose from her chair. Short and plump though she was, peasant of idiom, lacking poise, and dressed in shapeless wools, she stood before them with sudden impressiveness, stubborn, her legs rooted in safe conservative earth.

"Please to leave my house now and never come back," she said with astonishing firmness, but keeping a wary eye on them. "Your characters have wickedness in them. A bad air you have brought into my house. But your way you will have. I will not marry your father though pity for him is in my heart. A man with such daughters I could not marry. You would bring black shadows over our wedding and step over our way like witches. Dangerous women you are. Please to go now."

Marion was able to assume the calmly deprecating air of a lady faced by an incensed inferior. Gwen was less stately and began to bridle into a mien of retaliation, but she was only allowed to say: "My good woman, this is impertinence——" before Marion laid a restraining hand on her arm and smiled sweetly at Mrs. Parry: "I almost wish you would marry father. It would be an education for you and it would be interesting for us to watch him hurry you into your grave, especially as you own property."

"Off with you now." Mrs. Parry, drawn up squatly, pointed to the door.

"What a bad-mannered person," Gwen murmured, imitating Marion's unyielding calm as they went to the door.

"I expected it from the first," replied Marion.

"But why do they always have such bad tea?" said Gwen as if she was leaving a restaurant. "She's supposed to be well-off." Outside Marion scolded her for making this remark.

3

"For God's sake be natural," Kate growled. "This habit of giving yourself the airs of a duchess is getting on my nerves. . . . You're a penniless, garrulous, provincial old maid," she went on brutally, "and it's time you faced the fact."

"Natural?" Marion said tartly. "You call yourself natural, I suppose? Is it natural for a woman to wear farmer's breeches, use men's bad language, and . . . yes, go into the saloon bars of public-houses?" She ended in triumph.

Gwen stopped folding unironed bed-sheets out of the wash-basket and stared hard at Kate, who slunk over to the window. "Public-houses?" she exclaimed. "Is that true, Kate?"

Kate glowered at the window. Marion said: "She's getting herself talked about; she goes into common public-houses drinking beer on market-day at Tremartin. However hard I try to keep up tone in this family she seems determined to pull us down. If she had the money she'd become a drunkard."

Gwen, with a deliberate stride, went over to Kate and

smacked her face. "Take that, you hussy," she said in a low murmur. At once she went back to the wash-basket and resumed sorting out the washed, half-dried linen.

Kate, with a howl, had collapsed into the chair beside the window. But almost immediately she broke into guttural abuse of her sisters.

"Be quiet, Kate," Gwen said briskly.

"Kate, you *are* the youngest, you know," Marion preened herself, "and in a way Gwen and I take the place of your parents."

Gwen said: "Now who is going to iron these things? I've done my share, washing them. I'm sick to death of having more work put on me." The previous week, their father had announced that he would pay no more laundry bills: even the bed-sheets must be washed in the house.

"I can't iron sheets," Marion fluttered, "my wrists are too thin. I'll do some of the smalls, dear."

"Kate," called Gwen smoothly, "you'll do them, won't you? All except this pair." She had put aside two wrinkled, damp sheets.

Kate growled something unintelligible. Gwen took up the two sheets she had laid aside and prepared to leave the parlour. "I'm going to do his bed now," she said. She opened the door. The sound of a soprano voice singing to a piano accompaniment became more distinct. "Heavens, that girl," she remarked, "how she goes on and on with that tune. It's enough to drive one crazy. . . ." She hesitated, stepped back into the parlour and took up another couple of the wrinkled sheets. "She may as well have her pair put on now," she murmured. "Why should we iron for her?"

"Gwen, dear," Marion half-heartedly asked, "are they dry enough?"

"Good gracious, yes. Besides, she's as strong as a donkey—hark at her voice! I'd like to put her in the cellar."

"I must say," Marion listened with a look of experience, "she sings quite well. . . . Don't be long, Gwen. I expect

he'll be back from Tremartin with the afternoon bus." Left
alone with Kate, she said: "I hope you're not going to sulk,
dear. Gwen is high-tempered but she means well. We are
frightened you'll disgrace us in some way, you're so
temperamental——"

"And you're so two-faced." Kate was hunched up in her
chair as if she was licking her wounds.

"Well, I have to be." Marion considered her finger-nails
trimmed to long, fine points. "But never mind about
that. . . . Please, Kate," she resumed earnestly, "don't let
us down by becoming flighty. It's more necessary than ever
that we three keep together and don't do anything undignified outside. We've got to be respected."

"Do you think that woman is going to keep quiet about
father having an illegitimate child?" snapped Kate.

"I don't care if she doesn't. It might earn valuable
sympathy for us three, in case we have to act in some way
later. . . . Of course I didn't tell her," she added with an
air of yet having the trump card up her sleeve, "how father
earned his little fortune, because there was some danger that
it might reflect on us. After all, we are being kept by his
money."

He had not arrived back at the expected time. They did
not lay tea in the dining-room but shut themselves in their
parlour. Laura's cup of tea and a plate of bread and butter
was left for her in the kitchen. When she went there Gwen
nipped into the drawing-room and locked the piano. This
began another row. Laura burst furiously into the parlour
and demanded the key.

"We've heard enough of your voice for one afternoon,"
Gwen declared, flat. "What with the parrot and you I fail to
see the advantage of living in the quiet of the country."

"Give me that key." She was very pale.

Marion said: "It's really for your own good. You are
overstraining your voice."

"Give me that key."

"Give me that key!" mimicked Gwen.

"Once again, Laura," Marion said, "I must remind you the piano is mine."

Laura stood swollen with helpless rage. But the gleaming black of her eyes ranged over the tea-tray, paused on a knife. Gwen, with an easy move, stood confronting her: the little lurking smile was one of invitation. There was a cry, a rush, and Laura had vanished.

"God, why didn't you give her the key?" Kate said irritably. "There'll be more trouble to-night."

"Do you know," Gwen remarked, "I believe that girl is going to leave us. I've been keeping an eye on her lately. She's been writing to London, to a Tremartin girl who's already there."

"I don't blame her," Kate said.

"Father will attempt to stop her," Marion said. "Especially when he knows he cannot marry again."

"Without our consent," Kate added, heavily ironical.

"Kate, will you have the rest of the jam?" Gwen held out the dish. She had taken none herself though fond of it. Kate accepted it, recognising this as an apology for loss of temper. And after a cigarette she entirely ceased being surly and asked if the irons were being heated. Marion said she'd wash the tea-things. Gwen unlocked her own private drawer in the tallboy and offered both of them a chocolate-cream.

"I'd prefer a glass of beer," Kate laughed.

"Kate," smiled Gwen admiringly, "if you came home drunk one day I believe I would burst into tears."

"May I never live to see that day," Marion tittered.

Kate began to swagger about the room: "There's still drink in the cellar. Shall I go and get a bottle of something?"

"No, dear," Marion said, "we may need clear heads this evening."

"And we have seen enough of the evils of drink in this house," Gwen pronounced.

"I think you'd like to see me drunk," Kate strutted, very downright and masculine.

The atmosphere of harmony, of reunited understanding,

remained with them while they set about their tasks. At seven o'clock, when Kate lit the lamps, their father still had not returned. Two days had elapsed since the visit to Mrs. Parry. That morning a letter from Tremartin had arrived for him and Gwen managed to steam it open before he got it: Mrs. Parry formally invited him to call on her that afternoon. It was past nine o'clock when he arrived.

Cold supper had waited in the dining-room for over an hour. The sisters took theirs at eight o'clock; the gong was struck but Laura did not appear; she probably knew her father had not returned. After supper the sisters waited in their parlour. Only Kate, quite losing her swagger, became nervous; she bit her nails and smoked the last of her week's supply of cigarettes and went out more than once to the stable. Gwen sewed, Marion turned over the pages of a novel Kate had borrowed from the farm. The oil lamp burned warm and golden.

"There he is!" Kate exclaimed. "Go and tell him his supper is laid, Gwen."

"He can see that for himself. . . . If he has anything to say I hope he eats first. A hungry man is always more difficult. Where has that moth come from?" It banged itself against the glass funnel, kept glitteringly bright by her. "The window is closed."

"It must have come in with Kate," Marion said. "Catch it, Kate. Or it will settle for the winter somewhere. Catch it, Gwen."

But they heard his step in the passage. They glanced at each other in a last united understanding. The door opened. He stood there silent, looking at each of them in turn. He seemed tired, as if he had been walking for hours. As he did not speak, Gwen said: "Your supper is in the dining-room, father. We didn't wait." He stood there looking at them.

"I do wish you'd catch that moth, Kate," said Marion. "You know I never can catch them, and we can't afford to have our clothes eaten."

But Kate did not budge from the chair in which she was slumped.

"The three of you," their father said, "will leave this house to-morrow." His voice was weary and hollow. But the unflickering eyes did not move from them.

"What do you mean, father?" snapped Marion. "Don't be ridiculous." She tossed aside the book and rose, made a step or two across the room as if to examine him closely, and stopped. "Do you mean you are threatening to turn us out?"

Gwen clapped her hands in an effort to catch the moth. Kate watched, furtive in her chair. He stood looking at Marion penetratingly; he might have been seeing her for the first time. There was a sense of them measuring each other's strength. She did not flinch. He stepped closer to her, coming full into the room.

"Are you my daughter?" he asked in wonder.

"Father," she said. "I hope you're not ill? Would you like to rest a little and talk to us afterwards? Gwen has one of those tins of soup in the kitchen——"

"Ah, that's got you!" cried Gwen, swooping her fist. But she hadn't. The excited moth soared away.

"You heard me. . . . You will leave my house to-morrow," he repeated in that soft hollow voice. "The three of you."

"Father, of course you're unwell. What are you saying! You can't turn three grown women out into the lanes. . . . Why, the whole district would be scandalised." But she drew back a step.

Gwen turned from her concentrated scrutiny of the moth's antics to say: "The trouble with you, father, is that you've been so concerned with yourself and your own affairs that you haven't realised we've grown up. We're full-sized now and can't be dictated to——"

Kate broke in, nervously staccato: "I'm sure there's a law to protect us. The parish wouldn't grant us relief while we have a parent with the means to keep us."

Marion turned to Kate: "Do you think we're going to sleep in the workhouse to-morrow night then? Be quiet, dear. And leave that moth alone, Gwen."

Suddenly he screamed, raising an arm as though he would strike: "Demons! Why do you torment me! I will drag you by the hairs out of my house." Trembling, he advanced a step towards Marion.

She did not retreat. They were close now. "You torment yourself, father," she said, more slowly but watching him carefully. "You have never been a father to us. We would like to give you affection, if we could. But your conduct hasn't encouraged it." Her voice held a little mocking note. She stood unwavering.

"You will go to-morrow," he shouted in febrile rage, beginning to storm about the room, the weariness apparently gone. "You torment me, you torment Laura, you are not women but devils. If you do not go I will go myself, you will starve——"

"No," Marion said, "I'll take pianoforte pupils. We like this large house, father."

"We might take a paying guest or two," Gwen said, her attention returning to the moth, which was banging against the lamp again.

"I could take a job in Tremartin," Kate barked. The three seemed to speak in unison.

He turned from the window and stared at them in fury. Gwen pursued the moth, clapped her hands, and breathed triumphantly: "Got it."

"All this," Marion complained, "because we considered it our duty to warn that poor woman we would not welcome her and that you had no right to marry her, father!"

"I will destroy you," he screamed.

It was then that Marion lost her stony calmness and also screamed: "Do you think I could not destroy you! There is nothing I don't know about you. Nothing about your evil life in London. Nothing about your tainted money. I have held my tongue until now, I did not tell that woman all the truth. But I could disgrace you here, so that no decent person would look at you." It was she who stepped over to him now. "You call me a devil!" she raged, and she seemed to uncoil and lunge towards him. "Have you thought what you have done to us? Search your own bad soul——"

But he had thrust past her with a strange animal bellow. He picked up the lamp from the table and hurled it across the room towards the window. It fell among the half-drawn curtains. The crash of bowl and funnel as they reached the floor was hideous. A jagged flame shot somewhere in the air swift as a meteor and vanished. In the momentary black silence they heard his groan and rush from the room.

"The house will catch fire," Gwen shrieked.

"No," Kate's voice came, oddly calm. "Don't get excited. The flame went out. What a smell of paraffin!"

"Poor father," Marion's voice shook now, "I'm afraid I lost my temper too much." At once she left the room, as Gwen called hysterically to Kate to fetch another lamp.

He was in the hall, stalking about with quick jerking steps, flinging words at Laura, who shrank against the newel of the staircase.

"I did not create their souls. They are like the vermin that eat into the tree's substance and bring it down at last. . . . Go, go if you want to. Leave me alone with them."

"Father," Marion called, standing beyond the lamp's area of radiance, her head bent. "I am sorry I lost my temper. I beg you to forgive me." Behind her, at the entrance to the passage, Gwen and Kate hovered.

He had halted. He drew back a step, stopped again and looked across the hall at her. "What, what?" he stammered. Now there was something strangely pathetic in his lunging head. His face was haggard and old. The white hair was flung back like a prophet's. Laura watched with eyes round and large in fear.

Marion crossed the hall. Her head still hung in contrition. And she knelt before him, whimpering, the thin cool woman who walked with such pride. It was somehow dreadful, in a way the raging outbursts in the parlour had not been. He looked down at her in horror, shrinking into himself.

"Forgive me, father," her yielded voice entreated, "you drove me beyond myself. It was because we couldn't bear the thought of a stranger coming here. Don't marry again, father, don't tempt us into wicked actions. Let us stay here as we were before."

With a cry Laura turned and ran up the staircase. Gwen and Kate looked across the hall at their prostrate sister in surprise. But she was rising. She staggered a little as if she would faint. He had not spoken, only watched her penetratingly.

"Gwen?" called Marion, looking round blindly. She was weeping.

Gwen ran over to her. "Here I am, my darling," she whispered. She supported her faltering sister on her arm.

But suddenly, at her touch, Marion gave way to hysteria. "Why have we to live like this?" she shrieked. "I will go mad. Let him kill me, he wants us to die." She hung on to Gwen for a moment or two, but, writhing, slipped to the ground. There she uttered a long piercing scream. It rang round the hall. Gwen knelt beside her sister and attempted to lift her shoulders in an embrace; she whispered soothing endearments. Kate stood quite still. At the bend of the staircase Laura appeared for a moment, looked down in dread, and fled upstairs again.

He stepped over to the prostrate moaning woman. Gwen still tenderly struggled with her. "We must carry her upstairs, father," she said.

He looked down at his daughter. For a moment he hesitated as though to bend to her; his shaking hand moved out. And then he turned away.

"Tell her when she recovers," he said abruptly, "that you may continue to live in this house." He walked away, his voice rising as he mounted the stairs. "But from now you will live your lives separately from mine——"

"Kate," Gwen called, "come and help me. . . . Go and get those smelling salts."

They bore her to their parlour. She still whimpered and uttered wild cries, and she did not recover quickly. She lay on the sofa in slack exhaustion, her eyes closed, her nostrils blue. For the first time her skin looked old, her face faded. Gwen, after repeating their father's message, suggested they all went to bed. The smell of paraffin was thick; the shattered lamp lay where it had fallen.

"Sleep with me to-night, Gwen," Marion whimpered.

Even Gwen and Kate were uncertain of her. They were impressed by her look of age. She seemed to have really crumbled inside; a real terror seemed to have withered her. They went upstairs together.

There was a distinct atmosphere of peace in the house, the storm's aftermath. Gwen slept in her sister's bed. Marion, relaxed and her voice worn, asked where Laura had been: she seemed to remember seeing her in the hall when she followed her father there, but was not sure. "Something possessed me, Gwen," she whispered, "I wasn't myself, I was in a trance when I walked to him and knelt. Only a little bit of me knew what I was doing."

"I couldn't believe my eyes," Gwen said.

"Was that girl there?"

"Yes. But you scared the life out of her. She ran up-stairs."

In the morning Gwen found Laura's room empty. A letter for her father stood on the mantelshelf. Gwen opened the envelope. The letter only said she wished to take up a career in London, that she had somewhere to go there and would be quite safe, and that she hoped to see him some day in London. She enclosed an address. Gwen ran to Marion, who was taking breakfast in bed and still looking limp and woebegone.

"Poor thing," Marion said, indifferently. "She's got so little character, Heaven knows what will happen to her. It's her mother's strain coming out."

"Oh, as I said yesterday, she's strong as a donkey. . . . She must have carried her suitcase all the way to the village for the bus." Gwen was struck into a muse. "I'll quite miss her. She was nice to tease sometimes."

Later, after a full discussion with both her sisters, she took the note to her father. He was in the barn. "Father," she said casually and very carefully. "Laura seems to have gone. She left this sheet of paper in her room."

He took the note, read it in the dim light, his back to her. She waited. He crushed up the sheet and threw it into a corner. "Go away," he said; "why do you stand there?"

From that day he never spoke to them except to ask them some strictly necessary question or to make a concise statement about the domestic arrangements of the house.

Part II

THE DAUGHTERS

Chapter One

I

AT last, black in the dusk, she saw the tower and the clustering chimneys of her father's house. She stopped. There was time to turn back. But a few minutes later, opening the high double gate flanked with imitation turret-posts, she found herself trudging up the snow-thick drive as if filled by some inner urgency, though she kept well in the shadow of the evergreens. The trail of footprints she left wavered very unevenly. Still her mind hesitated. Why had she taken this uncertain journey of three hundred miles after such a long silence? She did not quite know.

That terrible scene, nine years ago, when she told him she was leaving! Afterwards, in a moment of perception, it had suddenly occurred to her that really he had been begging her to stay and not leave him alone with her stepsisters.

The evergreens had grown rank and unkempt. Beyond them the massive house, frowning with gables and its square castle-like tower giving it a boastful look, stood forbiddingly unilluminated. Its late-Victorian ugliness had always quarrelled with the quiet anciently pastoral landscape. But, proudly isolated, two miles from the village and the last house before the ascent to the wild mountains, it was the mansion of the district. Somehow, despite the suggestion of decay among the sagging gables, the fussy window-bays and the ivy-dark porch, it still generated an air of wealth attained by strident new means.

To-day, seeing it with new eyes, she realised its formidable pretentiousness. She wondered why her father bought it when he retired from London; she always thought of him as austere, spare-living, almost an anchorite. But perhaps he bought it to try and overcome her mother's objections to the country.

That there was no sign of life in the front windows did not surprise her. But she couldn't mount the five steps to that hooded porch with its two rusty cressets empty as skulls. There was not a footprint in the snow of the steps. Stealthily she crept to the huge bay-window on the left and peered in. A heavy gloom locked this drawing-room with its grand piano. She passed the low iron-barred cellar-grating which the withered dahlia and chrysanthemum bushes revealed, and, noiseless in the snow, came to the gabled end. There, startled, she drew up.

Low in the sky, an enormous moon stared at her. In the icily clear air its tawny yellow seemed to ring down on the earth with a physical power. She felt diminished under that primitive lunar stare. Its illumination flooded a kingdom of frozen blue roots and trees white as skeletons. There was no traffic in the world but this gaze into a glassy sphere where all life was petrified, as an anemone is stilled under ice. The silence was appalling.

She could still see, far off, the massed hills looming heavy with snow, an enclosing throw of whiteness strong as marble. But a wonderful, virginal beauty had transformed the earth. Here, where the curved lowlands ran down to the sea, the snow lay in dry, crisp lightness. The long walk from the village inn, on a glassy road, had been like plunging deeper and deeper into an unknown, magical world. All the trees and bushes bordering the lanes and in the tilted woods were laden with a marvellous filigree of glistening crystals, all around her was struck into a silent white enchantment, a still diamond-hard world of crystalline branches, grottoes webbed with stiff ceremonious lace, spectral caverns static in a strange bluey-white lustre. She had not met a soul; and every animal, bird and beetle seemed fled.

From a narrow corner window came a shaft of light. It lit a tall birch tree growing at the edge of the white lawn. Delaying the moment when she must look into the window, she stood gazing at this tree. She remembered it as slight and young and shivering. Now its wealth of lithe branches, under their burden of frozen snow, swept down to earth in a fountain of crystals. She crept towards it.

And at last, huddled against the wall, her face secret on the edge of the shaft, she peered into the window. With a small uneasy smile.

She saw three women in that familiar interior of red plush, heavy gold-framed pictures and a brassy oil lamp. The table was carelessly laid for tea; it also held a sewing-machine. This, her stepsisters' own parlour, wasn't changed. From outside it looked cosily inviting, domestically warm with the usages of traditional family life. Its three occupants were conversing. Kate sprawled on the old-fashioned red sofa, her legs stuck out like a man's; she wore breeches and woollen stockings with turn-back tops. Gwen, tall in a tight business-like dress, stood holding a length of material; she still looked the capable kind of woman who abounds in health. Marion sat in an arm-chair drinking tea in her careful lady-like way and, with her attenuated cheeks carelessly rouged, more than ever like a papery, crushed pink flower. All three somehow looked distinguished. But in a vaguely decadent way. Character and even physical attractiveness had certainly not been extinguished in them. They could have seemed drab. But they were not.

Laura, as she peered in, began to shiver. But still the uncertain smile hovered. She saw Marion, laying down her cup, put out her tongue at Kate with a prolonged and surprising deliberation. *Not* the action of a lady. Kate nonchalantly lit a cigarette.

But where was her father? Lying vanquished in bed upstairs? The three women looked such mistresses of themselves—yes, they had changed, they exuded an air of increased security. To the woman outside, the room seemed a little fortress from which all intruders would be ruthlessly repulsed. She drew back; her courage seemed to be oozing away. The oppression of her years in this house swept down on her again. They had defeated her in the past—had they succeeded at last with him? Where was he?

Swiftly she stepped away from the window, walked through the shaft of light and went to the back of the house. There were footprints here, and an enamel pail, a carelessly thrown heap of potato peelings, a frozen floor-cloth hanging from a nail. Looking around at the snow-covered out-houses and stable in the moon-dusk, her eye caught a light beginning to grow in a top window of the tower—an oil lamp just lit. Was he there? In her time the cold isolated tower-room had never been used, except for storing trunks, though her father had slept there during her mother's last illness.

The back door was unlocked. A candle guttered in the stony spacious kitchen. There was no fire in the old-fashioned range—they would have boiled the kettle on the oil stove. Passing through into a passage, dark and icy, she turned into another passage on the right, walking unhesitatingly now. She opened a door.

Kate's legs drew up in their breeches. Gwen's amber beads gleamed on the rise of her bosom. Marion remained static with the teapot she had lifted out of the hearth; afterwards she placed a hand on her heart. Laura, still smiling a little, stood a moment or two in the doorway. Then she walked in, with a deliberate and over-assured nonchalance.

No one said a word until Kate, in her hoarse, smoky voice exclaimed: "It's Laura!"

"Good gracious," Marion complained breathlessly, laying down the teapot without filling her cup, "why didn't you come to the front door? My heart is going pit-a-pat." Gwen laid her hand on the sewing-machine as if to verify a material fact in what might be a dream—"Why didn't you write or 'phone?" she then demanded sharply. "Creeping in like that!"

A clock struck too many notes. "It's still a disobedient clock," Laura smiled, glancing at her tiny watch. "How I used to like that old clock."

There was a silence. Of suspicion; of decision held in abeyance. She took off her gloves, hat and expensive fleecy coat, laid them on a chair, and shook out her crop of well-kept hair; she sat down, giving her stepsisters credit for not asking her to sit, in her own home. They were assessing her clothes and appearance; their eyes pounced on her wedding ring. . . . But from that silence rose, thick and pronounced, the assumption that she had come back a failure, perhaps penniless. They were not going to be taken in by fine clothes, not they! It was still too much in their mythology that a daughter who fled the parental tree in the way she had done was bound to come to some kind of disaster.

"You're married," barked Kate, nodding towards the ring.

"And divorced . . . Is there a cup of tea?"

Marion and Gwen drew in their breaths. The suspicion in the air acquired a new force. Gwen hurried to the kitchen for a clean cup. Then Marion, fluttering in her chair in the waiting silence, mysteriously whispered over her shoulder at nobody: "Yes, yes, Dora." Laura started at this. Kate took another loose cigarette from the pocket of her khaki cotton breeches and lit it from the other.

"Divorced!" Gwen exclaimed, hastening in again. She poured tea, handed the last slice of bread and butter.

"I divorced him. Thank you, Gwen . . . I arrived from London this afternoon," she went on, too easily; "I've left a friend at the Ruthin Arms; and my suitcase. I suppose I should have telephoned from there; I'm sorry."

"A woman friend?" Kate barked.

"No . . . I suppose I can stay here?" There was no reply to this, and she asked: "Where is father?"

The three glanced at each other. And a circle seemed to enclose them, an orbit from which this intruder must be kept. Laura waited. She began to frown. It was even a scowl, the young girl's scowl of years ago. The intervening years might not have happened, and she was alone again with three powers roused into a single alien force against her.

Still they did not reply. Laura looked at them in turn, waiting. Her short nose seemed thickened with temper. She was visibly making an effort to control herself—so far, after all, what was there to be angry about?

"Where is father?" she repeated, calmly.

"He won't want to see you," Gwen said at last. She sat down. Laura shivered in remembrance of the strength and physical warmth of this woman's superb body.

"No? . . . I saw a lamp being lit in the tower. I'll go up to him presently."

"He won't let you into his room," Kate said, in her smokily hoarse voice; "and he seldom comes down. We have to put a tray of food outside his door. . . . He won't let you in, d'you hear!" she continued in a swearing voice, as if she were riding a recalcitrant horse. "It's no use trying . . . What have you come back for?" she suddenly swooped.

And as rapidly the other two, completely recovered from their shock, reared in their chairs, Gwen exclaiming: "Yes, why have you come back?" Marion, with her more silky manner, but really the most stubborn of them, added: "It's rather impudent, coming back after all these years—and not a line from you. You haven't cared a button, have you! But *we've* had to put up with him; we couldn't run away to enjoy ourselves." She looked secretly at the other two, a pinched-in look of haughty censoriousness startling in such a rouged, artificial face.

"Well," Laura said, "he's had to put up with you too." They stared at her, each with the stare of the introverted egoist surprised by a revelation of his own soul. "Give me a cigarette, Kate, will you?" she went on, calmly it seemed. "I've left mine at the inn."

"I'm short of them," Kate shook her head.

Again there was a silence, and an air of biding time. It was broken by Marion, always apt to strike out on her own (except of course that the three were indissolubly united when threatened from without). She tittered: "Kate sold her horse for thirty pounds to keep herself in cigarettes. Father won't give her money for them."

"So it's no good you coming here for money," Gwen said, flat, "if that's what you want. He's worse than he used to be."

"He's mad," barked Kate then, direct to Laura, and as if after consideration she had made up her mind to speak. "You'd better know straight away."

"Quite mad," Marion said in her light stringy way.

"Mad as a hatter," chorused Gwen. "Padlocks and keys, sulks and tempers!" She added, with a peculiarly obsessive violence: "He's locked up the cellar. He wouldn't even let me take my daffodil bulbs down there. Three bowls I planted. . . . He goes down there of nights, when we're in bed, down into the dark. He says there are rats, and he made us get Mr. Ellis, the Council rat-catcher . . . 'No trace of rats,' said Mr. Ellis. But father said he saw the king rat come out—ugh," her fine body heaved, "he was only trying to frighten us . . . He's mad, "she repeated.

"Now you know," said Kate. And Marion cloudily murmured: "It's unfortunate. But considering what he's had on his mind——" She wagged her head.

"What has he had on his mind?" Laura asked.

The other two looked at Kate. Perhaps because of her masculinity and downrightness, Kate seemed to have attained to natural authority in the house now, though Laura, watching her, began to wonder if this hectoring manner of hers covered a complex mass of private indecisions. Now, blowing out cigarette smoke, she looked along her eyelids at her stepsister.

"Why have you come back?" she repeated, in a harshly parrying way.

"Why, to see you all . . . My old father and my three darling stepsisters."

"I don't know that we want to see you," replied Kate. In contrast to the active spite of the other two, a sort of morose indifference seemed to emanate from her.

"Yet I think you need a visitor. There's a horribly oppressive atmosphere here." She added, surprised herself by the sudden thought: "I was going to suggest—though of course I must ask father about it—that I bring the friend I left at the inn. You'll like him."

Gwen and Marion started, but Kate asked roughly: "Is he your lover?"

"Certainly not," Laura replied with such decisive sharpness that Kate flickered into a quick attention. And the other two rose from their chairs and hovered uncertainly. This was not the Laura they knew. This rounded, full-fleshed woman sitting there with a sort of thick, meditative assurance, her black eyes glinting, her full red lips curled in repudiation of them. This was not the clumsy young Laura of the sulky tears, the stormy distresses—and the fears of her grown-up stepsisters powerful in their united advantages and their secret knowledge. And yet the ghost of that girl was still there, behind the glint, in the undertones: it was like a hostile spirit not yet released. They watched her calculatingly.

"You seem to be very sure of yourself," Kate said, with her rough jeer. And, as though instinctively, the other two went nearer her where she sprawled on the red sofa. "We don't want visitors here; this is no house for visitors, with a madman on our hands. If I were you I'd go back to the inn now and leave us alone—as you've done for nine years."

"What, without seeing father?" she asked, apparently in rebuke. But it was costing her a great effort to maintain this calm.

Kate, in her turn, now made an effort and spoke more moderately: "Laura, it may interest you to know that years ago father forbade us to speak of you, and he's never referred to you since then. . . . But perhaps you've come back," she went on, her control breaking a little, "wondering if he's made a will?"

"Yes——" breathed the other two, "yes."

"Well," Laura said, dangerously, "I am his daughter."

"By his drunkard of a second wife." Marion exclaimed. "Who made his life a misery for him. Who shamed him." She gave a mysterious little titter. "But *we* know why he married her—the old ruffian." She laughed outright. "And it's not all we know."

"Shut up, you!" Kate barked. "You're a fool with your silly imagination and babble." But Gwen tried to cover this by asking at once, with a hypocritical air of tact: "What does your friend at the inn do? What work, I mean?"

"None." Laura's temper seemed quite cooled down.

"A rich man?" asked Marion, arrested. They still hovered about the sofa.

"I don't know about *rich*," Laura replied, cunning herself now. "But I expect you'd find him what is called a gentleman." Poor Alex!

"We haven't," sighed Marion, "had a gentleman in the house for many a long day. . . . No one comes here. It was quite a relief to see the rodent officer." And again, as if mutually agreed upon by all present, there hovered in the room a fragile air of biding time.

"Don't you ever go to Tremartin or the village now?" Laura asked, idly.

"Kate goes regularly for her cigarettes," Marion said.

"But church?"

The three glanced at each other—yet again with that significant look, blinded almost instantly. Even Marion was alert in this. "No, we don't go now," replied Gwen pursily—"and we have our reasons."

After another little pause, Kate asked: "Did you go in for singing after you left here?"

"Yes. I'm on the stage."

"The stage! You don't look like an actress to me. . . . Not a bit like your mother. With all her faults she did look an actress—and was one." Kate surveyed her unflamboyant stepsister up and down: the fixed dourness in her gaze passed beyond derision into total rejection.

"You mean I don't look a successful one—or just that you don't believe me?" She went on: "It's time you three got out into the world a little. You make one think of a trio of vindictive moles. . . . I had hoped to find you'd got kinder in disposition, but——" She stopped, hopelessly. How had their characters become so locked in hatred? There was a domination they had lacked the courage to escape. It had arrested any natural flowering. Did the sense of inert oppression in this house come from the horror that perhaps it was now too late for them to escape?

"Vindictive moles!" tittered Marion. "We must send for a mole-catcher next . . . I suppose you sing on the stage? Well, I'm sure *we've* never heard of you." Her own expensively trained voice vaguely dismissed this vocalist.

"Why did you divorce your husband?" resumed Kate with heavy directness.

"For the most common reason. He had a liking for variety . . . We were students together at the Academy of Music," she went on, feeling this had to be told. "We had our first engagements together; we went out to South Africa." But now she couldn't control the look of hatred she directed at them. "He met a woman there . . ." she concluded lamely. And exclaimed in irritation to Gwen and Marion: "Why do you keep standing there over the sofa? Can't you sit down?" But they ignored this.

"You're still in love with him!" Marion said, with the papery titter which yet somehow revealed her steely obstinacy.

Laura made an effort over her scattered forces. How they were subtly, insidiously exercising the old domination of her childhood. And she had given herself away now.

Mollified, they could almost accept her return; she *was* creeping home for sanctuary from something. Or because of some inner sense of failure.

"Well," said Kate, a little less roughly, "you always were a romantic fool, Laura . . . Yet," she added with a musing insolence, "you were a pretty little thing. I said to Gwen when you left here, 'She *might* do well for herself *if* she keeps her head screwed on tight.' . . . And here you are, a second-rate singer, a jilted wife, and with a dotty father who doesn't want to see you."

Laura sighed. She took out of her handbag a lipstick, compact and mirror, and, with the deft manner of the expert, used them. Oh, these half-sisters of hers! She had nearly allowed herself to be caught up again in their world. There was something remote about their existence that surely couldn't affect her now? And she had thought of Alex's possible reaction to them; she had tried to see them through his eyes. And this had pulled her up just in time. . . .

"Do you think all that improves your face?" Gwen asked.

"Don't be silly, Gwen." She snapped her bag decisively. "Now I want to see father. I'm sick of all this spite." But still she felt that somehow they had managed to get the upper hand.

Kate, apparently equally decisive, then flung a cigarette-end into the hearth and announced:

"I think, Laura, you're still a shallow little thing. Shallow like your mother was, though she was shallow in a big flashy way. . . . I still don't know why you've thought fit to come here, since you've no place here now. . . . Unless," she added, lighting yet another cigarette and coughing on its smoke, "you're just being calculating. But I tell you again, father doesn't want to see you. And he *is* mad." She uttered the last word with a cold-blooded bluntness, flicking ash off her breeches.

Laura, looking at her, sat in growing fear again. How far had this slumpy earthy-looking woman gone in a tragic identification with elemental things? Was her own sophisticated determination not to be affected by the sense of drama in the house really shallow and brittle compared with her stepsister's dark grimness? She had not believed these assertions of her father's madness. If there was madness in the house it was surely among these three—they were not individually mad but the thing bred between them, in this room where their father refused to come, had the nature of madness.

"In what way is he mad?" she asked, warily.

Marion and Gwen drew even closer to the sofa. Kate took no notice of them. Her eyes became fixed with a remote contempt on her stepsister across the room.

"We've already told you," she said in an unusually patient way, "that he has shut himself away. Some time ago it was religious mania but now he believes that religion can't help him—he thinks he's bound hopelessly to the Devil. There's something on his mind—he's ashamed of himself, I think. He won't let us go near him, and we can't get any money except the very barest expenses of the house——"

"Yes," Gwen bustled indignantly. "Something on his mind, true enough!" And Marion appeared to preen herself righteously: "The old ruffian; we're frightened he'll give his money away, he——"

"Shut up, you two!" shouted Kate in great irritation. "I *hate* the way you interrupt with your braying." And indeed she showed so markedly a masculine impatience with their prattle that again one could almost hear the lewd oaths behind her voice. . . . Laura saying nothing, she resumed: "He always was mean, of course, and thought of little but money. Perhaps he saw it didn't bring him what he wanted, and that is why his mind has gone to pieces——" She paused, as if heavily considering further revelations.

"Dora, be quiet," Marion murmured with a backward glance and a brush of her hand. "Yes, yes, dear, I understand; thank you, dear, but be quiet now." A complacent expression settled on her face, like someone in a very advantageous position.

"To whom are you talking, Marion?" asked Laura, glad of this further interruption.

"Dora, my guide. She's been with me ever since you came into the room."

"I see," Laura said carefully, willing not to offend in this. "She advises you, does she?"

"Dora has been a great help to me in our trouble," Marion said simply. "It's restful to know that the unseen is ever at hand with its counsel."

Kate made an impatient movement of her legs; Gwen looked vacant. But even in the old days Marion often possessed a bodiless air, as though she were half a resident of an abstract world. Perhaps this was because of her efforts to keep herself a lady unbesmirched by the earth. Now more than ever she had turned her back on unpleasantnesses and fixed her eyes on an astral kingdom where all was peace. Hence, for all her fluttering air, she was really tougher than her two sisters, who were at the mercy of the corporeal world's hard facts: she could well afford that papery titter of hers. Nevertheless she would faithfully support the other two in their earthly dealings, though without incurring responsibility for their inception. Thus she ate her cake and had it, which is the ultimate reward of successful religious belief.

Laura rose from her chair, tucking her handbag under her arm. "I think I'll go up to him now." She couldn't deal any more with Kate's tirades.

At once there was consternation. Kate jumped up from the sofa exclaiming: "I tell you he won't let you in." Gwen and Marion circled round the room as if they would pounce on the intruder. "Leave him alone," Gwen commanded, while Marion breathed: "I have been advised by my guide that his mind can't stand shocks." Gwen was close to the door now. Marion stood near the uncurtained window.

Behind her, out there in the silence, lay the white ribs of trees and empty marble fields.

Laura stood looking at them uncertainly. Oh, why hadn't she brought Alex with her! That ripe detachment of his would have aided her in coping with this. "But this is ridiculous," she said weakly. "Do you intend trying to prevent my seeing him?"

"He doesn't belong to you any more." Kate's voice was still raised. "Go away; you shall not go up those stairs." Marion circled round her, a tenacious painted wraith. And Gwen, taking up her stepsister's coat from the chair, said with an enticing smoothness: "If you like I'll come with you as far as the Common; you can see the lights of the village from there. I'll put on my goloshes . . . Come, Laura." She might have been speaking to a refractory child. The child of many years ago.

Laura stood as if transfixed in a dream. She was staring out of the window into the glassy bluish-white evening. A rigidity held her eyeballs.

She was remembering how, when she was fifteen, Gwen had carried her to the tower-room and locked her in for a whole day. The house had been laden with the perfume of the full-flowered garden hawthorns. Particularly she remembered—and it still brought back a sickening odour—Gwen's strong ruthless arms and breasts enclosing her as she struggled, and the sense of violation that had made her want to vomit. There had been a terrible realisation of the power of masterful, softly-enveloping flesh. . . . And years later, when romantically obsessed girls at the Academy and on the stage had yearned over her, she had fled from them with this same sick feeling. For years she could bear with calm the physical proximity only of men, though even they—at least among her lovers, would-be or otherwise—could cause a retreat. . . . Perhaps after all it was not surprising that Hugh, when he suggested the divorce, couldn't quite explain himself—and in any case, poor boy, he had few brains and less perception. Only Alex was never masterful: *he*, intelligently, usually sought her along less physical paths. (If only he were younger, less ripe!)

She sat down again; she felt she had at least an appearance of composure. But she had to wait a few seconds before saying: "Well, do you intend to lay hands on me? Pick me up bodily and throw me out of the house? You seem to think I'm still a——"

She couldn't finish. And the words were scarcely uttered when a paroxysm swept over her. Her voice sank like a dismembered cord, her face-muscles writhed, her limbs felt convulsed as though struggling among soft tentacles entwined over them. The prison, the prison! Yet far within the centre of this not unfamiliar nightmare there was a point of calm, and from there her being seemed to watch cunningly. But still she could not speak, while, as from a far distance like figures in sleep, the three watched her convulsions in the chair.

"You are perspiring," Gwen said, remotely. "Why are you pulling such faces? It's making you look ugly."

"Temper won't help you," Kate said, extraordinarily dim.

Slowly the paroxysm left her. It was like the sounds of drum-beats dwindling away down the corridors of her mind. Suddenly she felt icy cold. But wonderfully calm. The three women became focused in their proper perspective. She gazed at them, not with the disdain she felt, but with that fixed composure.

Meeting her gaze, Kate's expression changed; she seemed to wilt. Turning abruptly, she said with an air of blunt honesty: "We ask you to go, Laura, and not to come back troubling us. I think you've shown a want of feeling in turning up like this so casually. And father is in our care and we don't think it's wise for him to be disturbed. You always were a worry to him. Please go."

"And if you've come here," said Gwen in her capable schoolmistress manner, "wondering about money or a will, the best thing for you to do is to leave your address with Mr. Rowlands, our solicitor in Tremartin. If there'll be anything for you he'll let you know."

"You remember, dear," said Marion artificially, "that when you left here you said you'd never come back."

Kate repeated: "I tell you again you've no place here now."

"If father tells me that, I'll accept it," Laura said. And she was surprised at the ease of her voice. . . . But her thoughts were occupied in trying to formulate some way of getting upstairs without a disgusting scene. If they laid hands on her——

There was a distant slam of a door. The heavy snow-shrouded house seemed to waken. In the room the silence following her last remark took on a different quality. It was as if the strength of the three sisters was held in suspension. Slowly, almost furtively, they lifted their heads and listened. There were slouching footsteps on the bare passage-way flags; they came near the door and pattered away. Then a voice swept hollowly through the passage:

"Gwen, oil . . . get me oil."

Laura leapt from her chair to the door and ran into the passage.

But they did not follow—she had a glimpse of them as, grouped together, they stood struck into a statuesque listening. At the end of the passage she saw a yellow light flutter and vanish. She reached the icy hall. It was in darkness. But an angle of light was disappearing upwards.

2

He was ascending the wide staircase, a cloak thrown loosely over his shoulders, a candlestick in his hand. She saw his white hair, and a spasm of anguish quivered through her loins. She staggered against the staircase post; the wooden blackamoor stationed there, that held out a tray for visiting cards, crashed to the flags. He turned. He had reached the staircase bend where the arched stained-glass window gleamed dingily violet, rose and green. He peered down.

"Father . . ." she faltered.

He could see nothing. But she, she could see in the candle's light his blurred eyes, the hollow cheeks, the waxen skin. And why had he shaved off his beard? His face looked naked and exposed.

' I said bring me some oil."

Slowly she mounted a stair, another, her face lifted in supplication. But she was aware of a hovering of secret figures in the icy shadows at the side of the staircase. They were there like furies.

"It's Laura," she said. After a hesitation she mounted another stair. She saw his diminished figure, thin and, though he was a tall man, somehow smaller than the image in her memory. But she could not run to him. Her knee bent constrictedly as she took another step.

Muttering something, he had turned impatiently. She was aware of an old patriarchal fury; it mingled in her fibres, half petrifying her. But she called, louder: "Father, don't you know me? It's Laura."

Suspiciously he turned his face back again and peered down. "Laura?" he rasped. "My daughter Laura?"

She mounted the remaining stairs more swiftly. He held up the candlestick, his eyes peering greyly. Below him her face loomed into the yellow throw of light. But still he was suspicious. He was shrinking away from her approach.

"You've been away a long time," he said, querulous.

"Yes, father," she said humbly.

"What do you want?" he asked, louder now but in a strangely distant tone, like the hollow echo of a voice. They seemed to be speaking across an abyss of time.

"Want?" she murmured, in fear. "I don't want anything except to see you." Still he shrank away from her, into his dark cloak. She had broken too ruthlessly into his isolation. And a blade-like gleam had shot into the blurred eyes, now more alertly suspicious.

"You chose to go away," he said in a hard repudiating way. "You kept away for twelve years."

"*Nine*," she faltered. "I had to go away. I . . . I was frightened, father."

"Of what?" he demanded as if angry.

She could see no sign of welcome or forgiveness in his face. Yet that shrinking away from her—she felt it was not repulsion but a dread. She did not reply to his question. On this cold staircase, with those women crouching below in the dark, how could she explain that instinct of self-preservation which she knew now had driven her?

"Of me?" he insisted raspingly.

"No, father."

"Of your stepsisters?"

"No," she replied in a strong, swift voice. "I think I was frightened for my life here . . . Father," she asked, shiveringly, "it's very cold, can't I come up to your room?"

Again that blade-like gaze of suspicion. It startled her, coming from this aged shrunken man with his waxen pallor. And his face yielded nothing of affection or parental interest. It was as though he was contained utterly in himself now. If there was dissolution in this man he would die secret and alone.

"What do you wish to see me about?" he asked, cunning.

She felt hopeless. But she replied, even with resentment: "There's nothing special, father . . . I've just come on a visit." All this drama of the afternoon was exhausting her. She began to feel an irritable need to curb it. But how could it be done in this house with those three women prowling about in frustrated malice!

"Come up, then," he said, abruptly. "I'm living in the tower now. Those stepsisters of yours nearly demented me with their greed. . . . That Kate," he exclaimed, loudly grumbling as they climbed the last stairs, "with her ever-lasting cigarette stuck to her lips, pah!—and forever trying to make me buy her a motor-car . . . and Marion," he fumed, swishing angrily across the landing to the narrow archway that led to the tower staircase, "bringing her witches here. . . . And Gwen wanting to buy a private hotel at the seaside. . . ." He swerved round on his heel, so that drops of candle-wax shook on to his hand, and snapped: "Sometimes I think I've fathered three vipers . . . Have they told you what they've been trying to do to me?" he demanded, drawing himself up in a sudden rage of arrogance, there at the archway.

"No, father. But they haven't welcomed my coming here at all. They tried to keep me from seeing you."

"Ah, did they!" A fevered glitter flickered into his eyes; the protruding cheek-bones jerked. "They've tried to get me put away!"

She stared. Now he watched her face keenly. "Put away?" she breathed.

"Yes . . . declared insane! So that they can get control of my money. . . . They've been to the doctors—*two!* Got me to see one by a trick, some bumptious young lout with the face of a fish and the brain of a flea." Thin laughter blew through his nostrils. "Ah, but they didn't know then they'd have to get a J.P.'s signed order. . . . I would have gone to Court and shown them up for what they are!" His voice rose to a hollow cry of rage: "My own daughters!" Then, with another shocking cry—"They would crucify me!"

She leaned against the wall. He stepped over to her, staring into her face. It was like some elemental examination of the soul. But still there was no parental emotion, no tenderness in his regard. Had he gone far beyond the domain of the emotions, into some naked world of his own where he stood appallingly alone?

"Your face is honest," he whispered. "Yet who can tell!"

There were footsteps on the staircase below, an approaching light. "Quick," he said; "she's coming——" He hurried to the curling upper staircase and scampered up it with surprising—and pitiable—agility. She followed. He put a key in a door, turning to her with a chuckle. "I never let them in here. They got so angry too." They went in. He shut the door and locked it. A minute later a can was dumped outside and Gwen's voice called in a carefully obedient tone: "Your oil, father. When do you want me to bring your supper?"

He called back: "Lay supper for us all in the dining-room. Light a fire there . . . You hear?"

There was a silence, then the startled voice: "In the dining-room? For us all?"

"Yes. Plates for five. I will come down at eight o'clock." Before getting the can in he listened carefully to the retreating footsteps.

She looked round the square whitewashed room with its narrow mock-castle window in each wall. A small iron bedstead, scrupulously tidy and thick with blankets, stood in a corner. On a round table the oil lamp was becoming dim. There was one chair, a small desk littered with papers and a few books, an oil heater, and a tawny old-fashioned tin trunk which she recognised as the one he used to say had gone with him to London in 1895. She did not greet the aged-looking green parrot dozing, its weary plumage without gloss, in a cage on a stool in another corner. There were two pictures on the walls; one was a photograph of a graveyard memorial—a block of granite and a broken column—the other, in a thick dusty gold frame, an enlarged photograph of a chemist shop with a Victorian-looking façade. Both photographs were familiar to her; they used to hang in the drawing-room. While he took in the can and, after locking the door again, filled the heater, she stood gazing in the fading light at the chemist shop picture.

"About a year ago," she said, carefully conversational, "I passed that shop. I was visiting a friend at Hampstead. It's got the same front but it sells old china and foreign stamps now." She was determined, as far as she was concerned, to try and keep this meeting on a level ordinary plane. She had had enough for one day.

"Oh?" he said, interested. "The same front? Ah, I

should like to go to London and see that quarter again——"
But he shook his head. "Now the lamp. Shall have to put
the light out first——" He extinguished it, and in the red
and yellow glow of the heater lifted the can with thin—oh,
so tremblingly thin and white—fingers.

"Let me do it, father." She went to the table. Her heart
had begun to ache again. She couldn't bear this bleak
isolation, this awful lonely withdrawal into himself that the
room signified.

"I can do it—don't interfere!" he said fiercely.

"The district round there," she resumed, steadying her
voice, "has got very shabby. It's almost working-class now.
It wasn't like that in your time, was it?"

"It was a carriage-and-pair district!" he said proudly.

He relit the wick and turned it up. The light grew gently
in the dazzlingly polished funnel. There!" he chuckled.
"I do like a clear bright light. I always trim the wick . . .
You remember the parable of the Foolish Virgins?" The
light grew to a satiny brilliance. He gave a pleased chuckle
at its radiance. "Those three daughters of mine;" he went
on—"ah, I'll teach them a lesson yet!"

He lifted his head. Across the table he looked at her
with an old alertness. But she saw death in his face.

Chapter Two

I

WITHIN three hours the house had been transformed.
Laura went down the staircase into a yellow blaze of light
and the welcome of fires lit in rooms seldom used. The
word had gone forth. The prodigal daughter had returned.
Doors were open, bedsheets airing, a delicious smell of
cooking penetrated into the hall—was it from the boiled
ham and morello cherry pie which they had debated?
Already the wakened house glowed.

It was the announcement two hours ago that her friend Alex was arriving that had galvanised her stepsisters into activity. The extraordinary event set the domestic warfare in abeyance. After obtaining her father's permission to invite him, Laura had descended from the tower-room to the telephone and persuaded the inn people to bring him and her suitcase in their car. He arrived half an hour later. Marion was delegated to entertain him while the household preparations proceeded.

From the drawing-room her voice, a little cracked but still stylish and obviously trained, began—*"Gaze not on swans——"* The door was ajar; Laura walked in gravely. Her stepsister was seated at her grand piano—dressed in a wonderful flowing pink gown with faint silver rays, old-fashioned and romantic. Laura blinked a moment half amused, half admiring.

> *"Gaze not on swans in whose soft breast*
> *A full-hatched beauty seems to nest,*
> *Nor snow which, falling from the sky,*
> *Hovers in its virginity——"*

Alex sat in one of the shell-backed arm-chairs, listening with an air of comfortable courtesy, his round moony face placid. It seemed plain that the two had not jarred each other. But Alex could usually placate and amuse women; they found agreeable his aroma of insidious, rather decrepit non-moral ease blended with the faint but comfortable reek of an upbringing nourished on the beef, port and horsiness of upper-class Old England. The last male representative of an old war-ruined Kent family, he had rescued a little money from the crash.

"Charming . . . How these old airs soothe the nerves!" He looked at Laura and, though his tongue did not exactly hang out of his mouth, she felt an urge to bring a bowl of water.

"Is there sherry or something in the house, Marion?" she asked, with an effort.

Marion swished round on the piano stool, the pink and silver rays flowing iridescent. "We *think* that father still has a lot of bottles in the cellar. But we told you he keeps the door locked. Two padlocks as well! . . . Yes, yes, Dora; thank you," she murmured over her shoulder, and then to Alex, like a moth to the male visitor—"My guide likes that song too. . . . You must ask father when he comes down, Laura. He carries the keys with him."

Into Alex's eyes came a brief greenish flicker. With his Elizabethan kind of gusto for sombre histories he was scenting drama in this hag-ridden house. He had met the three sisters on his arrival. But their father had not yet come down. When Mansell walked into the drawing-room a few minutes later the guest rose and made his greetings, a man of the world meeting someone perfectly ordinary.

"You assist Laura in her work, I understand. Please make yourself as comfortable as you can and stay with us a while, if you will. My daughters here need company."

But the haggard white-haired man's delicately deranged eyes looked unseeing. His voice came in quick, frail jerks, the thin nervous hands were restless as his glances. He wore a black cut-away jacket, a not quite clean collar and wispy tie, and baggy sponge trousers.

Laura was moved by these efforts to dress for this occasion. But when he sat on the edge of a chair, it was as if he was ready for instant flight. He seemed a man possessed, a man who harbours against demonish assaults what tattered inner resources remained. He also looked a man whose total flesh had been scorched away in some cataclysm of the spirit. Watching from under her lids, she saw that Alex, beyond his composure, was impressed.

"Father, is there some sherry or something?" At his entrance Marion had silently drooped a little on the piano stool, an autumnal flower on the turn to decay.

"Yes, yes, of course . . . But I will have to fetch it." With a crafty gesture he felt in his jacket pocket and hurried out. At his disappearance Marion at once fluttered into life. She left the room murmuring something about glasses.

"She's gone to the kitchen to tell Kate and Gwen this further item of news. You see, Alex, he had entirely cut himself off from their lives—denies them all but the bare necessities."

"He looks ill," Alex said. "But I imagine he wouldn't admit it."

"What kind of illness do you mean?" she asked uneasily.

"I don't know. But I suspect a—a clot isn't it called? Something that moves to the brain and obliterates . . . My poor Laura, was it awful for you when you arrived?"

"My stepsisters wanted to turn me out before I saw him. . . . Of course," she added, as if ashamed, "they're completely unbalanced by their lives in this lonely house. They never see anyone. I'm afraid to-night is not going to be very pleasant or easy——"

"They're very much alive, Laura. . . . Family life," he sighed—"what horror it can contain! But it's fascinating," he mused. "There's an elemental squalor in family life which I find fascinating."

This slightly irritated Laura. Though she had wanted such detachment, had called on him in fear of being blindly swept into an emotional storm, his comment seemed cold-blooded, even offensive. There was great suffering in this house.

"I've hurt you," he said, with that curiously quick sensitivity to atmospherics often possessed by people well-endowed with flesh. And he began to squirm, his lips moving soundlessly, his greenish eyes unhappy. He began to stammer: "I think it's bad for you to be here. One should never deliberately resurrect the past. You don't belong here any more, Laura."

"Leave my father to those women! In his condition!" The gleam of her eyes became menacing. "I don't wonder I kept feeling I ought to return."

"I can see now that you've always been conscious of

your father. You only broke away physically . . . But I imagine your stepsisters couldn't do even that."

Marion came in with six glasses and a corkscrew on a tray. "Kate wants to know," she said, "if Mr. Gregory brought any cigarettes from the village."

"I've brought two hundred."

"Let her have ten," Laura said shrewishly.

He took out a gold case—a presentation from one of his rich friends in recognition of an accomplished bit of match-making very advantageous to one of the parties—and obediently counted out ten. Marion hurried with them to the kitchen. She returned saying: "Gwen's just gone up to change. Now we shan't be long. . . . We can't get servants to stay in such an isolated house," she explained easily to Alex.

She had left the door open. Across the hall a door slammed, a key was turned . . . and then the sound of two *clicks*.

Mansell came in carrying a couple of bottles. "Here is sherry, and a bottle of sloe gin. You will kindly open them, sir? . . . Marion, I've left two bottles of claret in the hall. Take them into the dining-room; they need to be slightly warmed." He had become more focused on the necessity of being host.

But he would not drink. Laura and Alex took gin, good glassfuls. The three sisters, when presently they entered together in a carefully arranged trio, took sherry. Kate looked impatiently drab in an ill-fitting brown dress; the silver buckle of one shoe was missing. She seemed like some great cat fuming interiorly and determined not to be approached. But Gwen, long gipsy-like pendants swinging from her ears, was superb in her flamingo red and old gold though the dress proclaimed a splendour long gone. And her fine carriage gave her an air of repose; no one would have thought she had been cooking for an hour and a domestic upheaval had gone through the house. Marion, in her carnival pink and silver, took on an air of increased confidence as she fluttered between her sisters. It was Laura, in the soft pale dress she had changed into after Alex's arrival with her suitcase, who began to look a little cancelled out as the trio of women spread themselves, mistresses of this drawing-room. The father sat as if unaware of the atmosphere of a dark festival.

Alex chattered nobly. It seemed that he had once spent four days snow-bound in a hut in Switzerland; the recital took on the epic quality of North Pole or Everest sufferings. Kate turned on him her eye of a sceptical tomcat; she helped herself to another sherry—it was evidently a treat—lit one cigarette from the other and at length deliberately put her hand down the loose opening of her dress and, yawning, scratched her back.

Yet she, like her two sisters, concentrated on Alex. He was an escape. They avoided looking at their father; only their stepsister glanced at him now and again as he sat withdrawn across the chasm separating him from other beings.

Gwen, with babbling aid from Marion, kept Alex's tongue on the move. "You've travelled a great deal?" she asked, stretching her fine throat as she took a sip of sherry. "Tell me, would you recommend Bruges for a holiday?"

"I would prefer Venice——" began Alex stoutly.

But in the dining-room, with the ponderous mahogany table laden with florid crockery, the brocaded curtains drawn against the snowy night, a log fire burning, oil paintings smokily black in their gold-crusted frames, claret in the glasses, and a simple but excellently cooked meal smoothly produced by the capable Gwen, the father's attention returned. His four daughters were breaking bread on either side of him. A gentlemanly guest was present.

"Do you believe in the Devil, sir?" he suddenly addressed Alex. "That is, do you find he is a power on earth and takes possession of certain persons in order to work here?"

"Oh yes," Alex replied at once. "I met him quite

recently. In a Regent's Park house. I had a distinct feeling that I was shaking hands with the Devil—or at least with one of his protean shapes. I've always thought that every wise person must be on the watch for these meetings."

"*I*," Mansell said, "saw him in Hampstead once. Afterwards, in a music-hall, I met one of his dependants——" He ruminated furtively for a moment, seemed about to proceed, but kept silent. The three sisters glanced at each other. Laura sat blankly, but fidgeted a little.

"When I was presented to him in Regent's Park," Alex said, taking salt, "he had just arrived from Germany. He gave me the impression of being one of those flitting, mysteriously international figures who look so respectable and economical in a Ritz kind of way . . . Flitting about sowing international mischief. But for all the evil in his eye he showed a great reverence for architecture and was much taken with the formation of a society for preserving England's building treasures; I gathered he was prepared to start with a generous donation. A most cultured and intelligent man; he showed every sign of possessing the good taste that so often goes with bad morals." He added judiciously: "It did occur to me, though, that he was only trying to show up God, who of course is so preoccupied with religious problems that He has little time for art."

Mansell leaned forward in lively attention. "But you must remember that God—if one believes in His existence——" he writhed a little, "created the universe—surely the first work of art?"

"Yes, yes—in His young loving days, before He began to preach. But we must not forget that He left the world in quite a raw state, so to speak, and it was man who hewed out of a block of God's crude stone the Venus of Milo."

Laura began to think this conversation totally random and erratic, passes in the dark. She knew Alex could turn on most of the conversation taps, but she was suspicious of this flow to-night. He seemed to be playing up to her father's disordered interests. . . . Yet, wasn't the old man roused into warmth and attention, wasn't he eased of this hateful obsession with his daughters?

"I think," Mansell said, as if tormented himself by this, "that you are a man with faith only in the absolutism of the earth? Animalism. That otherwise we are nothing?" His blurred eyes shone. "*Nothing*," he repeated, a hollow echo of anguish in his voice.

"Animalism? Oh no, no," Alex protested. "I believe that we are hunted by forces of good and evil that struggle for possession of us, and if we are truly alive we become acutely aware of these forces. And I believe too that we've all got to travel a road of mortification—and alone. And that everyone possesses a private little hell inside themselves." His head lolled back and forth mournfully, his loose insecure-looking mouth became pursed; for a moment he seemed to peer inwardly into his own little hell. "It is these private little hells that make up the total evil of the world. They're like tributaries, myriads of turbulent little streams of black bile running out and forming a great black central river. But now and again a man or a woman learns how to shut up their little hell and not impose it on the world or their neighbours. These are the true saints, the great warriors." And, laying down his glass after a mouthful of claret, he added solemnly: "When I've seen that hideous black river I could weep. I could weep and sit down in hopeless lamentation by those evil waters. . . . People's hatred of each other, individual and racial! They *want* the river, they *want* to see mass drownings in it. They want death, death, death."

Kate, who had continued to smoke during the meal despite a vehement frown from her father, gazed at Alex with a remote derision. Gwen's heavy grey eyes, coarse-speckled, were fixed on him in a sort of humbug of feminine salutation to the male. Only Marion looked as if she wished to interpose some prattle; once she murmured over her shoulder to her spiritual adviser. Laura seemed gone into some cloudy reservation of her own.

Their father held them in subjection. But now he suddenly turned on his three daughters ranged one side of the table—they had placed themselves together there—so that Laura felt a sick terror run through her again.

"You hear, you three? Have you listened to this gentleman? The road of mortification! You've got to travel it, and alone. Why do you try to drag me along with you? I have my own road. Why do you try and drag me into your hells?" Ammoniacally bleak, he barked out the last question startlingly.

Kate turned away her face in contempt. Gwen's grained eyes hardened: she flung down her napkin on the table. But Marion, with her air of harbouring an extra-terrestial advantage, sang: "Well, father, speaking for myself, I deny that I have a private little hell inside me. Remember," she careered on, "that I have the help of the spirit world——"

"Bah, you and your witches!" he interrupted rudely. He turned to Alex again: "I find the conceit of spiritualists shocking. And when you're not fools they're cowards. They turn their backs on this world or else pretend its problems can be solved by slipping their heads for a while into the spirit world—the modern ostrich." He seemed more normal now.

But Marion's toughness swung up through her flutterings. She would *not* be beaten down like this. Alex's opening mouth closed again as she swept on: "Don't you wish, father, you had my peace of mind? I think too it's vulgar of you to call me a witch. When I go to Mrs. Matthews for a séance we have Christian hymns, prayers and everything." Like a daring little girl putting out her tongue, she finished: "I expect it will surprise you to know that my guide Dora has been down into the cellar and told me what you've got there."

His eyes narrowed. "Well, what have I got there?" he flung, sneeringly.

"I won't be bullied into telling you," Marion tossed her head.

"Are you a father, sir?" Mansell turned terribly to Alex.

"No," Alex shook his head, smooth of face as if such a scene as this was in no way unusual. And before Mansell could say more he proceeded: "I am in favour of the spirit world's attention to our wants. It seems to be full of advisers, domestic servants, secretaries, nurses and doctors. I once knew a spiritualist who owned a faithful retinue of eight of these, though over here she could never keep a servant for very long. They were mixed of nationality but ever ready to help my acquaintance in this difficult world. One presumes they are very idle and bored over there."

Kate could no longer contain herself. "Have we finished?" she demanded, and, without waiting for a reply, bundled herself out of the room. Imposing, with a basilisk mien, Gwen followed. But Marion, lightly brushing a chiffon handkerchief over her corsage, got up quite elegantly and said: "Coffee will be waiting in the drawing-room."

Laura rose with an effort; she did not want to go.

"Stay, Laura, if you wish," her father said. He still fumed, his arched nose quiveringly sharp.

She sank back. She had been appalled by his outburst against her stepsisters, had even felt sorry for them. . . . But she realised again that he could no longer accept the ordinary traffic of family domesticity; he had attained some ruthless vision that made it impossible. Glancing at Alex, who was drinking the last of the second bottle of claret, she saw he was not a whit disturbed. He had behaved beautifully. She was grateful for his unruffled steering of the uncomfortable dinner.

"I will leave you presently," her father announced querulously; "I am going to my room. Laura, is there anything you wish to ask me?"

"Won't you come to the drawing-room with us and sit by the fire?" she pleaded. That dreadful tower-room with its oil heater, half-dead parrot and shut-up air! And he had eaten so abstemiously, drinking only a little water.

"You are no longer frightened of your stepsisters? You have your friend with you."

"Frightened of them?" she said, sharply. "Why, father, if I were, I think it would be best to face them."

He ignored this. "Sir," he turned to Alex, again obsessively, "my three daughters tried to get me declared insane. Do I strike you as being in that condition?"

At which Alex was at last confounded. All he could reply was a subdued, embarrassed: "No, no."

But Mansell was satisfied. He nodded and resumed with rather more quietude: "I must own that their conduct sometimes drove me to such anger that they were made spiteful. Your devil in Regent's Park! I have three she-devils under this very roof." Rising from the table, he cried: "But, who knows? they may be tribulations meant to cleanse me. . . . Laura," he turned fretfully, "how long are you going to stay home?"

"I don't know, father," she replied miserably. "I have no work at present."

"Do you want money?" he asked, arrested; perhaps steadied by a reminder of something material.

"No. I have just finished a very good engagement. I earned thirty pounds a week for eight months."

"Ah yes; you told me you were on the stage. Strange, strange—I should never think you had followed in your mother's footsteps; you are so different from her. Her singing voice was deep and full, before she ruined it with drink and it became stringy. . . . You're not inclined to drink, Laura?" he asked, parental for the first time since her return, if only vaguely. "There was a shocking amount of drinking and loose living on the stage in her day." Standing half musing, half attentive, he had spoken of his second wife as if she were wholly a distant recollection banished from his judgment.

"The stage is less spectacular now, father," Laura said. "I've even met actors and actresses who are strict vegetarians."

G

"But divorces are very common now, are they not?" Again he looked at her distantly, cut off yet fumbling. "You must have had your divorce very quickly after your marriage."

She was silent. Her plump small hand—it was one of those hands that proclaim a blind kindness, a perpetual giving out—ran her napkin ring back and forth.

Alex drank his last drop of claret. "Far too common," he said with some pomposity. "But divorce saved *me* from a fate worse than death."

"Are you two sweethearts?" he asked, startlingly. Again it was as though he appeared briefly out of his private, cut-off world, focusing for a moment on something concrete, but impatient to be gone again.

"No, father," Laura said at once.

"I would like to marry Laura," Alex said. "But Laura doesn't see eye to eye with me," he mourned.

His mind set on flight, her father backed a step or two towards the door. Yet still that fumbling held him; as if he waited to be released from some shock or paralysis. "I thought perhaps you were coming home for good, Laura. But you have your career, you will probably get married again, perhaps to this gentleman." As far as he was capable of identifying himself with activities beyond his obsessions it seemed clear he approved of Alex, unless it was only relief that a male element had arrived in the house. He went on: "You must not stay if it is too uncomfortable for you here. Your stepsisters rule the house, unfortunately." Was this terrible distance his punishment for her flight? She had bowed her head. "They have a great deal of power, the three of them together," he rambled on, his eyes beginning to gleam. "They want to destroy me. I cannot be responsible for what they might do to you. I cannot intrude"—he had got nearer the door—"I am too old!" he cried, fury beating up in his voice. "All my strength is needed to preserve myself against them." He opened the door.

She lifted her head. "I am not to see you again to-night, father?"

"What?" He paused, testy—"No. I need a great deal of rest."

"Can't I come to your room later on?" she pleaded.

He stood half turned in the doorway. Once more it was as though something struggled for awareness in his mind. And suddenly he looked furtive, his head gave a ducking movement, he seemed to shrink in stature, there in the doorway with the yellow hall light behind him. And, in a blinding flash, she saw that he *could* not give way and continue to live. A colossal effort of will was upholding him. If he gave way, broke down, it would be the final debacle. She had a nightmare vision of him crumbling physically and mentally, a total collapse of his faculties. And she wanted to go to him, press him against her bosom, flood him with her strength, let him bathe in the warmth of her blood. Across the room she stared at him. She half rose from her chair at the table, but sank back.

He had fled, leaving the door open.

Alex closed it. She blindly pushed her arms on the table, clattering the dishes and upsetting some fruit juice so that a red stain spread on the lace cloth; she laid her head unseeing on her arms, weeping. Alex stood with his lips moving soundlessly; his moony face seemed empty. He stood, apparently very controlled, even placid. Presently he said: "Of course he's dying, Laura."

"Yes," she moaned.

" 'They want to destroy me,' he said . . . The brood devouring the parent." His head lolled musingly. Then he added: "What has he done to deserve it?"

She looked up, startled. Her dilated eyes rested on him in intent enquiry. But Marion, opening the door, called with a hostessy composure: "Aren't you coming? The coffee is getting cold."

They followed her across the hall. Far away upstairs a door slammed.—"Father has returned to his room," Marion remarked. "I suppose he will be going down into the cellar presently . . . I do wish he wouldn't behave so peculiarly," she addressed Alex. "It makes it very trying for me and my sisters, but a visitor must think him mad. I expect you found him quite eccentric?"

"I have seen a great deal of eccentricity in my time," he boomed. "Families are rarely without it. In fact I think normality almost mythical."

Marion tittered. They were entering the drawing-room. "Still," she insisted, "it was exhausting for us all just now. To soothe us shall I play the piano? Sing? . . . Perhaps Laura," she put her head on one side, "will oblige with something from her stage repertoire."

"No," Laura scowled, going to a low stool near the fire.

Always the active one, Gwen sat embroidering peonies on a cushion cover; she smiled welcomingly at Alex. Kate, her buckleless shoe kicked off, sprawled in the big arm-chair. Perhaps Gwen had scolded her on her manner to Alex, for she asked him for a cigarette with less animosity. Marion poured two cups of coffee—"I don't think you take sugar, Laura? Are you alarmed of becoming fat?" Alex said he liked a fug, hot fires and no ventilation. The room was all that and he settled himself comfortably.

There, in the orbit of her stepsisters, Laura looked diminished; Alex noticed it interestedly. "Three baleful harpies," his eyes sent a message across to her, while his manner conveyed: "They are wonderful." He seldom retreated from the horrors of the twisted, earth-bound psyche. It was only under the influence of drugs that he was liable to indignant moral outburst. Now he made sociable enquiries about local life, showed deep interest in this countryside devoted to sheep and wool; he praised a Victorian water-colour hanging in a mother-of-pearl frame against the wallpaper of peacocks and chrysanthemums. He spread an air of domestic felicity.

Marion and Gwen kept him going; Kate, inscrutable, smoked. Laura sat crouched and silent before the fire.

When she slowly looked round into the big room it was as though she saw it as an interior behind glass where she could not penetrate; even Alex was removed into its dimension. Vaguely she saw Gwen go to the window and, a strong-flanked woman in her preposterous evening gown, lift a fold of the heavy plush curtain—"The moon makes the snow blue," she remarked, pensive. "I pity anyone without warmth and comfort to-night." Laura shuddered.

"I must go and water my daffodils," Gwen added. Passing Alex she showed her moist dentures: "My bulbs— I give them a nightcap . . . Kate, shall we clear the supper things now or later?"

"Now," Kate grunted. Hulking herself forward, glad to go, she went out with Gwen.

Marion sang 'The Rosary' at the piano, stopping half-way and swinging round with a pout: "But my voice is so weak now! Do you know, Mr. Gregory, I would have had quite a rich voice if I hadn't been weaned too early."

Laura laughed then. Her stepsister's eyes swerved on her frostily. It had always been Marion's complaint that her lack of Gwen and Kate's robustiousness was due to the fact that her mother did not provide her with nature's provender.

"You can laugh, Laura. We haven't all got your vulgar health."

"You've got vulgarity on the brain," Laura sniffed crudely. "Don't be silly, Marion; you were singing quite attractively—though I see you're still too much of a lady to drop your jaw as low as possible. In singing a voice must come *out*, you know! . . . Out, out."

Marion looked appealingly towards the door, as if to cry for her sisters. Since they had left the room, as Alex noticed, Laura had regained potency. It was Gwen she really feared: Gwen of the solid physique, the strong-lidded eyes, the smooth voice lurking blandly in the fine throat. Kate, for all her over-riding masculinity, seemed too much riddled by interior contradictions, too much at the mercy of her own temper, to possess much real danger.

"I'm not going to stay here to be insulted." Marion jumped off the stool. But even her fury was artificial, a bravura piece; she struck a pose as, preparing to swish her skirts to the door, she said: "I see, Laura, that going on the stage hasn't refined you."

"Don't you wish you had gone on the stage yourself?" jeered Laura before the door slammed. She fumed: "She was always the most maddening of them. . . . These fluffy women with the insides of bears!" But her own temper was giving her keen satisfaction. Her short, rather thick nose looked truculent.

This smack delivered, she returned to her reverie at the fireside, barely aware of Alex. He watched her as she sat crouched over the fire, her fingers vaguely combing her black crop of hair. Closed from him. He couldn't bear it.

His voice complained. "Laura, how different you are here. I suppose you are harking back to your childhood with them—resuming where you left off?" She seemed to pay no attention to this, and he went on insidiously: "They might overcome you again if I wasn't here. You agree now that I was quite right not to allow you to take this trip alone? No wonder my feet followed you with such instinctive urgency to Paddington station this morning."

"I suppose so," she murmured, far away. The wintry earth-sleep outside, moon-glazed, snow-quiet, sealed the house.

"I wonder have your impressive stepsisters left us alone intentionally? If so, how considerate of them."

She started. A door slammed upstairs. Then another, louder. Footsteps pattered. Again a slam. Still another! The house jerked with brief interior rousings, before closing again into the silence lying in thick whiteness outside, where the distant marble hills were frozen and the jagged sea lay in the moonlight like smashed ice. A last slam shivered down the walls.

"Are they preparing our beds?" Alex asked. "I like the thought of Gwen turning back my quilt with those

strong Lady Macbeth hands of hers . . . I can see Marion
fussing with hot-water bottles too; she's sweet."

"They seem to want us to go to bed," she murmured.

"Not yet," he said anxiously. "I can't sleep yet." The
whimpering was seeping back into his voice; his body
began to move restlessly. "I want to go upstairs for a
handkerchief," he whined, with a great air of telling the truth.

She swerved from the fire. "You behave yourself here!"
she warned darkly. But he was getting up. He went to the
door, but half turned to say, reproachfully: "You could
stop this if you liked." He had said it fifty times before.

She made an impatient movement, turning her back on
him. He went out. Relapsed into her dream, she did not
know how long she was left alone.

2

Again she started. There was a series of light thumping
sounds overhead. It stopped for a moment or two and was
resumed. It was like a carpet being tacked down in the
room above. The door opened and Gwen came in. She
left the door ajar.

"What is that noise?" Laura asked.

"Marion with her table-tapping. She gets extra messages
from the spirits that way . . . I saw Mr. Gregory going
into the bathroom. Will he wish to go to bed now? . . .
We keep country hours here," she placed Laura in the
status of a guest. "Your room is quite ready. I've put the
hot-water bottle into your bed." A tiny smile came and
went. But her attention seemed to stray back into the hall.

"We won't be going up yet; it's only half-past nine. Alex
keeps late hours."

"He *is* a lover of yours, of course?"

Laura watched her out of the corner of her eye. Gwen,
the teasing smile on her lips, was now hovering much too
close. The gold lace on her long fine arms hung metal stiff.

From the gown came a lavender odour, mingled with the faint warm odour of flesh.

But it was hawthorn blossom Laura smelled; again she breathed that odour which years ago impregnated this woman's strong breasts. Her eyes travelled down to the hands. They were the hands of a person who labours in the fields; there was something atavistic in their sinewy power, the large chill nails the colour of a dead cod's eye, the veins like thick mauve cords. Her hands annulled her handsomeness in the worn magnificent gown. Laura gave one glance at them and, very still, looked away. She turned her back on her stepsister's hovering face with its little smile.

But, through the persistent tapping overhead, she heard the heavy exhalations from that nose, aquiline like her father's.

"You are frightened of me, aren't you? That's why you brought your lover here."

"He is not my lover. I am not frightened of you. But I think you're an unpleasant woman." She spoke with a stilted calculation as if dreading her voice would falter.

"I daresay. You encourage something unpleasant in me." A laugh lurked down her voice. "I quite missed you after you'd run off—you coward. I found myself wishing you'd come back." Her breathing was louder.

"Oh, go away," Laura snapped; "leave me alone."

Gwen laughed openly. She moved to the piano and, collecting Marion's music-sheets into a neat pile, said: "Do you think you can resume any sort of place in this house now—though you never had a strong position here, did you!—*now*, when you're completely out of things? . . . And in any case you haven't got the brains or the stamina to deal with us."

"Does it infuriate you that father welcomed me?" Laura flounced. "But that's an unnecessary question, isn't it!"

"Father has no use for you." She shut the keyboard. "He's only seen you like a ghost or something, a shadow.

. . . Of course, he vaguely recognises you as his daughter and feels you should be given accommodation. But to-morrow he'll have forgotten you are here."

But Laura had jumped up. "I know more than you think," she almost shouted. "I know how cruel you are to him." Yet even to herself her statement seemed meaningless. The specific acts of cruelty had small importance in themselves—and he was capable of dealing with them. "*Why* do you torture him?" she cried tremblingly.

"How little you know!" Gwen paused, looking round the room for further tasks, not a whit affected by the outburst. "You're just a sentimental little idiot, as you always were." With bland generosity she added: "But, after all, how could you know about *his* cruelty to my mother, to take one instance? He's been quite a wicked man, has our father, quite a wicked man." She emptied an ash-tray into the fire. The overhead tapping stopped and was not resumed.

Laura shrank. She wanted to run out of the room. Even out of the house: for ever. They were so terribly in possession. Like the clawed, serpent-haired Gorgons, the three sisters held the house with their united malice. She watched in horror Gwen shake out a cushion and place it in diamond-shape solidity against a chair-back.

"So don't interfere where you've no business or understanding." She pricked up her ears, then smiled. "It's Mr. Gregory," she said, and, as Alex came in a minute later: "Well, Mr. Gregory, has your long journey tired you?"

Laura saw at once that he had taken a drug.

"To what long journey do you refer, Miss Gwen?" he wagged a finger. "The journey from the womb to death? If so, yes I am tired. But if you mean the one from Paddington station to your comfortable abode, certainly not. I hope to enjoy the pleasure of your company a few further hours yet. Where are your sisters? They have not deserted us, surely?"

Gwen listened to this with perfect serenity. She even folded him in a smile. "I was referring to the railway journey,

G*

Mr. Gregory. My sisters have gone up to their rooms; they asked me to say good-night to you. It is my turn to keep watch to-night." She reopened the door, which he had closed, and left it ajar.

"To keep watch, Miss Gwen?" There was a beady simmering in his eyes. "Your turn? But isn't life one long damnable keeping watch? On your money, your horse, your wife, your stomach, even your virtue. Haven't you ever sat down and realised that except in sleep one is never released from watching? The strain of it!"

"More reason for plenty of sleep then, surely." A calm roguishness tucked away in her face, she opened the glass of the marble clock and gave the key several vigorous turns. "I understand you are a man of leisure, Mr. Gregory. Were you born in the purple?"

"A mildewed purple, Miss Gwen. The moth had got in it before it was folded round this baby. . . . Won't you sit and have a little chat?" He took from his waistcoat pocket a small paper sachet, professionally folded. "Would you care for one of these? I think I can spare one," he said, the pang in his voice making the generosity more beautiful. "You won't get on the high-horse about it?" he asked with a rapid change to entreaty. "Like Laura does."

Laura, shrugging her shoulders, looked away hopelessly. Gwen asked, smiling: "What is it?"

"A scrap of magic. You inhale it into your nose like snuff. So much cleaner and simpler than drink, soaking oneself in vile liquors like swine at a trough, coarsely blowing oneself out with fermenting poisons. It's my only effeminacy; I agree with you it's more prevalent among women . . . You won't take it?" He sounded relieved; he had no idea how long he would be marooned in this strange house.

"A drug?" Gwen still smiled. "Yes, I'll try it." She took the white sachet.

"Do you realise it's cocaine?" said Laura idly, but staring in surprise.

"Hold your tongue, Laura," scolded Alex. "You're far too puritanic about drugs. You think like a policewoman sometimes . . . Sniff it up, Gwen. Off the back of your hand . . . Don't spill it!" he cried shrilly.

She didn't spill it. She inhaled every particle. Was she accustomed to it, Laura thought, was this one of her secrets? Marion with her escape into the spirit world, Kate with her seventy cigarettes a day (and what else!) . . . but was it possible that the composed, housewifely Gwen felt the need of such releases? And where would she get drugs here? That doctor! Hadn't he been agreeable to signing a declaration of her father's insanity? How much further was this doctor identified with the house?

"Lie down on the sofa, my dear, and take a perfect rest. Or will the drug make you garrulous? One can never tell. I'm afraid *I* get garrulous, at my stage."

Laura glanced at him quickly. The fool, to say that! She had begun to speculate on his real intention.

"I won't get garrulous and I don't need to lie down." She sat on the edge of a straight-backed chair near the door, the sinewy hands clasped on her knees. Looking statuesque.

Alex, with a preamble about the agreeable effects and conduct drugs caused, launched into an anecdote. One week-end in the 'twenties he was staying at an inn on the upper Thames which had become a haunt of elegant riff-raff of London and Oxford. At dinner the most spectacular guest had been a highly painted woman wearing a white satin gown and diamonds. She was of uncertain age, but her hilarious group of friends of both sexes were all young——

"All the guests went out on the lawn that perfect summer night. You know, dear Gwen, how the river flows so still on those tranquil nights, with the red of sunset on the water . . . one could weep! Willow herb fringed the bank, I could just see a field of poppies on the slope beyond the water meadows. In a niche of the black yew hedge was a Venus, done in the modern style, thick-faced, ponderous, of limb. The innkeeper, poor fellow, was an awful drunkard; his car crashed into a tree a year later, just after the inn went bankrupt—all the guests used to use the till in the bar themselves——"

Laura sighed. She had heard this one before but not so long-windedly. Gwen sat quite still, betraying nothing of her thoughts.

"Well, sitting there musing on the lawn I wanted to go to the Gents. There was a little bricked nook at the back, just outside the public bar where the local farm labourers still got their pints. It was empty. But I had barely got inside when the lady in white satin came sweeping in, her diamonds flashing. Of course I pretended not to notice, but I couldn't help seeing this person pick up those satin skirts and show every right to use the place. . . . He spat, as men often do in those places, and remarked to me quite gruffly: 'Denis might spare a drop of disinfectant here.'"

Laura lit a cigarette and smoked with an impatient air. Gwen smiled composedly but made no comment. Wagging his finger, Alex resumed:

"I was not surprised to find that man had been a warrior of Vimy Ridge. Rank of Major. His name was quite well known to me; I joined his party after the little incident. He took drugs, and under the influence he had a remarkable talent for dressing up in women's clothes. His wife told me that several times he had deceived even her. Once he dressed himself like an Edwardian princess, got the loan of an open barouche and coachman and drove through Piccadilly to the Royal Academy under a parasol and a hat crammed with sweet peas."

It was then that Gwen laughed outright, and enjoyably. "How very interesting," she gurgled in her throat.

There was a slight intensity in her voice, a delicate flush in her cheeks. She unscrewed her long decorative earrings and let them drop into her lap. Laura sat looking aloof. But she was aware that the flow of bland malignity from her stepsister had somehow ceased. "It's hot in this room," Gwen proceeded, unbuttoning the top hooks at the back of her gown and easing her fine bosom. But she preserved her calm poise, sitting on the chair's edge. Laura began to frown and to look more sedate. "Hush!" Gwen said, holding up her hand. "He's coming down, poor father."

Laura could hear nothing. Gwen slowly, calmly, rose and put out the Aladdin oil lamp under its parchment shade. The log fire gave a dull glow. She closed the door until only a chink showed, and came back into the room.

"Why does he have to go down into that cold cellar?" she mourned. "Laura, you had better look."

Alex got up with pursed lips. Laura dragged herself up unwillingly and peered through the chink. The hall light was still burning.

Her father walked—he seemed to glide noiselessly—down the hall-passage beyond the staircase. He carried a candle and wore a sort of sack with a girdle round the waist. She saw something pale move beneath the hem—his feet were bare! His white hair glistened; again at sight of it her pulses raced. There was something so desperately lonely about his figure. He turned a key in the inset door of the panelling enclosing the staircase, unlocked the two padlocks, and disappeared. The door shut quietly but there was the scrape of a turning key. He had not once looked round. There had been nothing furtive in the procedure. It was ten o'clock.

"Now will you believe he's mad?" Gwen said to her, sorrowfully.

"No. But he's ill." She felt a weary depression, as if indeed she could cope no longer.

"I would say," Alex said, in a pompous way, "he feels an urge towards some sort of repentance."

"I hope so," said Gwen, adding sensibly: "But why conceal himself down there? It's such a worry for us. We can't settle for the night till we know he has gone down. Anyone would think he deliberately tries to upset us." The grieving mildness of this complaint seemed genuine. "I must go and tell my sisters now," she added. "Good night." And without further delay she went out, erect and preoccupied, closing the door softly.

"Why did you give her that drug?" Laura demanded angrily.

"Give her, give her?" he parried. "She *took* it . . . A grand woman," he swept aside her impatience. "I was filled with admiration . . . Her lovely old dress, her ear-rings— oh, how she wanted to spread a peacock's tail. My heart bled for her, yes, bled. . . . As for you," he taunted— "how could you understand her! You with your passion for that trumpery Hugh of yours and your anæmic cinema soul, bah!"

These abusive attacks were familiar. It was useless trying to deal with them. (He had protested after one of them—"In drugs is truth.")

"Can't you see I want to be a saviour?" he bustled on. "And even you must have noticed how the drug humanised her. The strain she's been living under in this house! Perhaps she's gone so far in suffering that only drugs will save her now. So don't belittle them, you self-righteous little puritan."

He was trying to bait her into a scene. And she wanted no more. She rose to go to bed. But her movements had the ominousness of controlled wrath.

"I suppose," he jeered, "you see yourself as the heroine here? Your stepsisters as villainesses? *I* don't see it like that at all. I think your stepsisters are wonderful tragic figures—and a little bit comical sometimes, as all tragic figures can be. Don't be a prig, Laura. You have so much to be saved in yourself, you know." He wagged his finger.

"Put out the lamp when you want to go to bed," she said at the door.

"Don't go to bed yet," he whimpered.

"The worst of you dope-addicts is that you're such a drag on other people," she said coldly. "There's a form of bullying for attention in drug-taking."

"I've come here to protect you," he reminded her. "And I've already thawed Gwen." But she shut the door.

All the time her mind was anxiously on her father. Was he indeed mad? She crept down the dark hall and crouched at the cellar door. But there was no sound. She remembered the cellar as a large square room with dustily white-washed walls. It had a high barred window concealed in summer by undergrowth of the garden border skirting the house. She had been down there only once, cautiously following her father—when they came to live in the house Gwen used to threaten to lock her there with the rats, though she herself had always placed there her potted bulbs of hyacinth, tulips and daffodils. There was nothing there but an old rocking-horse left by the owners, a bamboo table, an iron safe, a wine bin, a heap of potatoes sprouting long roots, and a dry grey silence.

Not a sound. The padlocks had been removed; the door was locked from the inside. She wanted to knock, softly, softly; she wanted to plead with him, touch him with her arms, caress him with her warmth, press her lips into his haggard cheek. Take life into his death, let him carry away the kiss of love into his kingdom of death. She crouched at the door. But she could not knock.

Dragging herself away, she began to climb the staircase. A dim light shone in the grimy stained-glass window at the bend. The hall was very cold again. Pausing at the bend, she sensed some presence watching. She looked up. In a shadowy light a figure stood waiting, leaning against the landing banister and looking down. It was Gwen. Laura hesitated. Her impulse was to return downstairs to Alex. But she climbed the last stairs.

Gwen stood in the shaft of light coming from the open door of her room across the spacious landing. She stood unmoving in her opulent gown, watching Laura's approach with full heavy eyes, like the eyes of a statue. One hand lay lightly placed on the banister. The other, unexpectedly, held a half-smoked cigarette.

"Why are you standing there?" Laura was driven to speak as, after a further hesitation, she began to cross the landing to go into the passage leading to her room. She even had to stop again, though Gwen had given no indication of speaking—only watched her with those marbled eyes.

"You had better leave this house to-morrow. For your own peace of mind. Go back to your own life." She spoke evenly.

"I intend staying."

"If I were you I would go to-morrow. There's nothing for you here now. His mind is dead to you . . . I only want to be kind to you," she said, with a remote, calm consideration. "You are such a foolish little thing. You are made for happiness."

Laura had looked down the passage as if measuring the length. She turned her head back again. Her fear dwindled. She became less crouched in herself.

"I want to try and comfort him," she said slowly.

As if she had not heard, Gwen went on: "He's trying to save his soul from damnation. But it's too late. You don't know what he is." She stood like judgment. "He killed my mother. He tortured her. He may have murdered her. He married your mother because evil lust filled him. I would like to drag him through hell——"

But Laura turned. She almost ran down the passage to her room.

Chapter Three

I

HOW fortunate that she had put the sleeping tablets in her suitcase. Without them heaven knew what sort of night it would have been. She got out of bed feeling renewed but a little dim. Half-past eight! It was too much to expect them to send up tea. Someone passed the door half an hour ago. Shivering, she threw her thick fleecy coat over her pyjamas and let up the window blind. And she gave a little cry of delighted surprise. She had forgotten about yesterday's extraordinary snowy landscape.

And there it was again. But glitteringly beautiful in a silver morning light. The sky was blue as a sapphire. Yesterday, when the moon rose within the frozen dusk, the whitish-blue of death had locked the fields, woods and slopes. But now myriads of morning iridescences shimmered on the trees and hedgerows. The field's hard snow sparkled. A crystal mirror-light danced in the air. Far away, the mountains spread luminously immaculate. It was all brilliantly soothing, a flooding of the spirit with delicate radiance.

Yet, oh, it all looked cold, cold; diamond-cold. The tower-room would be icy cold. She began to shiver again. As she combed her hair there was a rough thump on the door and she called, almost cheerfully: "Yes, come in."

Kate, in her breeches and thick stockings, stood glowering in the doorway. "If you want breakfast," she said in her smoky voice, "it will be ready in ten minutes. Does that chap of yours want any? Baths will be later; the boiler's not going yet."

"Have a cigarette, Kate. What a wonderful morning. . . . No, don't disturb Alex; he doesn't eat breakfast and will appear when he wants to."

Kate couldn't resist the cigarette but, advancing, accepted it grudgingly. "Takes drugs, does he! Do you?" She gave a contemptuous glance at the expensive snaky dressing-gown flung on the bed, at the array of cosmetics, the pink feather slippers. The atmosphere of femininity seemed to disgust her.

"No," Laura replied. "Does Gwen?"

"Look here," Kate stood in dark restlessness, half turned to go, half compelled to stay, her downright manner pitiably shallow, "are you and this idiotic Mr. Gregory going to clear out to-day?"

Laura was using her powder-puff. "No, we're staying on. Perhaps for a week or two. Father said we could."

"And you expect us to cook and look after you, I suppose?"

"You're not threatening to down tools? Of course I shall do my share of the work. I'll cook lunch to-day."

"There's nothing in the house for lunch. We don't get any money to buy meat and things. We shall have bread and cheese."

"I have money. Perhaps you'll go on your bike to Tremartin—and get us all plenty of cigarettes?"

Kate stood in her divided glowering. And Laura, to her own surprise, felt a wave of compassion. The secret turmoil and suffering this woman must have experienced! Suffering ennobled, did it? More often it seemed to sow a disease of the spirit. But from what initial source had come this spiritual ruin in the house? Was Alex right when he said her stepsisters were tragic heroines? . . . She cautiously retreated from the further thought. But to-day she must see her father and try to fathom this mystery. And, yes, comfort him. Surely it was he who needed comfort most!

In the pause, with Kate standing there sulkily smoking the cigarette and trying to make up her mind, sounds of someone whistling came from outside. This galvanised Kate. "There's Glyn bringing the milk from the farm," she said rapidly. "He'll have cigarettes for me. Lend me five shillings, will you?" Laura took a ten-shilling note from her bag. Kate snatched it and hurried out.

A few minutes later, still in her pyjamas and fleecy coat, she went downstairs. The hall was very cold. No fire had been lit in the living-rooms. She went on down the dark stony passage to the kitchen. From there voices came, including a man's, young and rather high with a sing-song lilt. She pushed the baize-covered swing door open, not without a qualm. Another day of facing them.

The three were there. And a young man, or youth, who sat comfortably near the hearth with an air of basking in the sisters' attentions. Kate handed him a cup of tea. Marion, her face fully rouged, cut bread and butter. Gwen, in an overall, half attended to the fire in the huge grate. But they all concentrated on the young man, a private group at the warm end of the long table. Kate seemed mostly in possession of him. He gaped as Laura came in, disturbed out of his basking for a minute, but the sisters took no notice of her. She poured herself a cup of tea and sat down at the table, away from them. The young man, good-looking in a rustically-sly way and fundamentally self-assured as a young animal, still watched.

"When are they burying her?" Gwen asked him.

"To-morrow if the hearse can get up to Llanwern Cemetery," he said in his high tenor sing-song. "There's a place to have a cemetery, isn't it now!" His eyes, soft and liquid, half veered, challengingly now, to Laura. "Ten days they had to keep Meredith the Drover, that storm last year and the roads choked with snow. Mrs. Meredith had him shifted out of his coffin and laid in the snow to preserve him—aye indeed, saw him I did lying there in the garden with a robin-redbreast hopping over his waistcoat."

Laura took a piece of Marion's bread and butter off the centre plate. Except by the milk boy she was still ignored. But despite Kate's hovering about him in a bossy, possessive manner, he darted further glances, inquisitive, waiting to be encouraged. It was ludicrous; Laura wanted to laugh. Obviously his head had been turned by the flattering attentions of the three sisters, mistresses of the local big house, London-born, educated women. They had forced him into a coltish vanity. But he was not a lout; there was something elusively fine and subtle—a racial heritage—in the underflow of these glances and this musical voice.

When Marion attempted to take him bread and butter Kate snatched the plate from her. Marion gave her an angry push. Kate swung round barking: "Don't you push me." She looked murderous.

"Don't you snatch, then!" Marion cried shrilly but drawing herself up rather grandly.

"For heaven's sake, be quiet," Gwen protested, clattering

the poker into the fender. She resumed to the young man, who had gone on calmly drinking tea: "They can carry her up there on a bier surely?"

"Slippery as an eel the road is," he sang, "and steep! And saying everybody is they'll catch pneumonia, so high up the cemetery is."

"Yes," Gwen was proceeding, adroitly taking the young man's cup before Kate could reach it, "the Council didn't think of storms and snow-bound roads when they took that land. . . . Councillors," she began to bridle, "once they get put in they don't care. Little tin-pot gods. Ignoramuses! Remember when one said at a council meeting it would be a good thing if they bought a gondola for the lake in the Tremartin park, and that Mr. Saunders got up and said: Why not get two, so that we can breed from them?' . . . Hah!" The Council was an old obsession of hers. She was one of those who write long letters to the local newspaper; hers were remarkably well expressed. "That rat-catcher they sent here once," she proceeded—"'rodent officer', as he called himself—hah, a fat lot he knew about rats. Got the job just because he's married to the Chairman's niece. I've said before that——"

But Marion broke in rudely, sweeping towards the young man: "Did Mrs. Matthews say anything about the Wednesday séance? If the roads are still bad perhaps no one will go——"

"I wonder," Kate barked, "your guide Dora can't tell you if the séance will be on or not."

"That'll do, Kate." The eldest daughter drew herself up again.

Glyn rose. "No, she didn't say." He popped another glance at Laura, who poured herself a second cup of tea. "I will ask her to-morrow, Miss Marion—yes I will, if I remember." Kate went out with him. Her voice could be heard barking through the crystal air.

"None of us has had tea yet," Gwen, standing at the hearth like a domestic Agrippina, addressed her stepsister.

A raucously warring atmosphere remained in the air of the kitchen.

"I'm sorry I've helped myself; I was cold. Can't some more be made?"

"We have to be economical with our tea," Marion snapped. "None of us earns thirty pounds a week singing in rubbishy musical comedies . . . I had better get father's tray ready, Gwen." With an eldest-sister autocracy she had delivered the last word and did not expect retaliation. A wrinkled morning ill-temper lay in her face. She wore a tattered kimono embroidered with disintegrating dragons, and altogether she looked stringy this morning.

"You're more actressy than any actress I've seen," Laura tittered, with far too much malice. "You could earn your fifty pounds a week, in the provinces. But your make-up would have to be less *dabbed on*."

"Hold your tongue, you impudent bitch," Marion writhed round.

"How dare you speak to me like that," Laura shouted, also swift. "Do you want me to smack your face?"

"Here, you," Kate had appeared in the doorway, "none of that! You had better shut up—and I'd keep to your room, if I were you." She advanced towards Laura.

Gwen, also advancing, put in satirically: "She'll be calling to her lover for protection in a minute. But he won't hear; he's drugged."

All three were near her now. She jumped up, throwing back her chair so that it crashed to the floor. She was barely aware that she had snatched a knife from the table. It was Marion's sudden appearance of crumbling, a rather horrible shrinking and a white contracting of her face, that made her break into a hoot of laughter as she threw the knife back on the table. It was all so fantastic. These awful women trying to frighten her so stupidly as if she were still a child! They had retreated.

"You find us funny, do you?" Gwen remarked. She lifted the teapot lid and considered the interior.

"I think she's as dotty as father," Marion sank to a chair. "But it's not surprising, seeing what bad stock her mother was too."

Laura, pink-cheeked, gazed across at Marion as though in wonder. But her plump short body still shook with interior laughter. "Oh," she gasped, "you consider yourself very normal, I suppose . . . Oh dear!" She wiped her brilliant eyes.

"I think you had better go back to your room," Kate said.

"But I want some more breakfast. I've only had one piece of bread and butter."

"She always did eat," Gwen said. "Look how fat she is."

Laura sat down again at the table. "Please forgive me," she said weakly. "I couldn't help it. . . . And about the food, I'm going to give you quite enough money . . . Six guineas a week for me and Alex."

The atmosphere of the room suddenly changed. Again a wave of compassion swept over her. She felt almost sick. Gwen's expression became predatory. Kate looked shiftily withheld. Lifting a pouting face, Marion said: "You could well afford eight guineas."

Perhaps in an instinctive effort to let them save, in disgust of her, a remnant of pride, she replied: "Yes, I can well afford it, but I'm *not* giving you eight. Six is ample."

But she felt sick. Why was he keeping them so cruelly short of money! He was quite well-to-do. The meal last night had been good enough, but she suspected it had come from the last of a carefully hoarded stock.

"She's lent me ten shillings," Kate told her sisters, taking a packet of cigarettes from her breeches pocket.

"I want things from the chemist in Tremartin," Marion said fretfully.

"I have to wash my face in kitchen soap," declared Gwen to the room at large. "And *both* my pairs of shoes need heeling."

"I had to sell my horse," Kate addressed Laura direct.

"He was undernourished," asserted Marion, whose love of animals had always seemed sincere. "I was in two minds about writing to that Society. It would have served father right to be shown up. He ought to be prosecuted." She twisted up her lips firmly.

They sat together at the hearth end of the long table. Laura remained near the other end. Around her silk pyjamas, her coat, her elegantly kept hair and hands, hung a faint distillation of luxurious flowers. Her generous flesh might have been fed on peaches and asparagus. The distance between her and the three huddled sisters down the long table seemed immense.

"Perhaps," Gwen said, "you'll believe now how disgusting he is. I can understand him wanting to punish himself—yes, indeed!—but that he wants to drag us down with him into his mess—well, it's more than flesh and blood can stand."

Laura looked carefully blank. "The impression I get is that he wants to be left alone," she commented slowly. "He said at dinner last night that *you* were trying to drag him down into your hells."

"He's become so unbalanced," Gwen said, "that he imagines we torment him. I daresay he sees us as fiends— yes, fiends," she smiled dimly, "just because we've got our own lives to live and are not meek enough to give in to him now."

"Why didn't you live your own lives in the past?" Laura asked, still cautious. "As far as I can judge, you never did attempt to break away."

"Well, you *can't* judge," Kate barked impatiently. "You don't know enough."

Marion said with a dramatic gesture: "He laid a curse on us."

"Curse, my foot!" Kate swore. "The fact is that when we were children he was a domineering man who hated us because we were the children of our mother and tied him to memory of her. But he couldn't get rid of us, and we were a damnation that possessed him. So he tried to make us into obedient slaves. He succeeded up to a point—and of course he's paying the penalty now. *We* can't tear ourselves away from him—and, besides, we haven't got the cash to do it."

Laura had half suspected before that Kate possessed a calamitous sort of insight. In the dark twists and turns of neurosis were there gifts of shattering light? But it was melancholy that insight seemed not to affect the seer's own conduct. Kate was still caught in this horrible wheel. And neither Gwen nor Marion seemed to pay any attention to her pronouncements. Of course Gwen, all physique, blood-movement and domestic capability, never had displayed much brain-power. And Marion was almost entirely preoccupied in striking her attitudes and poses—was it lack of audience in this isolated place that had driven her to consort with spirits?

She asked, carefully: "Gwen, why did you say to me last night that father had killed your mother? In what way, killed her?"

"He hounded her to death," Gwen replied, placing into its basin the sugar-tongs Marion had flung on the table. "I told you—he wanted to marry your mother."

"You said more," Laura said with her careful calm; "you said 'He may have murdered her'."

"Did I?" Gwen also looked supremely calm now, secure in her bodily health. "Well, that must have been Mr. Gregory's drug. . . . But I expect you know there are dozens of ways of murdering a person?"

"He had the chemist shop then," Marion nodded her head rapidly. "He could have quite easily made mother ill giving her doses of things."

With a measured selection of her words, like the tramp of disciplined feet, Kate pronounced: "You are a fool, Marion, a fool, a fool, a fool. Christ, what a fool! And you, Gwen, you are not much better. Can't you see that Laura is playing a game? She is capable of telling father what you say."

"No," said Laura in a shocked voice.

"Are you sure you wouldn't?" Kate eyed her.

"Do you think he could stand such a thing in his state of health!" Laura exclaimed with much indignation.

Kate turned her eyes away in sharp contempt. After lighting a cigarette she sat shut away, while Gwen poured herself and Marion more tea. Laura sat smoking too. Under Alex's tuition she had become aware of the fantasies indulged in by the frustrated and the neurotic. But again she saw in astonishment that it was Kate, outwardly at least the oddest and most twisted of the three sisters, who picked some kind of way through this nightmare. Was it because she might possess a sort of double illumination—a feminine intuition and a masculine logic?

Her meditation was shattered by a quarrel at the table. Over sugar. Marion, stealthily, had been about to take three lumps, but Gwen snatched the bowl away and gave her one lump, hissing: "You greedy old thing, you know this is all we've got in the house." Marion protested with loud wails. But Kate lifted her head and cut through the squabble.

"Look here, Laura, you had better know what we know *is* fact." In an abrupt, gritty voice, silencing the other two, she proceeded: "He did treat my mother very badly. But I don't want to go into that, it's natural you can't feel about it as we do. What I want to tell you is that father is no angel. In his time he's been lucky not to be sent to prison. You don't know how he made his money?"

"He owned several houses in London, and there was the chemist shop——" Laura said, uneasily.

"The chemist's was only moderately successful. It didn't bring him enough to retire well before sixty with thirty thousand in the bank, after the sale of the houses. . . . He owned at least four houses," she said, "which were run for immoral purposes."

"Brothels," said Marion, pushing a prong back into her hair.

"Shut up, you." And Kate resumed to Laura, who sat

very still: "He was cunning enough not to run them himself. He had a partner, the Mr. Monks who had lived with your mother—a common sort of man; he was even allowed to come to our house sometimes and mix with *us;* my mother was obliged to give him tea."

"He used to bring us sweets," said Gwen, in a horrified way.

"But clever as this Mr. Monks was," Kate went on, "he was caught once. He was put in gaol for three months and fined fifty pounds. There were two charges; one for keeping an immoral house—it was in the Paddington district—and the other for receiving a stolen gold watch. Father managed to save his skin; he had to appear in court as owner of the house but pretended he knew nothing of what went on there. All this was before mother died. She was ill, had been ill for years. But father told her all about it. Of course it helped to kill her." She took out another cigarette. "Now, are you listening? . . . Well, he was having an affair with your mother all the time. You are an illegitimate child."

"Now you know," Gwen said, brushing crumbs from the table.

"We talked it over yesterday," Marion said. "Whether to tell you or not." Looking at the clock, she exclaimed: "It's time for his tray."

"I knew I was illegitimate," Laura said. They all stared at her, Kate searchingly. "I found my mother's marriage certificate a few months before I left here."

"Was it that made you go?" Gwen looked a little crestfallen. Slowly, methodically, she had begun to prepare the tray.

"Good heavens, no. Old-fashioned ill-treatment was one of the reasons." Laura smiled faintly. "Devils of stepsisters. The other reason was that I wanted to make a career for myself. I realised that father was too eccentric to concern himself with my wanting to go out into the world. . . . But it's news to me about the houses. I don't know what to think about it," she frowned; "it's repulsive of course but there must be more to know of the circumstances . . ." Her voice trailed away, troubled and uncertain.

"Greed for money, that's all there is to know," Kate barked. "Except that he's a double sort of man. He's got this religious streak; he was brought up pretty strictly— so we've gathered down here—chapel and the Bible and all that. You've heard how he talks about the Devil. Well, according to these religious notions, he sold himself to the Devil, because one part of him wanted money above every-thing—and there was your mother, he couldn't have got *her* without money——" Suddenly, with the inability of the neurotic to maintain concentration, she lost her harsh control. "He's a wicked old ruffian!" she shouted.

"No," Laura said, but warily. Knitting her brows, she asked: "What about the money—are you waiting for it? Money made as you've said?"

"We've got to live," Marion pouted. "We will put it to good uses. Someone has got to use it, now it's made; that's what money is for, and we can't help how it was made. *We* are not guilty. Aren't we stern with him, don't we disapprove of him?"

"You're guilty in knowing how the money was made," Laura said tartly. Again she felt a mad desire to strike Marion.

"Don't quibble," Kate cried in irritation. "Would *you* take it?"

"No," Laura replied, slowly.

"But you want time to think about it?"

"Of course she'd take it, after a lot of fuss with herself," Gwen said, cutting very thin slices of bread and butter for the tray. "She has come here wondering about the money."

"That's not true," Laura cried. "And all this about him—I've only heard your side, a vindictive side."

"Of course we're vindictive," Kate said impatiently. "He's starving us of all luxuries, even necessities. We can't stir a foot beyond this place. We want to go, Gwen wants to run a private hotel with Marion, I would like a garage . . . For all we know he's leaving his money to some charity."

"Then you'll be forced out into the world . . . . It's not too late!" Obscurely she felt a need to help them.

"Thank you," Kate said shortly, ' but we don't need your advice."

"How did you come to know all you've told me?"

"Spying," Kate answered tersely. "Listening at keyholes. Reading other people's letters. Besides what our mother confided in Marion before she died."

"Yes," Marion preened herself. "Mother was a quiet little woman but no fool. I was always her confidante. Besides, I used to study father closely myself, even when I was quite a child. A man who leads a double life is always interesting. I even used to admire him, as a foolish girl."

"I see," Laura said, pondering. "And you three are using all your knowledge to harass him. To hound him." But beyond her repudiating words she had a sinking awareness of some element of primitive justice fearfully at work.

"What do you expect us to do?" demanded Kate with extreme harshness. "Forgive him?"

"He is an old man. I believe he is dying. . . . And isn't it plain to you that he is suffering intensely?"

"He is suffering chiefly because he's a conceited man," Kate said, again making Laura very aware of her. "He thinks the Lord keeps a special eye on him. He's got an extravagant idea of his own importance. He's got a taste for the showy—for instance, we know what your mother was like in her younger days. Of course it was all bound up with his greed. But he couldn't even go on making money without believing the Devil was at his heels. Fussy isn't the word for it; perhaps maniac is. I suppose it's what religion can do to certain natures when it can't kill the natural amount of evil in them and turn them into saints; they're left with one foot in hell. . . ." She paused to light yet another cigarette. "And now," she tossed away the

other stub, "he can't die without making the biggest
fuss of all. This living in the tower, and that cellar business
at night! And making us suffer . . . Look at the way he
showed-off at the dinner-table last night before your friend
—bah, it turned my stomach over. But I suppose *you* wanted
to throw your arms round him and weep on his chest. You
didn't think of his insulting rudeness to us, I suppose?
Before a guest!" She ruminated for a while in smouldering
anger.

"Yes, I did." Laura spoke in a troubled, reduced voice.
"I hated it. But he's so ill." Then, in a stronger voice, she
said at last, looking accusingly at each in turn: "Did he
speak like that because you've attempted to get him declared
insane and put into an asylum?"

As on the previous day, Gwen and Marion drew nearer
to Kate where she sat. Kate gazed at Laura with unflickering eyes, smoking her cigarette calmly.

"He told you, then! Well, and what are asylums for?
He wouldn't be the first man to be put into one. He could
afford a high-class comfortable place. I expect you are as
sentimental about this as about other things. You don't
think he is sane, do you?"

"He's ill, he's tormented," she repeated helplessly. Then
swiftly: "He needs love."

"It's taken you nine years to come back to offer *that*,"
Gwen said.

"You were not willing," Marion put in shrewishly, "to
make a sacrifice of your life to love him and look after him.
And now you're at a loose end you come back for a holiday.
All very convenient. Love him enough and he'll leave you
everything."

Laura ignored these interruptions. Only Kate seemed
possible to be borne. She met, half fascinated, the challenge
in her eyes. And, elusively, she had a sense of a purity in
the air, a bleak but dazzling truthfulness hovering, waiting
to be caught. She said: "He is suspicious you want him put
away so that you can get control of his money . . . I don't

know about that. But what I do know is that he needs love. Perhaps forgiveness." Yet these words said, and looking at each of her stepsisters again, she felt a hopelessness, a despair. The dazzling elusive radiance could not be caught. There was no real escape from the hate generated in this house.

"Let him ask for forgiveness, then," Kate said. Marion nodded her head in rapid agreement, while Gwen added: "Yes, indeed. But he's not likely to. Not him!"

"No, he won't ask for it," Laura said. "It would be terrible for him to ask for it, terrible for him and for you."

"And we are to forgive him," Kate darkened again into malignity, "for all he did to our mother and to us? What a triumph for him, what a get-away with wickedness! . . . I suppose murder can be forgiven by a saint or God," she observed with her dreadful obsessional irony. "*We* could make a show of forgiveness too. But it wouldn't be honest," she sneered, "it wouldn't come from our black hearts. . . . Go and take his tray up," she finished with abrupt impatience, springing from her chair.

The circle had closed again. Her hopelessness became profound. And this revelation about her father's money— her mind retreated from it, refused to realise it: like an obscenity, one tried to ignore it. . . . But they, *they* had faced it. Or were they only using it now for their own ends?

"If you want a bath, Laura," Gwen was saying, "the water will be hot by now." Was there a note of relenting? Did she wish to placate someone who might become a power in the house? Laura watched her pour water into a small teapot. The tray was laid with a spotless lace cloth. There were little pots of honey and marmalade, though their own breakfast had consisted only of thick slices of bread spread thinly with butter. China and cutlery shone.

Marion said: "It's twenty minutes after the time he likes it. You had better hurry, Laura, or he'll get cantankerous

and begin shouting down the stairs." Kate stood gazing
fixedly at the baize swing door.

2

Carrying the tray upstairs she had a confused sense of
veering from her anger against her stepsisters. Yet the
intolerable harshness of these women against herself in the
past could not be forgotten. And she had never been a
match for their strong, excessive characters. Had she come
back not only in troubled awareness of her father but to
avenge herself? That she had fled the house nine years ago
had been their victory. And though in those nine years
she had plunged into gruelling work—and there were her
emotional entanglements—she saw now that she had not
succeeded in obliterating the powers of this house. One
could never run away into a new life. The past carried its
seeds into the future.

He must know that, she thought, as she climbed the last
stairs to the tower-room. Kate's long tirades, though
doubtless warped by her state of mind, were worth considering. *Was* the torment with which he was racked caused
only by the cruel hatred of daughters?—than which, of all
the grim psychopathic twistings, there is nothing more
fiendish.

She knocked at his door. A gentle, uneasy knock.
There were shuffling sounds, a delay. She knocked
again. "Yes, yes," came his voice, querulous; "what do you
want?" She remembered then he did not admit her stepsisters. "It's Laura," she called. "Can I come in?" There
was no reply. She waited and said: "I've got your breakfast,
father." There was a sound like a swift whirring of wings,
then a depleted little screech. The aged parrot. After another
interval the key was turned and he opened the door.

Careful to seem perfectly ordinary, she walked in saying:
"The tea will be getting cold. Gwen should have put a

cosy on the pot." He locked the door behind her. She placed the tray on the table and, like an affectionate daughter, poured the tea. "How are you this morning? It's wonderfully light in here with those four windows . . . Ah, you've lit your oil stove."

With the silver and blue morning pouring through the curtainless windows the room's monkish spareness seemed less bleak. He was dressed and had made his bed—if he had occupied it. He looked as if he had been down to the bathroom to wash, his shining white hair combed back neatly. But, hollow-cheeked, thin, his breath coming in half-stifled pants, he was giving her sideway glances, suspicious. Instinctively wary, she pretended not to notice and went on chattering. But there was something . . .

"Won't you come to the table, father?" She fetched the only chair from the little desk. "Polly hasn't lost her voice then." She went to the cage. "She's a faithful old thing . . . Polly, Polly!" But its green plumage, once so gay, was without gloss; the eye stared into the dull distance of eternity.

"Don't put the teapot on top of the stove," he exclaimed, going to the table; "it will stew."

She almost laughed in relief. Her nervousness vanished. And that jerky, candle-lit glimpse of him going down the hall to the cellar door last night seemed like something in a fitful dream. After removing the teapot she went to the window, glad to notice his hand—but how fleshlessly thin and blue-veined it was!—stretch for a piece of Gwen's finely-cut bread and butter.

"Oh, the morning, father, it looks so lovely, especially from up here."

There was a wide flowing view to the mountains glittering in the azure. Below, the clear-cut silver trees with their filigree of snow were fantastically beautiful. Distant fields were crystalline. Again the delicate lightness of the morning lifted her heart. Winter was beautiful. There was no sensual urge in the earth. Only this tranquil, shimmering quiet, like a promise of ineffable calm. From here it seemed to lie over all the kingdoms of the world. The mountains were spread with white peace.

Her elbows on the sill, she passed into a quiet muse, content to be there with him while he ate with an old man's frugality. Surely this awful tenseness in the house must sometimes be forgotten? She would turn presently and tell him about South Africa. And about her husband. She could talk of that now. Strange how since her arrival here Hugh was receding in her mind! She felt a release. This morning he even seemed a curious aberration, an error at which she could almost smile. Alex had been right about him; Hugh would never be able to yield a jot of himself to anyone; like Marion he needed audiences to nourish him. . . . Yet, yet, had she herself possessed a liberated heart to offer him?

She turned. He was sitting quite still at the table, haggard and stony. He seemed like a patriarch beyond time. About him was the awful, piteous dignity of old age, its loneliness so much more desolate in a man than in a woman. She stood unable to move further, her voice faltering: "Have you finished, father?"

Still with that stony gaze, he said: "I went downstairs this morning. They were late with my breakfast. I heard them talking to you in the kitchen. I stood listening at the door."

Her breasts moved in a flood of anguish. She took a step towards him but stopped again. He was unapproachable. But she was able to whisper: "You ought not to have listened, father. They are strange women." She went on in distraction: "And how cold it must have been, standing there in that draughty passage. You——"

Taking no notice of this, he spoke without any of his vehemence of the day before: "They can say I murdered their mother. Perhaps I did. I do not know." He paused, for his breathing was laboured. "She was a good woman. . . . Ha, they want to punish me, do they! Why can't

H

they see I have punished myself more than they ever can! Why do they vex me, why don't they go? . . . But since that night," he proceeded, in a soft hollow voice, "when I locked them out and they smashed the window to get in, I have seen they are part of my punishment and there is no escape from them." His voice rose to anger: "But who could tell they would want to steal my money, strip me, leave me a pariah dependent on them? Declared insane, indeed! Because I am searching for God!"

He turned his white face and, inwardly, she shrank from the piercing shine of those eyes from which the blurring of age had vanished. She could not approach him now, she dare not. There was something mystically unresolved about him, as about a man who has not quite left the transactions of the flesh and fully emerged into that other, tremendous light. He sat looking at her from far away, his soul unconnecting: it was as though she were the personification of something abstract. And he cried out:

"Regeneration! A man is only a fragment of what he can be, he is never concluded. I said I destroyed myself. But I only destroyed the evil fragment I was. A demon had possessed me. I allowed myself to flee from the divine source where a man can reach his fullest stature. But no man can belong wholly to the Devil; *that* is his punishment and torment." Impatience, a more human irritability, began to curb these cries. "*Their* father is dead—why will they shut their eyes to it and try to drag me down into their petty world? Why do they force me to retaliation and to waste my strength against them!"

She knew what Kate would have said to this—that he was trying to escape the material facts of those misdeeds of which she accused him. She stood in troubled doubt. She did not know enough of that dark past haunting the four people of this house. But she felt that she wanted to know no more. . . . And still she ached to go to him, to touch him. It seemed necessary to touch him. But still she could not penetrate into that bleak isolation surrounding him like an aura.

"Father," her voice stumbled, "you must rest. You must not allow yourself to be troubled any more. I . . . I want to stay with you and look after you." If only he would accept the blind comfort of her presence!

He rose from the chair, backing from her. His demeanour changed again. A feverish colour flowed into the hollow cheeks. The sharp nose quivered. "Kate told you all those things. She told you you were illegitimate . . . and you knew . . . you had ferreted among my papers," he went on with growing anger. "Women, they prowl about and try to drag one down, they are everlastingly looking for ways and means to reduce a man into their power . . . like your stepsisters." And he uttered the shocking cry she had heard yesterday. "My strength is waning! They batten on me, want to possess me, they twine their arms into me——"

"Let them go, then," she exclaimed quickly. "Give them money and let them go their own ways. They are destroying themselves with all this cruelty."

He gave her a look of startling craftiness. "Give them money, my money? For them to enjoy themselves and go to the Devil! Fine clothes and holidays—they, who wanted to put me in an asylum! And they would come back for more, never leave me alone." He thrust out his head, his voice sank to a whisper: "*They are always there.*"

Then, for a moment, she felt utterly defeated. But, with a piercing sense of vision, an uplifting of her whole being, she remembered the spiritual exaltation of his face and the victorious glow of his presence when he had spoken of regeneration. And she saw his death as a thing to be desired, a wonderful shattering of something corrupt, a release of pure luminous spirit. There could be no other destruction of all this desperate hatred, no other exit from this evil circle. Let him die But if only she could give him some touch of peace and love in his death.

"Father," she reiterated softly, "I want to settle here with you, I want to help you. I . . . I have not been happy while I was away——"

"I do not need your help. You think your stepsisters have got the better of me? I have my ways of punishing them." Again he was retreating from her.

"But you will let me stay?" she insisted.

"I told you yesterday you could stay." He turned his back on her.

She searched helplessly for words, and for the courage to say them. But all she could say was: "You will let me come and sit with you here in the evenings——" How could she tell him she wanted to flood him with love and devotion? She could not find the words: not yet. She must wait. . . . She watched him go to the little desk and, like a fussily busy man, sort out papers—there were many, in addition to copy books and something like a ledger. A calendar was pinned over the desk, the dates crossed out with blue pencil.

"Leave me alone now," he said fretfully; "I have work to do." He opened a drawer, took out an old purse and extracted a note. "Here, give this money to Gwen—an extra pound for the house expenses." It was startling, the swift change to this practical attention. "Mind, to Gwen! Not to Kate—she'll spend it on cigarettes." And, in a mutter: "She looks like a smoked ham."

Laura, taking the money, smiled eagerly. "Gwen is very efficient in the house——" she began tentatively, longing for some normal contact with him.

"So is the Devil," he retorted, turning back to the desk. "She's smart as a whip-lash . . . And that tongue of Kate's, that slut of a Marion with her witches . . . Did a man ever have such daughters?" As she collected the breakfast things on to the tray he went on mutteringly: "Give them money, indeed! Didn't they tell you how that money was made? *I* do not use it; it is lying untouched in the bank. I have two bank-accounts; I always did." He rapped his knuckles on the desk. "One would think they would be ashamed to accept such money—*I* have not touched it for years." His head looked round cunningly, as he bent over the desk. "You said you would not use the money—I heard you. You are virtuous, though you are my daughter and your mother's. But you would let them use it." And he gave a chuckle.

She heard that chuckle again as she slowly went out with the tray. But, turning at the door, she saw him standing motionless, looking into the shining morning at the window. Tall, aged and white. And somehow unconquered.

Chapter Four

I

T HEY were gathered round the hearth. As Laura walked in Marion looked across the room with the frigid annoyance of a lady disturbed by some clumsy parlourmaid. Gwen sat with her sewing-machine at the round table drawn up to the edge of the hearth-rug; a tape measure hung round her neck. Kate sprawled opposite Marion with every appearance of being interrupted in the delivery of a forthright opinion.

"Well, have you decided what to do?" Laura spoke in too high, too impatient a voice. It was two o'clock. He had not returned. Luncheon had been over nearly an hour; everyone, perhaps from nervous stress, had been hungry.

"This is our private sitting-room, Laura," sang Marion. "You might knock before coming in. You coolly walked in like that yesterday, after nine years and without a warning, and you made my heart jump *very badly*."

"One of these modern bad-mannered chits," Gwen

addressed her sewing-machine. "Casual and thoughtless. There's a typist in the Council offices just like her."

"You can't just sit here talking," Laura fumed impatiently. "We've got to do something." When, just before luncheon, it was found he had left the house—he had not been out for over a year—and she told them he had overheard their accusations in the kitchen that morning, Kate had calmly said she was not surprised, he often crept downstairs and listened at doors.

"What do you suggest we should do, then?" asked Gwen, inserting a hem under the needle. "Hire a dozen men to comb the woods? They wouldn't, not in this cold. Besides, father is cunning; he'd know where to hide."

"Don't work yourself up," Kate barked. "He has the right to leave the house when he wants. As I said, probably he's gone to Tremartin on some business or other."

"You know very well." Laura rapped back, "he's not in a fit state even to go down the drive. . . . How can you sit there so callously? We must all go out in different directions. There's sure to be some trace in the snow."

"I think," pronounced Marion with her preening air of owning a special advantage, "it would be imprudent to interfere. I have received advice. Go back to your friend, Laura; you're so excitable . . . You needn't look at me like that," she said primly.

The sewing-machine wheel whirred an accompaniment to Gwen's words: "She comes back here after all these years and upsets the house. *She's* to blame for his conduct."

"Perhaps I came just in time. Stop that damned machine."

"Temper, temper," Gwen smiled.

"Your nose is shining," Marion remarked. "Are you running short of powder? Kate brought me some from the chemist this morning, thanks to the money you've given us."

Kate exhaled smoke from her nostrils. "I don't know why you're so worked up, Laura. But of course you're not really accustomed to his tantrums. He was not so peculiar in your time here."

Laura sat down sharply. Her black eyes shot from one to the other; she seemed to be sniffing the air. "You're glad of this, aren't you! You've been waiting for more proof of his insanity. You want justification for making another attempt to get him certified."

The wheel stopped whirring. Marion, pushing a comb into her hair, looked enquiringly at Kate. Gwen shook out the cloth, while Kate lit a fresh cigarette from the other before asking: "Wouldn't you consider this flight—or whatever it is—to be proof? But it remains to be seen; as I said, he may have gone out on legitimate business. . . . However," she added, "in case he's just out of his mind and wandering about, I telephoned the policeman's cottage in the village a few minutes ago."

"I heard you," Laura burst out.

"So you've taken to eavesdropping too," Gwen smiled, pinching in another hem. "Mr. Gregory must think this isn't a pleasant house, with people crouching at doors."

"The policeman," Kate proceeded, "said he'd get in touch with the Tremartin station and the constables there would be asked to keep an eye open. A description of him is being circulated. . . . Father is not an inconspicuous figure, with his cloak and bare head."

Laura shivered. The notification of the police was of course a well-planned move of theirs. Yet it had to be done; she had meditated it herself but shrank from the act. She demanded distractedly: "But haven't you any idea of a possible destination? If none of you wants to go in search of him, Alex and I can."

"It will be dusk in a couple of hours," Kate said, "so you'd better hurry; there's so many miles to investigate, and all the woods. Then, of course, if you find him he may curse you for being an interfering hussy. . . . Still, don't let us stop you."

"It had occurred to me," Marion prattled, "that he's gone up to Llanwern cemetery; I don't know——" she glanced over her shoulder—"if my guide has put in into my head."

Laura rose swiftly.

"Don't forget," Kate was adding, "that whatever his mental condition father is physically a strong man. He's quite capable of protecting himself."

Laura exclaimed: "You wouldn't see that he's very ill. When I arrived yesterday I saw him as a dying man."

"You certainly arrived with a fresh eye," Kate idly conceded; "I don't know if it's an experienced one. You don't strike me as being particularly intelligent, but you certainly overflow with feeling." Laura moved to the door, slamming it behind her, though not before she caught Kate's final: "What a bore she is!"

The trio of furies, that she would never subdue! Whatever Alex said in their defence, how could their stony malice, their dehumanised lack of pity, be forgiven? They might be explained, but never forgiven. She went fuming down the passage and into the drawing-room.

"Well," he asked, turning, "how did you get on with them?"

"Come," she said savagely, "we're going for a walk."

"It sounds as though I'm a dog," he complained. "But, there, what is the country for? . . . Why, my dear, you look angry. When will you learn," he scolded, "to fight them with less feeling? . . . A cool ridicule is what you need, darling. The most telling weapon of all."

"I've tried it. But they're stone, stone——" The telephone rang in the hall. She hurried to the door.

But Kate was reaching the old-fashioned contraption screwed to the wall. She spoke measuredly to the caller. It sounded like news. Laura walked into the hall followed by Alex. Marion and Gwen stood hovering near Kate, who hung up the earpiece and announced:

"It was Watkins, the Tremartin police sergeant. Father was seen entering A. L. Lloyd's office in Jubilee Place just after twelve o'clock. He got off the bus there. The sergeant 'phoned Mr. Lloyd's office and found that father stayed there over an hour. They haven't traced him after that."

"A. L. Lloyd's office!" Marion said, breathless. "The solicitor! But he's never been to him before." Kate gave her an irritable glance. They all stood silent.

"Possibly," Alex suggested, "a call to this office will help?"

Gwen, perhaps to cover Kate's gesture of impatience, smiled: "You must find all these troubles of ours rather annoying, Mr. Gregory. When you've come to the country for rest!"

"I'll ring Mr. Lloyd," Laura stepped towards the local directory.

"I'm doing so myself," Kate brushed her aside. But she obtained no satisfaction from the office; only a verification that her father had been there. It wasn't known where he had gone afterwards, and they couldn't give the reason of his visit. After hanging up, she barked this out, and with her sisters went back abruptly to their parlour. The door closed with a marked sound of finality.

"They didn't want to tell her why he went there," Laura said. "I expect he warned this solicitor."

"Obviously he's capable of moving about and transacting business," Alex remarked in relief. "So need we go out now?"

"Yes. But don't come if you're tired. Go and lie down."

Fetching his hat and coat from the hall stand, he observed: "Since Englishwomen are notoriously more enamoured of dogs than anything else, your tone is sweet in my ears . . . oh, but you're only half English, aren't you? . . . We'd both better take a stick for those roads."

2

They set out. After the fireside the pallid chill stung. A frosty touch of brine, the breath of the Atlantic, whipped thinly in the air. Already the sun's opaque red disc swung low. Laura shivered and tightened the belt of her soft fleecy coat. But Alex, now he was really out, set his nose with docile indifference towards the arctic landscape. He did not ask their destination.

After an hour's slow climbing they came to a cross-roads. One road, hard and glassy, ran down steeply to Tremartin. The pinkish-white hills loomed nearer. Below, the world billowed in broad waves of snow warningly tinted with rose. A distant farmstead stood etched in black clarity. "We take this road," Laura said, and laboriously they climbed again. "Someone has been cycling here. . . . There's a keeper's lodge at the gates." But she could find no human footprints; only the running sprinkle of a rabbit's feet in the softer snow at the road's edge. A telephone wire swung above.

Keen and bitter, the chaste odour of the inner mountains beyond the foot-hills leapt down, an odour of manless solitudes. In the air lay the haunting chill of immense silences, an unearthly inner chill folded within the raw cold as the mysterious blue heart of a wintry flower lies wrapped in the coarser petals. The lip of the purplish-crimson sun touched a mountain shoulder. In this pure elemental zone the two figures trudging up looked forlorn, even devoid of meaning.

"Don't forget, Laura, the moon is apt to rise an hour later each night. I rely on you to tow me back safely from these heights; women are so clever at outwitting nature. . . . But you're looking pale, my dear," he bent solicitously. "Or is it only all this pallor around us? Perhaps the keeper will give us tea at the lodge."

At last they came to the place. Smoothly it tilted up to the white silences. Tall iron gates were closed before an avenue of yews stretching in black formality. Beyond were glimpses of tombstones and, in the distance, a fabulous totem with massive outspread wings, half woman, half bird, poised as though to swoop towards the gates. They went in by a little side gate open in the palings and stepped across to the lodge. Then Laura, with a quick start, drew up.

A pair of mackerel lay embedded in the snow beside the porch.

Alex was delighted. "They'll keep fresh. Those glazed stripes and dotted eyes in the snow!"

But for her the place and afternoon had become wholly phantasmagoric. "Shall we knock?" she asked uncertainly, looking cautiously at the door. A bicycle stood in the porch. "Shall we knock? Or go straight up . . . it's in the far corner." The deserted white silence hung like something palpable.

"Knock. The mackerel and bicycle somehow suggest a human being."

She mounted the three steps and banged the knocker. The *rat-tat* crashed into the silence. "Enough to waken the dead," Alex remarked. "What a very imaginative place for a cemetery! It's bardic." His cheeks glowed red; he had already remarked that the climb would benefit his liver. "Yes, completely bardic. And the long via dolorosa up here! Chastening for those members of the cortège who are not preoccupied with thoughts of the will."

The door scraped open. A lean elderly man in dirty corduroys and a black cardigan appeared. Isolated tufts of dead reddish hair clung to his brown-spotted pate; his neck was excessively stringy. He smoked a short charred pipe. "Aye?" he asked, without surprise and looking beyond Laura at the hovering Alex.

She had stepped back a pace, in agitation. But she asked, hurriedly: "Is my father here? Mr. Mansell Roberts."

He pointed his pipe up to the right. "Up there." And, in a sing-song voice stringy as his neck, went on volubly, but still addressing Alex: "Got a column over it. Half an hour ago he came, all the way from Tremartin he walked, a day like this and no hat or gloves. Not for over a year now I've seen him. Cleanest kept grave here it used to be. You a relation?" he asked Alex inquisitively. "Best take the old gentleman back home soon; not too champion he looked to me, no—— 'You come here on way out, Mr.

Roberts,' I said to him, 'and take a nog of rum.' Dominoes I used to play with him often——" When he removed his pipe a cleft lip was revealed.

But Laura was stepping sharply away. She pushed past Alex. The keeper with his clay-caked corduroys and stained cardigan, his stringy neck and cleft lip, even that foul pipe, filled her with amazed dread. His image was stored away in some cell of her memory: deep in the fold of a chaotic dream. She knew that lean male aloneness of his, that unwarmed isolation of his presence, and the blank unconsciousness of her. She stepped past the frozen mackerel, knowing now that they too belonged to her dreams, and plunged up between the yews. The keeper went on addressing Alex. His up and down voice, like some bronchial turkey's, beat on her ears.

Turning, she cried to Alex: "Stay there." Plunging into a path between the yews she stumbled on through cushions of snow. Her feet were ice-cold. Slabs of lettered marble, the reduction of voluminous lives to two informative lines and a hopeful verse clamped to enduring substance, reared both sides of her. Here and there were stumps of white-blotched evergreens or skeleton rose-bushes briefly glittering. An immense shaft of darkly crimson light burned diagonally across the whole place. Her mother was buried in the southward extreme. She passed a massive snow-lidded stone casket and remembered it was the memorial of her father's only local friend—they were the two moneyed men of the district. Mr. Llewellyn died a few months before she left home and she remembered he had instructed that a copy of his published biblical studies be placed under his head in the coffin.

Dazzled and strained by all the brilliant whiteness of that day, her eyes sought the high northward corner. Presently she saw his black cloak. It moved on the snow like a shadow. Climbing higher, her heart stood still. He was kneeling beneath the broken pillar, and he seemed to be digging; digging with his hands.

Had his mind indeed become shattered? *They* would be glad to know of this obsessed flight to the cemetery. It would make an impressive item in an official application. . . . Or had he come here to die? She plunged on blindly, up a path deep in dry, crisp snow. The geometrical paths and roads strictly intersecting the ranked graves, a scheme of robots calculating in council, filled her with a renewed terror. The place was like some claustrophobic dream in which memory still entangled her.

Noiseless in the snow, she approached the large square grave with its border of low chains, its thick broken column reared on a solid plinth and its two-stepped entrance. He could not see her. He knelt with his back to her, scooping the snow away with his hands. For a moment she felt a great fear. This, this was the final isolation, he was removed into the last dreadful loneliness. But at sight of his white glistening head, unprotected, her fear vanished, and she stumbled forward in a passion of entreating love. "Father," she whispered: but falteringly, undemanding.

"Father . . ." he echoed. But he did not turn.

And hoarsely, his breath exhaled in painful gusts, he muttered oblivious: "Evil, evil . . . I looked into the heart of the world and I found evil." Then he chuckled; but the chesty heave ended in a gasp. "They would tear me asunder, would they? they would break me, they would fill my name in a form and go to the courts . . ." She saw the knotted veins of his hands swell and palpitate. His voice rose thinly. "Their bowels are filled with hate. They have never walked in Jerusalem, but they have held converse with the Devil." With oblivious tenacity he scooped again, calling: "Father, hear me, aid me! Tell me the secret." He gasped, brushed snow from his knees as he leaned back staring at the moist green patch those trembling thin hands had cleared. His nose curved sharply, with the bleak nudity of the dying.

She stumbled past the looped chains. Her shadow fell across the grave. She mounted the two snow-covered steps. He looked up, with a gleam of his old alertness. But she saw no recognition in the eyes glaring at her. Suddenly he swayed, sagged, and fell clumsily into the snow. An incoherent muttering came from the grey lips.

She scrambled over to him, she kneeled and lifted his head into her arm. A calculating calm came to her. "Father," she said, "it's Laura; I've come to take you home."

"Laura?" he gasped, staring up at her intently. "My daughter Laura?"

"Yes. You will come with me? Look, it's getting late, it will be dark soon. Come home with me." She was conscious of a slackening of his body, an exhausted giving way. But his eyes were upturned to her in a terrible searching. "Come," she said. She made an effort to help him rise: she felt swift and strong.

But with a startlingly agile movement he pulled himself away from her and stood up. Cunning suspicion crossed his face. "They sent you?" he shouted, swaying. There was even that patriarchal arrogance in his face, a vestige of his old intolerance. A nerve beat in his temple.

"No," she replied quickly. "I thought I would walk here with Mr. Gregory to look for you—you remember Mr. Gregory, our visitor?"

"The van is at the gates?" he demanded.

"The van?" she repeated, startled. Then felt a gush of shame. What threats had they used in those brawls he must have suffered?

"They fetched that whippersnapper of a doctor," he shouted. "And went to the solicitor." Then again he chuckled hoarsely. "But I will beat them yet."

"*We* will beat them. But you mustn't leave me alone with them, father. . . . Let's go back now," she said, softly. And put a hand on his arm; he winced but did not shake her off. "Come; I'm cold." She guided him to the two steps. "We'll warm ourselves in the keeper's house. . . . Look, there's Mr. Gregory." With a wincing obedience, yet aloof and muttering under his breath, he allowed her to lead him.

Alex was standing far below in the darkening stretch of white. She waved beckoningly; he began to amble up. "You remember him," she went on, "the visitor you met last night?"

"Ha, the one who had met the Devil! Is he your husband?"

Her arm firmly guided him; she had picked up her walking-stick from beside the grave. "No, no," she chatted. "I divorced my husband; one day I'll tell you all about it."

Alex made no sign of there being anything extraordinary in this meeting with the tottering, bare-headed old man in such a place. With a brief peep at Laura he stepped to the other side of her father and took his arm. "How bitterly cold it is up here, sir," he said. "Laura, I've been having an interesting chat with the keeper; he's been a sailor."

"Hopkins, an old friend of mine," her father mumbled. "Crafty fellow who never got married; lives alone . . . not even a cat or dog."

They got him to the lodge. The keeper admitted them without remark or show of surprise. There was a bustling fire in his neat, tidy living-room. An oil lamp had just been lit. The first thing Laura noticed was a row of white china flowers on the mantelpiece; broken segments of those 'everlasting wreaths' which are protected by glass shades. The keeper drew a curled old-fashioned sofa closer to the fire; her father lay on it with an obedience that began to alarm her. Still without comment the keeper produced a half bottle of rum and one glass. But he began to talk of a funeral that without mishap had come up the slippery road from Tremartin that morning. He wasn't going to fill in the grave until the next day; his assistant from the village was in bed with influenza, and . . .

He had climbed that three-mile road on foot after leaving the solicitor's! But his physical strength had always been remarkable; she could not remember any illness, not even colds. After drinking the rum he lay submissive, closing his eyes. The keeper's chatter still went on, addressed exclusively to Alex; it was as if a woman was beyond his perception. She had to force herself to ask for the use of the telephone. It was to Alex he replied: "Aye, it's in the passage."

The son at the Ruthin Arms consented to attempt the trip to Llanwern; she asked him to bring rugs. Then she telephoned her stepsisters. Kate replied. "He was in the cemetery?" she asked, calm. "Well, I'm not surprised . . . No, of course we can't warm his bed, the tower-room is locked and he won't sleep anywhere else . . . 'Phone the doctor if you like, but I warn you that father is not likely to see him." She sounded impatient. Then she asked, carefully: "What was he doing in the cemetery?" But Laura rang off.

He seemed to be dozing. The blue tint had drained from his face, his breathing was easier. But the vein still quivered spasmodically in his temple. She sat watching him. The keeper went on talking ceaselessly to Alex, though he poured tea for her from a pot stewing on the hob, giving the cup to Alex to hand to her. She listened in a half daze, keeping exhaustion at bay, fearful of slipping completely into the sense of something phantasmagoric haunting her. The keeper turned up the lamp.

His Adam's apple skipping up and down his neck, the stringy voice running in turkey exclamations, he continued his recital to Alex: "—aye, only this morning we buried him. Knowing him well was Mr. Roberts here. Theological student he used to be but got jilted by this farmer's daughter. A year ago that was, and he climbed up to the chimney pot of his mother's cottage across there in the valley and wouldn't come down. Sat up there spitting and cursing. Then they fetched the gal that had sent her ring back to him, and like a love-bird she called to him, and down he comes when she promised to marry him next Easter. Then over to the Institute they got him. But wasted away like a candle he did there, and *she* soon married a milk-contractor with a thousand or two of pound notes in the bank. But a big wreath she sent to the funeral to-day, white harum lilies big as dunce's caps in it and a card with deepest sympathy very prominent——"

She got up and crossed to the latticed window. The ice-blue dusk was slipping into night. When would the car come! That high sing-song voice was driving her to hysteria.

She crossed to the hearth and nervously fingered the shiny white porcelain flowers on the mantelpiece. There were roses, lilies, tulips, and small anemones. Pallid cold flowers of death. Had they broken off from their horrible glass-shaded bouquets in some wintry storm and blown among the graves? She could feel the keeper's eyes on her back. Behind the row of flowers leaned wads of postcard views of the cemetery. A horn sounded at the gates.

She ran out. But the great iron gates were locked. The keeper loomed beside her into the throw of the car's head-lights. Silent and calm. But did she imagine laughter in that silence? Thin, nasal laughter blowing in ghostly mockery? He was unlocking the gates; the tufts of hair shone crimson. She ran back into the lodge.

"Father," she called, stroking his forehead. He muttered in his throat. She rubbed his hands, kept on calling. At last the lids lifted; he looked at her intently . . . but from ages away. Gently, she continued to call. After a while he slowly rose, looking about him with a kind of lightless-ness, as of someone arriving for annihilation. The un-illumined eyes paused vaguely on the clinging woman with her glow of flesh, her soft agony of entreaty. Recognition began to seep into their depths.

"Why did you follow me?" he whispered.

Her hand still on his arm, she begged, humbly: "You will come with me, won't you? Back home."

He gave her a slight push. And with a gleam of his arrogance, he said fretfully: "Let me go then. My parrot is locked in my room." And to Alex he said, lifting his nose in remote hauteur: "Sir, you are very kind to trouble with me and come here with my daughter." It was astonishing, as though another being had quickened within him, a miasmic mist lifted off his mind. "I do not need your help, Laura. Why do women always cling and follow?" And, hulking forward like some lonely creature removed from the fusses of the world, he walked to the door.

But the blast of cold outside made him stagger. Alex and Laura led him to the car. The keeper was talking to the driver. They got him into the back seat, where Laura sat wrapping him in rugs. A miniature lamp shone in the roof. The keeper went back for some scarf he gabbled about, Alex following him for his walking-stick and hat. A minute later the car curved slowly into the glassy white road. The headlamps explored a fantastically spectral lane of silver trees and bushes writhing away from the invading illumination.

Alex turned from his seat beside the young driver: "The keeper gave me this for you."

Already her father seemed to be dozing: in the dingy roof-light his face looked slack and thinly folded in on itself. Her fingers turned over and over the white china rose. Its smooth cold petals curled outwards in dead trim realism and a hint of green lay in its depths. She put it in her pocket.

3

The slow dangerous descent of the road was anguish to her. He dozed on there beside her; he was in her keeping. But there was a curious rasp in his breathing. What was his condition? She had not telephoned the doctor; she felt that sight of this apparent ally of her stepsisters would plunge him into some awful paroxysm. How would that night pass? Would *they* somehow take him into possession? She felt her own senses passing into unreality, vague and distorted, there in the car gliding down between streams of apparitional white-webbed trees, like a descent through legendary lanes to Hades. The huddled arrogant old man seemed to be passing out of her mind's grasp. Arrogant in his repudiation of human love. And surely mad.

Appalled, she faced that thought now. But still her mind began to raise defences . . . Wasn't it a madness that made sanity seem drably trivial, an affair of petty and brittle transactions with transient things? In a dim, not fully realised way, she apprehended his flight as something grand, a furious gesture of self-preserving defiance. And somewhere far away beyond these thoughts lurking drowsily in her mind was the urge that he should have been left to die. She was bringing him back to *their* power, to the blood-hatreds and the mysterious compulsion of expiation.

The car had glided to a standstill. Alex got out to open and close the drive gate. She fumbled for her father's hand under the rug. It was cold; she kept on rubbing it, calling to him as they drove up to the house. Not a light showed in any of the front windows, though the driver had sounded the horn in warning. Alex had to thump the door knocker thrice. At last a light hovered behind the narrow panels of variegated glass. Bolts were drawn.

Marion stood in the lamplight in an ornate, low-cut evening gown with—yes, a narrow old-fashioned train gleaming mauve behind her. Pearls round her throat and bangles on her wrists.

"Is he to be carried in?" she cried in thin efficiency, peering. "If so, have you the key of his room, Laura? Gwen is just filling a hot-water bottle in the kitchen. . . . Good gracious, it's very cold, Mr. Gregory; I need a shawl for my shoulders . . . Kate, Kate," she called; "where are you? You'd better come and help, dear——"

But their father, Laura holding his arm, was stepping out of the car. He stood breathing in slow, heavy suspiration, there below the three porch steps. In crouched hostility he stood looking into the doorway where the painted, remarkably-gowned woman retreated with her hand to her shivering, half-naked bosom.

"The first bitch-child," he breathed. "And the worst."

Then, a mournful funereal figure with his black cloak and bare head, he walked alone into his house, though he accepted the stick Laura held to him.

After a few words with the driver Laura and Alex followed. In the hall, Marion was exclaiming with a deprecatory gesture: "Why, father, how foolish of you to go out into the cold. We've had to consult the police——" Gwen stood in the centre of the bottom stair holding a furry-coated hot-water bottle. Above her Kate paused in the staircase bend, under the dim gleams of the stained-glass window; there was a cigarette in her fingers. Marion's words tinkled away meaninglessly. There was a moment's dead silence as he advanced towards the staircase.

Gwen did not move. Thick-limbed and bovinely watching, she stood on the stair. Without a word her father lifted the walking-stick high above his head. Laura darted forward in horror: afterwards she wondered why she made that rush, half in protection of Gwen. But Gwen, with calm if heavy dignity, moved aside to the banister and leaned composedly against the newel. He began to mount. Above, Kate shrank against the panelling of the wall-curve. And Marion fussed, as if oblivious: "Take him the hot-water bottle, Laura. We'll bring up a cup of beef tea presently. . . . Mr. Gregory, there's a fire in the drawing-room; poor man, go and warm yourself."

It was over. He climbed to the tower-room alone. Laura slowly followed.

The upper stairs and passages were dark. On the first landing she darted down to her room and lit a candle. But by the time she had reached the tower-room he was inside it. And the door was locked. And he would not admit her. In a furious voice broken with hoarse gasps he told her to lay the hot-water bottle on the mat. Slowly she went downstairs for the beef tea.

Then, in exhaustion, she found her patience coming to an end. She could battle no more. He had not taken the hot-water bottle when she returned with the beaker of steaming beef tea—Gwen had given it to her saying: "Do see that he drinks it all." At her loud knock and call he shouted in a frenzy of anger: "Yes, yes, I'm not deaf! Leave me alone I tell you . . . go away." She laid the beaker on the mat and crept downstairs again.

Chapter Five

I

MARION presiding, a tea-tray was laid in the drawing-room. "It's late for tea, Mr. Gregory," she sang, "but it will warm you. We've had ours, but kept these scones hot. . . . Laura," she turned, only slightly frosty, "kindly shut the door; there's a draught. Father locked you out, presumably?"

Laura left the door open—Gwen was crossing the hall with a jug of hot water—and sank to the chintz-covered stool beside the fireplace. Gwen laid the jug on the tray, took her bag of silks from the piano, and settled near the parchment shade of the Aladdin oil lamp. Kate, who wore flannel trousers, a white business-like shirt and a dark grey jacket, sat bunched into the shell-backed chair: she kept on glancing along her eyelids at Alex, who was strangely silent. The room's air, as of a conference about to open, seemed to come from her.

"Your tea, Laura," Marion said mechanically. "*Can* you eat a scone? Gwen made them this afternoon." In her ornate gown, her face fully rouged and the old artificial pearls yellow, she looked like someone in a grisly pantomime. Yet that self-assurance of hers, a well-trained if brittle poise, gave her a sort of tattered dignity.

"Well," Kate began, "he climbed that staircase as though

nothing was wrong with him except a fit of bad temper, didn't he! I've waited till he returned before deciding whether to ring Doctor Williams—you said you hadn't, Laura."

"Bad temper! my word," Gwen drew out her skeins of silk and square of canvas, "he's never threatened to strike me before."

Marion said, reminiscent: "Once, when I was a girl of seventeen, he smacked my face. I had disobeyed him about a young man who was courting me: a German." She gave a long sigh. "He was killed in the war—I didn't know it then, but I've had messages from him since."

There was a pause, broken by Gwen: "Mr. Gregory looks quite bewildered." It was untrue; he sat drinking tea in formal round-faced inscrutability; but she went on: "I don't wonder; it must be embarrassing for him to be drawn into these vexatious family bickerings. Accept our apologies, Mr. Gregory."

"Now tell us all about this afternoon." Marion, planting the tea-cosy over the pot, seemed to be addressing him.

Laura heaved round from the fire. "There's nothing to tell except that he left the house to get away from you three. It's possible he thought it was a way of ending his life."

Gwen laid down her skeins of silk and said: "I've often wondered if he'd commit suicide. . . . Laura, are you becoming more convinced that he has lost his reason?"

"She's so obstinate," Marion sighed, as Laura turned back to the fire without replying. "But we must allow she hasn't seen as much of him as we have. She doesn't know yet, for instance, that he locked us out one night and Kate had to batter down a window with a hatchet."

Kate heaved herself up. In her face her mind could be detected struggling at a leash. "The question is," she said in her grittily hoarse voice—"are we to consult the doctor or not? Laura, you've got to face unpleasant facts. After what's happened to-day, can you make up your mind? Do you think he's insane or not?"

Laura's face turned over her shoulder. "I told you this afternoon—I think he is dying."

"What?" Kate exclaimed. "When he climbed the staircase like that after being out all day in this bitter cold! I tell you again, you don't know how physically strong he is." She made an effort over her impatience. "I won't suggest that you think of our lives here alone with him; I'll only ask you to consider whether it's not best for his own sake to get him into a well-run, comfortable Home—Doctor Williams knows of an excellent one. And you might consider in addition that besides the first-class psychological treatment he would get, he would be rid of us—excepting you, of course; he might welcome *your* visits."

"You want my support, do you?" Laura said. "I'm to stand by you as a witness?"

"She still suspects we're only thinking of the money," Gwen said with immense offensiveness, while she selected a silk thread. To this Marion added: "Well, we've got to live, haven't we? *We* can't earn thirty pounds a week singing——"

Kate exploded. The demoniac wrath in her face seemed to burn with the agony of deeper, unuttered curses. "God damn you both," she howled to her sisters, "hold your stupid tongues! You go off the point like a couple of washerwomen. How many times have I told you not to interrupt with your braying, you——" She took a great breath, half choked.

"Now, Kate!" purred Gwen. Marion added affectionately: "You know, dear, giving way like that upsets your nerves." No doubt to allow Kate time to simmer down, she swerved to Alex with her turned-on hostessy lightness: "And you, Mr. Gregory, what do you think? We probably need a man's judgment and you've seen and heard enough about my father by now, surely?"

Laura saw he had no intention of being cornered like this; aware that the drama in this house was beyond the question of sanity, he was preparing to lift the dispute from the awful private warfare in the room. He pursed his lips, he squirmed a little, he peered. But at last he pronounced: "Clinical insanity is a difficult question for a lay person to judge, my dear Miss Marion. Particularly if he believes, as I do, that nowadays everybody is moving about in a vast asylum of crippled souls . . . I've come to the conclusion that hatred——" he pronounced the word with a soft boom—"outweighs all the other emotions in our so-called civilisation. And hatred, being the most self-destructive of the emotions, is surely insane?"

Handing back a tea-plate, he paused but showed every evidence of not yet being finished. No one else spoke.

Laura recognised his purpose in dropping, like a stone thrown into a hothouse stifling with heat and perverted plants, that word 'hatred'. She glanced cautiously at her stepsisters. Gwen looked blank, though the embroidery was laid down. Marion was all social attention but plainly unreceptive, a vestal of the tea-tray. Only Kate, her fury controlled, began to stir; there was a gleam in her eye. Alex went on:

"To take an example, think how nationalist hatreds can bring the insane destructions of war—meaningless, squalid destructions, to say nothing of the way war coarsens the human race. Yet, in an indirect way, nationalist hatred is impregnated into our schoolchildren. In the same way, personal hatreds, leading to obsessions and the need for satisfaction, inevitably corrupt the mind and bring diseases of the spirit——" He paused again.

Kate pounced. "You are suggesting of course that my sisters and I are diseased with hatred? Ourselves insane? Well, Mr. Gregory, it may be true, according to your notions. But,"—a contemptuous note began to fume in her voice—"we haven't deliberately stepped into this hatred and insanity, you know! Hasn't everything a cause? Do you think hatred just descended on us out of nowhere and nothing?"

He flicked into a careful awareness of her; there was

something of deference in his manner as he replied, pompous in his caution: "I do become conscious that in family life there are certain elemental blood-impulses that suggest that the domain of barbaric sacrifice and tooth-for-tooth vengeance is just round the corner of many a desirable modern residence." He coughed, gave a glance over his shoulder to that ghostly accusatory policeman dogging such utterances. "But I do think too," he protested, "that we can make an effort to escape these horrors—which surely lead to the torments of guilt and all that ruinous to-do of the blood-curse."

"Can we, can we escape them?" Upraised and taut, Kate looked starkly awakened. "Well, perhaps we can. But haven't we got to pay in some way? Become sort of eunuchs? Or take to drink or drugs or escapes into other vices? Anyhow, lose force, become effete . . . In the case of nations," she went on with a staccato mocking, "become decadent; second-rate powers." Then she gave her harsh laugh, gritty in her throat. "But you're quite right about blood sacrifice." She pointed a finger upwards. "Ours is upstairs. Hiding in the tower-room by day, down in the cellar at night—perhaps Laura can explain why? *I* think he's frightened out of his life. Guilt, true enough! That man killed my mother."

No one said a word. Kate's demeanour, indeed, did not encourage interruption, and she resumed almost at once, direct to Alex: "I'm telling you all this not because you may think us disagreeable women, wicked daughters"—again the hard laugh sounded in her throat, while he made a gesture of denial—"but because it's a personal relief to talk of it to you, someone outside the business, though of course Laura has told you a great deal already and she goes to you for help. . . . Do you want to listen?"

At his prompt assurance that he did, she proceeded: "As I tried to get into Laura's stubborn head this morning, our parent is a heartless, ostentatious vulgarian . . . A rude overriding creature," she added with ferocious emphasis, again making Laura become fixedly aware of this strange unknown stepsister, "a man who suddenly became conceited about the state of his soul. And because he suddenly took to trying to save this precious soul—or skin, perhaps—he wanted to drag *us* along with him as sacrifices— presumably he was influenced by the example of Abraham with his son; he's never got the Old Testament out of his system, wicked man though he's been. But after years of obedience to him my sisters and I began to put up a fight. We've been trying—perhaps too late—to put a spoke in his wheel—that's all *our* wickedness amounts to. He treated us abominably; he still does, for we haven't won yet. He starved us in all kinds of ways. Money was always an obsession of his. He made it in a disgusting way, and he made it to show-off and to buy a woman—Laura's mother, if she'll excuse me—a woman he destroyed and got into the grave as he did our mother." She paused, to light a cigarette, and possibly to allow this last revelation to sink into Laura, who however betrayed no sign of shock.

Then she resumed: "We haven't always been half starved. At one time we came in for some of the money. Marion is wearing evidence of it now, as you may have noticed, and Gwen could have all the expensive chocolates she wanted . . . Oh, at one time, he didn't stint us, providing we kept obediently in his power. But, more important than this cunning buying of us, he got us by breeding in us a feeling of shame. As children we did not know for certain that he was a wicked man, though Marion tells me *she* knew . . . yes, yes, Marion," she gave an impatient gesture, "don't interrupt, I'm saying it for you . . . But this secret atmosphere of something evil going on was thick in our home in London. We breathed it every day, and when we went out, if we didn't exactly hang our heads, we felt furtive. And when we made attempts to form friendships, then and later, it was without confidence and determination, showing no real fight. He had cut us off from the normal world."

A calm, hard indifference in her face now, she ruminated

fixedly for a minute before going on, flicking ash off her cigarette: "Then years later came this conversion, religious mania, or whatever it was—anyhow, fright of his money was part of it. He became miserly. Laura must know a little of that. But what she doesn't know is that the money that enabled her to run away to London was got from our father by her mother threatening to spread it about this district, his precious family birthplace, how he made his fortune. She could order from the victuallers in Tremartin as much drink as she wanted, and clothes from London too, but she could never get any sums of ready cash. But she got this four hundred pounds for Laura. Blackmail, it could be called, and she blackmailed a very guilty man. I can hear her shouting at him now; it was in this very room. Gwen and myself crouched outside that window: the three of us had a good system of espionage and we often worked in shifts. Of course we became very jealous about this four hundred pounds put into a bank in Laura's name; and as at this time he was so miserly with us, Laura can hardly blame us for certain unkind acts towards her, especially from Gwen." She added with a twist of ruthless honesty: "Gwen always had a peculiar 'down' on Laura; why I don't know . . . it was one of those . . . those things"—surprisingly woolly, she fumbled over the word—"that you get in families."

Embroidering again, Gwen put in: "It began when Laura came to us first, in London. She was such a stodgy child. Once I let her get lost in the middle of Hampstead Heath. But a policeman brought her home . . . I couldn't help it," she added with bland frankness; "she aggravated me."

"I'm glad," Laura said tartly.

"You were a sullen child, you know, dear!" Marion inserted with a distant, musing aloofness. "You used to talk and behave like a board-school child. You seemed quite rough to me."

"And I," Laura said, "thought you so artificial, I couldn't

believe you had anything but eau-de-Cologne in your veins."
The heavily insulting exchange was like something set going
by a clock.

"Oh stop that!" Kate raised her voice. "It leads nowhere.
Can't you see I'm trying to clear the air a little?" As though
she too had now begun to find him some sort of relief, she
turned again to Alex: "Well, after this conversion of our
father, we began to live like hermits here. We didn't
exactly starve—not physically at least—but we've got an
idea of what His Majesty's prisons must be like. It's true
I managed to get a horse out of him, but only because a
crony of his who was a local bigwig backed me up and father
was ashamed to show his meanness before this influential
man." A grimace crossed her face. "But eventually my
horse had to go. I couldn't afford to feed him properly.
My sisters and I used to quarrel badly about the spare cash
left from the housekeeping money. Marion"—the grimace
darkly flashed again—"particularly wanted her toilet
accessories and Gwen her weekly box of chocolates——"

Marion interrupted: "And you your cigarettes."

Kate suddenly shot up from her chair, as she had done
after her recital of the morning, extreme impatience dis-
torting her face. "Bah, why do I go on?" She crossed to
the fireplace, kicked a log into place and stood hulked
against the mantelshelf. Laura, crouched on the footstool
below her, looked up at her with a wondering, uneasy face.

"Well," Marion fumbled at her curled coiffure, "I think
you went on too long, Kate. Upsetting yourself. And very
likely boring Mr. Gregory."

"Far from it." Always a sign of turmoil within, his head
began to sway about, the tight-fitting soft collar constricting
the swollen neck. "But I cannot comment." He was
helpless in a flood of male compassion for her stepsisters;
and fearful of giving it expression.

Gwen, looking at him over her embroidery, said:
"Marion, did you say you could find Mr. Gregory a drink?"

"There's a little of that sloe gin," Marion tittered, with

an archness that inevitably made Laura tremble. "And a little sherry. Perhaps a *little* for us all . . . Mr. Gregory, your visit has done wonders for us." She swished away, the train rippling behind her.

Laura sat hopeless. The sense of being vanquished, of being unable to cope with all this bitterness, overwhelmed her again. This long monologue while the sick man was locked away alone in that room! Yet she couldn't run up to make another attempt to gain admittance. She couldn't move.

Kate had sat down again in her chair. Alex began, tentatively: "I was especially interested in your remark about your father never getting the Old Testament out of his system. I suspect he had a very black and white upbringing? . . . I do hope," he added, as Kate gazed silently at the cigarette in her stubby, brown-stained fingers, "that I don't seem impertinently inquisitive—or aloof?"

"No. You've brought a certain amount of relief to the house; it's like," she gave her hard laugh, "the relief of besieged people. . . . I didn't care for you at first, you seemed irritating and rather smug; but I've thought since that you're far from shallow." (He sent Laura a green little reminding glance.) "I expect the atmosphere of this house badly needs ventilation by an outsider. . . . Laura can't do it, she's swayed too much by her dislike of us, due to her ignorance—without meaning to do so, I'm sure, she's grated our nerves quite badly too."

After delivering this, with a morose hauteur suggesting she had no intention of working underhandedly for Laura's support in the question of their father's insanity, she continued: "Ventilation indeed! All this concern and talk about him! Anyone can see we're slaves to him. Haven't *we* troubles? Souls of our own?" A spasm of baulked rage came and went in her face before she turned again to Alex: "His upbringing was more than strict; it was downright evil. I expect you know how the teachings of the Bible can go to people's heads and make them drunk, if not worse. Father was reared in this district, and some time ago I got to know an old woman who knew him and my grandfather; she was a servant in their farm until my grandfather lost all his money in some coal-mining investment . . . 'The Bible for breakfast, dinner and supper it was,' she told me, 'and never a smile with anybody and the food just enough for chickens.' After the loss of his money it seems my grandfather went to pieces, he'd spend the whole day praying and reading the Bible, and the farm would have gone to rack and ruin but for my grandmother, who was physically tough as her son but who rarely spoke to anyone, not even to her husband and son—I expect even speech was a sin and a waste——"

"Old Mrs. Lewis," put in Marion, settling with the tray of drinks, "said our grandmother wasn't allowed to sit with her husband and son in the local chapel and she used to eat a raw swede out in the fields . . . Really," she bridled, "one would imagine women in these parts hadn't come out of the dark ages; it makes one boil." Bending ceremoniously over the tray of drinks in her low-cut gown and yellow pearls, she suggested at least an external progress in the long pilgrimage of women.

"She wasn't buried in the same grave as her husband either," Gwen said, stitching, "even though it was through her exertions the farm didn't go bankrupt. Our father wouldn't have it. Mrs. Lewis said it was the talk of the district. . . . Only a thimbleful for me, Marion. I have the supper to cook."

"Putting two and two together," Kate resumed, taking a glass, "I've come to the conclusion that, besides that Old Testament kind of life, our parent had never got this father of his out of his system; he never really died for him. I think he wanted to make money mainly because his father suffered so much over losing his own——"

"But he lost his head and made the money in a nasty way." Marion sat up primly sipping sherry. "Perhaps it's no wonder he's gone to pieces in his turn."

"Money," Gwen said, coaxing a purple thread into her needle, "is always a curse, they say . . . It's the most destructive weapon in the Devil's arsenal," she added with a schoolmistress gravity, causing an astonished silence in the room—Kate broke it with an impatient snort.

Once more carefully veering from the personal, Alex said: "I've sometimes wondered if it wasn't a grave error to translate and popularise the Bible. A magnificent book, but one to be handled with great care. Aren't most human beings, except, perhaps, artists, scholars and saints, unfit to read it? Its brew can go too potently to mortal heads. Or is its teaching too remotely alien for our assimilation?"

"Surely, Mr. Gregory," Marion leaned forward in argumentative crispness, "the country cannot be governed successfully without the Church?"

"Dear Miss Marion, I was referring to a very remote connection of the Church——"

But Laura got up, impatient as Kate. "Where is all this leading, sitting here talking and talking!" She moved about restlessly. "Turning him into a petty villain! Oh, it may be the truth. Or the partial truth—how can we know all the mysteries in a person's mind and soul?" She crossed from the window to the door, prowling as though caged. "The past can't be interfered with, anyhow." Her eyes seemed to give a little recoiling jerk from Marion. "The point is: in his condition he can't be allowed to go on isolating himself in that room."

"Exactly," said Kate, calm. "I began by trying to convince you that if he doesn't develop a serious illness from this bout to-day—and I don't think he will—then you'd better join us in the business of getting him into this place recommended by Dr. Williams. Because he will *not* allow any of us to look after him."

They all looked at Laura. She came back from the door and flung herself into a chair half hidden by the piano. She did not reply, and Kate went on: "The business is unpleasant; but, think, it's also a medical necessity, like going away to be treated for T.B. or something. There's a legal formality to be gone through, and probably your support will be a help in making this as quick as possible——"

Marion, pushing a cork into a bottle, said: "But then we've got to get him out of the house. Martha Jones over at the Garth told me that when her husband was taken away she had to get her married daughter Phillis to come all the way from Swansea to coax her father out into the car. He was very fond of Phillis and she said she was going to take him for a drive to the sea."

Laura rose and left the room. Kate was looking at Marion with a cold, glassy hopelessness. Alex examined his finger-nails, and even Gwen laid down her embroidery. In the desolate silence the ticking of the black marble clock became very audible.

2

She went up to her room and lay on the bed, crouching under the eiderdown. She couldn't stop herself trembling her arms and knees were beyond control . . . If she had lifted one of those bottles and brought it down on Marion's head! The impulse still raced along her blood. But would the inhuman doll-like creature have felt the blow?

She curled down; gradually the warmth eased her.

When presently she lit the candle and went up to the tower she found the beaker and hot-water bottle still outside the door. There was no sound, but a dim gleam of light showed under the door. Hesitantly, she tapped; there was no reply. She knocked louder, calling to him. Still no reply. She beat sharply. Then came a long low cry. It was like a wail from the innermost heart of man, an agonised protest against violation.

Yet she could not move away. "Father," she begged, "let me come in."

With a yell of fury, he answered: "Break down the door and still you shall not come in."

And she knew then that the crisis of his torment was at hand. It was in his voice, the long low cry of utter repudiation. She crept away, mechanically taking the beaker and hot-water bottle. Back in her room, she lay on the bed again, drawing the eiderdown round her shoulders, sunk into a paralysis of despair, accepting now that it was she who had brought about this final phase. Her arrival had ended a bitter truce. The stagnation of the house had been disturbed. Her stepsisters had wakened again to their hunt. And he—his agony had become newly focused. For she too belonged to the inescapable past. The past, the source and cause of these furious scenes in which all the joy and happiness of life seemed mocking illusions.

And now she could do no more to offer him ease. She must only wait.

Beyond the candlelight on the dressing-table the frosty moonlight of the window seemed to crackle. Alex came in. He sat on the bed's edge. His loose bulk, cloudy under the soft, considerate face, was unobtrusively tranquillising. But she almost burst into a hysterical cry at his first words:

"Gwen sent me up to ask if you like curried eggs. If not, there's cold brawn. Supper will be ready in half an hour. . . . We must eat," he said, faintly caressive. She had not replied.

"I'm trying to think whether I can sit at table with Marion," she half gasped at last.

"Oh, Marion . . . of course, behind those delightful pinks and whites she's a pure mass of cast iron. Do try and be more neutral about her. Then you can enjoy her, as I do."

"Enjoy her!" The eiderdown heaved.

"It's Kate I find intimidating. That brackish quality of hers, so strong I can taste it on my tongue. . . . But realistic, my word! She barks out her statements as if she's never, never made the mistake of going maudlin with pity.

Ah, Kate's inhumanly honest—no doubt that's why she's so alarming. She despises masks, she's never realised their necessary charm——"

"Realistic and honest? Are you coming round to the opinion that she's right in wanting to get my father . . . declared insane?" She had hesitated before the word 'declared'; she found it difficult to say 'certified'.

He peeped down at her and, after a pause, murmured: "I don't think it's going to be necessary to arrive at that opinion."

"I hope he dies soon," she whispered.

They spoke in low muted voices. Up here the house seemed withdrawn into a clear repose, those vitriolic angers dispersed like acrid fumes. In the candlelight she smiled up at him faintly. Yes, his presence was light as a feather. No thrusting forward of his personality—the essence of good-mannered affection. It was when he was like this that she realised, with self-rebuke, the value and rare beauty of his loyalty . . . and of his patience.

"I thought to-day, up there in that place, that he had already died," he went on. "Something essential had fled. But the battle his three daughters insist on is still going on somewhere, and he is forced to take his part in it. . . . Laura, they're fighting a ghost, though they won't accept it as that. You needn't hate them, darling. And, remember, there's no victory in wars between human beings. That old-fashioned organ the heart won't allow it. They're going to pay for all this warfare. In their turn."

"Aren't they paying already?"

"Partially. But they think their quarry hasn't been extinguished yet. It's when they're released from the chase that they're going to know the hollowness of victory . . . Poor things," he said, vaguely regretful, but adding, not without a glint of homage: "Impressive poor things."

"I couldn't stand all that cold-blooded talk of Kate's any longer," she said wretchedly. "And when Marion spoke about that man being enticed away, I felt the madhouse was already here and in a moment I would be smashing something on her head." She cowered down, beginning to shiver again.

"This room is very cold." He too shivered, peering round into the russet shadows. The candlelight picked out objects. "The cup of beef tea and hot-water bottle were not accepted, then? Emblems of mortality!" He plucked the eiderdown's edge. "What my visit has done to me is to give me a deeper awareness of the flight of time . . . and how people can lay waste to their souls . . . I've become more aware of the hour-glass—Laura, I'm getting cold." He lifted the eiderdown, lay beside her and, after a silence, resumed: "You're realising now, aren't you, that all this belongs to forces beyond your responsibility? You've seen you can do nothing now?"

He took her hand; it curled unresisting in his. Over the curve of her cheek, rounded as an apple, ran a single tear. Side by side they lay silent in the warmth. The candlelight curled over her still face, with its dark unflickering eyes slackened of tension, like a child's bereft of thought. But another tear, pinpointed with yellow candlelight, dropped. Minutes passed.

"What are you thinking?" he asked. "I just thought we are here like two marble figures on an old tomb. Man and wife in all but fact."

"I was reminding myself again what a comfort it is that you're in the house."

"I knew I had better come. One of those solar plexus notions."

"I wish we could marry," she whispered. "But I'm frightened of it. I'm frightened that I would have to leave you."

"You mean, if the god turns up?"

"I might meet another Hugh. Make the same mistake again. I feel one does."

"I would keep track of your footsteps. Waiting for you to look back."

After another pause, she said: "It's extraordinary how I somehow depend on you—yet resist the fact of your will and find it necessary to conceal my real self from you. You seem to give me all the advantages of an affectionate woman friend plus a male . . . what is the word I want? . . . positivism?—no."

"Protection?" His tone became musing. "The mystery, or charm, of woman is that though she's so much tougher and more self-reliant than man she needs the illusion of male protection. I think I give you this sense of protection . . . While I—where do I stand?"

"Yes, my poor Alex. But I can't help it. The emotion can't be forced into activity."

"You look upon me as a wreck," he accused. "A has-been . . . I think if you fell in love with me I would stop the drugs. But to do that you'd have to change your whole angle of thought. You'd have to become aware of me in a new way. Even then of course the love might not happen. But it might make marriage possible; bearable."

"We seem to be drifting toward a scheme of marriage."

"It would be pleasant. And probably not dramatic. My three hundred a year would become double in your hands. We'd have a flat in a Kensington back street, and when your stage fling is over you'd teach singing, so as not to be too preoccupied with me. . . . Of course if my erratic Aunt Matilda sees my value at last—and if I'm married to you she's fairly certain to become less undependable—she won't let me down in that for which all rich maiden aunts are cherished."

"I don't intend making an honest man of you for the sake of your aunt," she began to bridle.

"I wish it for myself, you woman. In a mature way, I am in love with you. That is," he began to boom in his old style, the little beat of self-ridicule in it, "your physical presence gives me pleasure which I am able to control—to a certain extent. I would never waste away in unrequited passion for you; but on the other hand, there's the nice feeling of placidity you give me." He turned on his side towards her. "If only you didn't have this hankering for elegant, handsome ragamuffins, I can imagine our marriage as a pleasing experience, taking into consideration your own statements of what I supply——"

She jumped out from under the eiderdown. "You'd better go downstairs," she said, and after lighting the other candle, began brushing her hair.

"I'm happy to see you less wretched," he patted her shoulder as he passed. She caught the greenish flicker of his eyes in the mirror. And both smiled constrainedly, almost shyly: in the sheet of glass the smile was like an understatement more loaded with meaning than a decisive phrase.

3

She took one of the oil lamps from the hall and went upstairs. After supper Marion had asked Alex if he was too tired for a game of whist.

From her room she climbed to the tower yet again. The slit of light still gleamed under the door. But still there was no sound. She tried to convince herself he slept in that narrow bed which she had noticed as well-covered and clean: the long exhausted sleep of the aged. After all, her stepsisters knew his habits better than she did; perhaps it was not extraordinary that his eccentricities did not disturb them. Old men could be extremely stubborn, cantankerous and wayward. . . . She crept away.

A vague need to be occupied with trivial tasks made her wash a pair of stockings in the bathroom. Her mind meandered dimly. She filled her own and Alex's hot-water bottles and took a bath. Gwen certainly kept the water on the boil. With one of those extravagances the most miserly allow themselves, he must still pay the coal-bills willingly.
. . . . To-morrow she would order some drink from the

Ruthin Arms: chiefly for Alex. And there was her char-woman to write to about the flat. And Gordon, her agent. She would surely be here some time. London seemed in a foreign country; her life there had become remote.

Lying in the heavy soft bed, nerve-eased from the bath, she began to read a yellowed paper-covered novel she had found in the wardrobe. She remembered that in the old days Kate was lent these romantic novels by the only friend she had made in the district—Flora, the loose-lipped buxom daughter over at Garth Farm who, in addition, occasionally lent her a horse. The two would discuss the love-lorn romances with shrieks of ribald laughter; they made parti-cularly unmerciful fun of the men in them.

She found this one sweet and charming, as life some-times was. But the print began to yield little meaning. She remembered turning out the lamp. And sinking, with a dim last thought of the tower-room, into warm darkness.

Was it in her dream she heard slamming doors? One after the other. It must have been.

She was climbing the staircase from the hall, and at the bend under the arched stained-glass window stood Hugh, scanning a sheet of music, his eyebrows raised in the familiar, consciously quizzical way. She passed him like a stranger: he did not lift his eyes, only ran his hand—his other familiar gesture—over those gold curls whose number he surely counted daily. . . . She was lying on the floor in an ice-cold shaft of moonlight and felt a tear run like oil over her cheek. Above her, hanging like a moon-frosted star, glittered the white china rose. Swaying, she walked down meaningless corridors in a paroxysm of grief . . . and knew that rise of stone steps opening to naked sky-arched heights.

Had she heard a screech? A long ragged screech torn sharply from some throat and yet vague, dimmed?

Where was she? Impenetrable darkness pressed on her like a weight. Her eyes opened, she looked round bewildered. And saw the moonlit window. The room was flooded with a silver grey. A mirror gleamed. She sank back in relief. The quivering relief of escape from the dead kingdom of dreams. A deep quietude filled the house. Yet at the edge of her awareness remained that screech. And she remembered striking a match and looking at her watch. It was a quarter-past twelve.

This only faintly surprised her. Like dusk stealing into a grove her mind began thickening again: she was only dimly aware of her struggle against it.

But she woke again. And immediately sprang out of bed. What was it—that noise like a crash? Was there a cry? For a second she stood quite still. The moonlight was dimmer. Then she ran to the door and through the short passage to the landing. She ran in pure instinct, without stopping to snatch her dressing-gown. Down the staircase into the darkness of the hall. Flashingly aware of the scorching iciness of a stretch of floor against her bare feet. Aware too of the creak of an opened door above, an enquiring voice—she thought Gwen's. And of other sounds, fainter but nearer.

Now she had to feel her way along the panelling of the staircase wall. Her hand reached space. The cellar door was wide open. Dank air touched her face.

A moan came up from that hidden silence. Again she stood still, in a piercing moment of dread. Then, her hand against the wall, she descended the flight of gritty wooden stairs. Carefully at first, step by step, then in quicker certainty. "Father?" she called. But it was a whisper. She heard the sound of heavy breathing . . . nearer.

Her bare foot stepped into a soft yield of flesh and she fell.

A scream rang round the buried walls. She had stepped on his face. She felt the burning print of his mouth, nose and eyes against the sole of her foot. She fell on to his body. She did not hear her own scream. But in that moment when she thudded against his body a cord seemed to snap within her mind. She uttered another cry: low, vibrant, like triumph. And easing herself she lay flat across his body and took his head within her hands, her fingers feeling into the soft white air.

She lifted the face to her own. In a passion of sorrow she embraced him. As though for ever. Her crushed breasts flooded him with her warmth. She breathed into his nostrils. And in her passion of regret, the hopeless sorrow of the living, she wept. "Father, father . . ."

He moaned. She felt him quicken. His eyelids moved under her forehead. She called to him, called in entreaty. And slowly, slowly an arm fell across her shoulders and pressed with a light, broken weight. She heard the faint groan within his throat. And the whisper: "Laura . . . my daughter, Laura . . . stay with me."

She heard too the patter of feet above. A call: "Are you there, Laura?" A dim shaft of light shook down. Then other voices, a stronger light. As she staggered to her feet the arm fell from her in limp slackness. In the growing light she saw his hand lay open on the ground. And the white face of death.

They were ranged on the steep flight of steps: Kate first, then Gwen, and Marion peering behind in brittle nervousness, a hair-net tight over her curled hair. Each wore a dressing-gown; each carried a candle. The light swarmed down on her raised face. They descended another step in unison. "We heard a scream——" Kate said.

They peered down in silence. His head lay under the last step: the eyes were closed. At once they descended the lower steps, cautiously stepping across the head. Laura knelt and lifted his head. She saw blood on her finger-tips.

The three candles lit the whole square whitewashed place. A coffin of unstained oak lay on two trestles below the high iron-barred grating of frosted glass; if the glass were smashed the coffin would not be seen from outside. The lid stood upright beside it. From a hook screwed into a ceiling-beam dangled a length of rope. A candle-stick lay fallen on its side in the middle of the floor. Except for the

iron safe which had been there always, and the bricked
wine-bin built into an alcove, there was nothing else.

"Well," Marion said, "*I'm* not surprised. I always said
he wanted to commit suicide, but he never had the courage.
. . . Yes, thank you, Dora," she whispered over her
shoulder.

"He must have got the coffin delivered when he gave us
the money to go away for that day trip," Gwen said. "The
same day that he put the padlocks on the cellar door."

"Will you fetch Alex?" Laura asked Kate, apparently
quite calm. Kate, after another glance round the place,
looked at her with all the satisfaction of one who has
clinched an argument, and tramped up the stairs.

He was breathing, through his mouth, with hard, broken
gasps. The pallor of his face was deadly. There was
nowhere to lift him. The sisters made no attempt to touch
him. "There's blood on your fingers," Marion pointed, and
gave Laura a handkerchief. His head raised into one arm
she stroked his forehead. In a soft crooning voice she
murmured the endearments used to a child.

She was glad they made no attempt to touch him. But,
while they waited, Marion and Gwen drew together as if
for mutual support and warmth. Gwen stood drawn up in a
fixed scrutiny of her father. By her side, Marion, drawing
her dressing-gown in, complained that she was cold. When
Laura looked up and angrily told them to telephone for the
doctor, Gwen said: "We'll see what Kate has to say. It's
no good losing our heads. He has always refused to see a
doctor."

Chapter Six

I

LAMPS were lit everywhere in the house. By the time she and Alex had carried him up and got him into bed—they took him to her own bed; it was still warm—the three sisters had dressed and were again mistresses of the house, completely prepared to take their rightful part in this last activity. Hot tea further pulled them together. Kate, a cigarette in her twitching fingers, telephoned the doctor. The log fire in the drawing-room was rekindled. For a while everyone was active, united in a common purpose. But Marion vanished for a while to confer with her favourite guide; she came forth from this looking delicately confident and at once found the last drop of brandy in the house. Finally, Gwen sat at watch beside the unconscious man. She had bathed the wound in the back of his head: blood was already thickly congealed into it. Kate lit a fire in the bedroom.

Laura gave way to their authority. They could do nothing to him now. He was surely beyond their interference. He had escaped.

So she concluded in the quietude that came to her, like a rest, when these activities were done. All of them must know this was the last. It was surely in his face. For a while each went in and out of the bedroom on tip-toe, spoke in hushed tones, examined with that aloof scrutiny of the living the gaunt, yellowish pale face with its rigidly closed eyes. But at intervals unintelligible mutterings came from the sunken mouth, and a faint tremble, like a struggle of his faculties, passed down his body.

But nothing could be done to him now.

Afterwards she sat alone with Alex in the drawing-room while they waited for the doctor. They talked in undertones, with long relapses into the silence dominating the house at last. When they spoke it was casually, with a careful after-the-event repudiation of the implications. He glanced at her curiously now and again. The glow in her cheeks, the brightness of her eyes, were not the evidences of distress.

"It certainly looks as though he intended to commit suicide," she murmured once. "But was he delirious when he came down from the tower-room? . . . He left both that door and the cellar door open, and usually he was careful to lock them behind him. Did he know what he was doing? And he must have fallen down those cellar steps——"

"There was no point in locking them if he intended committing suicide," Alex said. "Besides," he added, hesitant, "that parrot . . . !"

It was Gwen, carrying a candle, who had gone first to the tower-room and made the discovery. She came down and whispered it to her sisters on the landing. Kate, her tone carefully avoiding a 'Well, will you believe it now?' note, told Laura a few minutes later. Laura had taken the candle and gone up.

The parrot, its neck twisted, lay in the bottom of the cage. A drop of rheum oozed from the closed eye: the spread claws clutched the air disconsolately. The door of the cage was wide open. She remembered the screech that had seemed part of her dream.

The doctor did not arrive until two hours later, half-past three. Laura went into the hall. Marion was receiving him. His manner with her was knowledgeable and familiar. This was the man who had aided their attempts to put their father under guardianship. "Here is my stepsister from London," Marion waved a hand of dismissal. "Poor man, called out in the middle of a freezing night! Did you have a terrible journey up? The roads are still like glass, I believe. Would you like some tea or coffee at once?"

Laura immediately disliked this youngish man. He looked too much the clever, cerebral scientist intent on forging ahead and achieving his way at all costs. His head had the single-minded plunge of a beetle's. The world was clinical for such a man, people specimens. She was glad the possibility of a dispute with him was past.

She did not go upstairs with them but returned to the drawing-room. Presently Alex suggested that she should go up, but she shook her head. She did not even want to hear what the doctor had to say. And she had already taken her farewell: she had gone with him to the door of the final kingdom. She did not want to see his physical death. Let them watch round the bed. Let them possess what remained. Let them have the illusion of victory. Their reign had ended.

They were upstairs a long time. At last there were voices in the hall. But still she did not move. The front door opened and shut: a car whirred noisily. Marion and Kate came in.

"Father has been given an injection," Marion announced. "He will sleep comfortably for a while——" She paused: a fastidious look of withholding information crossed her face.

"He may even pass away in it," Kate added.

After an annoyed glance at her sister, Marion hurried on: "The doctor warned us he will probably not last long. He is suffering from shock and exposure. What can one expect? Of course I told the doctor about the cellar, and also about his going up to the cemetery this afternoon——"

"*Yesterday* afternoon," Kate corrected, continuing: "On the other hand, he may last a day or two. It seems his heart is not too bad, though pneumonia is threatening. . . . I always said he was strong," she reminded. "I shouldn't be surprised if he recovers." Marion gave a pout, as if she wanted to add: "To spite us."

"No," Laura said.

"Of course," Kate granted, "you said he was dying the morning after you arrived here."

"Laura coming back so casually and without a word of warning," said Marion, "*must* have started the shock in him. . . . Going out into the bitter cold like that this afternoon—a suicidal act, if you like! We did warn you when you arrived, Laura, that he was in a bad mental state, didn't we?"

But Laura kept quiet. Compassion, until now kept at bay, coursed out for them. Alex sat looking interestedly at the sisters. They had the air of persons setting out on a long-awaited expedition. But Kate made another attempt to wrest from her sister the authority she had retaken— "In the morning," she said crisply, "I shall ring up father's original solicitor and see what can be done about raising some money. Father, possibly, will never sign another cheque, and a house like this can't be run on a few shillings."

"I think, Kate," Marion said, "I had better go and see Mr. Rowlands in person. I am eldest daughter."

"But you are so unbusiness-like," Kate objected.

"I unbusiness-like? Why, you have to count on your fingers, you always were stupid with sums."

Really they were on the scent of that unexplained visit their father had been to the second Tremartin solicitor. Laura cut into the exchange, which was becoming sharper: "But I can let you have some money." No doubt it was Alex's presence that curbed Marion's snaky pounce: all she said, proudly, was: "I think we can arrange our affairs without further aid from you, Laura. You left this house nine years ago and you're practically a stranger."

"Don't be so idiotic, Marion," Kate barked, a mocking note down her voice. "You may yet find yourself turned out of this house by Laura."

Momentarily arrested by this, Marion exclaimed: "But surely the law of the land wouldn't allow it?"

Laura got up. "We're all becoming irritable from lack of sleep. What are the arrangements for nursing him?"

It was past four o'clock. She suggested that everyone went back to bed while she remained with her father. Kate went to consult Gwen and eventually this was agreed to.

Laura would be relieved at eight o'clock. Kate said the little spare room, now the only unoccupied one except the tower-room—which Laura refused—would be prepared for her. Laura saw, with indifference, that they wanted to be together in the day-time: the night nursing would be for her. Before settling herself for the night she wrote a cheque and put it on the kitchen-table: the licensee of the Ruthin Arms would cash it.

Alex whispered: "Shall I stay with you?" But she refused.

The lamps downstairs and on the landing were lowered: night closed on the house again. The parchment-shaded lamp threw a dimmed light across the bed.

For minutes she stood looking down at him. He was sunk far away into sleep. But it was that sleep recognisable as unnatural, unhaunted by the shadows of activity. Sunk in it, the cadaverous face lay oppressively released. She mourned over those bluish eye-sockets, the helpless cheek-bones, that curved nose once so proud, the yielded droop of the long pallid mouth. From his whole demeanour came an unendurable helplessness, a slaughter of all those attributes that assemble a face and announce 'I am I; I live.' A drop of liquid had obliterated the human miracle. An old man had lost his link with the living: this face announced 'For ever'.

He was utterly removed from her. Then, alone in those final hours of the night, she wept at last. Burningly and completely delivered to grief, she wept for him and for herself. She swayed unseeing about the room, she crouched by the bed on her knees, she found herself at the door.

But when it had passed and, cold and shivering, she lay on the hearthrug in the fire's glow, a mysterious silence began to enter her being. How long she lay there she did not know. A wonderful ease, clear and calm, became awake in her. She had touched the source of the spirit. And reassurance burned within the heart of that shattering light. It was like a rebirth.

Presently she rose and crossed to the bed. She looked down on him in purified calm. Cleansed and composed. This coming death was beautiful.

Lifting the window curtain, she stood looking out, waiting for morning. Was there a distant trembling of light, a stirring in the air? The snowy trees greyly cascaded, the marbled fields stretched dim. Frost-bright stars rode high and rayed, their flashing diamond-sharp: hard and certain, they flourished as if they would never crumble. The vast silence spread unbroken as eternity. But morning, a sphere of new-born radiance, would come. This night, with its unholy happening, would pass.

At eight o'clock Kate came in.

"He hasn't stirred," Laura said. At the reposeful, almost placid tone, Kate gave a sidelong glance at her stepsister. Coming from the bed, she said: "I shouldn't be surprised if he'll pull through."

"No," Laura shook her head.

"You sound as though you wanted him to die."

"I do." She drew the curtains. The slow morning light hung milkily pale, not yet glittering. There was no sign of a melting of the snow: still the trees stood stiffly white. The sky's blue arched faint but hard: it would be a day like yesterday. She felt an easy, pleasant need of sleep.

"I'm going straight to bed. Will you call me at three o'clock this afternoon? . . . Unless of course——" she hesitated, looking with calm speculation at the bed.

"You will be called if anything happens."

"No," Laura said, suddenly decisive, "don't call me for that."

Kate took up the coal-scuttle. "Gwen's just going to bury the parrot," she said. "She's out by the stable digging a hole."

2

He lived for four days. At intervals, day and night, he would rally and open his eyes with, at first, a ghostly vagueness that soon became almost fully quickened, often conscious of his surroundings and the identity of whoever was in the room. But the doctor, coming twice a day, assured the sisters there was no hope.

On the second morning—it was the day the snow melted, vanishing in a couple of hours in the quick spring-like sunshine—he woke and, with much of his old bitter querulousness, asked for his clothes. Kate had just come in to relieve Laura. At Kate's resolute refusal he began an attempt to get out of bed. Laura was still in the room, but, after taking a step towards the bed she stood quite still. She did not want to touch him. Neither, it seemed, could Kate. The door was open, and Gwen could be heard calling to Marion from the landing. Laura hurried to fetch her. By the time she returned he had got half-way out of bed: one leg dangled, but his head had fallen back on the bolster-end.

Gwen, tall and strong-limbed, advanced without hesitation: Kate retreated. Laura stood aloof in her indeterminate apathy, like a stranger outside the family circle. He watched that approach with a sudden frenzy in his eye, like the frenzy in a horse's eye. But his voice was only a whisper: "No, no."

"Father," Gwen said smoothly, bending over him, 'you're very weak. See—you can't lift yourself back." And slowly her sinewy hands went towards his body.

"Don't touch me!" It was the ghost of a scream. Laura quivered; but still she did not move.

"I must, father." And as, panting, he crumpled and went limp, Gwen lifted him back into the bed. He lay gasping, with the defeated hopelessness of the stricken. She wiped specks of foam from his lips. She smiled down at him, a faint smile of encouragement. "We must take care of you, father." She tidied the bed covers, vigorously tucking them in. "You'll never get well if you're disobedient."

It was after this he became completely submissive to the nursing of his three daughters. And he did not show any preference for Laura's company.

In the early evening of the second day she went into the room and found him talking to Alex, who had readily offered to take a share in the nursing. He seemed not to notice Laura's quiet entry. She sat down silent in the shadows beyond the fireplace, instinctively obliterating herself. Apparently fully aware—at least at first—of Alex's identity, he talked with a mixture of rational enquiry and febrile mystical flights. But within his voice was the whipping of an intense urgency.

"But do you think, sir," he asked, "that we make progress through a knowledge of sin? . . . Knowledge of one's own sins, I mean," he added.

"Progress to what?" Alex asked. He sounded perplexed but patient.

The sick man showed the impatience of the obsessed irritated by someone's curbing. Laura saw that he had less a need for discussion with another than for expressing his own vision.

"Progress, *progress* . . . The soul doesn't stand still, sir! . . . Can evil purify? . . . Evil, or the curse on mankind?" His breathing became difficult.

"Is there a curse?" Alex countered, musingly.

"Why do men do evil, then?" There was a cunning triumph in his voice. "Answer that!"

"All men?" Alex parried. "Perhaps evil comes from a glandular secretion, more prevalent in some human beings than others . . . or from purely racial creeds."

"No, no." The voice became testy, but, under the compulsion of sheer will, it rose: "Evil is a thing of the soul. That is why it can torment. And evil is proof that though we rose from the slime, there is *something else?*" He uttered the last two words in entreaty, questioningly, as if begging for verification. Yet he went on at once: "Or is it that the soul pays for the evils of the flesh? . . . A man is two men, and there is always war between them. A man is dazzled by the lusts of the flesh and they silence the soul for long, but they do not kill it. The flesh lusts after possessions and a man wastes himself in this lust, and the soul despises him——" In a troubled effort at concentration, he stopped. The yellow fleshless hand plucked at the bed cover.

Alex, to give him rest, commented: "But a man can think of the flesh as a happiness and not a curse, he can obtain possessions without guilt."

But Mansell writhed in quick repudiation. He even lifted his head. "It is death to live like that, death and damnation: a man returns to the pool of slime: the soul is choked in it." And his eyes had become unconnected now, as if no image of others was reflected there, and he proceeded without pause, the gasping gone from his voice: "You have seen the throat of a toad beating? Beating as though the life within longed to burst from its bondage? The toad that lives in the slime from where man came. It is the beating of the soul's embryo: it is the holy quivering of life longing to grow. Look into a toad's eyes and you will see there a feeble shadow of man's agony."

Alex was silent.

The head had sunk back into the pillow. And the voice almost whispered now, its strength dwindling, as it began a long monologue, some of which was lost in murmuring. He repeated more than once: "I am only a fragment." Snatches rose clearly: "Suffering has more meaning than joy, birth is always attended with pain." He said: "I loved only myself, and that was evil; I never dedicated my life to anyone, and that was madness." A whimper ran through the voice at: "But the soul's loneliness is the hardest punishment of God." He whispered: "I turned from the divine source and I was broken. I became like a hungry ass braying in the wilderness. God abandoned me." The voice rose again, as it pronounced: "The choice between good and evil, all men must make it, no man is free of it. Men choose evil because it gives them pride and power."

For a while he lay silent, his eyes almost closed. Then, startlingly, came a chuckle. And, in a voice totally different from the intensity of the other utterances, contemptuous, even coldly malevolent, he said: "Let the vultures take their prey."

In a few minutes he lapsed into a deep sleep: the regularity of the breathing proclaimed it. Laura rose and approached the bed. The hollow bony face, greyly yellow, seemed eternities away. But the white hair, still thick and vigorous, shone with vitality. Sight of it moved her strangely. She wanted to touch it. But she did not. Drawing away, she sank on to the hearth-rug beside Alex's chair; her head drooped.

Alex had turned up the lamp a little and noiselessly drawn the curtains. They talked in low voices, with the secret intimacy of the living in that room of death. He said, with a sigh: "This need of men to torture themselves! What a sense of sin your father has! Did he deliberately cultivate it in order to thwart or escape from his own nature?"

"How could he escape from his own nature?"

"Yes . . . but he's only realising that *now*. He must always have been a very religious man. But also a very proud one . . . I think I said before that I saw him as a man shaking his fist at God."

She was thinking 'For all his suffering, were not these last years the drama of birth?'

"He believes we progress through guilt. He bleeds and bleeds from a consciousness of guilt. . . . Was he such a wicked man?" Alex pondered. "This need to grovel . . . the obverse of the medal of man's proud sovereignty——" he gave his little ashamed gesture and peered over his shoulder. "*Was* he such a wicked man? Shut away in some cranny of his being surely there was the tenacious little shrub of goodness that is in everybody—I hope," he added.

"My stepsisters would deny it."

"Ah, your stepsisters!" He shook his head. "I mourn for them."

After a pause, she said: "He seems to have quite submitted to them. I saw Marion sponging his face and he didn't murmur."

Alex looked at her curiously. "There seems to be an armistice all round. You're allowing them a great deal of latitude. You and Kate seemed quite friendly with each other to-day."

"I . . ." she hesitated, "I think I feel nothing but pity for them now."

On which he commented: "I think it is wrong to see them as idly rancorous. There's something consecrated in their lives."

"Consecrated to evil vengeance," she allowed herself to reply, but still troubled.

"Vengeance perhaps," he admitted. "But I wouldn't be so certain of the evil . . . though of course," he added, "they may have inherited *that*—if one accepts your father's mythology."

Later, downstairs, he asked for a drink. Behind his flow of sympathetic attention and help during these days there seemed a vague unease. Laura sensed it. Was his own being shaken out of its philosophic sloth?

They all took a drink. In addition to brandy for her father, Laura had got several bottles of spirits up from the Ruthin Arms. Her stepsisters were always ready for a glass. Not that, in their cases, there was tension or exhaustion needing to be eased; rather, a subtle air of excitement, a subdued, unacknowledged atmosphere of festival, hovered about them. They were frequently in private consultation, and, on the whole, otherwise markedly polite to each other, even Kate giving an impression of impatience curbed.

Outside, too, the melting of the snow, the sunny spring-like mildness, wakened the house. The grass of the fields, freshened by the snow, shone brilliantly green. Gwen found some tiny unopened snowdrops: she had laughed as she brought them into the kitchen in her reddish, sinewy hand. "There'll be lambs soon," she said, pleasure hugging at her voice. When Laura suggested that the snowdrops be placed on their father's bedside table she did not demur.

In this current of serenity flowing through the house there were no disputes. Each accepted the task of nursing at the allotted time and appeared promptly in the bedroom; even Marion. (Indeed, Marion was constantly in and out of the room at other times.) Laura's apparent withdrawal from a hostile watching of them further eased the atmosphere. When she came on them obviously engaged in a secret whispering conference she seemed unconscious of it.

Once, going downstairs in her bedroom slippers for some milk, she heard them talking from outside the swing door of the kitchen and listened.

"But I wonder is she just acting?" Gwen said. "One mustn't forget she's been on the stage, though no one would think it."

"No, she isn't acting," Kate said in her downright way; "she's suffering from shock. She found him first, remember."

"Whatever it is," Marion said, "it's a relief to find her behaving herself; she had become very trying with her airs."

"Unless she *knows* something——" Gwen said hintingly. "Perhaps he told her something about the will."

"She's quite generous with her money," Marion said in a tone of distaste. "Oh dear, I will be glad when all this worry is over and we can be independent. I feel quite dazed with it all."

"Do you?" Kate gave a cynical laugh.

Laura having supplied money for the day-to-day expenses, and the doctor assuring them that their father would not last the week out, they had postponed the visit to the Tremartin solicitor.

On the fourth day Laura went into the bedroom after her sleep and found Marion alone but busy with her planchette contraption: she sat absorbed with it at the round table which she used for both this communication with the unseen and the tapping. Her father was asleep. It was five o'clock. The lamp was lit and the curtains drawn. Laura stood watching the board running on its castors over a sheet of paper. Two or three other scrawled sheets lay discarded on the floor. She picked one up: it was covered with pencilled whorls, angles, circles, and one or two broken words which shot off into slanting lines.

"Hush, dear," Marion said, though Laura had not spoken.

"*You must not worry about——*" Laura read, glancing over Marion's shoulder. The pencil stopped and ran skittishly across the paper, making a zig-zag design.

"You disturbed it," Marion pouted. "You're unsympathetic. The spirits always object to a materialistic presence."

"What do you call yourself, then?" Laura asked.

"I don't wish to argue with you, Laura. Will you put some coal on the fire?" She collected the sheets scattered on the table. Under one of them was a cheque book and a fountain pen. Since Laura made no attempt to put the coal on, she did it herself, clattering the scuttle and, perhaps in anger, threw the poker noisily back into the hearth.

They found their father's eyes full on them.

Recognition flickered laboriously into those bared eyes, like flecks of light into grey marbles. Marion, with a quick glide, reached the bedside. But Laura hung back: again she found herself unable to go to him. "You wish for something, father?" Marion asked, her head on one side. He only gazed at her penetratingly, almost with wonder. She went on, lightly: "Why, there's quite a stubble on your chin. I wonder could I shave you to-morrow morning?"

Still he did not speak. She turned the tiny vase on the bedside-table and, with that firm but coaxing seductiveness trained nurses use, said: "Have you seen the snowdrops

Gwen found for you? She went out searching everywhere for them."

"Bring your sisters," he said.

"They're resting, father, they're very tired from all the work and the nursing. If you've got anything to say I can tell them later."

The gleam in the watching, lidless eyes became sharp as a knife. A rasp grew in the hollow voice. "Bring your sisters."

"You must take a little brandy. The doctor came this afternoon and said it was doing you good." In a considerately fussy way she began to look for the bottle and glass. "Kate and I were talking to-day about getting champagne for you; the doctor said it would revive you. Do you think you could write a cheque? There are so many extra things to get. We found your cheque book in the tower-room."

Groaning, he slowly turned his head away from her. She could not get him to take the spoonful of brandy. But he reiterated, moaning into the pillows: "Bring your sisters."

Laura, with slow, almost dragging steps, went out. She found Kate and Gwen in their parlour. Gwen was cracking walnuts on the hearth-stone with a flat-iron—Kate had cycled to the village shop that morning. She told them that they'd better come upstairs. He wished to see them. At once they followed her. They went into the bedroom together.

But Kate, after a swift glance at the bed, immediately retreated to the closed door and stood with her back pressed against it. In the lamplight, dim at the far wall, her smudge of dark face looked flatly expressionless, but one hand gripped the door handle while the other dipped mechanically to a pocket in her brown cardigan jacket. Gwen, solid and tall, loomed at the other side of the bed opposite to where Marion, very much in charge of proceedings, stood. Laura did not approach the bed. She watched like someone cast out, retired from an event that did not concern her.

He had watched their entrance with a slow dumb scrutiny. But the vein beat in his temple. He was collecting strength to speak. His mouth opened but no word came; only the heavy, rasped breathing.

"You must take the brandy," Marion fussed. "I remember when mother was so ill I used to feed her with brandy—though *she* liked milk with it—and then she would talk to me quite a lot." At this Gwen gave a quick veiled look of approval at the eldest daughter. And he took the brandy. For a minute or two he lay panting. "I was telling father," Marion addressed Gwen across the bed, "we need some money for the extra expenses. I thought fifty pounds at the least are needed. And we owe Laura—what is it, Kate? . . . Why do you stand over there, dear? Father wishes to see you."

"We owe her seventeen pounds in all." The staccato grittiness of Kate's voice sounded like a warning.

"We can't afford a professional nurse," Gwen said. "The doctor said we need one."

Marion took up the cheque book from the round table. "The doctor said we could hire oxygen cylinders from the hospital too. He was quite surprised when I asked him how much they would cost. It looks so bad to stint money in an illness; we'll get talked about . . . I could write the rest if you just sign it, father. . . . Hand me the tray on that chair, Gwen." She uncapped the pen, tore out a cheque and laid it on the tray. "Take out father's arm," she told Gwen.

She fetched the lamp to the bedside table. Gwen took his arm from under the covers, and, while she lifted his head, Marion doubled the pillow for a raised support, and then held the tray before him. Gwen placed the pen in his hand. Beyond the softly illuminated bed Kate stood crouched, barely discernible, at the door.

He had watched the activities with an awareness into which wonder seemed roused. But submissive to them, to the touches of their hands. Was it the brandy that brought

a faint flush to those naked cheek-bones? His breathing was
easier. The thin withered fingers closed on the pen. Marion
and Gwen both held the tray firmly over the bed. And he
wrote. The two daughters watched. They arched their
necks as he laboriously traced the stalking letters.

Marion drew back with a long sigh. Gwen's strong neck
eased down. There was the sound of a match scraped
against its box. Kate lit a cigarette. The flame shook.

"Very well, father," reproached Marion thinly.

"It tires one's patience," Gwen said. "It tempts one to
tell everybody the truth about this house." She turned her
head: "Kate, he's written the word 'vultures' on the pay
line." She tore the cheque across. Laura was completely
ignored.

"Don't tear it up, dear," Marion exclaimed, swishing
towards her little table and casting a perplexed eye at the
planchette contraption. "We may need it as evidence.
Give it to me."

Gwen, after handing over the two pieces, unfolded the
pillow and let his head drop back into it. She might have
been looking down at a stranger of no particular interest.
"Why did you wish to see us?" she asked.

But the exertion had exhausted him. The gasping breath
returned. They waited. "Give him some more brandy,
Gwen," Marion suggested, sitting down and stretching her
feet to the fire. "Laura, you needn't stay; it isn't necessary
for *you* to be here." Laura did not move. Shrugging her
shoulders, Marion called across the room: "Kate, aren't you
cold over there?" Kate too did not move; neither did she
reply. Gwen went to the other side of the bed and poured
a spoonful of brandy.

He took it. The blurred eyes opened for a moment. They
waited.

"It *is* trying," Marion said fretfully. "But never mind.
What with the parrot and the cheque——" She nodded
schemingly. She was thinking of the possibility of having
to contest a fantastic will.

His voice began to mutter. There were other sounds in his throat, unknown, frightening. Sweat broke out on his forehead: again the vein beat in his temple. Gwen approached the bed. She whispered: "Is he going?" Marion rose from the chair and stretched her neck towards the bed. She did not advance, but her gaze shone unswerving. Even Kate stepped a pace from the door and, her face darkly unfathomable, stood watchful.

His body began to shudder. Suddenly he opened his eyes. And the voice, half strangled, hollow, broken, rose intolerably: "Always forgiveness . . . always she forgave me! Why did she forgive me! She never fought. Her eyes like a dog's . . . Sh . . ." the voice sank.

Advancing a step, Marion asked crisply: "Who, father?"

He stared at her. There was no strength in the gaze. But repudiation, the ghost of an eternal battle, shone somewhere in those blurring greynesses. "Your mother," he cried. "She sowed guilt in me. Always meek and not a word against me! Tearing me down! She asked to be destroyed."

"You destroyed her," Marion said, icily calm. "You murdered her." But within that calm something was stirring: like the faint tautening of a snake uncoiling from sleep.

As though riven by some last force, the long lean body writhed under the covers. "The weak tear down the strong, feed on them . . . They twine their roots into them, they eat into their strength . . . I had to destroy . . . But their poison remains for ever . . . She sowed guilt in me . . ." Like a withdrawing wave, he retreated into himself for fresh strength.

"Cant and humbug," Gwen said. She loomed over the bedside.

Marion, approaching yet another step, flung one mocking word: "Pharaoh!" But Kate slunk back to the wall and, leaning her shoulder against it, with shaking fingers lit a fresh cigarette from the butt of the other, which she ground under her heel on the floor-border beyond the carpet.

Laura retreated further into the shadows.

"You lived with that woman before mother died," Gwen pounced, immediately after Marion's taunt. "You were cruel as the hell you are going to. You married that woman. *She* dragged you down. You sold yourself to the Devil. . . . Burn in hell, damn you." She said it quietly and evenly, the pounce removed from her voice.

Only Marion was not to be recognised. For a flashing moment, a transfiguration of human attributes, she was like a being stripped and peeled of physical presence. The flesh of her face seemed burned away, her head was a livid skull. She was nothing but stark bone and elemental spirit. Death breathed from her. It was miraculous and momentary, a glimpse of the eternal. Almost at once this apparition vanished. She had reached the bedside.

Her long neck thrust out, she mewed: "Why did you have to destroy our lives too? Starving us, robbing us. Murderer," her voice rose shrilly, yet cracklingly thin. "Keep your money, take it down to hell with you . . . Vultures?" She gave a shrill laugh. "What did you expect us to be—cooing doves?"

But he had seen that death in her. She had struck. He withered, he curled up, he sagged. Obliteration was visible. His head sank back. A little gush of brownish liquid came from his mouth.

Laura looked round the room blindly, slowly, as one arriving from a dream. She heard Gwen's voice: "He's not gone yet . . . pass me that cloth, Marion." She walked haltingly, like an automaton, towards the door. Yet she paused to take the cigarette from Kate's lips as she passed her.

He died within an hour. The sisters remained in the room the entire time. When they heard the death rattle Laura was called. But she would not go upstairs. They came down together a little later, to the drawing-room. Marion, important as eldest daughter, announced the death

but said nothing else. Kate flung herself into a chair and
asked Alex if he had any cigarettes. She ignored Laura.

Gwen, for some reason, attempted to let down the three
portions of the venetian blinds of the bay window. They
were never used now. The large clattering middle portion
became crookedly stuck: she struggled with it. Kate, her
nerves very much on edge, began barking at her—why in
heaven's name did she want to lower the blinds in the middle
of the country? The blind remained askew half-way down.
Marion telephoned the doctor.

3

During the next three days Laura had brief businesslike
talks with her stepsisters, mostly on domestic matters, none
of them of importance. They treated her with a certain
amount of careful consideration. Were they perplexed, but
pleased, by the quiescence she had shown at last, as if she
acknowledged now their right to complaint? They informed her of whatever they considered necessary. She did
not interfere in any of the funeral and other arrangements,
and she told them she would be leaving the day after the
funeral. There was no longer any atmosphere of watching,
of listening at doors and figures hovering unexpectedly in
passages.

Awareness that important material facts would soon have
to be faced was put aside but lay behind every transaction
in the house.

The sisters were very busy. Even before their father died
they had searched the desk in the tower-room, but except
for the key of the cellar safe they found nothing of conse-
quence; there were only masses of bill receipts mingled with
sheets of writings on what seemed religious subjects.
Laura gathered—in the excitement of liberation the sisters
chattered quite openly—that the safe contained only the
house deeds and some jewellery of no great value. Marion,

exercising her authority as first child, took charge of both deeds and jewellery—"until matters are cleared up," she said, sweeping aside some remarks from Gwen and Kate. They also found the birth certificate: he was seventy-two.

They made another search but no will could be found. Gwen boldly asked Laura if she had any information to offer but Laura shook her head. As soon as the doctor made out the death certificate, on the morning following the death, Marion and Kate went with it to Tremartin. They returned with fifty pounds in cash, and after a private conference in their parlour Laura was called in. They informed her that, after a great bother, the new solicitor had privately lent them the money, but refused to let them see the will—it was deposited in the bank and he suggested the three sisters and their stepsister be assembled immediately after the funeral.

"He was a proper old fuss-pot," Marion pouted. "But I blame Kate; she would interrupt me, and she lost her temper." Kate, sitting on the red plush sofa, still looked malign. There was, too, a decided flush on Gwen's cheeks.

But their main information for Laura was that they had decided to bury their father in three, not four, days. "After all," Marion said, "it's only a matter of reopening that grave, and we have a coffin ready here——" Gwen interrupted to say: "Of course the lid will have to go back to be inscribed. I wonder had father paid for that? I don't remember seeing a receipted bill for it among those papers. We'll have to trust Bevan to be honest, though——" Kate cut in to tell Laura they had decided not to buy any mourning clothes, and Gwen interrupted again, saying: "We don't intend staying on here, so it doesn't matter what people think."

Laura, as briefly as possible, agreed to everything: she was glad her stay in the house would be cut by one day. They seemed almost glad of her presence in their room, they even tried to delay her. Their remarks markedly cut across each other's—like swords, she thought as she went out. But she was left with the distinct impression that they confidently inferred from the visit to the solicitor that nothing frightening awaited them in the will.

Money in hand, Marion hired the Ruthin Arms car the second day and went with Kate yet again to Tremartin. They took with them the coffin lid—Marion had arranged over the telephone to have the inscription done while they went shopping—and Gwen's list of articles needed, mostly food.

"It's a relief not to feel like Mother Hubbard," Gwen said, handing the list in the hall to Kate. She turned to the perfumed Marion to add: "Don't spend too much on scent now; you don't know how long that money's got to last us."

"Do you require anything in Tremartin, Laura?" Marion asked, not entirely without frostiness.

"Why don't you take Laura? *And* Mr. Gregory?" suggested Gwen, with a faintly jeering note for the latter name. "The lid can be tied behind." It stood ready against the wall.

An hour after they had gone, a reporter from the local paper arrived on a bicycle. Laura admitted him, took him into the drawing-room, and fetched Gwen from the kitchen. She went to the drawing-room with Laura very readily.

She gave information to the young man that the deceased, in addition to being a well-known London chemist and a leader in the religious life of that city, had owned several 'private temperance hotels' there, before obeying the call to return to his native land—'which he could never forget,' she added. She needed no promptings from the reporter, who must have known of her many letters to his newspaper. "He was married twice, first to a lady of local connections; his second wife was May Potter, the famous London actress. There are three daughters of the first marriage and, by the second, a fourth who hopes to be as famous on the stage as her mother." Standing authoritative, she obliterated Laura, who sat at her usual place before the fire.

The reporter looked up. "Miss Roberts," he said flatteringly, "one would think you'd been a reporter yourself. It's surprising how difficult these interviews are usually: people seem to want to hide their most simple affairs."

No doubt he was aware too of the nickname "Petticoat House". Gwen smiled and proceeded with automatic ease: "The deceased was a man of strong character, wilful at times and even eccentric, but always masterful, as his very successful business undertakings testify. He held to the old belief of ruling his home with a rod of iron. During recent years his health had failed and the three daughters of his first wife nursed him devotedly. They have remained unmarried." She shook out her skirt, gave him details of the interment, and concluded: "That is all, I think."

When they returned from Tremartin both Marion and Kate took annoyance that they had not been consulted about the press notice. "You should have told the reporter to come back, or kept him here," Kate barked, while Marion threatened to ring up the paper and ask for another visit.

The dispute took place at the late tea. But Alex pacified Marion; after Gwen had given an abridged version of the obituary, he said it sounded dignified.

More and more Marion had been accosting him with sociable flourishes. For herself, indeed, there seemed established between them a solid class understanding from which the rougher occupants of the house were unavoidably banished. More than once she expressed her pleasure that he had remained in the house during their time of trial.

"She's already got the manner of an heiress," he said to Laura during one of their walks together. "Do you think she has discovered something definite?"

"I think they suspect me of knowing more than I'm entitled to."

They were very quiet during these walks. She got out of the house as often as possible. The mild weather, with its spry hints of spring, continued. Once or twice, deftly he tried to encourage her to talk. He told her she had a curiously virginal look, adding: "And a virginal look is always sad. I can't bear it."

Presently he succeeded in making her relate the death scene in the bedroom: he insisted it was necessary to be vocal about it and not try to shut it away.

"Horrible and disgusting," he remarked when, haltingly, she had finished. "But perhaps it's for the best. A grim purification for them—I trust." He took her hand and patted it. "The upheavals of the heart are always a gamble."

"I couldn't stir," she faltered, "I couldn't raise a finger, a word. He belonged to them . . . and they shattered all my strength."

"Did you *want* to interfere?"

She said, after a pause: "I was prevented."

Later, he said: "People seem unable to prohibit the secretion of venom in themselves. It seems to be one of the by-products of civilisation—one of the profitable industries of the Devil, your father would have said. And there's always a period when it is spat out."

"Always?" she murmured.

"I'm told there are saints," he admitted.

After another long pause, when she had made an abrupt turn back to her house, she said: "He was cruel to them. . . . He was cruel to himself."

He took her hand in his again: it remained unresponsive but without resistance. She had passed through one of the crises of the spirit that leave a person apparently unchanged. Its result is not to be detected immediately; it may appear years hence in some act or decision that seems to be startlingly out of character. The only evidence of it now was the abandonment of warfare with her stepsisters.

During another walk she spoke of her father's excessive thriftiness after her mother's death—"But I can see now it was some sort of religious conversion, or flight from the world, the flesh and the devil. My mother's death freed him—or seemed to, as you would say. I remember the day before the funeral he arrived home after being out all day and how frightened I was. He came back like a man who has seen demons. I'm sure he left the house intending never to return. Why, I wonder, did he come back——?"

"Did he see there was no escape?"

"From that day, though he was never deliberately unkind to me, he more or less ignored me. I think I reminded him too much of my mother, I was connected with sin. Oh, I was so unhappy, lonely! His ignoring of me finally decided me to go away. Yet he was very angry at this. Did he want me only as a defence against his other daughters?"

"Or did he see you as a dangerous example of flouting his authority, his idea of himself as the father-god?" After a pause, he said, musingly: "His protests against your stepsisters dragging him down might have been fury at his failure to cut himself away from his worldly life. No man can live in the world and abandon it. But some try; it seems that even our brilliant developments in comforts and labour-saving devices cannot eradicate from men the instinct that used to send them into the desert to find, if not God, themselves." He peered suspiciously over his shoulder, and added: "But he was almost shockingly alive. Alive with a double life. He pushed his life as far as its limits allowed. Most men don't do that."

She said: "I'm glad he's dead."

"Glad too that your coming back precipitated it, as your stepsisters say?"

She did not go to the funeral. Her stepsisters, soberly clad (but not in black), decided to go. The only others in the cortège were the parish vicar, the new solicitor, the bank manager from Tremartin, and Alex. The former solicitor who had advised the sisters in the matter of their father's insanity did not attend. Laura remained in her room when the coffin was carried out. She lay on the bed.

And she had not gone to look at her father before the lid

K

was screwed down by the undertaker. Her stepsisters made a little ceremony of this last view. Alex, who wore a black tie Marion had bought for him in Tremartin, accepted their invitation.

One sleek black limousine arrived back before noon. The sisters, the solicitor, and Alex stepped out. The car was kept waiting to take the solicitor back to Tremartin. Laura removed the napkin from the neat pile of ham sandwiches already prepared by Gwen and placed in the diningroom. Alex opened the bottle of sherry. After a glass each had been drunk, Marion formally led the way to the drawingroom, where a bright fire burned. Alex went into the sisters' parlour.

The reading and discussion of the will did not take long. The solicitor, an easy-going family-looking man—Gwen remarked later that he was more like a market-stall keeper than a lawyer—first explained that he was consulted by their father only seven days ago. There was another will in existence, deposited in the Tremartin bank, which had been drawn up by Mr. Rowlands, his Tremartin colleague: after consultation with Mr. Rowlands, he had read this will now legally revoked by the present document. In the first will, drawn up nine years ago (Laura afterwards asked for its exact date and found it had been drawn up a few weeks after she had left the house), everything had been left to charities. This will, of course, could have been contested by the testator's dependants under the new Family Provision Act.

The three sisters sat with admirable restraint during this surely unnecessary, tormenting prelude. Laura sat staring at the solicitor's totally bald head, vari-coloured like a map of the world. She sat so dumpily in a chair that she looked laxly thick-set, even fat: sitting as far away as possible from the positions selected by the others, she also looked as if she wanted to disclaim all this business and run away.

The contents of the second will were brief.

Except for a separate item concerning Laura, the entire estate was to be divided between the three daughters in the proportions of two thirds for Marion, the remaining third to be shared equally between Gwen and Kate. (At this, Gwen began to rise from the sofa with a "What!" but was restrained both by Kate, who sat beside her, and a nicely rebuking glance from the solicitor.) They then heard a short sentence about the testator wishing to pay tribute to Marion's devotion to her mother. At this, Marion lowered her head, spread her fingers and carefully scrutinised her nails. Gwen's breathing could be heard. Kate lit a cigarette at last; and again the solicitor lifted a fatherly eyelid.

Laura was left all the money deposited in a separate bank account in Hampstead, London. This amounted to three thousand pounds odd, was her sole inheritance, and the testator wished it to be understood that this money was the profit of his chemist business. (Her stepsisters turned and looked at her in unison, each in a non-committal way.)

Credit in the Tremartin bank stood at close on twenty thousand pounds, in cash. "He never would do business with stocks and shares," Marion, in a pleasurably roused state now, remarked. The only other property of the testator was the freehold house, the proceeds of which, if sold, would be divided among Marion, Gwen and Kate in the same proportions. "It cost nearly five thousand," Marion also remarked.

And it was she who broke the concluding silence—that silence which resembles no other—by asking if the will could be disputed in any way.

"Not unless the beneficiaries of the first will," he replied, "decided to raise the objection that your father was not of sane mind when he made this second will. That is unlikely, I would say. After all, you are his daughters."

"Not of sane mind!" exclaimed Marion in extreme indignation. "Well, indeed! He may have been known to be a little eccentric, but it was due to failing health, though we couldn't persuade him to go into a nursing home for a while, and——"

But Gwen, statuesquely impassive now, had risen. "You won't delay time over the proving of the will, Mr. Lloyd? We need money. As it is, we may have to pledge some jewellery."

"You interrupt me, Gwen," rasped Marion.

"I suggest," said the solicitor, "you all come and see me to-morrow. You will not wish to go into smaller details to-day." The time was a quarter to one.

Marion took it upon herself to agree to this. And to the room at large she announced that she had never really worried about the will; her guide had assured her that all was well. Laura asked the solicitor if she could see him at Tremartin that afternoon as she wished to return to London the next morning: she fixed an appointment for four o'clock and left the room.

She went quickly up the staircase. Pausing at the bend, her frightened face half looked back for a moment. Then she remembered that Alex had gone into the sisters' parlour. But she did not go down. They were coming out of the drawing-room. After a minute she heard the car leave.

Later, Alex came upstairs. He said he had looked into the drawing-room but instantly gathered he intruded into a particularly private conference—"a real family one, I imagine."

"I wonder could we stay in the Ruthin Arms to-night?" she whispered. "Would it cause gossip. . . ."

"Of course we can't . . . come, come——" When he heard of the division for the three sisters, he commented that it seemed unfair. After a while, she became calmer.

The gong for luncheon was struck at half-past two. It was a very loud single blow. Going downstairs—at first she found herself going on tip-toe—she rang up the Ruthin Arms and asked for the car to arrive within half an hour.

Doubtless for Alex's benefit, a steely calm was maintained during the simple lunch of ham and cold potato salad. And, after all, it was the day of the funeral. Marion talked most, addressing Alex exclusively. Did he know the south of

France, and which were the nicest towns there?

"Judging by the state of Europe to-day," he observed, after she had further enquired about the Rhine, and said she had always wanted to hear opera at Milan, "the old peaceable trips, when one could forget England for a while, are finished."

"I would like to travel," she said heedlessly.

"Nowadays," he sighed, "somewhere like Bali is my dream."

"Too far for an unmarried woman," she shook her head. "One needs a husband for such outré journeys."

At this Kate got up and left the room abruptly. Gwen—yet she seemed to hear nothing of Marion's prattle—kept staring closely at her sister: she might have been seeing Marion after a very long absence. But Marion kept her luncheon composure, though her rather jibing assessments of Torquay and the Isle of Wight—her mind seemed unable to tear itself away from flight into a holiday—became rapid and now she did not wait for replies from Alex. Once Laura caught her giving a quick sideways glance at Gwen; an untypical glance. And momentarily she looked real.

Laura rose. "Here's the car. You are coming with me, Alex?"

"Oh, but you must wait for coffee——" Marion cried, almost shrilly.

They did not wait. Huddled in the large, decrepit car—the driver was glass-screened—she whispered: "I don't know whether to laugh or cry . . . But I do know I want to get away as soon as possible. Ought we to stay, though—do you think we would be any use?"

"Do they want us to stay?"

"I doubt it . . . But our presence might curb them in some way . . . Oh, I don't know," she said, shivering; "we couldn't stay here for ever."

"If they've got anything awful against each other, hadn't it better come out at once? If they break apart immediately it might be the best solution."

"Will they ever break apart? . . . Oh," she whispered, "the *passion* frozen over that lunch table . . . This trip to Tremartin," she went on, trembling in the cold, roomy car, "is really only a pretext to get away. I've got little to say to the solicitor. But I want to pay him the fifty pounds they borrowed—he's really a nice fatherly old thing, I liked him——"

"Fatherly . . ." he used the word with a darting glance at her.

"Then I'm going to tell them I've done this," she went on, heedless.

"You want to drop a seed into their hearts?" he smiled, pursing up his lips.

She stayed in Tremartin as long as possible. She gave her London address to the solicitor and settled the loan, thanking him for his aid and remarking that her stepsisters hadn't consulted her about it. "Very decided characters they have," he twinkled, spreading his well-filled waistcoat, "very decided. I admire them. Poor ladies left alone now . . . but not for long, I'm sure, not now!" he beamed, giving a meaning, rather uxorious little laugh. With a start Laura realised that her stepsisters would be considered rich in this district: and even Marion couldn't be more than forty-five, older though she looked.

She sent a telegram to her charwoman to prepare the flat for the next day. They took tea in the town. "I'm left with well under two hundred pounds in the bank," she said, scanning her cheque book in the hotel. "I shall have to be looking for work."

"There's your legacy, you can raise money on that till it's through. Don't work till it's gone. Take a long rest, sit back and blow through your money."

"Oh, no," she said prudently. "I want to work—heavens, how I want to work." And to lose herself in the anonymity of London. . . .

"Work, no doubt, is a partial escape," he squirmed again. "If only you were star material!"

"That will do, Alex," she frowned.

"Laura, dear, I'm only trying to prevent any possible heartburnings. I also want to seem fatherly and protective, like that comfortable-looking solicitor. I do think you're a born worker very conscious of a career. But I also think you're a born married woman. I wonder will you be able to compose the two? Or be forced to make a choice?"

"Look after your own heartburnings," she said.

After leaving the hotel she stopped sharply at the side window of a fruiterer's and darted into the shop without a word. Such a display of flowers was unusual in that place. There were extravagant sprays of white lilac, rich dusky carnations, mimosa and wide-petalled violets, besides the more expected tulips, scarlet and white, small frail daffodils and jonquils, and bowls of hyacinths thickly curling out their moist azure and pink. She bought an armful of the cut flowers and a half-guinea pot of hyacinths.

"The best show in the hospital they'll make," nodded the fruiterer as she leaned her face, as if starved, into the glow. "All fresh in to-day."

Alex bought a pineapple. They picked up the car in the market place. Dusk was falling when they entered the drive. As they approached the house she saw the drawing-room curtains being drawn with sharp, untidy haste. The crooked venetian blind had been mastered. After ordering the car for the morning she walked into the house—Alex found the front door unlocked, though the sisters always bolted it at four o'clock—with the look of one suspiciously sniffing the air. For a moment or two she stood uncertainly in the shadowed hall, the loose flowers in her arm. Alex laid the pot of hyacinths and the pineapple on the marble-topped wall-table. Raised voices came from the drawing-room.

"They're in conference," he remarked.

She heaped the flowers on the table, slowly.

"Go into the drawing-room," he said. "I'll find a vase."

"I want to run away," she whispered.

"No . . . go to them."

"It will be useless." She stepped hesitatingly to the darkening staircase. Despite the shut-away clashing voices coming from the drawing-room, the house seemed deserted, a hollow dwelling of echoes. The smell of the flowers, wintry flowers unwarmed by sun, rose earthily thick. The falling night was like some menace closing on the house.

Suddenly she turned from the staircase and swiftly crossed the hall to the drawing-room door.

As soon as she entered the room—a cosy fire burned, and the remains of tea were on the black, gold-fringed enamel tray—Marion wailed to her: "Where have you been all this time? Going out on the day of your father's funeral! Where's Mr. Gregory?" She was not at all herself; the wail was utterly disconsolate.

"Mr. Gregory, indeed!" Gwen breathed. Standing forbidding, there still thrashed about her an air of having towered in the room long and victoriously. "Mr. Gregory indeed! You ought to be ashamed of yourself," she slowly leaned her head towards Marion, "the way you make yourself cheap before that man." And, in ghastly accuracy, she mimicked her sister's social prattle: " 'One needs a husband for such outré journeys. . . .' "

Marion lifted a scrappy lace handkerchief to her nose. Her cosmetics were faintly smudged. The blue tint in her face was pale but true. "They've been so unpleasant to me, Laura! Can I help it if father left me the greater share?"

"No, you can't," rapped Kate. "But if you think you can get away with it you're mistaken." She sat hard and resolute. Somehow her look of morose determination was more threatening than Gwen's merely physical power. "Have you had tea, Laura?" she snapped. "Yes? Then sit down."

"We're quite aware," Gwen turned to her stepsister with an inviting little smile, "that you've turned forgiving to us. Kate happened to telephone that solicitor just after you'd left his office and he told us about the fifty pounds."

"Very kind of you, I'm sure," Kate's voice relented a dour shade. "Marion will have to pay you back when her money is through."

"I don't want it back," Laura said, inattentive to the matter. Repelled by Marion's sickening look of collapse, she was still trying to get her bearings.

"Because our money is tainted?" Gwen asked with a dramatic look of interest.

Laura made an impatient gesture; perhaps it was one of evasion. Marion, swaying her head like one in genuine grief, said stringily: "But we didn't make the money." Even more repellently she seemed to be trying to force her way back into her sisters' favour; she looked appealingly at them in turn.

Kate looked back at her with the slow look of one profoundly stirred. Then, switching her face away and each word tramping out in slow deliberation, she said: "That woman is either a great fool or the world's most complete hypocrite."

Laura, steadying her voice, asked: "What exactly are you quarrelling about?"

She saw that she was a relief to them; they were passionately in need of a sort of judge. With that last vulgarity of human beings in high dispute they wanted to exhibit their indignation.

Kate began a reply to Laura's question. But at once Gwen's voice swam deliberately over the youngest sister's words. For a minute their utterances battled interwined. Then Kate, glaring, stopped abruptly. But Gwen, that look of victory gleaming along her aquiline nose, was still not satisfied: she immediately stopped her address to Laura and pounced: "You override one too often, Kate. You've had far too much of a say the last few days."

She drew herself up for the factual accusation. "The way you try to get hold of Glyn when he brings the milk, for instance! You overbore me this morning, didn't you? . . . You never will let me talk," a spot began to smoulder in her cheeks: she seemed to have forgotten Laura. "You always think you're so clever and everyone else stupid. You've been trying for a long time to get the upper hand here, haven't you? And lazy too—my goodness, *lazy.*" Her voice rose as she thrust out her head. "Who does all the hard work of this house, eh, who's been the housekeeper, cook and general servant, while you loll about smoking cigarettes and treating everybody as fools?"

Kate sneered: "Yes, I do think you're stupid; I've often wished I could change my opinion." It was mild for her. And the hard masculine downrightness was wholly gone— had Gwen called the bluff of a bully? Something else, however, lurked down her voice: a murderous suffering.

During this Marion sat back with a little gasp of easing herself. But she still looked tearful: her voice quavered as she unwisely interfered: "Yes, Kate is far too rude to everybody."

"You hold your tongue, you!" shouted Kate hoarsely. With blindly fumbling fingers she felt for her cigarettes under the cushion of her chair.

"Bossy and lazy and insulting——" Gwen went on madly.

Laura began to feel hysteria rousing in herself. She could not remain unaffected by this quivering heavily-charged air. But, making a determined effort to get herself heard, she exclaimed: "Oh, for heaven's sake, are you going to tell me exactly what all this is about?"

Gwen, triumphant for the moment, returned to her: "It started because of Marion. We've been having things out with her . . . She locked herself in her room after lunch," she said parenthetically, "but we got her out, we got her out; besides, she wanted her tea . . . Do you know what she wants to do? She wants to leave Kate and I in the lurch and just run about enjoying herself! And she used to agree to our plans for after father's death, the old fox. We were going to open a good class private hotel somewhere by the sea, with Kate starting a garage in the same place—though," she put in with a gibe, "*she*'d have to work harder than she does now. . . . But Marion said——" and again she mimicked the prattle with devilish accuracy—" 'Oh,' she said, 'Oh, I'll come and stay with you sometimes in the summer' . . . Oh yes, she'd come and play the lady, would she, sitting about on the front all day on her money——"

"I never said that!" Marion whimpered, sickeningly dwindled again. Laura even began to wish she'd return to the old irritating Marion. This reaching to her true foundations made her both repulsive and unnatural.

"Well, that's what you meant." Gwen, like some savage bird superb in its natural instinct, swooped on her again, so that Marion cowered down in her chair. "You know very well, selfish slut that you are, that you want to run away from your duties. But, whatever Kate does—and she's likely to gamble away her money on horse-racing— *I* would track you down," her body curved over the shrinking Marion; "*I* would disgrace you wherever you were. You've got hold of all that money by some trick or other, robbing me who slaved in this house *and* in London, while you sat about painted up like a shilling doll and just as useless——" She stopped to draw a breath.

"Just because I said a word or two about taking a holiday!" wailed Marion. "But I knew you and Kate were waiting to attack me."

Then, unable to bear it any longer, Laura cried: "Can't you see that father made that will to punish the three of you? He wanted you to hate each other, he wanted you to tear each other to pieces." The words flew wildly across to them. And struck.

Arrested, each of them gave her a wide-eyed attention. There was quite a long silence. They needed time to cool down before they could attend to this. But Laura was getting up from her chair.

"What do you mean?" Kate asked, in an abrupt but interested way.

Half turned to the door, Laura said haltingly: "That will was a last attempt to strike at you. Not only did he believe that money would corrupt, but by dividing it unfairly he wanted to make you tear each other to pieces. . . . He particularly wanted to punish Marion. He wanted you to destroy each other with malice."

There was another silence. Then Gwen asked, carefully: "Are you sure you're not jealous that you've been left less than any of us?" Laura gave a disdainful gesture. But it was Marion who perked up most definitely. She asked: "Did father tell you all this, Laura?"

Laura turned fully to them. Her look at Marion was open but inscrutable. "Yes," she said, perhaps too calmly.

"It's a lie," Marion cried shrilly. "He paid a tribute to me in the will! . . . You accuse *us* of hatred! Do you think I don't know how you hate me?"

"Not now," Laura replied, going to the door. "I only feel sorry for you." Her hand on the door knob, she turned again. A compulsion held her. "I think your conduct to father was partly justified," she said in a slow, compelled way. "Except that there's another law—of forgiveness. And in some way father was trying to find forgiveness. He suffered a great deal."

"Forgiveness?" Kate rapped. "You said he made that will to be revenged on us, deliberately to sow discord."

"Yes. Because you gave no sign of forgiveness; you tortured him to the last. In his proud and maddened way he sought forgiveness, and he didn't find it. Someone must give way first. He was old, and he was your father. It would have been easier for you to give way. Why couldn't you see that by submitting you would have gained the true victory, not only over him but over yourselves?" She gave them a swift glance. "Is it too late now?"

They looked at her in silence. It was too much to expect them to reply to this just then. But Gwen had drawn nearer her sisters; she stood between them. And once again there seemed to flow from them a single force united against an intruder. Yet in their eyes was speculation. Had they really been brought to a pause? Would new happier paths wind for them out of this halt? Or would they close themselves fast in their iron circle? It was impossible to tell; not yet. Save for this aloof speculation and this silence, they gave no sign.

She stood with her fingers twisting the door handle. The silence became oppressive. Yet still she couldn't go at once. Her voice said—she listened to it as to another person's— "I've been telling you this because that will shocks me. If I were in your place, Marion, I would divide the money equally . . . Then," she dared further, "you ought to go separate ways, at least for a time . . . And——" now she became startled at her own words—"if you want to come and stay with me in London for a while . . ." She couldn't finish the sentence, a shyness inhibited her. But, after a struggle, she added: ". . . separately, I mean." She gave a nervous laugh. "You're too overwhelming for me together. And you overwhelm each other." She was ready to go then.

"Well——!" Marion said, non-committal and looking away while she fingered at a prong in her hair. At once she seemed the old Marion again, false, artificial, mannered. And assured.

Gwen remarked: "This is forgiveness, indeed!—with conditions."

"I expect there's going to be need for correspondence between us," Kate said, equally non-committal. "But thank you for your invitation."

Laura glanced at the black marble clock and said: "I've decided to go back to London to-night, with the last train. I'm going to pack now." And she went out quickly.

When she found Alex and told him of this sudden decision, he protested: "But we'll land in London cold and hungry in the early hours of the morning!" He hated sudden movements.

"I've had enough. We're going to-night. Or at least

I am; you can stay on with them if you like, of course. Go and consult Marion; I'm sure you'll find her more than agreeable."

"This is no time for idle jests," he complained.

"Will you ring up the Ruthin Arms and ask for the car to be here in an hour?" She plucked his sleeve. "And, oh, darling, in case I forget—you've been very good to me here . . . and *for* me. Thank you for coming." She hurried up the stairs.

An hour later she looked over the landing banister and saw that the three were assembled in the hall. The car had arrived. Alex descended bumping her suitcase and carrying his own bulging portfolio. As he reached the hall Gwen held out to him a little corded paper package. "Have you room for this, Mr. Gregory?" Her voice floated up, loud and deliberate. "It's ham sandwiches: poor man, you'll be hungry on that awful night train. . . . This is just like Laura," she added commiseratively.

Marion sang: "When she left home before, she practically *ran* away. She's so headstrong." Kate, a cigarette askew from her lips, slouched aloof beyond the lamp's radiance.

As she began to go down—the delay was deliberate— Marion was proceeding: "You've been a comfort to us in our loss. Thank you for your kind sympathy." Fingering her pearls, the mask adjusted again, she looked at him pensively. She had been upstairs and made up the mask.

"You sound like an acknowledgement in the newspaper, Marion," barked Kate, coming full into the lamplight. "Mr. Gregory has had a hard time here. We must apologise."

Gwen smiled at him. "We must try and make up for it another time, if Mr. Gregory will pay us a visit, wherever we are. Henceforth," she launched into one of her school-mistress pronouncements, "we hope to experience the benefits of civilised existence . . . Ah, here's Laura . . . You look very flushed, Laura. Surely that coat is a little tight? I could have altered it for you. You've put on weight in your week here."

"The flowers are beautiful," Marion sang, peering at the cascade on the marble-topped table. "Thank you, Laura." She swept across to her and held out a small flat face-powder box tied with string. "This will go in your handbag. Don't lose it—no, there's no time to explain. Open it in the train."

"If they catch it," Kate rapped. "There's no time to waste." She glanced at Laura: the gritty voice was not hostile.

They moved out to the porch. Laura's head was down, her face unrevealed. Beyond a remark about the time, she had said nothing. But her three stepsisters retained their calm. Alex shook hands with them and descended the steps with the suitcase. On the top step Laura turned her head and, looking beyond them into the yellow hall, said: "Good-bye." She went down the steps hurriedly, head still down.

Marion, waving a lace handkerchief in hostess exhibition, sang: "You will write?" Gwen loomed solidly statuesque, her large sinewy hands clasped below her stomach, the streaming light catching a dimly tight smile. But Kate, like someone divided between retreat and advance, lurked secret in the shadows of the porch. "Good-bye, good-bye," Marion waved, drawn up centrally. No one would have guessed her débacle of an hour ago.

The car's headlights swerved into the drive, the unkempt evergreens shone brilliant. Beyond glass the driver sat impersonal. Laura did not look round for a last glimpse of the dark house with its tower and clusters of chimneys.

"This is cowardice," she faltered.

"That term," he grumbled, "can be applied to the instinct of self-preservation."

"But I . . . I think I stopped that awful quarrel this evening." Her voice was insecure. "I think I made them see there's a way out."

He shook his head. "Are they so malleable? Do people escape from themselves and bury the past so definitely?"

"No, but can't they be shocked into different . . . different ways of living? It will be some time before they change. And meanwhile they're going to quarrel like mad. But won't it be only superficial quarrelling?"

"You're weeping," he said, noticing a few tears rolling down her cheeks. "They won't be weeping."

He made no gesture towards her. She wept all the way to the station, crouching in her corner and sobbing helplessly to herself. Detached, he remarked: "It's been a week of strain and tension for you. But he had to die, and it was good that you went back and ended all that mental agony."

"Yes," she said, weeping.

He found an empty compartment in the unpopular night train. She sat huddled and still. The journey would take six hours. "What did Marion give you?" he reminded her. She opened her eyes, revived, and took out of her bag the little flat box. It contained, embedded in cotton wool, her mother's eight rings, including the wedding ring. She kept trying them on her fingers, silent and wondering, closed from him. Sensitively biding his time, he took no notice. When she lifted her face she looked at him helplessly: as if ust then she found the windings and recesses of the human heart too mysterious for her understanding.